meant for you

BY SAMANTHA LEIGH

Valentine Bay Series
Ready For You
Meant For You
Perfect For You
Only For You

Aster Springs Series
Wallflower
Sunshine

meant for you

samantha leigh

Cover design by Echo Grayce at Wildheart Graphics
Editing by Killing It Write
Proofreading by My Notes in the Margin

A catalogue record for this book is available from the National Library of Australia

ISBN: 978-0-6455703-4-2 (paperback)
ISBN: 978-0-6455703-3-5 (e-book)

To those of us who learned the hard way when to listen to our heads and when to follow our hearts.

AUTHOR'S NOTE

My books are low on angst and big on feel-good vibes, but they occasionally touch on topics that may be difficult for some readers. To access a complete list of content warnings for all my books, including *Meant For You*, please visit my website at samanthaleighbooks.com or use the QR code below. And most importantly, take care of yourself.

1

LOGAN

"THIS IS FUCKING surreal, Rossetti."

I ran a hand through my hair and stared up at the old building that housed The Salty Stop, the best pub in Valentine Bay. It hadn't changed much in the four years since I'd last been here, but standing in front of it now was an out-of-body experience.

"It's fucking *awesome*." My best mate, Luca Rossetti, flung an arm around my neck and dragged me into a headlock. I winced against the knuckles he rubbed into my scalp.

"Get off me, dickhead." I shoved him away and pretended to dust off my clothes, ignoring the fact that the dark grey suit he'd been working in all day looked a million bucks better than the blue jeans and white T-shirt I'd thrown on for the occasion. "This is a big night. The moment the Bay welcomes back its prodigal son. I have to look presentable."

SAMANTHA LEIGH

Luca raised his hands, palms up. "My mistake." Then he cocked his head, perfectly coiffed dark hair not moving an inch. "You nervous, Reeve?"

I snorted and dismissed the way my stomach tightened—just a little. "Why would I be nervous?"

"No reason." He shook his head and grabbed me in a rough hug. "Four years is too long for you to be in the UK without visiting us. Welcome home, man. And in case I haven't said it yet, thanks for coming all this way for my wedding and for agreeing to be my best man. It's bloody good to have you back."

I tightened my arms around my best friend. "Wouldn't let anyone else have the job. You know that."

He let go and set his hand on the heavy pub door. Even on this side of it, I could hear the muffled sounds of live music and raucous conversation, the tinkling clatter of schooners and wine glasses. "Ready?" Luca asked.

"Wait up!" a voice bellowed from up the street.

I turned to see Isaac Greene—another of my best, oldest mates—jogging towards us. The dark-haired giant threw his enormous arms around me, and I clapped him on the back.

"Fuck, mate," I grunted. "You're huge."

"That's what she said," he answered with a grin.

I shook my head. "Walked right into that one."

Isaac glanced over my shoulder and back again. "Where's the wife?"

"Uh, Bek's not coming. She's slammed at work, and it's too far between London and Sydney to travel for any time less than the fortnight they were willing to give her."

2

"That's a shame. I was looking forward to meeting her."

I smiled tightly. "Yeah, next time." I swept my arm forwards, gesturing at the pub door. "Okay, Rossetti. Lead the way."

Luca pushed on the door, we stepped through, and I was thrown back ten years to the day I turned eighteen and bought my first legal beer in this very room. The pub had been updated since then with eye-catching murals on the walls where there used to be kitsch posters and neon signs. The bar itself was new, a beautiful expanse of solid timber set on black metalwork cabinetry filled with glasses, cocktail shakers, dish towels and barware, but the bones were the same. The way the tables were laid out. The small, elevated stage to the right. The exposed brick. The worn floorboards. The cushy booths. The smells of spilled beer and roasting garlic ...

I was home.

"Reeve!" a woman shrieked from the crowd. "You're here!"

Only our old friend, Abbie Ellison, could pitch her voice in a way it'd carry over the din of a crowded bar. No sooner had her screech busted my eardrums than the woman herself crashed into me. I wrapped my arms around her narrow waist and reeled at her nostalgic scent—a signature mix of sunscreen and coconut oil. Abbie had smelled that way since we were fourteen.

"Hey, Ellison." I set my hands around her shoulders and held her at arm's length. Her blonde hair fell in gentle waves down her back, her skin was sun-bronzed, and she wore short denim cut-offs with a casual tank. "You look good."

"Of course, I do. I'm a yogi now." She grabbed my hand and pulled me towards our usual booth, and we began snaking our way to the rear of the room. "Come on. The whole crew is here tonight to see you."

"Careful with that arm, Ellison," Luca said, following us. "Don't overwhelm him so much he goes home before the wedding."

"*Pfft*!" Abbie yanked my arm so hard it ached at the socket. "Reeve *is* home."

Never had something sounded so true and so terrifying.

The booth was full of people, and the sight of so many familiar faces brought a smile to my lips. Spotting Joshua Ford with an unfamiliar, dark-haired girl tucked into the crook of his arm, I shoved Luca aside and took hold of Josh's free hand. "Ford!"

He grinned at me and slid out of the booth, scooping up his new girlfriend as he moved. They got to their feet, and Josh pulled me in for a rough, one-armed hug.

"Jesus, it's good to have you back." He let me go and gestured at his girlfriend. "Reeve, this is Jones."

She was tiny, with big green eyes and a shy smile. She stuck out her hand, and I shook it. "First name's Emily," she said. "I'm so happy to finally meet you." Josh grinned at her like he'd had a lobotomy. Poor guy.

"And I'm Logan," I said to her. "Nice to meet you."

Another member of our high-school crowd, Will Kidd, launched himself at my back, coming from the direction of the bar. "Holy shit, Reeve," he exclaimed. "You made it."

I shook him off my shoulders, then grasped him in a quick hug. I still couldn't believe Will owned this place now. He might have always been on the brink of dropping out of high school, but Will had never been stupid. Book smart? Not so much, but I wasn't surprised by his obvious aptitude for business.

"Hey, Kidd. The place is looking great. I'm impressed."

Will rubbed the back of his neck and glanced around the enormous room. "Thanks. I appreciate that." Noticing that the queue at the bar was starting to build, he grimaced and jerked his chin in that direction. "I'll be over there until closing time, then I'll have time for a proper chat. Good to have you back."

I clapped him on the arm. "Thanks, mate."

"Hey! Babe!" Abbie shouted, pausing Will's retreat. "Send over another pitcher of your bottomless margaritas and something yummy from the kitchen." Her eyes widened. "Oh! I know! I'll have a plate of those scrumptious fried potatoes you gave me last week."

"Hey. *Babe*," Will replied. "I'm working. Come see me at the bar like everybody else."

Abbie winked and blew him a kiss as he rolled his eyes, then left us behind.

"And this," Luca said, kissing the wrist of a tall, attractive brunette I'd never met before, "is my Tash."

I shook her free hand. "Congratulations on the engagement, Tash. Rossetti is a lucky guy."

Tash elbowed Luca in the ribs. "You hear that, honey?"

5

"I did, and I am." He dropped a quick kiss on her mouth.

All the love in the air was enough to drive a man to drink, and I had six more weeks of this shit to deal with.

As subtly as possible, I scanned the room—the bar, the other booths, the tables, the dance floor—but I couldn't find the face I was looking for.

"Is this all of us?" I asked as we squeezed into our booth.

"Almost." Abbie picked up her margarita and took a sip, cocking an eyebrow at me over the rim. "We're just waiting on Frost. She had a staff meeting after school, but she'll be here later."

I had no time to acknowledge the palpitation in my chest before Abbie's gaze flickered to Luca and Tash, then back again, her small smile slipping a little. Of course. Luca and Tash—his new fiancée—sharing a table with Jessica Frost, his ex-girlfriend? The party tonight was going to be awkward as fuck, and everybody knew it.

"Right." I cleared my throat and stood again. "Another round? Kidd knows what you're all drinking?"

Josh and Abbie raised their glasses in my direction and nodded, so I headed over to the bar. The queue was four people along and three people deep, and after a quick look at Will, who was filling glasses as fast as he could while doing his best not to look harassed, I worked my way around the crowd and joined him on the serving side.

"Need a hand?" I asked, not waiting for an answer before I cleaned away a stack of dirty glasses, then leaned towards the closest customers. "What can I get you?"

6

It took me a short, awkward minute to find my way around, but I'd been working in bars for the last two years, and I'd always been able to get the feel of new places quickly. Isaac appeared five minutes later to retrieve the round of drinks I'd offered to buy for everyone, and then he left us to it. If Will noticed me hunting around for a glass or a bottle, he'd pull it out and set it down without a look or a word in my direction, and for the next half an hour, we worked side by side. Cocktails were shaken, beers were pulled, tapas were ordered, and I flirted a little when the situation required it, but I kept an eye on the front door the whole time.

After the happy hour rush passed, Will flung his dish towel over a shoulder and leaned against the counter. "Holy hell, Reeve. Thanks. I owe you one."

I grabbed another cloth and began mopping up spills along the bar. The timber really was beautiful—reclaimed Sydney Blue Gum by the look of it, stained and polished to a deep, reddish glow and bearing the small, storytelling scars of rough hits and broken glass. "Happy to help, but why the one-man show? This place is packed. You could do with extra staff."

Will crossed his arms and dropped his head back. "It never used to be a problem, but things picked up this year." He jerked his head towards the booth filled with our friends, and I used it as an excuse to check again for new faces. Well, one new face. "Jones is a photographer, and she took some shots of the pub to use in her portfolio. She's good, and her stuff has taken off on socials. Now the council is flogging the joint as one of their must-see tourist attractions. The extra income is awesome, don't get me wrong, but for fuck's sake, the weekends are killing me."

I took another look at Josh and Emily. She was still snuggled under his arm, and he was whispering something in her ear that made her blush.

"It's good to see him happy," I said.

Will glanced over as well. "You have no idea. We'd started to think he'd never move past Maggie."

We let the silence sit for a minute, and I knew Will was thinking the same things I was. Maggie had been Josh's high school sweetheart, but she'd died in a car accident four years earlier. I'd already been in the UK for two years by then, and her funeral was the only time I'd returned to my hometown in the last six years. We all loved Maggie, but Josh had struggled more than anyone after her death. It was a relief to see him with somebody after all this time.

Finally, I shrugged. "Well, I'm available to help out behind the bar while I'm here."

Will shook his head. "I appreciate the offer—I really do—but you're back for Rossetti's wedding and a break, not to work."

I moved a step closer and dropped my chin. "How about a trade? Let me crash with you while I'm here. I don't think I'll survive a month and a half with Rossetti and Tash, and as much as they tell me I'm welcome, it's not really a good time for house guests."

Will smirked. "Yeah, that sounds painful. What about your parents' place?"

"No can do. It's been leased to a family while Mum and Dad are on their world cruise, and there are still ten weeks left on the agreement."

"I guess that settles it." Will thrust out a hand for me to shake. "It's a deal, but you're on my couch. I'm in the loft upstairs, and it's not a big place."

"Sounds good to me. And you'll let me help out here when you need it?"

"Oh, fine." Will turned to serve someone. "Rush hours only."

I saluted him. "Yes, boss."

After he poured two lagers and a glass of house red and sent his customer on her way, Will turned to me. "So, where's Bek?"

"Uh, she's not going to make it. Work can't spare her long enough to make the trip."

"That sucks, Reeve. Would have been good to meet her."

"Yeah. Next time."

Will cocked his head to the side. "So, you've been working bars in the UK or what?"

"Uh, yeah." I busied myself with a tray of dirty glasses, then started reorganising the buckets of cocktail garnishes. "On and off for a couple of years."

"The artisan furniture business didn't work out?"

I wiped my hands on a dish towel, then folded it and laid it on the counter. "It got old. Came time to pack it in and do something else."

Will looked around at his bar. "I hope this place never feels old. I'm in debt to my eyeballs."

"Still got plans to open that brewery?"

"You bet. I'm small-batch brewing IPA already. Here." He snatched a bottle of amber ale from a small, glass-fronted fridge underneath the counter. "Tell me what you think."

I cracked the top and took a small sip, just enough to appreciate the bubbles on my tongue. The beer was bitter, fruity, and fucking strong. "Good work, mate. That's brilliant."

He ran a hand through his light brown hair. "Thanks. Now get out of here. You must be jet-lagged as all shit. Hang in there, and I'll be free in a few hours. Then we can catch up properly."

"Sounds good." I pointed over my shoulder to an open door that led to a well-lit hallway. "Bathrooms are through there, right?"

"Through the door, up the hall and on the right. Can't miss them. I'll give you the grand tour tomorrow morning before opening."

I left the beer behind the bar, checked our party in the booth one more time for newcomers, then made my way across the room, manoeuvring around tables and chairs, pressing myself between people standing around with drinks in their hands. The Stop was busier than I'd ever seen it, with a crowd I wasn't used to. Now that Will had mentioned the tourists, I noticed I was nodding my head and excusing myself past more unfamiliar faces than recognisable ones.

Finally, in the empty hallway, I started towards the men's room. The heavy emergency exit door at the other end opened as I got closer, giving me a peek out at the lamp-lit service street that ran behind the building. A woman fell into the hall, the weight of the door unbalancing her as she juggled a couple of large bags and a phone. I took a few steps closer, intending to help her, but then she straightened and looked at me. Her large, chocolate-brown eyes widened, and we both froze.

She was the very picture of an uppity, know-it-all schoolteacher at the end of a long day, her neat white shirt unbuttoned at the neck, a tight navy pencil skirt hugging the curves of her hips, sensible tan flats on her feet. She wore black-rimmed glasses high on her narrow nose—the way she always had. Her ash-brown waves were twisted into a knot on the top of her head, a few curls falling free about her face—just the way I remembered. Her open mouth was full and inviting, and I ran my eyes over her lips. I remembered them as well.

This woman had been a pain in my arse for more years than I cared to remember. She'd also been the star of every naughty librarian fantasy I'd had in the last decade and more. The girl with a chip on her shoulder so sharp it cut me whenever I got too close. My best friend's ex-girlfriend—the woman I'd always wanted and would never, ever have. Now here she was, close enough to touch.

Jessica fucking Frost.

2

JESS

LOGAN FREAKING REEVE.

He sauntered towards me like a live-action cologne commercial. How was it possible that he'd gotten hotter in the four years since I'd seen him last? His blue jeans were just the right kind of snug, his white T-shirt strained across his broad chest and built arms—lines of black ink peeked out beneath the edge of the fabric; that was new—and he'd grown a little scruff along his sharp jawline, let his blond hair grow longer. He moved closer and closer, and all I could do was gawk. He took my bags from me, slung them over his shoulder, and looked down at my toes.

"Nice shoes."

Spell. Broken.

"Get lost, Reeve. These are designer."

Smirking, he took another look while I tried not to shift my feet. "My mistake." He tweaked my glasses. "Has anyone ever told you, you look like a librarian in these?"

I scowled and adjusted my specs. "Yes, actually. One person in particular." I glared, leaving no question that the person I referred to was him. "Not that I need to explain myself to you, but I've come straight from work. I'm ducking in the back way to freshen up, get changed, and put my contact lenses in."

"I'm always up for stories about you ducking in the back way."

The cocky half-smile on his face was too sexy, the quirked eyebrow too cute, and the jerk knew it.

"Oh, my *God*. You're as awful as ever. Now, are you going to let me pass or not?"

He moved aside and held out my bags. "I beg your pardon. Should I wait for you here or meet you at the booth?"

I snatched my things and stormed towards the bathroom. "Booth, please. I don't want to worry about you loitering out here like a weirdo. Someone might call to have you arrested."

His eyebrows drew in a little, and his mouth turned down at the corners. "I forgot what a royal punish you are," he said, but as I pushed on the bathroom door, he stopped me with a hand on mine and added, "It's good to see you, Frost."

I closed my eyes and sucked in a flustered breath. "Yeah, it's good to see you, too. Now go away."

Logan chuckled and let me go, and I threw myself into the bathroom. With the door closed behind me, I dropped my bags and leaned my head against it. I'd been dreading tonight for the entire day, and it was shaping up to be even worse than I'd imagined.

I locked the door and stripped off my work clothes, swapping them for something casual—a pair of white dress shorts that stopped mid-thigh and a floaty, long-sleeved blouse. I undid the knot in my hair, letting the waves settle around my shoulders and fluffing it up at the roots, then I dug out my lenses and put them in. Giving my face the once over, I brushed my teeth, reapplied some gloss, and rummaged around for shoes. I'd packed a pair of strappy heels because my legs would look better in the shorts if I lengthened my calves, but now it was going to look like I wore them because Logan had made fun of my ballet flats. I hesitated with them in my hands.

Ah, screw it. I put on the heels, twisted and buckled the straps around my ankles, and tried not to think about them.

A bang on the bathroom door startled me. I yanked it, ready to assault Logan with my very best death stare, and found Luca standing in the hallway. Damn, he was a good-looking man. Dark hair, darker eyes, smooth caramel skin. He was still in his work suit—dark grey, with a light blue shirt unbuttoned at the neck. Luca Rossetti had been built for suits.

Momentarily confused, I looked past him, up and down the corridor for his fiancée.

"Tash is at the bar for the next round," he explained. "Logan mentioned you were here, so I came to see if you wanted something to drink."

"Oh." I stepped out of the bathroom and let the door swing shut behind me. I didn't want to give anyone—especially Natasha, his soon-to-be-wife—any reason to believe Luca and I were doing anything we shouldn't have been. "Thanks. Margarita, please."

"Coming right up." He made as if to leave, then stalled. "I'm glad you're here tonight."

I smiled as brightly as I could. "Logan's back for the first time in years. How could I miss his reunion party?"

Luca ran a hand over his clean jaw. "Fair call, but what I mean is, I'm glad we can all be together. You, me, Tash …"

There was an awkward beat, then we tried to speak at the same time.

"How's work—"

"How are the wedding plans—"

We both laughed self-consciously before Luca sighed, crossed his arms, and leaned a shoulder against the wall beside me. "We were friends long before we were a couple, and I'd like to be again."

"We *are* friends," I reassured him. "And we haven't been a couple for more than three years."

"I know, but I don't want things to be weird between us. There are going to be a lot of situations coming up where the three of us need to be in the same room together."

I thought back a few months to one such occasion—a bonfire on the beach to celebrate Josh and Emily's fake wedding. To cope with the prospect of partying alongside Luca and his new girlfriend, I'd drunk more than my usual two cocktails, but Natasha had felt the same way about spending time with me, and we'd both ended up arm in arm on a patch of sand marked out for a dance floor.

"The two of you have been living in the Bay for six months," I pointed out. "There have already been a handful of those types of situations."

"You're not wrong."

"And I think they went all right."

He cocked an eyebrow, apparently remembering the same night I was, and he chuckled. "Point taken."

"We're good, Rossetti." I deliberately used his last name because we both knew what it meant. He was firmly in the friend zone. "I like Natasha, and I wish you both well."

He smiled, but there was a touch of sadness in the way his mouth didn't curl right. "Thanks, Frost."

I nodded, then stared at my toes, painted pink and poking out the tops of my silver sandals.

"How's work?" he asked.

"It's good. Busy."

"Yeah, sure. Fancy school like that, it's to be expected."

"Mm."

"Parents?"

"Mum and Dad are fine. Same as always."

"Good, good. And your grandmother's house? How are the renovations going?"

I didn't miss that the topics he wanted to know about were the very things I'd given as reasons why I couldn't go with him to Sydney when he moved there three years earlier. My job at the nearby private school was too new and too good an opportunity to let go. My parents lived in the Bay, they were my only family, and they didn't want me to leave. I'd just inherited Gran's rundown Californian bungalow and had grand plans to renovate the place and make it my dream home. Our dream home—Luca's and mine.

"Renovations are coming along great," I lied. "The place is going to look incredible when I'm done."

"Can't wait to see it."

I nodded and lifted my shoulders, then let them drop. The silence was too loud, and warning lights started flashing in my brain. *Don't ask! Don't ask!* And what did my treacherous mouth do? It jumped off the ledge without attaching the bungee cord and asked Luca the questions that had been haunting me for years.

"Do you think if I'd come to Sydney with you, things would be different?"

Luca sighed and shook his head. "I can't answer that."

"Do you think we wasted seven years on a relationship that was never going to last?"

"No. Not a minute of my time with you was a waste."

I smiled, ignoring the tears in my eyes, and praying he would, too. And, of course, he did. Luca was nothing if not a gentleman. "Thanks," I croaked.

He put a gentle hand on my arm, then pushed himself off the wall. "See you in there."

I watched his retreating back for a torturous second before disappearing into the bathroom again. Grabbing a few squares of toilet paper, I blotted at my eyes.

Another thump on the door interrupted me, but this time it was Abbie and Emily on the other side. They stood there with a drink for each of them plus one for me, uncertainty plastered all over their earnest faces.

"I'm *fine*," I said, taking the pink margarita Abbie offered and drinking half of it in a single swallow. They followed me back into the bathroom and locked the door behind them.

"Logan told us you were in here, and we passed Luca on the way through," Emily said, looking around at my abandoned clothes on the floor. I set my drink down on the vanity, crouched down, and began to pack everything away.

"Rossetti looked like someone just kicked his puppy," Abbie commented.

I huffed humourlessly, neatly folding my white silk blouse. "You're close. I asked him if things might have been different had I moved with him to Sydney. He was diplomatic enough to not say either way, but"—I sighed, then placed my shirt in a bag—"Natasha is his person, and he knows it."

Emily stroked the back of my hair as I busied myself tidying away the rest of my things. When I raised my head, Abbie was staring at me with eyes narrowed to slits. "What?" I asked.

"How many dates have you been on in the last three years?"

I pulled my clothes back out of the bag and began to refold each item. "I don't know. A few."

"Jessica Jane Frost. Look at me."

I met Abbie's honey-brown eyes.

"How. Many?"

I sighed and zipped up my bag, then stood and crossed my arms over my chest. "Eight."

"And how many of those were second dates?"

I glared at her. She already knew the answers to her questions. She just wanted me to say them out loud. "Two."

"And how many of these eight dates with six different men were set up by your mother?"

My glare turned into a scowl. "All of them."

"And how many proceeded to a romp in the sack?"

I mumbled something unintelligible under my breath.

Abbie cupped a hand around one ear and leaned towards me. "Sorry? You'll have to speak up. I don't speak *shame*."

I threw up my hands. "None! None, okay? None of them. Is that what you want to hear?"

"Fuck, no. I want to hear you've been having sex so animal you kept it from me to save our friendship from going up in the flames of my violent, jealous rage."

Emily looked at me with wide green eyes. "You haven't had sex in three *years*?" she whispered.

I pursed my lips. She didn't have to look so horrified. "Define sex."

Abbie smacked the vanity with a loud *crack*. "That's enough." Then she stuck out her hand, palm up. "Give me your phone."

Fishing my smartphone out of my handbag, I held it back as I asked, "Why?"

Abbie snatched it from my grip. "Give it here. I'll tell you after."

19

Of course, she knew my passcode, and soon she was swiping and tapping and frowning at the screen, the tip of her tongue poking out between her teeth. I exchanged a glance with Emily, who shrugged her shoulders and took a delicate sip of her white wine. The pre-timed air freshener on the wall released a noisy puff of forest glen-scented mist, and I wrinkled my nose at the synthetic smell. Finally, Abbie returned my phone.

"Congratulations, you've joined the land of the hot and horny. I've set you up with an online dating profile."

I rolled my eyes and opened the app, then groaned at the information Abbie had keyed in. "I'm deleting this."

"Don't you dare."

"I'm with Abbie on this one," Emily agreed. "Just give it a few weeks to see how it goes. It's time you moved on from Luca."

A familiar feeling of resignation settled in my gut. "I *have* moved on from Luca."

"Great, so prove it with a few dates," Abbie said, jumping up to sit on the vanity.

I rolled my eyes and shoved my phone out of sight. I'd delete the app later when she wasn't around to catch me.

"So, Reeve looks good," Abbie observed, sipping her margarita. "The years have been kind to him."

"What is it with the men in Valentine Bay?" Emily asked. "They're all unnaturally attractive—not that I'm complaining."

Abbie groaned. "Please, keep that to yourself. Their heads are big enough already."

I finished my cocktail in one big slurp. "Abbie's right. Logan, especially, doesn't need to hear how gorgeous he is. He's the worst of the lot of them."

"I don't know," Abbie replied. "Will's ego would give Logan's a run for its money."

I tilted my head to the side, considering it. "You might be right," I admitted.

Emily grinned at Abbie, and her eyes danced as she sipped her white wine. "Maybe if you and Will gave up your pact to marry each other if you're both still single by the time you hit thirty-five, he would stop sleeping around and start taking his love life a little more seriously."

Abbie choked on her margarita, then sputtered as she smacked her chest. "Who said anything about *marrying* the guy? What has he said to you?"

Emily chuckled. "Forget I mentioned it."

"No way. I'll be taking it up with him later," Abbie grumbled peevishly under her breath. "Marriage? What the fuck, Kidd?"

"Was there a reason you brought liquor to me in a public bathroom?" I asked, looking into my empty glass with regret. Something told me I'd be needing more than two of these tonight. Again.

"We thought you could use a nip of liquid courage," Abbie said.

I relaxed against the vanity, pressed against her hip. "Is it that bad out there?"

"It doesn't have to be," Emily said, sandwiching me in on the other side.

I closed my eyes, sucked in a breath, then nodded once. No more dwelling on Luca Rossetti.

"Emily's right," Abbie said. "And you know what's going to turn a bad night into a good one? No—a fantastic one?" She flicked the side of my cocktail glass with one red, manicured nail. "A pitcher of Will's notorious bottomless margaritas." She slung an arm around my shoulders, then Emily did the same. "Come on, Frost. Let's get you drunk."

3

JESS

BEEP. BEEP. BEEP.

Shut up! Shut up! Shut up!

I thrust an arm out from under my bedcovers and groped around in the direction of the obnoxious horn sounding out of my phone, but all I did was knock it off my bedside table and onto the floor. Groaning as I rolled myself off the mattress, tangling up in the covers and taking them down with me, I landed with a thud on the thick wool rug. The *beep, beep, beep* sounded even louder in my ear now, and I felt around again, refusing to open my eyes and face the sunlight glowing red on the other side of my eyelids. My head hurt. My feet hurt. Everything in between hurt. Curse Abbie Ellison and Will's bottomless margaritas. I was never drinking again.

Beep. Beep. Beep.

Why couldn't the world just go away for one day?

Doing my best to swallow with a tongue that felt like sandpaper and tasted like death, I dragged the duvet down over my head, retracted my arm with my phone in hand, and peeled open my eyes, checking the screen and swiping to silence the alarm. It was ten o'clock. I had an hour to sort myself out before my parents arrived for Sunday brunch.

It took me less than thirty seconds to set my priorities. Make the bed, tidy the house, wipe down the kitchen, stack the dishwasher … I'd dart out and pick up some pastries from the French bakery on Main Street, then take a quick shower and change before they arrived at eleven.

It'd be tight. I had to get up. Now.

Resting my cheek on the carpet for a glorious thirty seconds more, I pushed myself up and set about my tasks, downing two aspirin and two glasses of water while swiping a soapy sponge over the kitchen surfaces. I stole two minutes to brush my teeth before heading to the bakery, but in the end, the timing was just right. I was twisting my hair into a knot with only six minutes to spare when a knock sounded on the front door.

It wasn't my parents. "Oh! Hello, Dot."

"Hello, dear. Is now a bad time?"

Dorothy March was my next-door neighbour and my grandmother's lifelong friend. Dot was well into her eighties, though you never would have guessed it. Small and lean with ironically pink-rinsed hair and wrinkled skin stretched tight over sinewy limbs, Dot did senior aerobics three times a week and participated in competitive lawn bowls on Sundays. She lived in '80s-era

24

activewear unless she was out to tea with her invitation-only book club, mysteriously called the VBFYRRRBC, when she'd pull out a gorgeous vintage get-up—which she always paired with the latest sneakers. Just like Gran, Dot's husband had passed a decade earlier, but he had been the fifth man she'd married—or maybe it was the sixth—and for reasons I'd never felt comfortable asking her about, she'd never had children.

I liked Dot. She'd filled the role of an eccentric great aunt while I was growing up, sneaking me sugar when I wasn't supposed to eat it and talking to me about boys as though she were my older sister instead of my grandmother's best friend. Since I'd moved into my gran's house three years ago, Dot would pop around to see me a few times a week, usually for one of a handful of reasons: to give me food, to ask for help reaching things on high shelves, to get IT support for her tech adventures, or, like the good old days, to talk about boys.

Today, she was kitted out in white Lycra tights with a high-cut pink-print leotard on the outside and a baggy sweatshirt over the top. I bit back a smile as I wished I was half as fearless as Dot. She also had her smartphone in one hand.

"Not a bad time at all," I said, ignoring the throb behind my eyes. "Do you need help with your phone?"

She offered it to me, and I swiped the screen. I already knew her passcode.

"Yes. I'm trying to do that TikTok thing."

"Ah. Let me download the app for you."

She clicked her tongue. "I've already done that. No, I'm looking for a particular filter. Here, let me show you what I mean."

I watched over her shoulder, keeping one eye on the time, as she tapped and swiped. In the end, I wasn't sure who taught who what, but we resolved her filter issue. Actually, *she* resolved her filter issue while I nodded along, and not for the first time, I suspected Dot March invented reasons to visit me just so she'd have someone to talk to.

"Well, I'm glad we got that sorted for you, but you might want to head home. Mum and Dad are on their way over for Sunday brunch."

Dot grimaced, then rearranged her face into an over-the-top smile. As much as she'd loved my grandmother, and as much as she fussed over me, Dot had never warmed to my mother—or rather, my mother had never warmed to Dot.

"I've got lawn bowls in an hour at the club," she said, "so as much as I'd like to, I can't stay." She winked and gripped my fingers to say goodbye, then started down the steps. I knew better than to offer her my arm, as much as I wanted to.

With perfect timing, just as Dot disappeared into her house—a mirror image of my own little bungalow, but in somewhat better condition—my parents' car swung onto the drive.

"Oh, darling," my mother said, sweeping inside and planting a kiss on my cheek. Hands grasping my upper arms, she pulled me back and examined me with narrowed eyes. "You look terrible. Are you sick?"

"No, but thanks for noticing. I didn't sleep well last night."

"Now, don't get snippy." She patted at her blonde bob. "I'm your mother. It's my right to be concerned."

I bit the inside of my cheek. "Sorry. Come in."

Dad walked in next, landing a peck on the other side of my face. He was dressed in his usual khaki pants and a white polo shirt that strained over his growing middle. I closed the door and followed them down the short hall to the dining nook.

"Pastries from *Le Gâteaux D'Amour*?" Mum asked, setting her handbag over the back of a dining chair and perusing the spread I'd set out on the table. "Your father hoped we'd be having that yummy quiche you made last week. He hasn't stopped talking about it, have you, Michael?"

"It's fine, Sandra. These raisin scrolls look delicious."

I swallowed a sigh and disappeared into the kitchen. "Tea?" I called out.

"And juice," Dad replied, "if you have it."

I opened the fridge and checked the contents. "I've got orange juice. Will that do?"

"No apple?" Mum called back.

"Sorry. I'm fresh out."

There was subdued muttering, and I gripped the fridge door, waiting for the outcome of deliberations.

"Orange juice is fine," Dad replied.

I filled the kettle, swiped three glasses from a cupboard, and took the juice bottle back to the table.

Mum had loaded Dad's plate with pastries but only taken a small slice of brioche for herself. She delicately coated it with strawberry jam as I poured us all glasses of juice, then sat there looking around the house instead of at her plate. Familiar anxiety wormed its way through my belly, and I braced myself.

"It's just so *old*, isn't it?" she commented.

"That's part of its charm," I replied, running my eyes over the ornate—if stained—ceilings, the thin carpets and battered hardwood floors, the faded walls, the leadlight windows.

Mum pursed her lips. "Is it, though? Your grandmother let it go to ruin. Not a thing in here has been updated in fifty years or more. Look at that kitchen. Just look at it! The cupboard doors are falling off, and that linoleum is pulling up around the edges."

"It's functional enough for now." I helped myself to a croissant even though I wasn't sure I could keep it down.

Mum wobbled her generous hips, making the chair underneath her creak ominously. "And this furniture. I don't know why you haven't replaced the dining setting, at least. It's all junk."

I picked at my pastry, then took a sip of orange juice. "It's not junk. It just needs a little TLC."

Mum harrumphed, but she couldn't argue with me on that point. I'd shown her the websites that proved most of the pieces in my grandmother's old collection were classic, well-made mid-century items that, if they were refurbished well enough and restored to their original glory, would be worth a lot on the second-hand furniture market, but Mum insisted on disparaging all of it every time she visited. I suspected it was her rocky relationship with her mother-in-law that compelled her to be so bitter. That, and the fact Gran left the house to me and not to Mum and Dad like they'd expected.

"Well, your father and I have been talking about that," she went on.

I stole a glance at Dad, who was focussed on his meal, then returned my attention to Mum. She fiddled with her napkin as her lips thinned.

"Talking about what? The furniture?"

"Yes, and the house. It's too much for one person, Jessica, especially a single young woman like you, with no partner and only one salary. We know you had big plans for this place when you were with Luca, but you lost him a long time ago, and now he's gone and proposed to *that girl*—"

"Natasha." Mum's head jerked around at the interruption, but I couldn't help myself. "*That girl's* name is Natasha."

Mum put a hand over one of mine and squeezed it hard. "We all know it should have been you. Luca is going to make a wonderful husband and father, and he would have been the ideal partner to help you tackle these renovations. On your own, I just can't see how you're going to manage it."

I ground my molars together, hating the way my nose stung with the promise of tears. "I still have big plans for this place. My break-up with Luca didn't change that. I haven't started on anything yet, but I will soon."

Dad smiled sympathetically. "You've been here for three years, sweetheart, and you haven't even torn up the old carpets yet." His gaze flickered to Mum and away again, like he might be about to get in trouble. "Perhaps I could help you—"

"We've talked about that, Michael." Mum hitched her shoulders and avoided looking at both Dad and me. "The physical labour would be too great a strain on your heart."

Dad slumped a little, gave me an apologetic grimace, and forked a lump of sugary scroll into his mouth. This wasn't about his heart.

"So, what do you suggest I do?" I asked. The kettle in the kitchen began to sing, but I ignored it.

"You could sell it," Mum replied. "I've already spoken to a real estate agent who says that with the size of the land, someone would snap this property up at a very good price. Probably knock down this ratty old cottage and start over."

"It's structurally sound," I argued. "I had the inspections and assessments done when I moved in."

Her nose wrinkled as she rubbed her fingertips on the tablecloth. "Yes, well, if you ask me, there's not much to salvage here, really, and with the profit you would make, you could buy something newer and more modern. Give yourself the chance to focus on more important things, like finding a husband."

I stuffed a piece of pastry in my mouth, then pushed my chair back and went to the kitchen to make the tea.

Were they right? *Should* I give up on this place—just take the money and run?

Gran had always promised me this house would be mine when she passed, though I'd been sworn to secrecy, even as a child. I'd fantasised about what I would make of it, how I would install a bright, quirky kitchen, convert the poky formal dining room into an extra bedroom, put a long, lovely pool in the backyard ... I had binders of notes and dozens of Pinterest boards bursting with ideas, and the potential of creating a family home with the soul of my beautiful grandmother at the heart of it warmed me from the inside out.

When I turned eighteen and began a relationship with Luca, my dreams about the house shifted to include him too, and for a long time, I couldn't imagine this house without him standing in it right alongside me.

After we broke up—just months after Gran passed and I officially inherited the property—I waited like an idiot for more than a *year* for Luca to change his mind and come home to me. I couldn't bring myself to make changes to the house I always believed would be ours. What if he didn't like the tile I chose for the bathroom? What if he wanted carpets in the bedrooms? It was better to wait, I'd decided, until we could do it all together.

Then came Natasha and an engagement ring. Hers, not mine.

Maybe my mother was right. I'd had to let Luca go. Perhaps it was time to let the house go, too.

I returned to the table with three mugs of steaming tea, and Mum picked up the conversation as though I'd never left the room. "Before you argue, hear us out.

We only have your best interests at heart, and if you think about it, you'll realise that as long as you've listened to us, your life has been in much better shape. We got you through high school, choosing your classes and setting a study schedule that got you into the best university. We encouraged you to be with Luca when there were, perhaps, less suitable options available to you. We supported your relationship with him, welcomed him into our family, and if you remember correctly, we advised against you letting him leave for Sydney when he did."

I carefully arranged my face to stillness and stared at a spot on the wall just past my mother's head. I knew what my parents thought about me—that I had no idea how to be an adult, I didn't have the sense or the strength to build a successful life, my judgement was poor, my intuition was shaky, and I was better off deferring to them instead of chancing things on my own and coping with the consequences—but would the constant reminders ever stop?

They'd never stopped treating me as though I were a twelve-year-old kid, and in some ways, I'd never stopped feeling like one.

Mum didn't notice my attempt to zone out her noise. "If you'd just listened to me at the time," she went on. "If you'd convinced Luca to stay here in the Bay with you, where he belongs—which is obvious now because isn't he back here? And with a new girl, no less?" She shook her head and clicked her tongue. "If you'd just stood your ground, you wouldn't be in this mess."

"What mess is that?" I managed to ask.

"A single woman facing down thirty, who has nothing in her life outside of a job teaching other people's children and a house that's falling down around her ears."

"I love my job."

"Yes, I know, and thank heavens I had the connections to get you the interview at Saint Andrew's College. At least I can tell the ladies at church that you're teaching at a private school now instead of that hellhole they try to pass off as a premier public learning institution."

My molars were almost ground to dust, but I let her comments pass. I'd heard it all before. "And I love this house."

Mum pulled a card out of her purse and handed it to me. "This is the name and number of the real estate agent I spoke to last week. If you call him and give him my name, he'll have all your details on file. Even better, he has a brand-new townhouse for sale right now, just down the road from your father and me. Wouldn't that be wonderful?"

I took the card and stared at it blankly. Sell Gran's house and move into a place on the same street as my parents? My stomach began to battle against my mouthful of croissant.

Mum set a hand to my forehead and frowned as she leaned in to get a better look at my eyes. "Are you sure you're not sick?"

I pulled away from her touch. "I went out for a few drinks last night."

"With Abigail?" she asked tersely.

"Yes, with Abbie."

Mum sighed wearily. "There's another bad choice, Jessica. She's always been a bad influence on you."

"So, my life is a list of bad choices, is that right?"

"Of course not! I didn't say that. Did I say that, Michael? Did I?"

Dad opened his mouth, but Mum charged on.

"I said you've got a good job at a great school, and you have a lot of money sitting here in this house, which you should sell to make your life easier."

My jaw dropped. The woman was a master at spin.

"I also said," she added, "that things would be a lot easier for you if you listened to my advice."

"Which is what exactly? Sell the house, find new friends, and beg Luca to take me back?"

Mum shrugged. "It's too late for that last one now. If you recall, I *did* suggest you talk to him as soon as he got back from Sydney *before* he put a ring on *that girl's* hand. Perhaps, if you'd done that—"

"Thanks for the card," I interrupted, forcing myself to be polite—even though I wanted to scream—and holding up the card for the real estate agent. "I appreciate your input, and you've given me a lot to think about."

"Are we done?" she asked, staring down at the brioche she still hadn't touched.

"*I* am." I pushed my plate away. "I think I'm going to be sick, then go back to bed."

Mum *tsk*ed under her breath, but she stood, and Dad

did the same. As I ushered them to the door, she kept on talking.

"Oh! I almost forgot. I bumped into Anita Dewey at the supermarket on Thursday. Her nephew is on the market—thirty-five years old, an accountant, quite handsome in the picture she showed me. I said you'd be available for a date next week."

"N—"

"And before you say no," she cut in, "have a think about what we were just talking about. *Choices*."

My nostrils flared, but I bit my tongue.

I held the front door open as my parents gave me their brief kisses goodbye. I tolerated the affection, but I needed them to go already. Sunday brunches were always painful, but today felt like I'd had surgery without anaesthetic.

"And can you believe it?" Mum said, stopping on the top step of the verandah. "Maria Rossetti phoned me yesterday to ask if I wanted chicken or fish at the wedding reception. Behaving as though there was no bad blood between us— pretending that her son didn't dump my daughter and pick up with someone else!"

"Luca and I are friends, Mum," I said, rubbing a weary hand over my forehead. "I'm going to the wedding, too. It was nice of Mrs Rossetti to ask you and Dad. You've always been on good terms."

"She was showing off," Mum replied. "Rubbing it in. She'll get grandchildren before I do, and she knows it."

"I heard Logan Reeve is back in town for the wedding," Dad said, trying to move down the steps and along the

35

front path in a way that took Mum with him, but she stayed rooted to the spot. "Have you seen him yet?"

"Michael!" Mum snapped. Her eyes cut to me and away again as she hissed under her breath, "What were we just saying earlier about *unsuitable* options?"

"What are you talking about?" I asked, my eyes bouncing between the two of them. "What options? There's never been anything between Logan and me."

Mum shot Dad a look that would have frozen the blood in a lesser man's veins.

"Of course not," she said. "You're too smart for a boy like that."

I stood on the porch, staring over into the neighbours' yards, long after my parents had left. Mornings with my mother often left me shell shocked, but today had been hit after hit after hit. Luca. My job. The house. Dating. Logan.

Logan.

What the hell did she mean by "unsuitable options"? I wracked my brain and tried to recall the details of that part of our conversation, but my head felt stuffed with cottonwool, and the pieces wouldn't fit together. Nobody knew about Logan and me—not that there had ever been a Logan and me. Well, not exactly.

I wasn't only stunned. I was also pissed off, and that was new. Maybe it was a combination of the dull throb from a waning hangover headache, a stomach that wanted to throw up *and* hoover in a cheap, greasy cheeseburger, plus the accusation that everything wrong in my life was attributable to the fact I hadn't listened to *her*, but I wanted nothing more in that moment than to do the opposite of everything my mother had just told me I should.

Somewhere, a voice told me that was immature and stupid. Mum's advice was probably sensible and appropriate. If I followed it, maybe I'd finally have my shit together. I could sell this house and buy something boring, let her set me up with another uptight accountant, pop out three kids, then quit my job, and try to ignore the fact that the uptight accountant was now cheating on me.

But I really, *really* didn't want her to be right. If she was, then I was officially incapable of creating a life that would make me happy, and the smart thing would be just to give up now.

Should I just give up now?

Perhaps the answer was yes, but giving up didn't mean giving in, did it? I could go out with a bang. If I was destined to live a miserable, lonely life teaching other people's kids and eating microwave meals every night until my own cats ate my corpse, I was going to have a lot of hot *unsuitable* sex while I still had hips and end my days in a house that looked like it belonged on some other sucker's Pinterest board.

I grabbed my purse and my glasses, slammed the front door behind me, and got in my hatchback. First things first: I opened my dating app, swiped right on a bunch of suitably *unsuitable* profiles, then tossed the phone into my bag. Next, I reversed the car down the driveway and headed into town. I knew nothing about interior design outside of what looked good on the pages of a magazine, but I didn't care anymore. For better or worse, this broken little house was mine, and the renovations started today.

4

LOGAN

FIRST THING I did the morning after the party—my first full day back in the Bay—was sneak out early for coffee. Will was snoring in the loft above me, but it was already past six o'clock and jet lag had me by the balls, so I threw on some clothes, ran my fingers through my hair, and headed straight to old Tony's Place.

Tony's coffee shop—ingeniously called Tony's Place—had always had the best coffee, and it was the only place in town guaranteed to be open this early on a Sunday. A little bell jingled as I opened the door, and old Tony—round and ruddy cheeked, with thick hair dyed a suspicious shade of brown and an impressive walrus moustache hiding his top lip—threw up his hands at the sight of me.

"Logan! You're back!"

I reached over the counter and shook his hand. "Yeah, for Luca's wedding next month."

Tony pulled out a takeaway coffee cup, and I held up two fingers to indicate he should add another.

"Luca and Tash," Tony said, getting to work on the coffee. "Good-looking couple."

I nodded. "That they are."

"You best man?"

"You know it."

I sensed someone sneaking towards me and had to stifle a groan when I turned and saw Dawn Linley blinking up at me. With her smooth face and only a hint of lines around her eyes to give away the fact she was over forty, Dawn looked like a twiggy, pointy-nosed bird in a long braided blonde wig and faded denim overalls, old sandals on her feet. Past experience told me she was getting ready to poke her beak in where it wasn't wanted.

"Logan! It's good to see you. It's been too long."

"Four years, give or take. How are you, Dawn? You're looking good."

She flapped a hand at me. "Thank you, honey. You here for Luca's wedding, I assume?"

"Absolutely. Can't let my best mate get married without a best man."

She squeezed my upper arm with a grip like a vice. "You may need to think about sticking around for a while. I suspect Josh and Emily will be next down the aisle, and soon."

"Is it that serious, do you think?"

"Oh, I know. I'm the reason they're together, after all. I set them up."

I glanced over Dawn's head to Tony, who was fitting plastic lids on the coffee cups and shaking his head at me. I bit back a smile.

"That's not how I heard it," I said to Dawn. "Josh tells me he helped Emily when she was having trouble with her ex."

"Well, yes, technically speaking." Dawn pursed her lips. "But who do you think planned the fake wedding?"

"Nobody but you has the skill to pull that off."

She smiled and reached up to pat my cheek. "Thank you." Dawn considered me for a minute, her head cocked to one side, then sighed. "If only you were single. My niece would be perfect for you."

I cleared my throat, set some cash on the counter, and picked up the coffee cups. "Yeah, shame about that—*and* the fact I live on the other side of the world."

"What's your wife's name again? Make sure you introduce us while you're here. I'd love to meet her."

"Bek, but she couldn't make it. Work. You know how it is."

Dawn blinked, and her big blue eyes darted to my hand. "And no wedding ring?"

I looked down at my left hand. Shit.

"Uh, no. It's, uh, in my wallet."

"Right." She narrowed her eyes. "Two coffees?"

I sucked in a breath, searching for patience. "One for me, and one for Kidd."

"Oh. You're staying with Will! How nice. Do you boys have plenty to eat?"

"Coffee first," I said, raising the cups to make a point. "Good to see you, Dawn. Take care." I sidestepped her, shouted a thanks to Tony over my shoulder, and all but ran out onto Main Street. From the corner of my eye, I spotted Dawn watching as I powered past the tall coffee shop windows, and I wondered how long it would be before everyone in the Bay knew Logan Reeve was back—without his wife or his wedding ring.

When I got back to the loft, Will was slumped on the couch, looking bleary eyed and green around the gills.

"Thank you, God," he said, taking a coffee from me.

I couldn't help myself. "That's what she said."

Will rolled his eyes, then groaned. "How can you be so chipper this early? I feel like my brain is seeping out my ears. Literally, grey matter leaking from my head." He wiped a cheek and looked at his fingers.

I sat opposite him, set my ankle on the opposite knee, and took a loud slurp of coffee. "Do you need a lecture on the dangers of alcohol at your age? You're a few months off twenty-nine, and you own a bloody bar, for Christ's sake."

He took a ginger sip of his coffee, then set it on the coffee table and leaned his head on the back of the sofa. "Can't believe you don't drink, Reeve. You're a fucking traitor."

I smiled thinly. "Working in bars, I've seen too many smart people get too many beers into them and do too many stupid things." *I've* done too many stupid things, I amended silently. "That shit sobers you up quick smart."

"Yeah, I suppose so." He rubbed his face with two open hands, then threw back another mouthful of coffee.

"Let me shower, and I'll give you that tour of the bar I mentioned."

I checked my watch. "You've got an hour. I'm meeting Luca for a surf."

"You two are nuts. The morning after is for sleeping in and throwing up." Will dragged himself to his feet. "Just give me fifteen minutes."

Thirty minutes later, we were downstairs—Will feeling slightly more human after coffee, a shower, and three pieces of heavily buttered toast—and I had a better idea of how he ran things at The Salty Stop.

"It's a great venue," I told him when he'd run me through the kitchen and service areas. I examined the joinery again and slid a palm over the smooth face of the bar.

"Thanks. With the exposed brick and the refurbished floors, I had plenty to work with when I took it over, but I'm glad you appreciate the new additions."

"Who did the renovations?"

"A guy over in Scarborough Cove," Will said, referring to a coastal town about twenty minutes north of the Bay. "Benjamin Pope."

"Yeah, I know him. He does good stuff."

"I'm stoked with what we came up with." Will looked around the room, satisfaction shining on his face, but then he grimaced and hiked his thumb at the door that led up to the dual function rooms above. "Unfortunately, the rooms upstairs aren't so pretty."

I followed him up the worn carpeted staircase, thinking if it were me, the carpet would have been the first thing to go.

"I'd rip up the carpet," Will said as if reading my mind, "but I don't have the budget to pay someone to refurbish the boards underneath, nor the time to do it myself."

At the top, he took me through both private dining spaces, the first smaller and more intimate with space to comfortably hold a party of up to twenty people, and the second much larger, with a stage for a band and floor-to-ceiling windows along one side that offered up panoramic views of the Bay. Both spaces were worn and tired, the threadbare navy carpets pulling up around the edges and a musty staleness in the air. It was a time capsule of the seventies, and not much of it good. None of the contemporary, industrial vibe that made The Stop what it was downstairs had filtered up to these rooms.

I examined the flaky painted walls and pulled back the carpet to get a better look at the timber floors. I ran my hands over the worn window frames and noted the panes of glass were murky at the edges. It'd take time and skill, not tons of cash, to make these rooms suitable for hire. The floors were solid; they just needed to be stripped back, sanded, and polished. The walls could have done with a coat of paint. Same with the window frames. The glass set in them would do for now—after a thorough clean—though if it were my place to renovate, I'd install panels of louvred glass to capitalise on the ocean breeze. New light fittings in keeping with the theme of the bar downstairs, plus a few more wall murals, and Will wouldn't recognize these rooms. I was confident that even if the makeover was, for the most part, cosmetic, my friend would be able to hugely improve his events business.

After two rounds of both rooms, we stood in the centre of the larger one, the long banquet tables and high-backed dining chairs stacked against one wall. Will rubbed his jaw as he looked around. "Nobody's lining up to hire these spaces the way they are, but I'll get to them one day."

"Restore the floors? Paint the walls?" I asked.

"To start," Will agreed with a nod. "Just got to find the time to get it done—or come up with the money to hire Ben Pope to come back and do it."

I considered it for all of three seconds. "Why don't you let me have a crack at the floors while I'm here?"

"You're on holiday, Reeve, and you've already conned me into letting you behind the bar. It's too much already."

I shrugged. "I've got six weeks to fill, and the floors will only be a couple of days' worth of work. At the very least, it'll keep me busy when I'm not doing wedding stuff, and let's be honest—what is there for me to do other than sort out the bucks' night and remember the rings on the day?"

Will frowned, but his eyes kept roaming. I knew he wanted to say yes, so I took it as a given.

"I'll swing past the hardware store after my surf this morning. You got the funds for equipment hire and supplies?"

"Yeah, I can manage that much." He squinted at me. "You sure you want to do this?"

The thought of spending the next six weeks with nothing better to do than stare at the walls of Will's loft and listen to Luca and Tash rant about their wedding like they were the first couple in history to get hitched made my skin feel too tight. I was happier when my hands and mind were occupied, and I enjoyed this kind of distraction. I'd given up my carpentry trade two years ago, and I'd never admit it out loud, but not a day went by when I didn't miss the work.

"Positive."

Will stuck out a hand, and I shook it. "Deal," he said. "I really appreciate this."

"You're doing me a favour, Kidd." I clapped him on the back. "Trust me."

The waves were decent, and my first surf in Valentine Bay in four years felt like a rebirth. I'd chased swells across Europe—Portugal and Spain, a few spots in France, still others in Denmark, a couple of solid options in England itself—but nothing beat the coast of my hometown. Luca and I were out for a little more than two hours before we called the session done and paddled back in.

"That was fucking fantastic," I said, walking out of the ocean. We hit dry sand, and I shook the water from my hair, then pulled down the zip on my wetsuit. Yanking my arms free and letting the suit dangle from my waist, I soaked up the gentle June sun.

Luca nodded and wiped the water from his face with one open hand, then set his board in the sand. "I needed that. The closer we get to the wedding, the more worked up Tash becomes about seating arrangements and music selections and flower girl dresses. I thought we had it all figured out, and now she's questioning everything. I'm a patient man, but fuck. A wedding's enough to send anyone mad."

I huffed out a laugh. "And that's just the beginning."

He shook his head. "I forget you've already done this. You've got a *wife*, Reeve. I'm getting *married*. How did that even happen? I'm pretty sure we were fifteen years old just last week."

I shrugged and forced a laugh.

"I'll have to hit you up for advice while you're here," he continued. "Four years with a ring on your finger must have taught you something."

"You'd think so, wouldn't you?"

Luca quirked an eyebrow, and I landed a playful punch on his shoulder.

"Since when have I ever been able to teach you anything, Mr Most Likely to Succeed? Five minutes as a married man, and you'll be giving me lessons. I guarantee it."

Luca snorted, and I started up the sand towards Main Street, wanting to put an end to his line of questioning. He followed a few steps behind, our boards hefted under our arms.

I waited beside his car and watched Luca strap his board to the roof racks, then he pulled out a towel, removed his wetsuit, and dried himself off. I did the same with a second towel he threw my way, then I held out my hand to say goodbye. Luca grasped it, but when he didn't let go right away, I knew he was about to ask me for a favour.

"You're giving me your please-and-thank-you handshake," I accused, trying to pull my fingers free without any luck. "I'm already your best man. I promised not to lose the wedding bands. I told Tash I wouldn't get you a stripper, but I crossed my fingers when I said it, so we're all good there. What more is there for me to do?"

Luca gave my fingers a tight final squeeze, then dropped his hand. "This is why we're best friends, Reeve. We know each other inside out. I know you're a decent, generous guy, no matter what everyone else says."

I groaned. "This isn't going to be good, is it?"

"It's about Jess."

My heart constricted, causing actual physical pain for the split second it took me to remember to breathe. "No."

"Hear me out."

"No."

"I need to know she's okay."

"Uh, you saw her just last night. She was fine."

He gave me a withering look. "Are you serious?"

No, I wasn't serious. Jess had drunk her weight in margaritas last night, and Isaac had had to carry her home. Literally.

"Could you talk to her?" Luca asked.

I tipped my head back, squinting at the clear blue sky, and sucked in a deep breath. "That is the worst idea you've ever had, Rossetti. No, really. Worse than your plan to wear board shorts and bow ties to the Year Twelve formal.

Worse than the cheap beer you made us drink at the after-party. Worse than—"

"She needs somebody. She won't admit it, but she does."

"Uh, she *has* somebody. Blonde hair, best friend, about this tall"—I held my hand just below chin level—"first name rhymes with *stabby*."

"Abbie's the reason Jess needed to be stretchered out last night! And every night they're together lately. Jess cannot hold her drink—we both know that—and the bottomless margaritas are becoming a habit. It's all because of Tash and me and the wedding … Jess puts on a good front, but I'm worried about her."

"Oh, man. Don't say that." I fumbled for an alternative. "Can't Isaac do it? Or Josh?"

"I'm asking *you*, as my best friend and my best man. Please? Just a conversation. A friendly check-in today, maybe another one later in the week. If I know you're watching out for her, it'll put my mind at ease, so I can focus on the things I'm supposed to focus on, like Tash and the wedding, for instance."

My posture collapsed, my shoulders slumped, and Luca grinned at me. "Knew I could count on you. Thanks, mate. I appreciate it. Drop in on her later this afternoon, but don't make it too obvious, all right?"

"Oh, sure," I snapped. "Nothing suspicious about me showing up at Jess's place for an uninvited social call. I'm sure she'll welcome me with open arms." Then drive a knife between my shoulder blades. "The woman despises me, Rossetti."

"You could try being *nice* to her for a change. That might help your cause."

"For Christ's sake! It's your cause, not mine."

Luca grinned and checked his watch. "I've got to get back and help Tash with revisions for the menu. Call me later and let me know how things go?"

"Leave now before I change my mind," I grumbled.

His smile stretched wider, and I scowled. At the rumble of laughter in his chest, I spun away and started the climb up the street to Will's loft. I'd stow my board, take a shower and change, then drive his work truck over to the hardware store for the equipment and supplies I'd need to start on the floors in the function rooms. I'd get something to eat after that, take an afternoon nap—jet lag be damned— and then maybe, *maybe*, I'd think about Jess. I'd had years of practice putting that woman out of my mind. What difference were a couple more hours going to make?

5

LOGAN

THREE HOURS LATER, I stood at the service desk at Valentine Bay's largest hardware store, Spies and Sons, and signed off on the equipment hire order I'd just made.

"Thanks, Burt. I'll pick it up tomorrow morning at eight o'clock."

Burt the Third, named after his father and grandfather, all of whom had owned the hardware store since it opened in 1931, tipped the brim of his cap at me, which I took to mean all was settled with my request to borrow a drum sander and floor edger for the work I'd be doing at The Stop. With my phone held in front of me, where I could read from a list of the supplies I'd need to do not only the floors but a few other quick fixes around the function rooms, I wandered deeper into the store, taking my time to check out each aisle as I went. I loved hardware stores the way some people loved bookshops—the smells, the energy, the possibilities—but I hadn't had a good enough reason to browse in one for a long time. I planned on taking my time on this visit. The fact it was delaying my stopover at Jess's house on the way home was out of my control. Shopping was important, and Jessica Frost could—and would—wait.

Luckily for me, Will's toolbox and general maintenance supplies were shameful, so I had a long list of things I wanted to collect. For the floors alone, I needed a good hammer, a nail punch, three types of sandpaper—the floors were worse off than I originally thought, and they were going to need at least three passes—sealant and brushes, a lambswool applicator, and safety equipment. As I pushed the oversized trolley up and down the wide aisles, I was happier than a kid at Christmas.

I'd traversed half the store when I saw her standing up ahead, her eyes darting between the screen on her phone and a tall wall of paint card samples, her top teeth clamped down on her bottom lip. Jessica. She wore those fucking glasses again, short shorts, a baggy jumper and white sneakers, and I scolded my dick for assuming I'd downloaded another picture from the spank bank. Drawing to a stop a few metres away, I watched her for a minute while the heat in my pants abated, and I deliberated whether it was better to "check in" on her now, in a public place covered with security cameras, or later at her home, where she could murder me without witnesses.

But before I gathered my nerve, she swivelled her head in the opposite direction, looking for something or someone, then back around. Right at me. Her mouth opened in a little "o," then her brows drew down, and she scowled. Finally, she stuck her nose in the air and returned to her paint perusal.

I pushed my trolley forwards, then stopped and planted myself beside her, mirroring her stance and glaring up at the rainbow wall. Still, she refused to acknowledge me.

"Sunshine yellow," I declared.

She huffed out a breath. "What?"

I pulled a card from the wall, coloured a cheery shade of buttery yellow, and handed it to her. "To brighten up your day, grumpy pants."

Jess rolled her eyes, then slammed the card into its slot on the display. "Please leave me alone. I'm not in the mood to deal with you today."

"Hungover?"

She snorted. "To start."

"What brings you to Spies?"

"None of your business." She walked a few steps up the aisle, eyes glued to the colours fanned out in front of us.

I shadowed her. "Doing some painting, are you?"

"Oh my God, Reeve. Why do you care? Just stick the boot in, get it over with, and get lost." Then she sniffled, took two more paces away from me, and crossed her arms, blinking hard and by all appearances captivated by the wall and only the wall.

The longer I watched her, the more I realised how uncertain she looked, with her brows drawn down and nose twitching, and I didn't anticipate the flip in my stomach. She was a superior goody-two-shoes who knew too much, relaxed too little, and pissed me off without even trying, but at least when she was snapping my head off, I didn't feel so guilty about pushing her buttons. This Jess—the uneasy, uncertain Jess—didn't sit well with me.

Something was wrong, and as much as I hated to admit it, it had to be about Luca. That's where I was supposed to come in, right?

"For fuck's sake, Frost," I growled, following her. "Forget about Rossetti. You're too good for him anyway."

She stared at me, jaw on her chest, then laughed humourlessly. "Wow. Nobody asked you, but thanks for the heartless, inappropriate, unhelpful advice." She turned away, then mumbled, "I guess it's the day for it."

I ran a hand through my hair. "Look, all I mean is, he doesn't deserve any more of your time or tears—or whatever this is," I added under my breath, wishing the floor would open up and swallow me whole—or better yet, open up under wherever Luca was standing at that very moment and suck him into the fiery bowels of hell.

Jess covered her face with her hands, stood there for long enough that I started to panic, then dropped her arms. Her eyes were bloodshot, the tip of her nose red and swollen, and she huffed out a laugh. "Of all the people I could run into today, why did it have to be you?"

I sauntered over and slung an arm around her shoulders. "Of all the hardware stores in all the towns in all the world, she walks into mine."

Her laugh this time was still weak but genuine. I let her go, faced the paints, and crossed my arms. "Really, Frost. What's going on here?"

She sighed and threw her phone into her bag. "You know Gran's old place? The brown-brick bungalow on Figtree Road?"

"Yeah, I remember it. Fantastic position. Loads of potential."

She looked up at me, a surprised smile playing at the corner of her pretty mouth. "That's the one. Gran left it to me when she passed three years ago, and I've been saving for the renovations. And today, I'm going to start on them."

I frowned, wondering if she was having me on. "And you're beginning with paint?"

"Yes?" At the look on my face, she flushed beet red and dropped her eyes. "I guess the correct answer is no."

I rubbed the back of my neck and resisted the impulse to make fun of her. Jessica Frost always knew better than everyone else. She'd been awarded top marks in every subject at school, had her life mapped out from the age of fifteen, and was never short of snark when she lectured me on all the reasons I was wrong about something. Now was the perfect chance to knock that chip right off her shoulder, and I couldn't take it.

"Uh, do you have plans to extend the place?"

She rolled her lips. "Maybe."

"Maybe?"

She fished out her phone again and opened an app, scrolling through picture after picture of designer digs.

"I like this," she said, pointing at an incredible mid-century modern kitchen with timber-faced cabinets and a quirky feature tile. "And this," she added, swiping through to a bright Deco-style living space with a brick-faced fireplace and soaring ceilings. "I like the retro feel," she said, pulling up an image of a cosy vintage bedroom. "And this for outside," she said, showing me a manicured yard with lush green shrubs around a Mediterranean blue pool. It was fun and fresh and off the wall, an eclectic mix of classic and contemporary, and I liked it all.

"You've got good taste, Frost," I said. "Who's your project manager?"

"My what?"

"Your project manager. If you want to extend, you'll need architectural drawings and a builder, too. You've got a good eye, so you might be able to do the interiors yourself, but a consultation with a designer would probably set your mind at ease about the big-money decisions. I hear Josh wants to get out of the ambulance service and into landscaping, so he can probably help you with the yard design. Either way, you'll have to plan for a big budget."

"Oh." She clicked off her phone, stowed it away, and shrugged. "I'll have to think about all that, I suppose." Biting a lip, she returned her attention to the paint samples.

Well, shit. Couldn't keep my big mouth shut, could I? Luca had asked me to check in on her, boost her spirits if I found her feeling like crap, and right on brand for Logan Reeve, I'd run my mouth and made her feel worse. As if that should have been possible, given the gallons of tequila she'd mainlined last night.

"Do you mind if I take a look at the place?" I asked.

She narrowed her eyes and crossed her arms under her breasts. I ignored the way they lifted when she did it. My cock, I'm sorry to say, did not.

"Why?"

"Because I might be able to give you some pointers about where to start with the renovations. Give you an idea of what's possible and what's not. Show you where you can save some cash. Put you in touch with the right people so you can get shit done."

She wriggled the tip of her nose in that adorable way she had whenever she contemplated something she considered a bad decision.

"Why are you grinning at me like that?" she snapped. "Is this a trick? Are you going to follow me home, then steal my mail or something?"

I schooled my face. "Who the fuck is grinning, Frost? Do you want my help or not?"

Jesus Christ, you moron. I could not screw this up so badly that I'd have to tell Luca I made the former love of his life break down in the middle of Spies and Sons.

"Do I want your *help*?" she scoffed. "No!"

"Tough shit," I snapped. "You're getting it. Now tag along while I sort out this stuff I had to buy for The Stop, then I'll follow you back to your place. Don't argue with me."

Her eyes flashed fire. "Why do you do this to me? Isn't there someone else in this town you can torture?

"No. It's only fun because it's you."

As she huffed out a breath, I cursed my best friend for dragging me into his mess and stormed off towards the registers. It took her a minute, but Jess followed eventually, and I didn't know whether to laugh or cry.

6

JESS

_____

"WELL," I SAID, throwing up my arms and letting them land with a smack on my thighs. "This is it."

Logan followed me through the front door of my house, down the boxy hall and straight past the closed doors, his eyes roving everywhere at once.

"Good bones," he said, swiping a *pain au chocolat* from the dining table as he wandered past the dining nook, into the laundry room, then back the way we'd come to explore the rooms we'd missed.

I left him to it and picked at the abandoned brunch. It wouldn't take long to complete a full circuit. The house wasn't big, just a modest kitchen attached to a dining nook and living space, two good-sized bedrooms, and the boxed-in formal family and dining rooms. One bathroom. A 1980s add-on laundry-and-utility room with an extra powder room. An enormous back porch, plus an oversized detached garage in the yard that was currently filled with all the other stuff Gran had left me, and I'd been avoiding clearing out.

If I was honest with myself, it wasn't just my decade-old dream of sharing this house with Luca that had derailed my renovation plans. It was also the sheer volume of work required to turn my vision board into reality, plus the stomach-twisting overwhelm I felt at the thought of doing it alone. I didn't want to ask my friends or parents to pitch in, though. Something about remodelling this house felt too intimate to share with Abbie or Emily, and I was certain that if my mother got involved, nothing would keep her from co-opting my dreams and making them her own.

I hadn't begun the work because I didn't know if I was capable of finishing the job by myself.

My performance at the hardware store notwithstanding, I *did* know renovations didn't begin with paint. That's why I'd had a structural assessment done when I'd moved in. Ugh. I hated that I'd looked like an idiot in front of Logan. I made a point of never letting that happen—he enjoyed it too much—but he'd caught me in a bad moment. I was simply trying to think of things I could manage without asking for help, and painting a room seemed a good place to start. There was no need for him to make me feel so inadequate, but he did, often and without any effort. Logan Reeve—knocking my confidence since we were fifteen.

I can't believe I'd let him follow me home.

He circled back around and stepped out the back door, and I moved to where I could watch him through the kitchen window. I thought I saw Dot next door, peeking out at him through her curtains before ducking out of view again, but I couldn't be sure. Logan did a quick round of the yard, peering through the filthy windows of the garage to get a look inside, then beelining back to the house, a look of determination tightening his jaw and furrowing his brow. I clasped my hands in front of me, feeling butterflies about his prognosis.

It surprised me a little that I cared so much what Logan thought about my house. Maybe I needed validation after the conversation I'd had with my parents that morning. Hearing from Logan—a qualified and, I could begrudgingly admit, gifted carpenter—that he believed in the place would give me a lifeline to hang onto when my parents inevitably tried to convince me to give it all up and sell.

"Well, you've certainly got your work cut out for you," Logan said, scooping up another pastry. "But if you're after a fixer-upper, you couldn't buy any better than this. Good position on an attractive street, fantastic views from out front, plenty of space to build out back, and enough good stuff in the original house to hold on to if you wanted to retain some of that 1930s character—which I think you should, by the way. The timber fretwork and the bay windows, the high ceilings and ornate roses. The verandah, too. The entire front of the house, really. It has great proportions. The bedrooms are plenty roomy enough to keep as they are." He crouched down and lifted a corner of the already lifted linoleum floor. "Floors will probably be salvageable, too."

My stomach hit the ground with relief, and he quirked an eyebrow at the breath I released in a long, noisy puff.

Next, he ran his hand over the old, dark timber dining table. "And you're sitting on a fucking treasure trove of mid-century furniture here." He caressed the dining chairs, and I watched the way his strong, tanned fingers stroked the wood, the pattern of the pale blue veins under his smooth skin, and how reverently and competently he moved. My mouth was dry again. Stupid hangover. I picked up my leftover orange juice and polished it off.

"This is an original Featherstone dining setting, did you know that?" he asked, not taking his eyes off the dining chairs.

I shook my head. "I've tried to Google most of the furniture in here but couldn't put a name to this."

He nodded towards an armchair in the living space, with its curvy frame and webbed-style leather upholstery and a matching footrest set in front. "That's a Snelling chair. A real one."

I watched as he gravitated towards the chair, then beyond it to the chest of drawers Gran had used as a sideboard.

"Fred Ward," Logan said, brushing his fingers along the top. "This and the shelves over there. And don't get me started on the Parker furniture—the sofa, the television unit, the little hall table." He shook his head. "It's like a museum in here."

"Is that good?" I asked, the tone of his voice making me suddenly wary that he was dragging out some kind of elaborate joke.

He chuckled and shook his head. "It depends on who you ask, I suppose. If you ask me, it's fucking incredible."

"There's a ton more stuff in the garage. Did you want to look at that, too?"

I didn't miss the way his eyes lit up, so I went straight to the kitchen and opened the drawer holding my spare keys. Logan followed, watching over my shoulder and standing close enough I could feel the heat pulsing from his skin, smell the sugar from the cinnamon scroll on his lips. I kept my head down and my focus on the mess inside the drawer, but from the corner of my eye, I saw him grimace around at the broken cabinets.

"The sooner you get started on this place, the better, Frost."

"Aha!" I held up the key to the garage, glad for an excuse to ignore his comment and the flare of terror I felt at the prospect of trying to work out how to replace an entire kitchen. "Follow me."

As I led the way outside, the curtains definitely twitched next door at Dot's place, and I wondered how long it would take for my surrogate aunt to knock on my door and invite herself in for a cup of tea with a side of gossip.

I jiggled the key in the padlock on the garage door, and once it was loose, Logan pulled the heavy timber doors wide open. At the sight of what had to be a lifetime of Gran's junk stacked and stored in this one big room, Logan grunted.

"I haven't got around to sorting it out yet," I explained, feeling the heat of embarrassment.

Logan ran a hand through his hair and let out a gusty breath. "Don't blame you, Frost. This is going to be a mission." He stepped inside, where it was dark and dusty, and put a hand on the closest piece of furniture. "But it'll be worth it in the end."

"You think?" I gazed around at the piles of boxes and furniture, at the dust motes dancing in the air, at the gritty concrete under my feet—anywhere but meeting Logan's clear grey eyes. The dust tickled my nose and made my eyes water, and I cleared my throat, blinking against the sting. "I'll get to it eventually."

After he closed the doors, Logan watched me with a speculative tilt to his head while I clicked the padlock into place. Could he sense my uncertainty about this place? The way it made me nervous? I avoided his gaze for as long as I could, then finally, I had to ask, "What are you looking at?"

He paused for a beat, then poked my cheek and said, "Ever heard of napkins? You've got food on your face."

"Ugh!" Swiping at him and then at my mouth to dislodge any crumbs from my sneaky croissant, I stormed back to the house. This was why I kept my guard up around Logan. The man was as charismatic as sin, too beautiful for his own good, and he had noxious sexual pheromones oozing from every pore, but he was a dick, most often when I least expected it, which is why I forced myself to *always* expect it. I kicked myself for forgetting, even for a moment.

Stalking up the back porch, inside and straight through the house, I stood with the front door wide open as I waited for Logan to catch up.

"So, uh, listen," he said, crowding me in the doorway. "I can help clean out the garage while I'm in town. You need someone who knows what they're looking at, so they can decide what needs to be tossed and what's valuable enough to keep or refurbish. It won't take that long once I get started." He used his thumb and forefinger to squeeze my bicep. "A little muscle will go a long way in a situation like this."

I jerked my arm away and opened my mouth to refuse—loudly and violently—when he raised his hand to stall me.

"I can do it when you're at work. You won't even know I'm here."

"Why on Earth would you do that—a favour for me involving manual labour on your holiday?" I jerked my chin at the car he had parked on my driveway, where the parcel tray was packed with gear for whatever work Logan had volunteered to do for Will. "You've already got enough on your plate with The Stop."

His bottom teeth caught his full upper lip, and he glanced at the car, then back at me. Holy crap, he was close. If I breathed any deeper, my nipples were going to brush the cotton of his shirt, and now he'd gone and mentioned *muscles*, I was hyper-aware of the size of his biceps, the lines of his forearms, the broad expanse of his chest. And why did he have to smell so good? Like citrus and earthy, woodsy spices. Damn, I hated him.

I had to crane my neck to meet his eyes, but I did it. Defiantly, and with all the heat I could conjure. I thought of my meddling parents, Luca and Natasha's wedding, the dream house I desperately wanted but might never have, all the unsuitable sex waiting for me on my smartphone, and my ultimate death by cat, and I unleashed every ounce of my anger and frustration and *need* on Logan's pretty, perfect face.

His eyes narrowed, his jaw clenched, and his hands fisted at his sides. "Oh, for fuck's sake," he mumbled, then he was leaping off the porch and shouting at me over his shoulder. "I'll be back on Wednesday morning. Early. Leave the key under the mat or something. Don't make me break the lock."

"Don't you dare!" I screeched as he got in the car, slammed the door behind him, and revved the engine. "Do you hear me, Logan Reeve? Don't you dare come back here. I'll call Greene and have you arrested for trespassing. You know he'll do it."

But he was already down the driveway and pulling out onto the road.

Stomping back inside and slamming the door behind me, I grabbed the last of the pastries and the warm bottle of orange juice, then went straight to my bedroom, where I disappeared under the covers. I resisted the urge to raid my goodie drawer and indulge in certain *unsuitable* fantasies about Logan Reeve and committed my fingers to a disappointing spiral on my dating app instead. When my stomach growled, I ate stale brioche for dinner, but I didn't leave the security of my bed until my alarm went off at six o'clock the next morning.

7

LOGAN

I SCHEDULED EVERY waking hour of the next two days so my brain wouldn't have time to think and my body would be exhausted enough to sleep. It wasn't hard to keep busy. To start, I woke early and went for a run, which served three important purposes.

One, my route took me straight past Tony's Place, where I stopped for a morning coffee to enjoy on the beach while watching the sunrise. Not a bad way to begin the day.

Two, I made a point of passing Jess's house—once on the way out of town and once on the way back in—to clock the time she left to go to work. Both mornings she was gone by seven-thirty, which was when I planned to arrive on Wednesday to start work on her garage. I even drove past in the afternoons so I'd know when to expect her home. Both days, she wasn't in the door before five, so I'd make sure I was gone long before then. I'd meant it when I told her I'd only be there when she wasn't. The less time we spent together, the better, which brought me to purpose number three.

Running helped expel the fuck-ton of sexual frustration I felt now that Jessica Frost had returned to my immediate orbit. She was every bit as hostile—and hot—as I remembered. More, if that was possible. The woman was wound so bloody tight, and I don't know why that was such a turn-on, but all her spit and fire had me climbing the walls. Morning sprints helped me manage the morning wood. Well, sprints and a little self-care.

The hours between stalking, I spent upstairs at The Stop, hard at work on the floors. It wasn't a difficult job, but it was physically taxing, and I welcomed the strain on my muscles. The simple, repetitious movements were soothing, and I lost myself in the process of punching nails, sanding edges, running the drum sander over the boards, filling gaps with a mixture of sawdust and resin, and starting the process again with finer sandpaper. It was going to be more than two days of work, but I'd made a good start, and the rest could wait until after I'd finished with Jess's garage.

I was an idiot for volunteering to help her out. No, not volunteering. Insisting. *Demanding*. If I could take the offer back, I would, but all I could think in that moment was Jess was way out of her depth and too proud to admit it. Under normal circumstances, I took pleasure in knocking Miss Know-It-All down a peg or two—those types of opportunities came along so rarely that I had to make the most of them when they did—but Luca's voice sounded in my head right about the time she teared up in the garage. *She needs somebody, and she won't admit it.*

I knew a little something about that.

Luca showed up at The Stop just after lunch on Monday to ask how things had gone. I took a break and poured us ginger ales, and we settled in at a booth.

"How's work?" I asked, eyeing his suit. The man worked as a corporate communications consultant or something like that. I'd never really understood his job, but he made a shitload of money and always wore a suit, even though I didn't believe it was necessary. His thick, dark hair was always freshly cut and styled with product, no matter that it made him stand out among the casual culture of the Bay, and his hands were always clean and smooth—a side effect of his white-collar job. Luca was a good guy, and I loved him like a brother, but he wasted way too much energy on looking good, and I liked to tell him so every chance I got.

"It's good, but don't change the subject," he said, taking a long swallow of his drink.

I snorted. "We weren't on a subject. You just got here."

"I'm here to ask about Jess, dumbass, and you know it. How did it go?"

I ran a hand through my dusty hair and leaned back against the leather-upholstered seat. "As fate would have it, I bumped into her at Burt's hardware store yesterday afternoon. She was shopping for paint."

Luca cocked an eyebrow. "For the renovations?"

"Ha! What renovations? The woman has done nothing to that place."

He shook his head. "I thought as much. I asked her about it the other night, and Jess is a terrible liar, but I'm surprised she confided in you, of all people."

I stamped down a flare of irritation and made my shrug casual. "Yeah, then I followed her back to her place, and she showed me around."

Luca frowned, and I hid my smile behind my glass. We were as close as brothers, true, but that also meant there was a friendly rivalry that tethered us as powerfully as any of the good stuff. I usually let that shit go—I learned long ago not to compete with Luca; my self-esteem had taken enough hits by the time we were twelve for me to understand nobody saw Logan Reeve when Luca Rossetti was around—but anything that shook his world view was a good thing. It kept his feet on the ground and his head out of his arse. Let him chew on the fact that Jess, who swooned at the sound of his name, had kept something from him and shared it with me, the guy she'd walk over broken glass to avoid.

"It's a big job," I continued, "but if she gets it right, the house will be a beauty when it's done." I took another swallow of ginger ale. "I'm clearing out the garage in the meantime. Her grandmother stored about fifty years of junk in there, and it's too big a job for Jess. I'll work out what to keep and what to toss, sort out what's left over. One less thing for her to worry about."

"And you'll be around to keep a closer eye on her." Luca nodded, then gave me a grateful smile. "I appreciate that."

I cleared my throat. "Yeah, well, I need something to keep me busy while I'm here. I'll stay out of her way for the most part."

"You know, renovating that house would be right up your alley. Jess could use your skills while you're here."

Fuck. I should have kept my big mouth shut. Give a man enough rope, and he'll hang himself. "Forget it," I said.

"You need something to do, she needs to get things done, and the best part, you'll be around to make sure she's okay. Makes sense if you ask me."

I sipped my drink. "Don't think I did."

"Just consider it, will you?"

I grunted, and Luca played with his glass on the table, turning it in circles and staring straight through it. "It's weird how things turn out, isn't it? After everything we've been through, Jess feels like a sister now."

"Ouch. Don't let Jess hear you say that."

"Maybe it would be better if she did. Then she'd move on."

"You're engaged to someone else, Rossetti. I think she gets the message."

"You might be right." Luca checked his watch, then downed the rest of his drink. "I have to get back to work." We stood, and he shook my hand, refusing to let go immediately. I scowled at him, but he laughed. "Not a favour, this time. Just a word of advice. I know Jess isn't your favourite person, but give her a chance, will you? And stop riling her up, for Christ's sake. You make things a hundred times worse than they need to be."

He released my grip, and I shoved my hands in my pockets. "Jess made up her mind about me a long time ago. I don't think six weeks of good behaviour is going to change a dozen years of bad blood."

"Just go easy on her, okay?"

"Leave it with me, okay?"

He chuckled. "Will do. Talk to you later, Reeve."

Late the next afternoon, just as I was packing up my gear for the day and getting ready to drive past Jess's house for reconnaissance, my phone lit up with a call from Bek. I checked the time and answered it with a grin.

"Hey, what are you doing out of bed this early?"

"Ugh. Damien dragged me out for his morning boot camp. Sadist thinks burpees are an acceptable way to start the week. Needless to say, that won't be happening again."

"Obviously. And how is my favourite personal trainer?"

"He's good. We're good. I just called to make sure you're settling in okay."

I stared around at the coating of dust on the floor and walls of the smaller function room, then down at my filthy clothes. "Settling in fine. Keeping busy."

"I thought we agreed you'd try to relax a little while you're there. Go slow. Chill out."

"I'm happier when I'm busy. You know me."

"Yes, I do. That's why I'm calling."

"I'm fine."

I didn't mention it to Luca at the time, but I understood exactly what he meant when he said he cared for Jess the way he cared for his sister. That was the exact way I felt about my ex-wife—except she seemed to think it was her job to look out for me instead of the other way around.

"Oh, God. I know that tone," Bek said. "What's wrong?"

"Nothing, but I suppose you should know. There hasn't been a good time to let anyone know we've split up."

"Logan."

"Don't worry. I'll clear it up. I just didn't want to shit on the happy wedding vibes with a divorce announcement."

She sighed. "That makes sense, and it's up to you how and when you tell your friends, but for what it's worth, I think you should do it while you're there." There was a pause. "Have you told your parents?"

"Uh, not yet."

"Logan! You promised. It's been two years."

No, my parents didn't know about my divorce—nobody back home did—nor did they know that my furniture business had folded, and I'd been working in bars for two years. It wasn't the kind of thing I wanted to talk about over the phone. Or ever, really.

"I'll tell them. I will. Don't worry about it."

"I'm not worried about that. I'm worried about *you*."

"Well, you don't need to be. Everything's great."

There was a pause, and I pictured her on the other end of the line, tugging at her bottom lip the way she did when she was working up the nerve to say something she knew I didn't want to hear.

"Just ask," I said with a sigh.

Another beat, and then, "Have you seen Jess?"

Something caught in my throat, and I cleared it quickly. "Yeah."

"And?"

"And ... what?"

It sounded ridiculous, but my ex-wife was the only person who knew about my complicated feelings for Jess. I'd confided in Bek to make her feel better when I'd fucked up my life, my business, and my marriage with one too many whiskeys, and she'd fallen in love with her personal trainer. We'd gotten married too fast and for all the wrong reasons, and that was entirely on me, but it was going to be okay, I'd told her. I wanted her to be happy, and we couldn't help who we wanted—or who we didn't.

"*And*," she said. "What was it like?"

"Bek, I love you, and I'm happy to talk to you about almost anything, but in the same way I don't want to hear the finer details about you and Damien, I don't want to talk to you about Jess and me."

"So there *is* a you and Jess."

"What? No! I didn't say that."

"But whatever it is, it's hot, right?"

I groaned. "Bek, I have to go. I'll call you in a couple of weeks, okay?"

"Logan, wait."

"What is it?"

"I'm going to keep saying this until it sticks. You're a

wonderful man, and you deserve to be happy. Stop putting yourself second."

I huffed out an uncomfortable chuckle. "Is that what I do?"

"Worse than that. You take yourself out of the running because you think you'll never win first place, but life's not a race, and it's not about the destination."

"Someone needs to limit your access to the self-help section," I muttered.

"Logan, stop it. You're good enough, okay? You're more than good enough. You're one of the best men I've ever met. Tell her how you feel."

My skin started to itch. It was the dust. I needed a shower. "I appreciate the advice, Bek, but I really have to go. Thanks for calling."

"If I don't hear from you soon, I'm calling back."

Just like a bloody sister. "I wouldn't expect anything less."

In the beginning, my plan to avoid Jess worked perfectly. She was gone when I got to her place in the mornings— and she was sensible enough to leave the key under the mat like I asked—and I was out of there well before five in the afternoon. One person I couldn't dodge, however, was old Dorothy March next door.

She materialised like a phantom on the first day, with a white-bread ham sandwich on a plate in one hand and a glass of iced lemonade in the other.

"Holy shit!" I exclaimed, startled to find her standing in the middle of the yard, watching me, dressed in a baggy fluoro-yellow tracksuit set off by a tight halo of pink, fluffy hair and a fluoro-pink sweatband.

"I'm sorry to scare you, Logan. I saw you through my kitchen window and thought you might want something to eat."

I brushed off my hands and accepted the plate, tearing into the sandwich. I hadn't thought to pack myself lunch. "Cheers, Mrs March. I appreciate it. How have you been?"

"Oh, you know me. Keeping busy. Gym, the VBFYRRRBC, check in on Jess. Repeat."

Grinning, I ripped another bite of the sandwich. "The VBFYRRRBC still going strong, is it? How do I get an invitation? I'm dying to know what all those letters stand for."

"You don't meet the eligibility criteria for my book club."

"You'll let me know when I do?"

She flapped her hand. "Of course, dear. And how are you?"

"Can't complain." I ripped another bite of the sandwich.

"You're back for Luca's wedding, I assume?"

"Yep, and to spend time with the old crew."

Dot shook her head. "Sad business all that, wasn't it? With Luca and Jess, I mean."

I swallowed my mouthful of bread with effort. "Some relationships just don't work out, I guess."

Her head dropped to one side, and her eyes grew speculative. "I'm old enough to recognise experience when I hear it."

I swapped the empty plate for the lemonade, and she watched me with narrowed eyes as I chugged the entire glass. My conversation with Bek was still fresh in my mind, so when I finally met Dot's gaze, and she held it fast, I broke first.

"Yeah, I know something about it, but I'd rather not talk about it if it's all the same to you."

She accepted the empty glass, tucked it under her arm, and used her free hand to pat my cheek. "I remember you, Logan, and I always knew you were a good boy. It might not feel like it now, but things always work out in the end, especially for good people. You'll see."

I cleared my throat, surprised at the heat creeping up my neck. Old people in this town had never called me a *good boy*. Luca had been the good boy, and if I was lucky, they'd refer to me as *the good boy's friend*. The sidekick. More often than not, I disappeared altogether, blown out by his shining light. I didn't know why I compared myself to Luca in that moment with Dot. I thought I'd outgrown that shit. Being home was doing a number on my head.

"Nice talking to you, Mrs March, but I have to get back to work."

"Of course. I didn't mean to interrupt your day. Just feed you is all."

I spent three days lugging furniture and boxes in and out of that garage, rearranging what could be kept, stacking personal items along one wall so Jess and her parents could sort through them, and starting a pile of rubbish that grew so large it was going to require professional disposal.

Mrs March fed me every day, twice a day, but after that first conversation, she left a plate where I could find it instead of stopping me while I worked.

The biggest surprise of the whole task occurred when I finally reached the back of the garage and found a door that led through to an old workshop. At some point in the past, the person who lived at the property must have been a carpenter of sorts. There were benches fitted to the walls, plus another right in the middle, a handful of old, rusty tools, and bits and pieces of unfinished projects. I spent more time than I should have exploring, looking for anything that might still have use. I was distracted, and perhaps that was the reason I not only lost track of the time but also missed the sound of Jess's car pulling up the driveway. She must have come home and headed straight inside because it was almost six when I realised it was way past time for me to leave, and she hadn't popped her head in to say hello.

Not that I expected her to. That wasn't our arrangement.

I locked up the garage, ducked my head and powered out to the car, praying we wouldn't make awkward eye contact through a window or something, when movement at the front door flickered in the corner of my eye. I had to look up then. It was Jess, of course, and saying hello now would be unavoidable. I planned to wave, then leave, but the sight of her stopped me dead in my tracks.

"What?" Jess said, smoothing her black mini shorts over her hips, then collecting her ash brown waves in her hands and pulling them over one shoulder. "What are you looking at?" She parked her hands on her hips. "There's no food on my face this time, Reeve. I just got out of the shower."

"Uh, no. It's nothing."

I took a few steps closer just to get a better look. Her legs were miles long, ending in back strappy heels that twisted around her ankles and halfway up her calves. She wore a loose, pale pink tank with a scoop neckline and a leather jacket over the top that gave her a cute grunge vibe. The weather wasn't warm enough for so little clothing, so her hard nipples poked at the thin fabric of her top, and she'd coated her lips in a shade of red I hadn't seen her wear before. I'd *never* seen her look like this, and the impact was decimating.

"Are you going somewhere?" I asked, hoping she didn't notice the adolescent crack in my voice.

She flicked her hair back and started down the porch steps, and against my will, I was swept up into one of those slow-motion movie sequences. All that needed to happen now was for a rush of water to spill over Jess's chest, soaking her clothes and exposing her pink, peaked nipples, drenching her hair as she tipped back her head and shook it out, droplets flying everywhere. My pants strained as blood rushed to my dick. I blinked once or twice, and the fantasy dissolved, but by that time, she was standing right in front of me, glaring daggers. She smelled like soap, clean and floral, and I resisted the urge to run my tongue along her collarbone. Just one taste.

"Not that it's any of your business," she said, "but I have a date."

She had a *date*? Guess Luca had nothing to worry about—Jess was certainly moving on—but I didn't feel great about her going out looking the way she did. Anyone who saw her in those shorts was going to have one thing on his mind. I should know. My head—and cock—had already taken me there.

"You're meeting a guy?" I asked, knowing I sounded like a jerk, yet unable to stop the words before they tumbled out. "Wearing that?"

The fire in her eyes dimmed a little, and she ran her hands over her hips again. Did she know how that drew the eyes?

"Yes," she said. "Why? What's wrong with it?"

"Nothing, if you're going for a fired-up sex fiend kind of look."

I wanted a rewind button. I wanted one right now. A shadow of uncertainty passed across her face, and a crease popped up between her brows, but then they furrowed into a furious glower, and her eyes were throwing knives again.

"Yes, arsehole. That's exactly the *kind of look* I was going for. Now get out of my way. I've got somewhere to be."

"Who's the guy?" I asked as she pushed past me and slid into the driver's seat of her little red hatchback.

"You don't know him."

"Do you?"

She smiled, slow and deliberate. "I will after tonight."

The car door slammed, she backed out onto the street, and I watched her with my car keys biting into my clenched fist. I should let her go. Jess was smart, and she'd been taking care of herself for years. It wasn't my place to assume she needed a protector.

But she didn't even know this guy. *Fuck.*

I'd made a promise to Luca that I'd watch out for her, and that was the story I told myself as I threw myself into my car and sped towards The Stop. I'd have to give Will a lame excuse about why I couldn't help out behind the bar because no matter how long it took, I was determined to spend the rest of the night searching for Jess and whatever creep was scheming his way into her pants. Luca relied on me, and I couldn't let him down, but even I wasn't stupid enough to think for a second that's all this was about. Jessica Frost drove me nuts in every sense of the word, and until I was safe again on the other side of the world, it was increasingly impossible to pretend otherwise.

8

JESS

I DIDN'T KNOW how I felt about this date. It was the first one I'd set up myself since—well, ever. I'd been with Luca since high school, and the six guys I'd been out with after our break-up had all been introduced to me by my mother. Not one of them ticked my box, if you know what I mean. Only two had had promise, but both crashed and burned on second dates—I'd had little in common with the first guy and no chemistry with the other. So, all up, it had been nine months since I'd been out with a man, and the sad part was, I wasn't all that bothered. Dating felt like a chore, not an adventure, but I was determined to change things. Enter Zachary—my first real date in a really long time.

So yes, I was nervous. And a little excited. I'd given myself a serious pep talk before walking out the door, trying to add a little Abbie to my attitude. I could be cool with casual sex. I was a year off thirty, for crying out loud, and the number of men I'd slept with could be counted on one *finger*, not one hand. If I had any chance of getting Luca out of my system once and for all, I had to get another man *into* my system, or so Abbie told me. Her logic might have been crude, but even I had to admit, she wasn't wrong.

So, that would explain the *fired-up sex fiend* look, thank you very much.

As I drove towards The Stop, I tried not to fume at the way Logan had looked me up and down with horror in his eyes. Oh, how repulsive! Plain old Jessica trying to look sexy. Well, what did he know? My outfit had been pre-approved by both Abbie and Emily, so I was fairly confident I had the balance right. The red lips had been a late addition, sure, but I'd been feeling brave when I painted them on. Hell, I was *still* feeling brave. I wasn't going to let Logan mess with my head. Not tonight of all nights. I was calling the shots, and I was doing things nobody believed I was capable of, including—maybe especially—me.

I parked the car, checked my make-up in the rear-view mirror, then stepped out, purse clutched in one hand. The cool air sent goosebumps rippling across my skin, and my heart thumped in my ears, but I sucked in a breath and blew it out again in a long, steady rhythm. This evening was going to be great, but as I pushed against the familiar door of The Stop, I felt a wave of relief that I'd chosen Will's bar to meet Zachary for the first time. My behaviour tonight might be more reckless than usual, but I couldn't stop myself from planning ahead. If anything went wrong, I could excuse myself to go to the ladies' room, then ask Will to run interference. None of this meant I was scared. It was simply good sense.

I stepped inside and was embraced by warmth, music, and conversation, which helped settle my nerves. Scanning the bar and lifting my hand in a quick wave to Will, I located Zachary, who waited for me in a booth as we'd agreed. After picking my way through the crowd, I slid into the cushioned seat on the opposite side of the table, hoping he didn't notice my flush of self-consciousness as his bright blue eyes swept up and down my body, lingering on my thighs before making a stopover at my chest. That should have pleased me—at least, I thought it should have—but all I could think was, I wished I'd worn jeans. And a bra.

Zachary reached over and held out a hand. "Nice to meet you, Tess. You look smoking."

"Oh, um, thank you. And it's Jess," I corrected, shaking his hand.

"Shit, right. Sorry. Drink?"

"Uh, sure. Thanks. Margarita?"

"Coming right up."

Zachary made his way over to the bar while I removed my jacket and took the opportunity to get a better look at him. He wore tight blue jeans that hugged his butt and a black collared shirt, cuffed to sit halfway up his forearms. So far, so good. His hair was almost black in the moody light of the bar, and it had that naturally tousled look that could only be achieved with deceptively large quantities of hair product and time. He was clean-shaven, which I liked, and tall, also a plus. All in all, the package was definitely acceptable.

But just as I started to feel a little more at ease, Zachary leaned into the bar to buy our drinks and I noticed it wasn't Will who took his order. It was Logan.

What the actual hell?

My glance darted all over, searching for Will and maybe a hint to explain why Logan was pouring drinks and not the man who owned the place. And there I found him, flashing his boyish grin and irresistible dimples at a group of giggling women on the other side of the room. Since when did The Stop have table service?

The important thing was, Will was still here. That was good. I could pretend Logan didn't exist and focus on my date.

Zachary carried our drinks to our table, but over his shoulder, Logan glared at his back. Oh, my God. He was going to ruin this for me just because he could.

With a cocktail in my hand and a mouthful of it in my belly, I forced myself to relax. Zachary had parked himself on my side of the booth this time, and I resisted the urge to scoot away. At least the cologne he wore smelled nice, even if it was a little strong.

"So, Zachary, what do you do for work?" I asked.

"Call me Zach," he said, taking a swallow of his pint. "I own my own business. I'm an entertainer."

"Oh." Was I meant to read between the lines? I looked at the size of his arms and the obvious muscle under his shirt, and my cheeks grew warm. I took a sip of my drink to cool down.

Zach smirked at my discomfort. "I love doing that when I meet new people. Women always assume I'm a stripper. I'm not. I dress up as superheroes for kids' parties. Spiderman. Batman. That sort of thing."

I expelled a loud sigh, then panicked that he might be offended at my relief. If anything, he only seemed amused.

"The thing is, Tess, I've got to work hard to fill out a superhero costume, you know? I've got the body of a stripper under here. Trust me."

I licked my lips and examined his chest again, then took another gulp of my drink. I couldn't even string together enough words to correct him on my name. Again.

Zach stretched his arm along the back of the booth. "So, you live around here?"

"Uh, yes. Not far. You're from Sydney, right?"

"Yeah, but I've got friends over in Scarborough Cove. If things don't go well tonight, I'll crash with them instead."

Holy crap. He was talking about sex. With me. Tonight. Zach's arm dropped off the back of the seat and over my shoulder. His fingers brushed up and down my arm, and I tried hard to like it. I really did.

"Nice place," he commented, looking around the pub.

"A friend of mine owns it. I come here all the time."

He lifted his near-empty beer glass and tipped his chin

at my finished margarita. "Excellent. Think you can swing the next round on the house?"

"Oh." I looked over at the bar at just the wrong moment. Logan was staring at me, but when I met his eyes, he turned away to serve another customer. "I could try, I guess."

"That's my girl."

My stomach heaved at the endearment, and then it tightened violently as Zachary wrapped two large hands around my waist and dragged me across his lap to the open side of the booth. I squealed and swung my legs around, avoiding the way he leaned into me as if angling for a kiss. Snatching up my purse and starting for the bar, I searched for Will but couldn't see him anywhere. That left me with Logan. Fuck my life.

I waited my turn at the bar, then stepped up and set my purse on it, fingers clasped on top. Logan wiped his hands on a towel, then flung it over his shoulder. "You look uncomfortable."

I'd expected a smart-arse comment and opened my mouth to bite back, but he delivered his line without heat, and I stalled for a second. "Well, I'm not," I said.

"No?"

"No. Everything's going just the way I want it to. Another round, please."

Logan pulled a pint for Zach and set it in front of me, then started mixing my margarita. Not a single emotion played across his face. "Say the word, and I'll get you out of here."

Again, my mouth opened, and I had to close it with a snap. I smacked my money on the bar, stuck my purse under one arm, and picked up the drinks. "That won't be necessary. And why are you here on the bar, anyway? Where's Will?"

Logan looked up and around the room. "He's here somewhere, but it's busy, so I'm helping out."

"Right." I glanced over at Zachary, who was leering at me again, and I turned back to the bar, blinking and biting my lip, staring into my drink, wishing I didn't have to go back there.

"I'm right here," Logan murmured.

"Just my luck. Stay out of my love life, Reeve. All right?"

"Fine." He stalked up the bar to tend to another customer while I took another breath, glued a smile on my face, and returned to my date.

Zachary grinned up at me as I set our drinks on the table. He made just enough room for me to sit down, patting the seat to indicate I should squeeze in beside him, so I did, but I was forced to press up against him or else fall on the floor. With one hand, he took a slug of his beer. The other he set on my thigh, and slowly it moved higher and higher until he was north enough to run a finger beneath the fabric of my barely there shorts.

"Uh, what are you doing?" I asked.

Zachary leaned in and swept the tip of his nose along my neck. "You're such a fucking tease, Tess. I can't help it."

My head jerked up, and I searched desperately for Logan. I don't know what he saw when our eyes met, but he froze mid-pour, launched himself over the bar, and bolted for my table.

"Sorry to interrupt your night," he announced, sounding anything but remorseful. His gaze landed on Zachary's fingers underneath my shorts, and his nostrils flared. "Jess, there's a cop outside about to tow your car. Looks like you parked it in a no-stopping zone."

Zachary pulled away, but his hand didn't leave my thigh. "Is this the friend who owns the pub?" He looked Logan up and down. "We're kind of busy here. Do you mind moving Tess's car for her? Go on, sweetheart. Give him your keys."

"I can't ask him to do that," I said. "It's too busy for Logan to leave right now. Don't worry. It'll just take a minute."

I slid out of my seat, collected my purse and jacket, and let Logan usher me outside. I saw him tip his chin at Will, who was back at the bar pouring drinks, and then we were outside in the cool, fresh air, and I was blinking back tears.

"Go home," Logan said. "I'll tell the dipshit inside you had to leave. Headache or something."

"Yeah, okay. Thanks." I pressed the button on my central locking and opened the car door, but Logan put a hand on it, and I stopped. Here came the *I told you so*, and I really, *really* didn't want to hear that right now. "What?" I asked sharply.

"I've nearly finished the garage. Can I come by Sunday morning to talk you through it?"

"Oh. Sure, I guess."

"Eight o'clock okay?"

"Yeah, okay. Fine."

"Have a good night."

I scoffed quietly, unsurprised that he managed to get a final, sneaky dig in, and slid in behind the wheel.

Soon enough, I was on my way home much sooner than I had expected. What a complete disaster. Served me right for listening to Abbie.

And there it was again. More undeniable proof I had no freaking idea what I was doing. I was a paint-by-numbers kind of girl, someone who coloured inside the lines and would never make a pretty picture of her life working freehand. The sad part was, the paint-by-numbers life I used to have wasn't exactly a masterpiece, either. I was sick of being told what to do, sick of ticking boxes, but I didn't know how to run my life otherwise.

As I looked in the rear vision mirror, I saw Logan standing on the street outside The Stop, watching me go. He was still there when I turned the corner and left Main Street behind.

9

JESS

HE KNOCKED ON my door on Sunday morning at eight o'clock on the dot. I was showered and dressed in my standard weekend wardrobe, but my hair was a wet knot on the top of my head, and I had my glasses on. I tried not to wear my contact lenses all day, every day, but I was hoping Logan would take the glasses as bait. I'd rather be tormented about those, like the good old days, than deal with the fallout of my date.

"Morning," I greeted him.

"Hey, Frost." He tweaked my glasses like I knew he would. "Ever thought about buying less-obvious frames?"

"Shut up, Reeve. These are a *look*. It's not my fault you don't get it."

He raised his palms. "My apologies. I didn't realise you were so into fashion."

I looked down at my baggy tee, torn jeans, and worn-in sneakers at the same time he did and knew we both came away with the same conclusion. I wasn't exactly stylish.

I crossed my arms and jutted out one hip. "Are we going to get started in the garage or what?"

Logan's lips twitched, but he refrained from commenting as he led me out to the backyard and past an enormous pile of rubbish that he'd covered with big blue tarps.

"I've watched this get bigger and bigger every day," I commented as I gestured at the heap.

"Yeah, there was a bunch of furniture that wasn't worth saving. Some rolls of rotten fabrics. Tons of mouldy books and magazines. You're welcome to go through it, but I don't think there's anything you'll want to keep."

"I trust you," I replied.

Logan quirked an eyebrow at me. "Can I get that in writing?"

"No. I already take it back."

He chuckled, then unlocked the padlock and yanked open the garage doors. I gasped at the transformation inside.

There was a wide aisle all the way to the back of the room, where a door stood open. One side of the garage was filled with neatly ordered furniture, the other stacked high with boxes and bags. Logan pointed to that section first.

"Personal items that you'll need to sort through yourself. Photo albums and letters and official paperwork. I didn't look too closely at anything, so good chance there'll be even more to throw away once you've gone through it."

I decided instantly to hand that job over to my parents.

They would know better than I would what was important enough to keep.

Logan gestured at the furniture. "This all has enough going for it to fix and keep or sell if you want to."

I ran a hand over an old armchair with holes in the upholstery. "Do you mean DIY?"

Logan grinned at the uncertainty in my voice. "If you want to give it a go, sure, or you could sell them the way they are at upcycle markets or direct to artisan carpenters. I used to do a lot of this kind of work back in London. Plenty of people have the money but not the time to fix vintage furniture."

"Did you enjoy it?"

"Uh, yeah. Most of the time. Preferred making my own stuff, but sometimes you have to take the work you're offered when you can get it."

"Makes sense." I walked past the furniture, all the way to the end of the garage, and stuck my head through the opened door. "What's this?"

Logan crept up behind me, and I startled when he put his big, warm hands on my shoulders and squeezed. He moved me aside and stepped into the room, but even after his hands were gone, I could feel the heat of his skin on mine. The sensation poured over me like syrup, tingling and burning its way to my core.

"This is the best part," he said. "Someone built a workshop in here, and it's the last bit of work I have to do. Sorting out the tools and clearing away the grime and dust. It should only take a couple of hours."

I checked my watch. My parents weren't due for brunch for more than two hours, and Logan had already done enough work on his own. It felt like the right thing to do to offer to pitch in. "I've got time now if you want some help?"

Logan rubbed his neck and looked around. "Uh, you don't have anything better to do with your Sunday morning?"

"Not really. Mum and Dad will be here at about eleven, so I'm free until then."

There was an uncomfortable beat before he agreed. "Okay, then. Sure. Let's do it."

"Great. Where do I start?"

Under Logan's direction, I helped him toss a bunch of old tools, save a smaller collection of things that were in better condition, clean out cupboards and wipe down benches, and reorganise the bits and pieces he wanted to keep. By the end of it, I was covered in dust and sweat, but it felt good to work my muscles. In fact, I kind of enjoyed it.

"Thanks, Frost," he said. "You cut my workload in half."

"Really?" I don't know why his praise made me feel so good.

"No, not really. By a third, at best. More like a quarter. You ask more fucking questions than a five-year-old."

"Get lost," I grumbled, pushing him out the door and through the garage. "I did good today."

"Yeah, sure. Maybe you did."

I walked him around the house and out to where Will's car was parked on the driveway. "Thanks for the help," I said. "You didn't have to do this."

He ran a hand through his hair, and puffs of dust sprang out where his fingers pulled through. "No problem."

"So, I guess I'll see you around. At the wedding, at least."

"Yeah, the wedding. Of course."

When he didn't get in his car, I waited for him to bring up Zachary. Rub my nose in the fact he'd had to run to my rescue. There was no way he'd be able to resist getting one up on me. I knew the way Logan Reeve worked.

"Frost, promise me you won't go on any more dates with strangers you meet on dating apps."

And there it was.

"I said it before, and I'll say it again. Who I date—or who I sleep with—is not your concern."

I wasn't about to give him the satisfaction of knowing I'd already deleted the app from my phone.

"You made it my concern on Friday night."

"That was bad luck. I appreciate you being there, but that's the whole reason I went to The Stop in the first place. I knew I'd have Will there to bail me out."

He scoffed. "The fact you prepared for disaster proves to me you do not want to be doing shit like that."

"Like what?"

"Dressing up for dickheads who just want to get in your pants."

"Do you know what I really hate? More than unsolicited dating advice from a man who can't stand me?"

Logan's eyes flashed, and a vein throbbed in his neck. "What?"

"Unsolicited advice from happily married arseholes who think finding a soulmate is easy! It's not, all right? It's the hardest, most heartbreaking thing most people will ever have to do. I do not need a lecture on the best way to find love from some smug bastard who has a wife to go home to when all this wedding bullshit is over!"

Logan's chest heaved with the fast, shallow breaths of someone who was monumentally pissed off. "Who said anything about love? You were out there on Friday night looking for someone to fuck!"

I reared back as if slapped, and someone cleared their throat, loudly and deliberately, a little way off to my left. My parents were standing there, watching with horrified eyes.

Oh, boy.

"Mr Frost," Logan said. "Mrs Frost." He extended a hand to first my father, then my mother, who accepted it with a sour twist to her mouth. "I was just leaving. It's nice to see you again. Have a good day."

Logan jumped in his car, slammed the door, and took off down the street, leaving behind an awkward silence and a band around my chest that made it hard for me to breathe.

"What was Logan Reeve doing here?" Mum asked.

Apparently, my parents were going to ignore the conversation they'd accidentally overheard. I was okay with that. I swallowed thickly, not sure if I was choking on shock or shame, and watched Logan drive away. "He's been helping me clear out the garage."

"What? Why would he do that?"

"I don't know. He offered. I accepted. Nothing sinister."

I started inside, heading to the kitchen, where I pulled out the quiche I'd made the day before and put in the oven this morning to reheat. I concentrated on breathing—in and out and again.

"Oh, quiche," Dad murmured, rubbing his hands together.

"That boy is bad news," Mum said, taking a seat at the dining table.

"He's hardly a boy anymore, Sandra," Dad commented.

"Oh, I noticed. And were those tattoos on his arms?"

"Maybe," I replied. "I haven't paid attention."

I cut slices of quiche, plated them, and poured juice. Dad dug right in, and I picked at mine, but there was no stopping my mother's mouth.

"Why is he sniffing around here? What does he want?"

The last thing I wanted to be doing right then was defending Logan, but I didn't like my mother's tone. "He doesn't want anything, and he's not *sniffing around*. He's a friend who I haven't seen in years."

"He's married, Jessica. Don't debase yourself by becoming the other woman."

I dropped my fork, and it hit my plate with a loud *clang*. "Why would you say something like that? I'm not interested, and even if I were, Logan's not a cheater or a liar—and neither am I."

"I thought you had better judgement than this, and if not *then*, at least now that you're older." Mum shook her head and scooped up a small bite of her meal.

"Better judgement than when? You're going to have to explain this to me because I have no idea what you're on about."

Mum dabbed her lips with a napkin, then set it down. "Very well. You were always a featherhead when it came to Logan Reeve, even though Luca was a much better match. Logan had no goals, no vision, no plans for his future, and he was a bad influence. How many classes did he fail? How many days was he caught truant from school—taking you with him, I might add?"

"That was one time!"

"When has he ever applied himself to anything worthwhile?" she demanded. "And just when he might have been able to make something of himself with his construction apprenticeship, he ran off to Europe and never came back. He's unreliable, Jessica. Always has been and always will be."

"That's not—"

"He wasn't right for you then," she interrupted, "and he's not right for you now."

Mum spoke as if she knew something she shouldn't, and I shifted in my seat. "I've never had a thing for Logan."

A small smile played across her mouth, and that confirmed my suspicions.

"Logan is here for Luca's wedding," I said firmly, "then he's going home to London to be with his wife. Nothing has ever happened between the two of us, and it never will. I don't know what fantasy land you're living in, but you can stop talking about it. Now."

Mum shook her head. "Fine. Shall we discuss the house, then? I spoke to the real estate agent again, and he hasn't heard from you. Why haven't you called?"

"I haven't decided what I want to do with the house yet," I lied. Sometimes it was easier to let my mother think she was getting her way rather than come right out and argue with her.

She exchanged a look with my father, then gave him a slight nod. He cleared his throat and put down his fork.

"Now, sweetheart. Your mother and I have been talking, and we've decided you need a little push."

My glance bounced between the two of them. "I don't understand."

"Three years is more than enough time to fix up this house," he went on, "and it hasn't happened. So, just like we did when you were younger, when you listened to us and your life was ... on track ... we're setting you a task and giving you a deadline to motivate you."

My pulse sped up. "What task? What deadline?"

Mum shifted in her chair. "If you're serious about keeping this house, we want you to prove to us you can make something of it. We're giving you ten weeks to do what you should have already done—ten weeks to create your dream home."

"You're both crazy," I scoffed.

My mother pursed her lips. "Are we the crazy ones, or are you? Holding onto this property and doing nothing with it—does that make sense?"

"I can't renovate a whole house in ten weeks!"

"You're right, you can't," Mum agreed, "but if you count the three years you've lived here so far, you've had more than enough time."

"You want me to fail," I accused. My chest felt tight again, and it was hard to fill my lungs.

Mum put a hand over mine. "Now, darling, it's not about failing. It's about convincing you to give up this dream and find a new one. A more realistic one."

"You realise I'm a grown woman, right? I don't have to go along with this."

"You're right," Dad said. "You don't have to take on this challenge, but maybe you should."

Mum's mouth flattened. "Prove to us you know better than we do, Jessica. Prove to me I'm wrong because I don't think I am, and the sooner you come to terms with it, the better."

A rebellious burn rushed through my body, chasing the hot humiliation of Logan's earlier reproach. "Fine, have it your way, but I don't need ten weeks. I'll do it in five."

"Now, don't be like that," Mum replied.

"Like what? I know how I want the house to look—I even went to pick out paint samples last week—and the mid-year break is coming up at school. It's the perfect time to get things done."

Dad frowned. "Jessica, you don't have to—"

My mother thrust her manicured hand at me. "Deal. Thirty-five days."

I gritted my teeth and placed my hand in hers, and the look of triumph on her face made me want to scream.

"Oh, I'm so glad that's out of the way," she said. "Now, I wanted to talk to you about your dress for the wedding. What do you think about wearing cream? Not white—*of course* not white—but something neutral?"

I let her words rush past me, adding as little as I could to keep the conversation flowing, and the hour dragged on as if it would never end until finally, I was waving them goodbye from the front door.

As soon as I was on my own, I slammed the front door, stomped to the spare bedroom, and dug around for the box I used to store sentimental things from my past. Awards and trophies, old school reports and birthday cards, notes passed in class and stuffed toys traded with friends. Finally, I found what I was looking for. First, the binder I used to file my renovation notes before I shelved my plans indefinitely, and second, my high school diary.

I put the binder to the side, dread settling like a weight in my stomach as I considered the stupid agreement I'd made with my parents. I was going to regret that decision, but poor choices and self-flagellation had become the theme songs of my life.

Instead, I opened my old diary and flicked through the pages, my eyes tripping again and again on the large red love hearts and the messages scrawled inside them.

Jessica Frost loves Logan Reeve.

JF + LR.

Logan Reeve 4EVA.

I'd seen it all before, but not for a long time, and looking at it today put a sour burn in my throat. It was the only answer I could come up with to explain my mother's coy behaviour. At some time in the past, she must have read my diary. I wish I could say I was surprised, but it was right on brand. The woman had no boundaries and nothing in my life was sacred as far as she was concerned. Frustration boiled again in my veins.

Well, if she'd bothered to keep reading, she'd have learned that any feelings I might have had for Logan had been well and truly shelved by the time we graduated high school. I'd stopped writing in my diary after that because I didn't need anything printed in ink to recall the lessons I'd learned in those formative years. I took the diary with me as I left the room, tucking it away in my underwear drawer. I knew it then, just as I knew it now: Logan Reeve couldn't stand me, and the feeling was definitely mutual.

10

LOGAN

I DID A great job ignoring the world for the next few days. I surfed every morning, ran for an hour every afternoon, spent more time than strictly necessary finishing Will's floors, and sent my temporary boss upstairs to the loft after happy hour every night, manning the bar for him while he got on with things he never had time to do otherwise. When I offered to cover for him, and he reluctantly accepted even though it wasn't the weekend, I thought for sure he'd take the chance to line up a couple of dates. But on the third night, when I dragged myself upstairs after closing time and found him once again sitting at his dining table, elbow-deep in accounting reports and paperwork, I poured Will a whiskey, got myself an iced tea, and asked him what the hell was going on.

Will accepted the drink and slumped back in his chair, taking a sip and sitting silently for a minute. I waited, looking around at his small loft apartment—the bedroom upstairs, the small second bedroom he used for storage, the tiny but neat kitchen, and the open-plan living areas. It was a bachelor pad but a modest one.

"Thanks for the floors, Reeve," he said finally, gazing into his tumbler and swirling the amber liquid around. "They look great."

"Really? By the look on your face, you'd think I coated them in red paint and studded them with rusty nails." He snorted, and I leaned forward, elbows resting on my knees. "What's the problem?"

"Not the floors. Seriously. They're perfect, and I owe you one." He met my stare, and when I said nothing, he rolled his eyes. "Nobody's ever mistaken me for the serious type, right? But, fuck. I want this bar to succeed. No, I want more than that. I want to expand, I want to open my brewery, and I *don't* want to be watching every dollar so bloody closely." He looked over at me from underneath his furrowed brow. "Makes me sound like an arrogant arsehole, doesn't it?"

I mirrored his posture, relaxing into the hard-back dining chair. "Not at all. Sounds like a sweet dream."

He chuckled under his breath. "Yeah. Just a dream."

"What the fuck's wrong with that? Every big win begins as a dream. You have to start somewhere." I hesitated, watching him nurse his whiskey. "But why all the pressure?"

Will threw back the last mouthful and smacked the empty glass onto the table. "Ever feel like the years get away from you?"

I snorted, ignoring the pit his words punched in my stomach. Every day felt like another chance slipping through my fingers. "We're young. There's plenty of time to do what we want to do."

"Maybe you're right. Maybe it's all Luca and Tash's wedding talk, and now Josh and Emily settling down. You're already four years into a marriage. We're growing up, man. At least everyone else is, and I'm trying to catch up."

Now didn't feel like the right time to admit I wasn't only old enough to be married but also divorced with a failed business on my résumé and a lonely life waiting for me on the other side of the world. Will needed me to build him up, not drag him down.

"Finding a partner isn't the only way—or even a *good* way—to measure progress or success," I offered. "You're the only one of us with a pub to his name, and business is doing well, isn't it?"

"It is," he admitted with a shrug. "But it's taken a lot of work to shake my reputation as a playboy, you know? Will Kidd: always in it for a good time. It'd be nice to be taken seriously for a change. I'm done with screwing around, acting like a stupid teenager all the time." He gestured to the piles of paperwork. "Doesn't change the fact that all this would be easier if I had someone to share it with."

I nodded slowly. "I get that."

Rolling my glass between my palms, I replayed for the millionth time my last conversation with Jess. The way I'd spoken to her and the look on her face afterwards. The hurt in her wide brown eyes. There's no way she could have known how her words would scratch at a wound I'd hesitate to call healed, but Will was right—I was way too old to be lashing out like a rejected kid, and that's exactly what I'd done.

"Thanks for the chat," Will said. "I appreciate the ear." Then he set an ankle on the opposite knee, crossed his arms, and stared at me with a knowing smirk on his face.

I narrowed my eyes at him. "What?"

"There's one more way we know we're getting older."

"Oh, shit." I knew where this was headed.

"Don't think you're getting out of it."

I set my elbows on my knees and put my face in my hands. "I thought for sure you'd forget."

"You haven't had a birthday here in six years. There was no way in hell we'd let this one pass without a party."

"It's not even an important birthday. I'll be twenty-nine, for fuck's sake. What's the big deal?"

"Some might say that the last year of your twenties is worth celebrating, but that's not what this is about." He stretched towards me and set a hand on my shoulder. "We've missed you, Reeve. It's good to have you home. Let us throw you a party."

I spared a small, fast smile for him, then sat up. "Fine."

"Glad to hear that because Abbie's already organised everything. Bonfire on the beach this Friday night, just like the good old days."

"Yeah, right. I bet this town still finds any excuse to get drunk and kick up drama around a fire."

"The man speaks the truth," Will agreed with a grin. "The crew even convinced me to close the bar and direct customers to the beach if they want drinks, so it'll be a big one."

Knowing what I did now about how hard he was working to solidify his business, the gesture hit home. "Thanks, Kidd. Sounds like a good night." I looked into my empty glass, wishing I had something to wet my throat. "So, all the usual suspects will be there?"

"You bet. Abbie, Josh and Emily, Isaac, Luca and Tash, Jess, plus anyone else who wanders past. It'll be a good night."

"Yeah. Sounds like it."

I took our dirty glasses to the kitchen while Will returned to death-by-accounting. I scrubbed them and set them on the drying rack, then dropped onto the couch and scrolled mindlessly through my phone. Anything to avoid *thinking*.

Since I'd messed things up so royally at Jess's place, and because avoidance was my MO, I'd considered ignoring her entirely until the wedding, and even on the big day, there'd be so much happening I could probably stay out of her way.

I imagined not speaking to her again before flying back to London, and the idea of it—having her so close for the next month and not letting myself so much as look at her, then leaving without knowing when or if I'd ever see her again—made every muscle in my body pull tight. But now that she'd be at my birthday party and that option was off the table, I'd have to come up with another plan.

Was I capable of having a functional friendship with Jess, one that wasn't weighed down with more than a decade of hostility and emotional baggage? I still had a promise to Luca I had to keep, plus I owed Jess an apology—or at least, an explanation. Those reasons alone were enough for me to admit that if there were any hope things might improve, I was going to have to be the one to make the first move.

She was avoiding me.

Walking onto the south end of the beach for the first time in years was like stepping into a time machine. Every sight, scent, and sensation was familiar. The raging blaze in the ash-caked ring of stones the Bay always used for parties. The black sky filling up with stars in patterns that spelled out my childhood. The bodies dancing to thumping music that cocooned us like walls of good vibrations. The beer and cocktails exchanging hands. The sharp chill in the air. The laughter. If someone had tapped me on the shoulder and told me I was eighteen again, I might have believed them.

The party had started at eight and two hours into it, every one of the fifty-odd guests had sought me out to shake my hand, exchange a story, and wish me a happy birthday. Everyone except for Jess. It was the kind of fuss I hated, but given that Valentine Bay would use any excuse to set the sand on fire, I wasn't the centre of attention for long before the music was blaring, the drinks were flowing, and everyone had forgotten that I was the reason they were there.

And the entire time, Jess kept moving around, scooting away if I got anywhere near her, finding someone else to talk to or somewhere else to be like she had an anti-Logan radar switched on at maximum strength.

"Cheers," Isaac said, strolling over from the bar and handing me a brown glass bottle before taking a slug out of his own.

"Thanks, man, but I'd rather not drink."

"I know," he replied with a wink. "It's a mocktail. Some sugary shit Will put together."

Taking a hesitant draw and not hating the pineapple-flavoured concoction, I crossed my arms over my chest and stood shoulder to shoulder with my old friend, gazing out over the orange-lit and shadowed throng. My focus drifted towards Jess and away again, back and forth, never losing track of where she was at any given moment.

"Not working tonight?" I asked.

"Nope. I'm on the early shift tomorrow."

"No date?" The grunt Isaac gave me had me turning my head, and I grinned at the familiar chagrin on his face. "Friend-zoned again?"

"Starting to wonder what the fuck is wrong with me," he growled, the sound reverberating around his barrel of a chest.

"Nothing, man," I laughed, punching his arm. "Nothing at all."

Whatever Isaac was going to say next was cut off by a thready call over my shoulder.

"Oh, Logan! There you are!"

Mrs March came tottering over, picking her way across the sand, circling the fire and beelining straight for me. As I turned to greet her, I noted Jess was in yet another new position, tucked up against Abbie on a wide driftwood log, snuggled under a wool blanket wrapped around their shoulders. Abbie's back was turned a little away from Jess, her attention all on Will, who had closed the bar half an hour earlier and was now three drinks into his night. One look, and I could tell he was trying to lure Abbie onto the dance floor, and I nudged Isaac with an elbow, jerking my chin to direct his attention that way.

It had always been the same: Will and Abbie flirted like teenagers, insisted nothing was going on between them, and played the field as though it were the truth. Yet, get enough alcohol into him, and Will begged Abbie for more every time. She refused every time, too, often leading to theatrics from the both of them, but the next day, they went on with life as though the pleading and the rejecting had never happened. If I wasn't so messed up over Jess, I'd have said Will and Abbie's relationship was the most bizarre I'd ever seen.

"Hi, Mrs March," I said to Jess's neighbour. "Thanks for coming."

"Oh, it's a pleasure."

I leaned down so she could plant a kiss on my cheek, and she grabbed my hand, pressing a folded note into my palm.

"Happy birthday, Logan. Now don't spend it all at once, you hear?"

Glancing down at the money in my hand, I tucked the five-dollar note into my pocket. "Wouldn't dream of it. Thank you."

"You're welcome. Now, what have you been up to this week? I haven't seen you at Jessica's house since Sunday."

"That's right." I peeked at Jess, and our eyes met, but she looked away. "I finished with her garage, and that's that, I guess."

"I'm glad to hear you're not busy because I could use your help."

"Oh, yeah? How's that?"

"The timber boards on my front porch are loose. Dreadful wobble, and I almost fell two days ago. Would you be kind enough to stop by and take a look at them?"

"Of course. No problem. How does tomorrow sound?"

Feeling an itch between my shoulder blades knowing that Jess was out of sight, I turned to see her extracting herself from the blanket, wrapping it tighter around Abbie, and giving both her and Will kisses on their cheeks. She was wearing jeans and boots, a cute grey knit beanie on her head, her cheeks flushed from the combination of cool air and heat from the fire.

"Tomorrow would be wonderful," Dot replied. "Is seven o'clock too early for you? I have an aerobics class at ten-thirty, then VBFYRRRBC in the afternoon."

"Huh?" I was distracted, watching Jess wrap her arms around Josh and Emily, who were canoodling on another of the fallen logs. Was she leaving? "Sorry, Mrs March. Sure. Seven is fine."

"Oh, good." She patted my cheek the way she had in Jess's backyard. "Don't stay out too late tonight. It's chilly."

"Don't worry, I won't. I think the party's starting to break up anyway."

She looked at her watch. "Well, goodness me! Look at the time. I best be off. I'll see you tomorrow, young man, and don't worry about breakfast. I'll feed you when you get there."

I waved in her direction as the old woman wandered over to a group of similarly senior partygoers, and they started to make their way to the nearest path to the street, but in the thirty seconds I'd been distracted, Isaac had drifted off, and I'd lost sight of Jess. Shit.

Scanning the faces still around the fire and then looking for movement along the distant street, I spotted her walking away along the sand, headed towards an exit point further north. Her stride was long and fast, her head was bowed and her shoulders hunched, and I knew she was trying to get away before she had to face me. Twin grappling hooks of guilt and affection clamped onto my ankles and tugged. Hard.

Jogging to catch up to her, we were halfway up the beach, equal distances between the fire and the street, before I was close enough to call her name. When she didn't respond, I ran a little faster and reached out to stop her with a hand on her shoulder. She spun around and crossed her arms.

"What?"

"You're leaving?" I asked. "Without even telling me happy birthday?"

Jess said nothing for a long minute, and her dark eyes were cool. What I wouldn't have done for her usual heat. I relished the rush of her frustration and fury, and I didn't want her to look at me with nothing behind her eyes.

"Happy birthday," she said, spinning and stalking away again.

"Wait!"

She didn't, and I went after her again. "Jess!"

When she didn't stop, I shouted after her. "Bek and I broke up!"

That froze Jess on the spot, but she didn't turn around straightaway. I watched her back, too scared to move in case I spooked her, and waited for her to come to me. Releasing a breath when she turned, looking at me but not coming closer, I slowly took a step, then another. When she didn't run away, I closed the distance, stopping close enough to touch her if I wanted to.

"You said I was a smug bastard with a wife to go home to when the wedding is over, but it's not true."

"Part of it is," she mumbled.

I tried not to smile, but it was hard. Insults were good. Insults were fire where before there was ice. "Not the part about being divorced and single."

"When?"

"Two years ago."

"I'm sorry." She crossed her arms over her chest and looked up at me. "Why haven't you told anyone?"

"I haven't found the right time."

"It didn't happen yesterday."

"No, but it's also not the kind of thing you share in a text message."

"You could have called."

"You're right. I could have, but I didn't, and now I don't want to ruin Luca's wedding with divorce talk."

Her eyes narrowed, and her nose twitched. A bad decision was imminent.

"So, why are you telling me? And why now?"

Shit.

"The truth?" She rolled her eyes, and I ran a hand down my face. "Give me a break, would you? I'm trying to apologise."

"Well, you're not very good at it."

"That's because I don't have to do it very often."

She huffed out a laugh. "Holy crap, you're full of yourself."

I took a calming breath. "I shouldn't have spoken to you the way I did. It was rude and insensitive, and I don't know any more than you do about finding love. All right?"

She looked down at her feet and kicked at the sand. "All right. Thank you."

That was it? It was that easy?

"What about the other stuff you said? About the way I dress and who I date."

Nope. It wasn't that easy.

114

I frowned, but I'd started with the truth, and I was going to stick with it. "No, I don't apologise for that. I still don't think you should be dressing up for dickheads who just want to sleep with you."

"Typical." She blinked a few times, lifted her shoulders and dropped them again, then looked out across the ocean. The tips of the heaving waves glinted silvery under the moon, and the sounds of music and laughter floated to us over the gentle roar of the waves. "Thanks for trusting me enough to tell me about Bek, and I really am sorry things didn't work out. I won't say anything if that's what you want."

"Yeah, thanks. I appreciate that."

"Happy birthday, Reeve. I'll see you around."

She was halfway to her car before I realised that was it. Huh. I thought an apology and confession of heartbreak would have made a bigger splash.

I waited until I was sure she got in her car and pulled away before returning to the bonfire. I wasn't in the mood for it anymore, but I didn't feel like going back to the loft yet, either. I did my best to distract myself with loud music, drunk conversation, and cold appetisers, but disappointment made a home in my gut, and I still hadn't shaken it by morning.

11

JESS

FUCK. BULLSHIT. BULLSHIT. Fuck. Fuck.

I lugged my little ladder to the other end of the long window in the second bedroom, where I'd begun my renovations—because the room had a door I could close if my experiments went awry. Climbing onto the top rung and reaching up on my toes, I tried to set the white metal curtain rod in its bracket. I'd drilled them in myself, and they were almost even. At least they weren't so uneven anyone would notice. I had one end of the rod inserted on the opposite end of the window, but every time I tried to set the pole, the other side would slip out and fall to the floor. I'd been at this curtain caper for two hours and achieved nothing, and the only other things I had to show for a week of renovating were discounted curtains still in the packaging plus a stack of carpet swatches in the corner—and I wasn't even sure I wanted to install carpet.

I tried not to panic that the first five days of my agreement with my parents had flown by while I was plugging through the last week of school before the break. Teaching at a private college had plenty of perks—the big one was access to more classroom resources than I'd ever thought possible, but the other was the extended mid-year holiday. Under usual circumstances, my students would be out for three weeks, and so would I, and before last Sunday's fateful brunch, I'd planned to spend my time off doing not much other than binge-reading the dozen romance novels queued up on my e-reader.

But then, three days ago, after an impulsive night of online shopping and with a delivery of pretty, gauzy curtains headed my way, I'd managed to arrange a substitute to cover my classes for the first two weeks back in session, making up for the five days I'd lost so far. So, I'd signed off on Friday afternoon feeling hopeful and prepared to spend the next thirty days breaking fingernails and dreaming of nothing other than my house and how it was going to feel to flip my parents the proverbial bird on The Day I Proved Them Wrong.

Now, with the trouble I'd had teaching myself to use a power drill and trying to install a single set of freaking curtains, I was beginning to think reveal day was more likely to go down as The Day of Great Regret. There I'd stand amid the rubble of all my grand plans and admit to everyone I had no idea how to find my own dates, have casual sex, put up a curtain, demolish a kitchen, or figure out a way to stand up to my parents.

I slipped the curtain rod into the bracket, and sure enough, the opposite end fell right out again. As it hit the floorboards with a tinny thud, I clenched my jaw, strained my arms, and tried to heave it up again. The rod wasn't heavy, and neither were the curtains, but the pole was long and awkward, and in an ideal world, I'd have someone there to set it straight so that both ends could be locked in at the same time. But it wasn't an ideal world, and I didn't have someone there, and if I was going to show my parents that I could live my life on my terms, I had to do this on my own.

Bracing my knees and preparing for one final attempt to get the rod in place, I hoisted it. The curtains slipped down the pole towards me and somehow caught on my ankle, and before I knew it, I was shrieking like a banshee and careening backwards as the rod slammed through the glass window with an ear-shattering crash. I landed painfully on my arse, jarred an elbow trying to break my fall, and lay there in the aftermath, eyes closed, shrouded in torn gossamer fabric that I'd bought for fifty percent off, feeling the sharp bite of broken glass under my skin, and spiralling into a familiar pit of despair. Oh, hello, misery. I know you.

Then it got worse.

A resonant, urgent voice shouted from somewhere outside. "Jess! Jess, are you all right? Where are you?"

Fuck. My. Life.

"Go away!" I screeched.

The crunch of footsteps outside grew louder, and I squeezed my lids closed tighter. This was not happening.

"What the hell happened?" Logan asked, his voice clear as day through the broken window.

"Nothing. Go away!"

Dot's voice piped up. "I'll fetch my spare key, and we'll go in the front door. You wait here, Logan, and keep an eye on her."

"Will do. Thanks, Mrs March."

I listened to the shuffling retreat of my old neighbour, but when silence followed, I cracked one eye to look up at the window. Logan stared down at me, a small smile playing at the corner of his mouth. "Oh, my God," I moaned. "I can't deal with you today."

I started to roll to the side, but a shard of glass stabbed into my upper arm, and I hissed. Then Logan spoke again. "Don't move until I can get in there and help you."

Returning to my back and wincing at the sting in my arm, I tried to glare at him, though my eyes were still closed, so it was more of a telepathic glare teamed with a vicious nose-scrunch.

"I don't need your help."

"Tough luck, now lay still." Another pause, and then he said, "Mrs March is back. I'm going around the front. Don't move, Frost."

I wanted to move—I wanted to jump to my feet and bolt in the other direction—so I tried, but another sliver of glass cutting into my palm stopped me. Please, please, please, tell me this was someone else's life.

"All right, I'm here," Logan said moments later. He stepped carefully into the room, his shoes crunching over the pieces of broken window, and I inhaled sharply as he crouched beside me, carefully slid his hard arms under my head and my knees, and lifted me off the floor.

Pulled in tight against his chest, his arms pressing our bodies together, I couldn't think straight enough to protest. His skin was hot. His hands were firm. He smelled divine, the way a man should, and if I turned my head a little, I was close enough to brush my nose against his neck and graze that spot where a thick blue vein beat under his skin. I could tilt my head a little, put my lips over the pulse, and say hello to it with my tongue. Then …

"Can I help you?" he murmured, watching me from the side of his eye.

Damn it. Why did the idiot have to tell me he was divorced? I couldn't cope with the change in his circumstance. All the ways I'd refused to think about him—the *unsuitable* scenarios I'd refused to entertain—were raving in my head, blowing party whistles and throwing streamers in the comeback celebration of the century.

Logan carried me straight to the dining nook, where he lowered me onto a chair. "Where's your first aid kit?"

It was in the cupboard above the fridge, but when I tried to stand, he glowered at me. "Sit down. I'll get it."

"I feel like a slice of the banana bread I baked for morning tea," Dot announced, clapping her hands and scooting for the door. "I'll go home and get it, then come back and make us all a pot of tea." She gave me a meaningful look. "And then, I expect you to tell us what's going on here."

I huffed out a sigh but knew better than to argue. On her way out, she passed Logan coming out of the kitchen, and he set the first aid kit on the table before crouching in front of me.

"Let me see your arm," he said.

"You're overreacting," I grumbled. "I can take care of it myself."

"Fine." He stood up, crossed his arms over his chest, and watched me with a steady grey gaze. "Go for it."

Though his eyes felt hot and knowing he was staring caused a fine line of moisture to spring up along my spine, I did my best to pretend he wasn't there as I dug through the kit, pulled out antiseptic and bandaids, some gauze, and then tweezers. I had two cuts: one on my upper arm, the other on my palm. First, I wiped away most of the blood, then checked both wounds for glass. I had to use the tweezers to extract a small splinter from my hand and a much larger one from my arm. I bit back a gasp at the sting and kept ignoring Logan's disconcerting stare, as well as the way a muscle ticked in his jaw. Next, I applied antiseptic without too much difficulty, but when it was time to attach bandages, I couldn't manage with just one hand. The sticky sides kept attaching to each other, and I'd thrown away five when Logan finally said something.

"Would you like me to help?"

I took a breath, considered how stupid I'd look if I refused, then thrust the box in his direction.

He knelt beside me, and I concentrated on my arm as he tore open the packaging. And then, his hands were there. He'd always had long fingers and tan skin, but the little brown freckle on his left ring finger startled me, triggering memories I'd buried more than a decade ago. I'd first noticed that freckle when we were fifteen and had been assigned as partners for our school's PE dance program. He'd been unusually awkward in those classes, tripping over his feet and flushing when he had to put his hand on my waist, but I'd been unable to look away from the sight of my hand grasped in his, that freckle flashing as we moved through the steps. It was just as hard to tear my eyes away from it now.

Logan handled me with confidence, setting a cover over the cut on my palm first. His fingers were gentle, and I wondered if I imagined the way they lingered, if he'd meant to brush my wrist like that. He repeated the process on my arm, and I was almost certain he took more time than he needed. In another life, I'd have begged for that touch, and despite my best efforts to ignore the butter-like melt between my legs, goosebumps rippled over my arm as his fingertips grazed my skin.

"All done," he said, his voice gravelly.

"Thank you," I murmured on an exhaled breath.

"You're welcome."

"All right, then!" Dot exclaimed, bustling in with a platter in her hands. "Let's get that kettle on."

Logan sprung up and away as though he'd been caught with his hand in the cookie jar, and I refused to acknowledge the flush in my cheeks as I left him tidying away the first aid kit and followed my neighbour into the kitchen. I pulled out plates while she organised cups, and within a few minutes, we were seated around the dining room table, my guests looking at me with expectation.

I hadn't told anyone about the bargain with my parents, or my date with Zachary for that matter—I judged myself harshly enough on both counts, and I'd been avoiding Abbie and Emily so I wouldn't have to share all the gory details of my recent mistakes—and while I really didn't want to spill my guts with Logan in the audience, there was a relief in getting this pressure off my chest. I'd been stupid to let myself get trapped in this agreement, but I was so fed up with my parents behaving as though I was little more than a child. Renovating an entire house in thirty-five days might be a risky, ridiculous way to prove it to them, but somehow, I had to make it very clear I was capable of making my own decisions. Good decisions. The right decisions for me.

"Okay, here's the thing. I had a discussion with my parents last week about the house. Their opinion is that it's too much work for one person and that if I ever had any intention of improving it and keeping it for myself, I would have finished the renovations by now. It's been three years, and not much has changed, so they're adamant I should sell it."

Dot snorted. "Ignore them. What's the rush, I say? You're happy here, and you'll get to it when you get to it."

I glanced up at Logan, who looked at me as though he knew there was more to it, and I shifted on my chair. "Well, that's not an option anymore. The discussion sort of escalated into an ultimatum, and I made a bet, sort of, that I could finish the house in five weeks."

"Five weeks?" Dot looked about ready to fall off her chair.

Logan took a sip of his tea but said nothing.

"Try to understand, Dot. My mother thinks my life is one long series of missteps and that anything good to my name is all her doing. I have to show her she's wrong, and I have to prove to myself I'm capable of creating something wonderful—by myself and for myself."

My voice cracked, and I scrubbed at my eyes. Bloody hell. Now was not the time to get emotional. There was no way Logan would be able to resist rubbing this in, and I couldn't waste my energy on tears if I had any hope of giving it back to him.

"Five weeks is doable," he said.

My head jerked in his direction, and I narrowed my eyes, waiting for the punchline.

"What?" he said. "It's doable."

I bit my lip, then confessed, "That was on Sunday. I'm already down to thirty days."

He shrugged and forked up a mouthful of cake. "Still doable. You got a notebook and a pen?"

I frowned but went to the kitchen, retrieving what he needed from a drawer and setting it on the table in front of him. Sliding back into my chair, I swapped a curious look with Dot, who set her swollen hand on mine and squeezed.

"We'll make it work," she said with a wink.

I had no idea what a woman almost into her nineties thought she was going to do to help me renovate my house—I couldn't very well put her on the end of a paintbrush—but even if all Dot could give me was moral support, I'd take it.

Logan had the pen in his hand, hovering over the paper. "You'll have to shelve any plans you might have had to extend the place, but working with the footprint you've got now, what ideas do you have?"

"I wanted to close in the dining room and turn it into a third bedroom?" I said it like a question, feeling inadequate in the face of Logan's obvious skill as well as vulnerable after today's renovation progress took such a destructive turn.

Logan scrawled down a note on the page. "Next?"

His manner gave me a little confidence. "Refinish the floors. Paint the walls."

He wrote down the first item, then the second, one line under the other. "What else?"

"New bathroom," I said with a grimace. "New kitchen."

Logan put them on the list without hesitation. "And then?"

"Open up the back—put in glass doors that let in more light."

"The back porch needs fixing, too," Dot offered. "And the yards need some TLC."

Logan wrote it all down. "Laundry room?" he asked.

"Fresh paint and new cabinetry?" I replied. "Oh, and tiling, too."

When he'd added that to the list, he asked one last time. "Is that all?"

I collected my curls and pulled them over one shoulder, giving my hands something to do. The cut in my palm pulled a little, but it didn't hurt too badly.

"The roof is new, and I had a structural report done when I moved in, thinking I'd renovate straightaway. I want to make the second bedroom a study, but that only requires fresh paint and the right furniture. So ... yes, I think that's it. Aside from, you know, the cosmetic things. New art, light fittings, rugs—"

"Curtains?" he deadpanned.

"Shut up."

"Now, children," Dot said. "Don't bicker. I think we're in excellent hands with Logan here. He'll get things done."

"What?" My head whipped back and forth to Dot, then Logan, and back again. "Logan's not doing anything. Well, he's writing a list, and he's giving me his *opinion*—which I never asked for, by the way—but that's it. This is my project. I have to do this on my own."

"You going to tile the bathroom?" he asked.

"Well, no. I'll hire someone."

"You going to rip out the kitchen?"

"Again, no. I'll hire someone for that, too."

"You going to move the power sockets, redirect the plumbing, install the oven ...? Hang the curtains?"

"I— *No*." My cheeks caught flame, my nostrils flared, and my eyes threw blades as sharp as the glass carpeting my spare bedroom floor—and the bastard just grinned

126

at me. "I'm going to *hire* people," I enunciated so he'd understand.

"Awesome. I'm your carpenter."

"I don't need a carpenter."

"That dining room wall going to fill in itself? The back wall miraculously grow glass? The kitchen going to demo on its own and put in its own cabinetry? The floors going to sand and polish up like magic?"

Ah, crap.

"I'll find someone else."

"Good luck," Logan said, sticking the pen over one ear and returning to his cake. "Will had to go all the way to Scarborough Cove to find someone to work on The Stop, and still had to wait three months to get on the guy's books. He bloody cost an arm and a leg, too. What's your budget, by the way?"

I told him. I'd saved a good amount of cash specifically for this house, so money wasn't going to be an issue. What I didn't have was time.

"Thirty days, Frost," Logan said, turning the notepad towards me and tapping the list. "What's it going to be?"

I looked at Dot, and she rolled her lips together, refusing to give me the answer. I thought about it for a full minute, the room silent as the verdict came down, and my nose twitched nervously.

"Okay, fine. Fine!" I pointed a finger at Logan, ignoring the smug, sexy smile on his face. "But this is my house, and I'm going to make all the decisions. You have to do what I say when I say it. Understand?"

He chuckled, then bit it back when I opened my mouth again to take it all back.

"Understood. You're the master, and I'm your willing servant."

I crossed my arms and slumped back in my chair. "Good."

"Just a suggestion?" he said, waiting for my curt nod to continue. "We should get started right away. We'll clean out that room now, then head down to the hardware store to organise equipment to refurbish the floors and prep the walls. Next week, I'll make some calls and get all the necessary trades lined up." He cocked an eyebrow at me. "Do you have brunch with your parents tomorrow?"

I looked sideways at Dot, then down at the table. "Uh, no. I've put a pause on those. I think I need a break from Mum and Dad."

Dot stood and put a hand on my shoulder, then pressed a kiss to the crown of my head. "Smart girl," she said. "Now, I won't be any help on the tools, but I can keep you two fed. Don't worry about cooking for the next month, all right? I'll take care of everything."

"Dot, I can't—"

She raised a finger. "It's the least I can do, and your grandmother would have wanted me to help. Can't have her haunting me in my final days because I let her only granddaughter down. I'd never get any sleep."

"Thanks, Dot."

She winked at me, then at Logan, and her stooped, pink-tracksuit-clad figure disappeared down the hall.

"I'll return tonight with your dinner!" she called before the sound of the front door closing behind her floated back through the house.

Logan shifted on his chair, taking the list and staring at it so hard I expected smoke to curl up from where his eyes bored holes through the paper. "I'll make an appointment at the showroom for early next week so you can choose joinery, tiles, and finishes. I'll take measurements sometime before then."

It wasn't too late. I could still back out—if that's what I wanted. "You don't have to do this," I said.

Logan shook his head slightly, still consumed by the words on the paper. "You're doing me a favour, Frost. I've got a month to fill before I head home, and I'm happier when my hands are busy."

Against my will, I looked at those hands, seeking that one little freckle and feeling something loosen in my skin when I found it. "Okay. Thanks." I clasped my hands under the table. The memory of his fingertips on my skin lingered, the remembered impulse to put my mouth on him stirred *things* inside me, and the air felt loaded, the way it did just before a summer storm swept in off the ocean.

Abruptly, Logan got to his feet, his chair scraping back on the linoleum floor. "Where do you keep your broom?"

I sent him to the laundry while I cleared away our dirty dishes, and a confronting realisation dawned on me. I'd just sentenced myself to thirty days of hard time in the same house as Logan Reeve ... and the idea didn't irritate me. I wasn't dreading it or trying to think of a way out of it.

The situation was worse than that, though. Much worse. I felt safe, like Logan had put me in the driver's seat and clicked on my seatbelt, then climbed in next to me to make sure I knew where to go. I *wanted* him around, and the butterflies in my stomach unsettled me in a way that hating him never had.

12

LOGAN

I PULLED WILL'S work truck into the parking lot of the region's largest renovation showroom early on Monday morning. There were a few cars already there, but Jess's hatchback wasn't among them, so after checking the time and realising she wouldn't arrive for another twenty minutes, I thumbed through the contacts list on my phone.

Two weeks into my trip and, whether or not I'd meant to do it, I'd settled into a kind of domesticity I hadn't experienced in a long time—not since the early days of my marriage, and even then, it would have been a stretch to call what Bek and I had together domestic bliss. As my thoughts brushed against that time of my life and quickly recoiled, I was reminded again why I liked to keep busy. It stopped me from dwelling on the realities of my life.

That meant my mornings began early with a run and a coffee at Tony's. Depending on their schedules, either

Luca, Isaac, Will, or Josh joined me for a surf—and hell, it was good to have saltwater on my skin every day—then I'd throw myself into whatever task I'd managed to set up to keep my body moving and my brain preoccupied. In the first week, it had been refinishing the floors at The Stop. The week after that, Jess's garage. I'd been staring down an empty to-do list when she'd told Dot and me about the mess she'd gotten herself into with her parents, and at the time, I'd felt two polar opposite responses. One, she'd acted on impulse and was in way over her head, and wasn't that just so unlike her? So yes, the option to tell her as much did occur to me, but the desire to hassle her was doused by response number two: the urge to help. As a bonus, the project might be the distraction I needed if I wanted to get in and out of the Bay with my sanity still intact. It was only after the deal was done that I considered thirty days of non-stop Frost might actually drive me crazy.

But in the end, it was her tears that had me speaking before I could stop and weigh my words. I had no idea her parents were so tough on her, and I wondered if her teenaged smart mouth and know-it-all attitude were things she'd been forced into or roles she played to cope with the pressure. Finding her collapsed in a room of broken glass hadn't helped. I wasn't used to seeing Jess vulnerable, and if there was anything I could do to prevent her from feeling that way again, I was going to do it.

So, what could I have done differently? Nothing, that's what. Luca would have expected me to hang around to make sure Jess wasn't overwhelmed by not only the emotional challenge of dealing with his wedding to Tash but also the stress of transforming her house to please her uptight parents. She couldn't even hang a curtain, for fuck's sake, and I noticed those brackets she'd installed— so uneven that the rod was going to be steep enough for surfing.

No, I was doing the right thing—the *only* thing. Left to her own devices, the woman was likely to saw off a hand trying to cut lumber.

That was my story, and I was sticking to it.

Phone in hand, I found the name I was looking for and hit dial. The voice that answered was rough, brusque, and familiar, and I hadn't heard it in more than six years. "Ryan Micallef."

"Boss, it's Logan Reeve."

With the crashes of construction playing in the background, my old employer was silent so long I thought he'd either misheard me or forgotten who I was, but as the noise receded and I picked up the sounds of footsteps moving to a quieter location, he finally replied.

"Can you repeat that? I thought you said this was Logan Reeve, but you can't be. Logan Reeve was the best apprentice I've ever had—taught him everything I knew and then some—and when he was done with me, he up and left for colder pastures. Haven't heard from the prick since."

I chuckled. "Fuck off. I sent you a Christmas card that one time."

"I wouldn't know. The missus opens all my mail. So what, you're back in town? Looking for work? I've got something you can start on yesterday. Just give me the word."

I'd completed my apprenticeship with Ryan, so I'd known him since I was eighteen. He owned the most successful construction business along this stretch of the coast, was a genius with timber, and a decent guy, one of the best I'd ever met, but his job offer still took me by surprise. I was glad he couldn't see me grin as warmth bloomed in my chest.

"I appreciate that, but my problem's just the opposite. I'm only back for a month or so for a mate's wedding, and I'm helping out an old friend with her house renovations while I'm here. We're on a tight deadline, and I need to line up contractors as soon as possible."

"What do you need?"

"Someone to help with demo this week. Electrical and plumbing for the rough-in after that. Maybe an apprentice, if you've got one to spare, to help with the window and joinery installation later on."

The sound of Ryan sucking his teeth drifted from my phone, and I recalled the way his mouth danced when he was thinking through project logistics.

"Big place?" he asked.

"No. It's an old Californian bungalow. Near enough to the original footprint and no plans to extend."

"Right-o. I'll send you Paul for demo on Wednesday, and I'll let Baz and Brody know you'll need them for electrical and plumbing in the next week or so."

I huffed out a breath of relief. "Thanks, mate. I owe you one."

Ryan laughed. "Yeah, you do, which is why I'm also giving you my second-year apprentice for help with the install. He's almost learned one end of a hammer from the other, and he's on a winning streak at the moment: three days without screwing up. See if you can send him back to me a little improved, will you?"

Not for the first time—but for the first time in a long while—I couldn't tell if Ryan was pulling my leg, but beggars couldn't be choosers. I'd have to take my chances with the kid.

"It's a deal. Thanks, Boss. I appreciate it."

"Ah, what I wouldn't give to be your boss again, so quit rubbing it in. Call me Ryan."

I tongued the inside of my cheek, fighting another grin. "Okay. Thanks, Ryan."

After I'd hung up, I texted him Jess's address, and he sent me the names and numbers of the tradespeople he'd offered to loan me. I didn't know them, but a lot could change in six years. Again, a sense that something was missing bubbled to the surface. I loved my work, whether it was flipping a house or spending hours shaping a piece of timber into something special, but it wasn't something I could give my heart to anymore. There were only so many hits a man could take.

I'd been sitting still too long and my thoughts were getting away from me, so when Jess's red car flashed into the drive, I leaped out of my own and walked over to meet her.

"Morning," I greeted her, appreciating the torn jeans and tight tank she wore and nodding at the thick binder she had tucked under one arm. "This isn't the library. We're not here to study."

Her nose lifted into the air as she slammed the car door and clicked her key to activate the central locking. "These are my renovation notes. I wanted to bring them all with me when choosing finishes."

I followed her through the automatic doors of the renovation centre. "Good thinking."

"Oh," she said, sounding surprised. "Thanks."

Standing inside the enormous warehouse-style showroom with aisles of display kitchens on one side, bathrooms on the other, and rows of samples beyond, Jess came to a standstill, and her perfect mouth dropped open. "Where do we start?" she asked breathily.

"At the beginning." I headed for the far-right side of the store. "We'll take a look around, see if there's anything that jumps out at you, then locate a consultant to lock in all the details."

When she didn't follow, I turned back and watched as her focus flitted across the room, to the binder in her hands, to the front doors, and back again before she gathered resolve around herself like a blanket and marched over to me. "Let's go."

I'd decided that if renovating a house had any chance of building Jess's self-confidence, I couldn't say too much on this visit. She had made it very clear she wanted to do this on her own, and I was determined to do my best to behave like her employee or, perhaps, a supportive friend with no skin in the game, but ten minutes into our tour, she'd asked me at least thirty questions.

"Frost," I said, drawing to a stop. "Look at me."

With her bottom lip caught between her teeth in a way that made me blink, Jess met my eyes with a faint crease between her brows. I curled my hands around her narrow shoulders and dipped my head to meet her at eye level, but her gaze dropped to my mouth, her lip popped free of her teeth, and her tongue slid into view in a way that demanded my attention—and the attention of the guy in my pants. Forcing myself to focus, I waited until her eyes lifted to mine and said what I had planned to say in a voice that was huskier than I'd intended.

"I promise not to let you choose anything ugly, all right? You've got a great eye, you've done your research, and you can do this."

She glanced at a simple coastal-look kitchen set up beside us, all cool whites, chrome edges, and zero personality. "My style is a little ... different ... to most of the stuff in here."

"Good. A lot of this shit is boring and made for people who don't want to think too hard. You're not like everyone else, so your house shouldn't be like anyone else's either. Stop second-guessing yourself."

She gave me a small nod. "Promise you'll speak up if I get something really wrong?"

"I promise."

"Okay. Let's try again."

I must have said something right because, after that, she breezed through the place. I held her binder open while she scanned and touched and contemplated every cupboard door, every handle, every tile, every tap, then made a notation in her files. It was a long morning, but I enjoyed watching the transformation in her. I gave her my honest opinions when she asked for them, prompted her to explain why she was drawn to certain colours or textures when her certainty wavered, and encouraged her to refer to the pictures on her phone app when she dithered between options. Her shoulders relaxed, she smiled and laughed, she made jokes and gave me a hard time until we'd not only done a full circuit but rounded back to review her top choices, and we were looking for a sales consultant to place an order.

A middle-aged man wearing a company-branded polo shirt and with more grey than brown in his hair noticed us first, and he came bustling over with his arm outstretched.

"Hi, there. I'm Tom. Can I help you?"

I stared at the hand pointing in my direction, shook it briefly and said, "I'm not the one with the cash, buddy."

"Oh." Embarrassment brightened his cheeks—and stayed my irritation—as he offered his hand to Jess. "Nice to meet you. Can I offer you some assistance?"

Jess glanced at me once, quickly and with a question on her face, and I dipped my chin to reassure her. I didn't even have to fake it. I loved everything Jess picked out and had given my advice when she was veering into territories of regret, so I knew the end result was going to be a showstopper. Her house was going to look a lot like something I'd put together if I were fixing it up myself—a clever, quirky mash-up of mid-century lines and colours layered over contemporary materials and textures. I might have been more pumped than Jess to get started.

You got this, I mouthed.

"Yes, thank you," she said to Tom. "I need to place an order."

Tom showed us to a utilitarian desk, switched on the screen of his old computer, and Jess began to discuss her options. I'd taken all the necessary measurements the day before, so when it came time to mock up the kitchen design and choose finishes for the bathroom, we were able to confirm the details in one session. It took close to two hours—and I gave myself points for not decking the guy when he quirked an eyebrow at some of Jess's more unusual colour schemes—but I grinned at the look on her face when we finally stood, and she thrust her hand in Tom's direction.

"Thanks for your help, Tom. And you're sure we can get all the materials on rush orders?"

"Absolutely." He handed over a printed copy of our inventory. "Don't worry about a thing. I'll personally make sure everything gets to you as soon as possible."

Sure, he would. In one unexpected appointment, Jess had helped him reach his commission targets for the next three months.

"I've never had so much fun spending so much money," Jess said as we made our way towards the front exit doors of the store. "I'm excited. Are you excited?"

"Yeah, sure."

"And you like what I chose?"

"Do *you* like what you chose?"

She gave me a withering look. "I'm asking you as a friend. Do you like it?"

"A friend, hey? Okay, okay." I laughed at her glare. "Yes, I liked it. I told you, you've got good taste."

"Even the tile for the bathroom?" Her nose wiggled. "It's not too late to go back and change it. Perhaps something a little less bright."

"No. You'll drive yourself crazy if you keep questioning everything. Full steam ahead, Frost."

"You're right. Thanks."

As we passed the registers near the large glass automatic doors, a rangy dark-haired guy in a collared shirt and jeans, with black-rimmed glasses on his nose, did a double take in our direction, then settled his gaze on Jess. Frowning that the dipshit would be so obvious with his drool, I angled away a little, blocking his line of vision and shortening our route to the exit, but he stepped out of the queue and right into our path.

"Jess," he said.

"Miles! Hi. What are you doing here?"

He hefted the large box under his arm. "Heated towel rack. I've become used to warm towels in the morning, but the place I've moved into doesn't have one."

What numpty needed *warm towels* after his shower? Grow a set of balls, mate.

"Oh, I didn't know you moved," Jess replied, handing

me her binder and tucking a lock of hair behind her ear.

"Yeah. New apartment, new job. You know how it is."

Jess giggled. Was she *flirting*?

"Don't go getting any ideas about my job," she said. "It's a two-week stint, no more than that."

"Don't worry. Nobody could take your place."

Miles looked at me quickly—once, twice, and again. I responded with a blank look until Jess finally took the hint.

"Oh! Logan, this is my colleague, Miles McKay. He agreed to take my classes for two weeks next term so I can focus on the house. Miles, this is Logan Reeve. He's my, uh, project manager?"

She said it like a question, so I took it upon myself to respond.

"Really?" I put my hand out for Miles to shake. It was like gripping a dead fish. "I thought we were friends, Frost."

"Well, yeah, sure. Of course. Friend and project manager."

She was flustered, there was a flush in her cheeks, and I realised that, yes, Jess was indeed flirting.

"For the renovations," Miles said, visibly relaxing now that he knew I wasn't a boyfriend-type person. "How are they going, Jess?"

"Good. We were just—"

"Well, nice to meet you, Miles," I cut in, "but we're on a deadline and can't stop to chat. Enjoy your hot towels."

I slung an arm around Jess's neck and dragged her towards the doors.

"Oh, okay. Bye, Miles," she called over her shoulder.

I didn't have to look back to know the frustration on Miles's face would have been enough to have me strut out of there like a fucking rooster.

When we hit the bitumen of the parking lot, I started in the direction of Jess's car, not dropping my arm straightaway. The dumbass inside might be paying attention, and I wanted him to get the hint that I may not be *the boyfriend*, but Jess also wasn't his for the taking. Funnily enough, she didn't shrug me off until we were a handful of paces from her hatchback.

"That was rude," she said, pushing my arm away and hitting the button on her central locking. The car responded with a *beep beep*.

I shrugged. "The guy's a muppet. You can do better."

Her nostrils flared, and she opened her mouth, but we'd arrived at her car, and I reached around to open her door.

"Get in. I'll see you back at the house."

"Ugh! You are the most irritating man I've ever known, Reeve. For real. I just want to strangle you right now."

I smirked. "Kinky."

I don't know why, but I took a step closer, close enough that the tips of her breasts grazed my chest, close enough that my eyes burned into hers with the honest—and entirely inappropriate—heat of my attraction, but not so close she'd feel the ridge of my erection protesting the confines of my pants.

Breath hitched in her chest, and the roses in her cheeks bloomed brighter, but I only had a second to wonder what it meant before she snatched the binder from my hands, flung herself behind the wheel, and slammed the door in my face.

I watched as she drove away, and only after she'd cleared the driveway did I figure it out. I'd just made Jessica Frost *blush*. I never made her blush. I made her furious, yes. Annoyed, often. Flushed with rage, all the time. But a *blush*? That was new, and I liked it. I liked it so much, I looked forward to doing it again.

Soon.

13

JESS

I HAD NO idea how I made it home. One minute, I was speeding away from Logan with his smouldering grey eyes, my nipples aching and my thighs clenching, and the next, I was pulling into my driveway, turning off the car engine, and looking up at my house in a daze.

Logan had been *kind* today. He'd been encouraging and given me confidence, and I'd enjoyed being with him. More than that, I'd had *fun*. Then, *bam*! He'd assaulted me with all his jacked-up sexual innuendo, and my usual snark deserted me. I snapped back when Logan teased me and I never, *ever* blushed, but it had been an unexpectedly good day. My defences were down, and I was having a hard time putting them back up.

No. Scratch that. I was having a hard time making myself *want* to put them back up. What I wanted was Logan's hands on me. His mouth on mine. My bare skin pressed against his. I wanted to feel his arm, hot and possessive, around my shoulders again. I wanted much more than his arm, hot and possessive …

A wet pulse between my legs made me groan just as Logan turned his car into the driveway and parked behind me. I stepped out of the car, retrieved my bag and binder, and beelined for the front door, stalling in the hallway as I was hit with the mouth-watering fragrance of a dinner I didn't prepare.

"Oh, God. What is that smell?" Logan moaned behind me.

"I have no idea, but I want some."

I led him to the kitchen, where we found a chicken with vegetables roasting in the oven and a note from Dot instructing when to take it out and how to make a gravy. I plucked up the piece of paper and held it up so Logan could read it. "Food will be ready in fifteen minutes."

"Your neighbour is an angel. I'm starving."

I set plates and cutlery on the table, then turned to the fridge and inspected my pathetic liquor inventory. "I've got a couple of beers and half a bottle of white wine," I said to Logan, who was sitting in a dining chair now, his long legs stretched out in front of him, his solid arms crossed over his broad chest, the ink on his biceps coiling out from underneath the sleeves of his tight black T-shirt. Clearing my throat, I stuck my head in the fridge in a bid to avoid his eyes and cool myself down. "What can I get you?"

"Water is fine."

"The no-drinking thing," I said as I filled a goblet of wine for myself, then poured us both chilled water from the fridge. "Is that new? You never used to say no to a beer."

"Whiskey," he replied, taking a gulp of the water.

When he didn't elaborate and I couldn't catch his eye, I started serving the meal. What would another five minutes in the oven matter? It was probably ready now, and we didn't need gravy.

"I'm sorry," I apologised over the crash of the oven door closing and the clash of the metal roasting pan hitting the riveted stovetop. "I didn't mean to stick my nose in. You don't have to talk about it if you don't want to."

He was silent for as long as it took me to plate up food for us both, and by the time I set it on the table and took a seat, I felt like an idiot. I'd overstepped a boundary, and all the progress we'd made today felt as cooked as the poor bird on my fork.

"I never used to say no to a *whiskey*," he said, starting on his meal and talking between mouthfuls. "But one day, things weren't going well in my marriage, I had some disappointments in my business, and I became a little too friendly with the single malt. It was a shit time of my life, but that's no excuse. When Bek told me she was leaving me for our personal trainer and business dried up altogether, I realised I'd fucked up my entire life by choosing oblivion over reality. Haven't touched the hard stuff since."

"Oh." I poked my fork at my potatoes. "I'm really sorry, Logan."

He shrugged. "I'm not. I'll have a beer now and then if I feel like it, but I rarely do."

Playing with the food on my plate, I tried hard to resist the urge to ask more, but in the end, I couldn't stop myself. "What happened with Bek?"

The grin he flashed at me quadrupled my pulse rate. "Haven't I spilled enough blood for one day, Frost?"

"Okay. Sorry," I replied, mortified that my cheeks were aflame again. "Let's talk about the house. What next?"

He noticed my blush—the bastard—and he made a show of it, too. His crooked smile sent heat raging to my hairline, so I got to my feet to fetch more wine from the fridge.

"Good news," he said, and I could hear the smirk in his voice. "I have someone coming to help with demo in a couple of days, but that means we have to have everything squared away in here by tomorrow night."

"Oh." I looked around, not wanting to have to ask him what he meant, then realised it was inevitable. "What do we need to do?"

His smile grew wider. "We'll need to pack up the kitchen and clear out the bathroom. We're knocking out the back wall, too, and we might as well take the porch with it. I'll build you another one."

I stared at him incredulously. "You'll build me another one? You say it like it's nothing. *Poof!* Just like that."

Logan paused until he had my attention, then he dropped his chin and cocked an eyebrow. "Nothing I do is *just like that*."

Oh, shit. Understanding dawned on me. He was doing this on *purpose*. Logan Reeve was flirting with me. It wasn't a new experience exactly, but in the past, he'd only made these kinds of comments to piss me off, tormenting me for his own twisted pleasure, and this was the part where I was supposed to get mad. But now? Now I wanted more.

"Well, I guess I'll just have to take your word for it," I said archly, returning to the table.

His lips tipped up on one side. "I guess you will."

I returned the conversation to the renovations. "Is there anything we can get started on today?"

Logan squinted as he checked the colour of the sky through the window, then the time on the old clock on the wall. It was approaching late afternoon. "After we get these dishes done, we can transfer all your kitchen gear into boxes. We'll do the same in the bathroom. The furniture can go out to the garage, but it might be a tight squeeze in there for all the boxes, too. Can we keep them in here somewhere?"

"Will the spare bedroom work?"

"Perfect."

We made a good team for the next six hours or so, working quickly enough that instead of leaving anything to the next day, we made the silent agreement to just keep going. We emptied all the kitchen cupboards, doing the same in the bathroom and laundry room, then stacked all my dining and living room furniture in the garage. Logan had been right about the tight fit, so we rearranged the junk I already had stored in the spare room and dragged the storage boxes in there. By the time we were done, the sky was dark, and I was exhausted. I collapsed on the floor of the second bedroom and slumped against a stack of boxes, my back against one wall.

"I'm sleeping here tonight," I announced, resting my cheek against a plastic tub and closing my eyes.

I listened as Logan walked away, heard him open the fridge and return, then I cracked my lids when he nudged my arm with the cool, wet glass of a beer bottle. I took it gratefully, and he clinked his own bottle against the side.

"Cheers," he said, taking a long gulp.

I took a welcome draw of my own. "So, it's a night for a beer, huh?"

"You looked like you needed one, and I couldn't let you drink alone." He slid down the wall opposite me and set his beer to the side. "You do know you can't stay here after the back wall comes down and the kitchen's gone, right?"

"I—" I frowned, then took another sip. I hadn't thought about it, which seemed ridiculous now, but I wasn't going to admit it. "Of course. I'll stay with Dot. She'll love the company."

Logan nodded. "Sounds like a plan."

His gaze drifted around the room, noting all the boxes— those we'd just added and the ones here before. "You've got a lot of crap, Frost." He opened the lid of the storage box closest to him and pulled out a teddy bear that had seen better days. "What the fuck do you need this for?"

Outraged, I straightened from my slump. "That's Mr Templeton. I've had him since I was a baby. What would you have me do with him? Throw him away?"

Logan rolled his eyes. "Calm down." He returned the bear and pulled out a stack of old Christmas cards. "You do not need Christmas cards from the neighbours you had twenty years ago. Come on."

Although I agreed with him, I wasn't going to give him the satisfaction of saying so. "They're memories, Reeve," I said with a deliberate lift of my chin. "Every card is a memento of my childhood."

"Who the hell wants to remember their childhood?" he muttered, pawing through the box until his eyes lit up and he pulled out a thick glossy book. "I haven't seen this for … Actually, maybe ever."

He held up our old school yearbook, and I snorted as I leaned back against the wall. "You have seen it. You *signed* it."

"I did?" He flicked through it, and I waited for him to find his signature in there, underneath the smartarse message he'd written for me. It only took him a minute.

"'See you round, Frost'," he read out loud. "'How will I cut my food without a never-ending supply of your razor-sharp wit? Guess I'll have to make do like everyone else and invest in a set of steak knives.'" He had the good grace to wince. "Ouch."

"Typical Logan Reeve," I replied.

He hummed and flicked through more pages. "Who the hell put this together? I don't remember half these photos being taken— Oh! Ha! He did win Most Likely to Succeed. I knew it."

I nodded, but Logan was already flipping the page over. He'd been referring to Luca. Even as a teenager, the guy had been a star in every sense—perfect academic record, competitive on the football field, active in extracurricular groups, like the school newspaper and debate club. For the first time, I wondered if Logan had ever minded being best friends with someone who shone so brightly.

"Hey, check this out," he said. "There's a truth or dare article in here."

"I remember that."

"I don't." His eyebrows drew down as he read the responses, and I dropped my head back against the wall, admiring the planes of his face. The line of his jaw, the shape of his mouth, the smooth stretch of tanned skin down his neck, the sexy scruff on his cheeks. He was beautiful.

He chuckled. "You're in here, Frost. You chose truth, and they asked you three questions. Do you remember your answers?"

Of course I did, but I snorted delicately. "No."

Logan glanced up at me, his chin still dipped for reading, disbelief pulling up one eyebrow. "Don't believe you. Here, let's do it. Question one. First high school A-grade?"

I stared at him blankly, debating whether to admit I did recall the answers I gave ten years ago, then rolled my eyes. "Year Seven English. Shakespeare essay."

"Correct."

When he tried to ask the next question, I stopped him. "Your turn. First A-grade?"

It was his turn to snort. "Still waiting. Question two. First high school party?"

"Abbie's thirteenth. Do you remember it?"

He squinted and looked at the ceiling. "Ice skating? Or was it bowling?"

"Bowling," I confirmed, then I laughed. "All you boys looked like clowns in your shorts with socks and those two-toned shoes. All tall and skinny, with big, floppy feet. Remember?"

"You know what they say about big feet," he quipped.

I met his stare and raised him an eyebrow. "Another thing I'll just have to take your word for."

He smirked. "Touché, Frost. And I guess that party was my first one too. Okay, last question. First high school friend?"

"That's such a stupid question. Everyone in this town has been friends from the womb. I don't think anyone made a new friend in high school."

Logan tossed the yearbook back into the box. "True. How about the lack of imagination, eh? For something that should have read like a gossip column, that was tame."

"Oh, yeah? And what would you have suggested?"

Picking up his beer and taking a small swallow, Logan contemplated his answer, then pointed the neck of his bottle at me. "First high school failure?"

"Year Nine PE," I answered. "Volleyball. Couldn't get that bloody ball over the net."

"Year Seven English," Logan countered. "Shakespeare essay."

"First high school cigarette?" I offered.

"Hmm ... I think Will swiped two from his dad's packet sometime in Year Nine, and the boys and I lit up at the lookout. Never did like it much. You?"

"Maggie got her hands on one in Year Eight. One puff, and I was coughing for an hour."

"Year Eight? Never would have thought you capable of it. First time you cut classes?"

I gasped in mock indignation. "I never cut class!"

"Liar. As I recall, you didn't need much convincing to join me, Will, and Abbie when we went to the movies instead of double history."

"Fine. Year Ten, when you, me, Will, and Abbie went to the movies instead of double history. You?"

"Uh, Year Eight," he said. "Skipped out on maths four Fridays in a row before anyone caught on."

"First drink?" I asked.

"Cheap cask wine at Josh's sixteenth birthday party."

"Same," I admitted.

"First kiss?" he asked.

"You."

We were batting back and forth so rapidly that my answer was out before I could stop it, and it crashed like a car wreck we couldn't look away from.

"I— What?" he said, eyes round and body still.

"You," I repeated, my heart beating hard enough that the word came out like a challenge.

"But … What?"

I took a deep swallow of my beer, buying time to compose myself and push aside the pang of hurt that he didn't remember.

"Maggie's sixteenth birthday party. We played a game of spin the bottle. You landed on me, and we kissed." The look on his face was worth a million words, and I shook my head, laughing under my breath. "You don't remember."

"No, I remember," he replied, running a hand through his hair. "But I had no idea that was your first kiss."

I shrugged. "First and second."

"Yeah, right." His mouth twitched. "What were the chances of me landing on you twice?"

"I don't know, but two kisses must have been more than enough because you left the game after that."

He frowned. "That's right. I did."

"I found you making out with Bianca Ripa about twenty minutes later."

"You *found* me?"

"Mm-hm." I took another drink of beer, draining the bottle.

"Were you … *looking* for me?"

I shrugged. "I thought you might want to kiss me some more, but obviously, I wasn't good at it or something."

"Uh, no. That was not the case at all."

The air in the room grew thick. "It's fine," I said. "We don't need to rehash memories that are more than ten years old. We were kids. It didn't mean anything then, and it doesn't mean anything now."

Logan frowned at the bottle in his hands, one thumb picking at the corner of the sodden label. "Right."

"Well, it's getting late," I said, pushing myself to my feet. "My beer is done, and this is the second-last night I'm going to spend in my own bed for a while. Now is probably a good time to call it a day."

He didn't move.

"Uh, thanks for all your help at the showroom and with the house," I continued, needing him to go so this torment would end. "I didn't expect to have a good time, but I did. I'll see you in two days for demolition?"

Slowly, he stood. "Sure. No problem, Frost."

Logan was quiet as he followed me to the front door. I opened it and stepped out, holding it for him, but when he was level with me on the porch, he stopped and stared out into the street, something in his thoughts furrowing his brow.

"Logan—"

It took me a startled moment to realise the soft, hot lips on mine belonged to Logan Reeve. They were gentle and curious, capturing the top, then the bottom, taking care not to assume too much. I leaned into it, responding with surprise and desire, and he took the cue, slipping a warm hand around my neck and brushing a thumb across my cheek.

I opened my mouth a little, inviting more, and he slanted his mouth over mine, stroking my tongue with his own. I moaned at the feel of his stubbled skin against my mouth, and I couldn't stop the way my body melted against his or

155

the way my hands latched onto fistfuls of his shirt. His free hand made its way down the curve of my back, over my hip, landing on my arse and squeezing gently. I may have whimpered as I pressed my hips against him, feeling the hard length of his cock against my stomach and getting wet at the promise of it.

And then his lips were gone, and my vision swam with the closeness of his earnest gaze. His hands cradled my face as he searched for something in my eyes.

"Kissing you means something," he said. "Then, now, and always."

Launching himself off the porch and throwing himself into his car, Logan was gone before my head stopped spinning, but it would be a long time yet before my blood quit racing, and I wasn't sure I ever wanted it to.

14

LOGAN

"IF I DIDN'T know better, I'd say you had woman troubles."

I dragged my attention away from the horizon and glanced at Isaac, who was floating on his surfboard beside me, sitting with a leg on either side as we waited behind the waves for our next break. "Huh?"

Isaac chuckled. "You've been staring out to nowhere for fifteen minutes, and in my experience—which is limited, I'll admit—a look like the one on your face is usually reserved for a man with woman problems. Everything okay with Bek? Is she unhappy about the separation?"

At first, I assumed he meant the divorce, but then I remembered my friends had no idea my wife was now my ex. Isaac must have been referring to the distance between Bek and me with her in the UK and me home in Valentine Bay. I rubbed my face with two hands, then dragged my fingers through my damp hair.

"Bek and I split up." Not content with the reasonable volume of sympathetic shock on Isaac's face, I turned the dial. "Two years ago."

Ding ding ding. Maximum horror.

"Fuck, mate. I'm sorry. I wish you'd said something."

Shrugging, I looked back out to the end of the ocean. "I should have, but it's not something I wanted to talk about."

"Even now?"

"Even now." Admitting to Isaac I hadn't confided in him when it mattered made me feel like shit, and I owed him more than that, so I sighed. "It's actually fine. We're still friends. She ended up marrying our personal trainer, and he's a decent guy. It all worked out in the end."

"You've got a twisted definition of things working out." Isaac shook his head. "I'm really sorry, man."

"Thanks. I appreciate it."

"So …"

"What?"

"Will mentioned you've been working in pubs over there for a while, and now you tell me you've split up with Bek. Is there a reason you're still living in London? You could be divorced and pulling beers anywhere, including here, where you have mates."

"Fuck off. I've got friends in the UK."

"I didn't mean it like that. More like, is there someone else keeping you in London when you could have come home two years ago?"

That was the problem with sharing. Once you started,

it was hard to stop. "Yeah, there's someone who's been keeping me in London," I replied.

"Reeve, that's awesome."

"Not really. She's been on the scene for a while, but nothing's ever come of it."

Isaac huffed under his breath. "I know that story. So, what are you saying? Is this girl worth staying in the UK for—or is there a chance you'll give up and come home?"

"I wish I knew how to answer that, Greene."

I laid flat on my board and prepared to paddle in for the next set. The sea was cranking, the waves were clean, and I wasn't taking advantage of the conditions. I was too preoccupied with the memory of Jess's mouth, the way her lips were soft under mine, how she'd opened up and asked for more. I'd replayed the feeling of her tits pressed against my chest over and over, her fists in my shirt, the moment I squeezed her arse, and the whimper in her throat.

I couldn't answer Isaac's question because the girl keeping me on the other side of the world was also the only girl who could ever give me reason enough to come home.

I knocked on her door a little more than an hour later. I'm not sure what I hoped to gain by turning up unannounced, but I had to see her again. I'd detoured past the hardware store on my way over and picked up a dozen paint samples, giving me a valid excuse to be there and a story to get me through the door.

Jess opened it after my first knock, and I grinned at the state of her. She was dressed in old denim cut-offs that showed off her toned legs, and a tight tee strained over her generous chest. Her curls were coming loose around her forehead, and she had paint smudges on her nose and hands. Then there were the glasses, as good as a red flag to my bull of a dick. I couldn't pretend anymore, not even to myself. The only reason I was there was to put my hands on her again. My hands and my mouth, and that was just to start.

Too bad I had little experience being around Jess if it didn't involve tormenting her and even less idea how to go about things after that kiss.

Smirking and nodding at the bright spot of muddy green on the tip of her nose, I said, "You're supposed to paint the walls, Frost. Not your face."

Her smile wilted, replaced by a glower. "What are you doing here?"

I hefted the box in my arms. "Great minds think alike. I picked up paint samples based on your colour selections at the showroom. I thought we could get some squares up on the walls. Best to move around the house, let them dry, see them in several different lights before making a final decision."

"I know all that." She turned and walked into the house, leaving the door open behind her, so I took it as an invitation to follow. She headed straight to the empty living area, where she'd brushed four large squares of earthy, olive-toned greens on one wall and another quartet of subtle greys in different shades on the opposite side of the room.

"I like them," I observed, "but I'm a little surprised at how subdued they are."

She planted her feet, crossed her arms, and looked at the wall. "That's me, isn't it? The girl who plays it safe and paints by numbers." She pointed at a stack of magazines in the corner that I'd missed, open and tabbed with brightly coloured sticky tabs. "I'm following the suggestions in those articles there."

"Well, I think I misunderstood the assignment. The ones I bought are a little bolder."

Jess glanced sideways at the tiny tins in the open-faced box in my arms, packed in tight with brushes and painting supplies, and she wiggled her nose. "Okay. Let's try them."

Pleased to see that she'd covered the floors in plastic drop sheets, I scooped up a screwdriver and leveraged open the lids of the cans.

"Wow," she breathed. "You weren't joking about bold."

"Nope."

I'd chosen four colours, three slightly varied shades for each: mustard-hued golds, fire-engine reds, harvest-bright oranges and rich, deep turquoises.

"Keep in mind these are meant to be the feature," I reminded her when her forehead crinkled with a worried frown. "And you can pair one with the grey paint you like best to tone things down."

The tip of her nose twitched adorably as she contemplated her choices. "Fine. Let's just get them on the walls."

I enjoyed working alongside Jess. She was focussed and intent on perfection, as always—brushing out neat squares, labelling them immediately, moving around the room to catch the light in different ways, and repeating the process over again—but today, it didn't irritate me. The opposite, in fact. I could have watched her for hours as she pulled out a pen and paper to compute all the combinations possible given the colours she had to choose from and added streaks of her grey paints next to the swatches I'd supplied to compare different compositions.

And I liked *watching* her work. She licked her lips when she concentrated and pushed her glasses higher onto the bridge of her nose often enough that my dick commandeered the majority of my blood supply. I began to wonder if it was my swollen cock or the paint fumes that had me so lightheaded. When she reached up on her toes to paint a section higher up, her calves and thighs tightened, and her shirt rode up enough to flash her flat stomach. It was the hottest tease I'd ever seen.

"There. Last one," she said with a sigh, scanning the room with a satisfied gleam in her eyes, a brush topped with red paint dangling from her hand.

I tore my eyes from her to look around at the walls, sharing the sense of a job finally finished, but shit, the room had grown hot. Hours of non-stop painting, plus Jess's constant proximity, had turned the temperature up to almost intolerable. I ran a hand through my damp hair, then lifted the hem of my shirt to wipe my face.

When I dropped it, Jess was staring at me. I wanted to

believe she was impressed by my abs, but all I could focus on were the fresh layers of paint on her body—streaks of red and gold and blue over her arms, her thighs, her shirt, her face.

"Good work, Frost," I said, reaching out and rubbing at a stripe on her cheek with my thumb. "You managed to get more paint on your face than the walls. I'm proud of you."

Her breath froze, and my hand lingered on her skin. Wanting to lean in and kiss her again but not knowing if I should, I stepped a little closer, my lips hovering over her upturned mouth as I waited for something in her expression to tell me *yes*.

As the pulse in her neck fluttered, she took off her glasses, lifted her brush, and swept a thin line of red paint across my black shirt.

"Good work, Reeve," she said, her voice low. "You managed to get more paint on your clothes than the walls. I'm proud of you."

Something shifted in her eyes. They grew hot in a way that didn't give me a *yes* so much as an *I dare you*, and fuck if I've ever backed down from a dare.

I crushed my lips to hers, groaning as I covered her mouth with mine, then stroked her tongue, grabbing fistfuls of her hair and gripping them tighter. I kissed her hard and desperately because I *was* hard—and desperate. Jess responded by opening her mouth and asking for more without words. I gave it to her, bruising our mouths as I devoured her like a starved man. My dick pulsed thickly as she kissed me back with just as much appetite.

Kissing her mouth was nowhere near enough. Dragging my lips to her earlobe, circling it with my tongue and trailing luscious swirls along her neck, I landed kiss after kiss along her collarbone, stopping in the hollow of her throat and licking it gently. Jess twined her fingers in my hair, dropped her head back, and moaned.

"Jesus, I love that sound," I mumbled against her skin, disentangling my fingers from her hair and sliding my hands over her hips and under the hem of her T-shirt. When the tips of my fingers grazed the hot skin of her belly, she moaned again, seeking my mouth with her own, and I kissed her as I explored higher and higher, running my palms over her ribcage, cupping one lace-covered breast, and pressing into the small of her back with the other so her body curved against mine.

"Mm," she whimpered against my mouth. "More."

A growl tore through my chest as a decade of desire broke free of its cage.

I palmed her breast and pulled down the fabric of her bra, tweaking her budded nipple hard enough that she cried out. It drove me insane enough that I had to get my mouth on her, and when I tugged at the bottom of her shirt, she raised her arms above her head and let me peel it off her. Oh, Jesus. "I knew your tits would be perfect," I whispered.

Yanking at her bra, I freed both breasts, each peaked with a tight pink nipple that felt like heaven under my tongue. I sucked on one, then the other, flicking them hard enough to make her gasp, and kept my hands roaming those parts of her my mouth couldn't reach.

"Keep going," she begged.

I sank to my knees, unbuttoned her shorts, and dragged them down her legs. Running my palms up over her ankles and brushing the curve of her calves, I explored higher with a firm, greedy touch. "I knew your thighs would be perfect, too."

Cupping her arse and giving her a warning with one fast, tight squeeze, I pulled her hips towards me and attached my mouth to her pussy, groaning when she opened her thighs and I found the white cotton of her panties already soaked. I kissed the hot apex between her legs, running my tongue over her folds, tickling the skin along the back of her legs and teasing the crease of her perfect arse.

"Oh, that feels good," she panted. "More."

She wanted more, and I wanted to give it. I ripped at her underwear, tearing them down her legs and flinging them across the room. "Oh, fuck," I breathed, seeing all of her for the first time. "Your pussy is perfect." I dived into her, sweeping the tip of my tongue up her centre, teasing her open as I worked my way to the top, groaning with satisfaction at the sweetness of her.

"Oh, God. The way you *taste*," I moaned against her. Wrapping my lips around her swollen clit, I sucked with increasing pressure until her knees wobbled and she fell forwards, bracing herself on my shoulders.

"Yes," she gasped. "*Yes!*"

Getting to my feet, I hoisted her up so she could wrap her legs around my waist. She felt my erection immediately and rocked her hips against it, grinding and chasing relief.

I kissed her to muffle my groan as I kneaded her arse and carried her to the bedroom.

Kneeling on the bed and laying her down, I took a moment to appreciate the incredible picture of Jessica Frost naked beneath me.

Fuck if I ever thought this would happen in my lifetime.

I lay down beside her, mouthing her jaw and her neck as I traced my fingertips down her body until they reached her slick seam. I gently opened her up before sinking one finger inside her. "Oh, God, you're so tight," I moaned.

"Don't stop," she whispered, opening her legs wider.

I added a second finger and pushed deeper, searching for that soft spot that would set off a riot. My thumb played with her clit in tight circles, and I took a nipple into my mouth again as her back arched off the bed and her hands clawed at the sheets.

The wetness around my hand intensified, and I knew she was close when the muscles of her core trembled around my fingers. I increased the pressure on her clit, curled my fingers deep inside, and watched her face with rapture as she cried out with her orgasm, the pulse of her pussy milking my hand the way I wanted it to milk my dick.

"Oh, Jesus," she moaned. "I'm coming!"

The sight of Jess coming apart underneath me, my fingers inside her all she needed, was the hottest moment of my life—and I was still fully dressed.

"Have you had enough?" I murmured, lining her collarbone with kisses.

I glanced up at her as she caught her lip between her teeth, and I braced myself for inevitable rejection, but she surprised me with a husky whisper. "I've wanted— No. I've had nowhere near enough. I want more."

Relief and desire tightened my chest as I stood, reached around to the back of my neck, and pulled off my shirt.

Jess licked her lips as she sat up and moved closer, perching on the edge of the bed with her knees on either side of me. She ran her hands up over my chest, then traced the lines of ink needled into my arms before running her hands down again to the ridges of my abs, tracking lower and lower until she hit my V-lines. She followed them south until she was unbuttoning my jeans and unzipping my fly, pulling my underwear down just enough to release my cock. It sprang out, and heat crept up her chest and neck, into her cheeks, as she hesitantly wrapped her fingers around me, stroked once, twice, slowly, reverently, and with increasing confidence. Then she looked up at me from underneath her lashes, leaned forward, and lapped at the drop of moisture beading at the slit. I almost blew my load all over her chest.

With a pained moan, I kissed her as deeply as I could, taking her head in my hands and feeling her palms on my hips. Every place her skin touched mine felt like fire on my body, electricity sparking at every nerve ending from head to toe.

"Do you have protection?" she whispered.

"Are you sure you want to do this?" I answered, needing to hear her say it. *Say it, Jess. Say you want me.*

"I want to do this," she replied, her hands gripping my waist as she looked up at me. "I want you."

Magic words, Frost.

I scrambled for my jeans, found the condom in my wallet, and Jess's generous chest rose and fell with the fast, shallow breaths of desire as she watched me roll it on. Every single second of the wait coiled me tighter and tighter, the heat of her gaze on my dick ratcheting up the anticipation in my blood.

"Lie back, baby," I said, and she complied, reclining on the crisp white bedcovers, her ash brown curls a wild tangled mess around her face, her cheeks flushed and her eyes glassy from her first climax. I took hold of her knees and widened her thighs, grazing a knuckle against her wetness one more time, eliciting a shiver that sent ripples undulating across every inch of her flesh. Jess was fucking perfect, and she wanted me inside her.

Setting my cock against her entrance, I eased into her, giving her one slow wet inch at a time while I watched the play of pain and pleasure flicker across her face. I breathed deeply, battling for control as her snug walls stretched to accommodate my size, but little moans from her throat coaxed me deeper until I was buried to the hilt.

"Oh God, how do you feel so good?" she moaned.

Grunting, fighting against my most animalistic urges, I started to rock, deep and slow inside her, though it cost me my last penny in patience.

"Harder," she said, and I wished she wouldn't. I started to grind into her, stimulating her clit with the base of my cock.

Jess grabbed my face with two hands, kissed me with a sharp nip to my bottom lip, and gave me one of her hottest, sharpest glares. "Faster. Harder. *More*."

"Oh, fuck, Frost," I groaned. "You don't know what you're asking for. If I let go, I'm going to ruin this perfect little pussy."

"Prove it."

My cock throbbed at the challenge, and I drew back and thrust again, pumping in and out, hard and fast and rough, slamming into her with every drop of my need and rage and possession. Her tits bounced with every jolt, and her whimpers were ecstasy bordering on agony, but she gripped my arse and drove me deeper.

How long had I wanted this? How many times had I dreamed of it?

"Fast enough?" I growled. "Hard enough?"

"Yes," she cried, her body convulsing with every thrust. "Oh, God, yes!"

Feeling her core tighten again, I pistoned hard enough that she might not walk tomorrow, but she bucked underneath me as I took her to the top. Her channel squeezed around me, my cock thickened and pulsed, and when she bit her lip, I murmured against her ear. "You want to scream, baby?"

She nodded, eyes closed tight, trying to stifle her moan.

"Then scream."

At the sound of her climax, the pressure at the base of my spine built to boiling point—too much—and the room went dark as I unloaded everything I had inside her. My relief went on and on, tearing growls from my chest that I could only hear after the first violent throes of my orgasm had subsided. When it was done, I collapsed beside her, my face against the mattress, the smell of her hair in my nose, breathing what felt like my last gasps of life.

We lay like that for God knew how long, catching our breaths, reliving the memory, until our panting faded away, and Jess blew out a heavy sigh.

"So, that just happened," she whispered, brushing her fingertips along my spine.

Thank God I wasn't the only one awestruck by that experience.

"Uh, yeah, it did." I carefully lifted myself off her body, sweat and rainbow spatters of paint mingling on our sticky skin, and rolled away. "Are you okay?"

"Yes," she sighed. "I'm good. I'm … good."

Smiling at the lazy lull of her voice, a lull that spoke of satisfaction and satiation, I pushed myself off the bed. "I'll be right back."

Cleaning myself up and returning to the bedroom, I found Jess laying in the same position, eyes closed, breathing evenly. I crept forward and leaned over her, grinning at the painted vision of her, colours flaking away where they had dried or smudging where our bodies had sweated and rubbed against them. I wondered if she'd fallen asleep.

"Stop staring at me, weirdo," she mumbled.

"Thought I might have knocked you out or something," I deadpanned, stretching out on my side next to her, my head propped in one hand so I could look down at her face.

Her mouth twitched. "Not quite."

She kept her eyes closed, and I took the opportunity to sweep my eyes up and down her glorious body, damp and soft and flushed.

"What are you thinking?" I asked.

"I'm thinking those were the best orgasms I've ever had—"

"Thank you."

A crease popped up between her brows. "And we should probably never do that again."

"What? Why the fuck not?"

She did open her eyes then, looking at me like I was an idiot. "Really?"

I fell onto my back, put a hand underneath my head, and stared up into nothing. She was right for a hundred reasons. I lived on the other side of the world. I was a loser with nothing to offer her—no job, no goals, no dreams— and Jessica Frost was too fucking good for me. And at the top of the list: she was my best friend's ex.

But I'd kissed her first, right? That had to count for something.

"So, we did it," she said, sounding like a schoolteacher summarising an important lecture. "It's done. We got whatever it was out of our systems, the itch has been well and truly scratched, and nobody ever needs to know. We can go back to hating each other now, okay?"

Something caught in my throat and made swallowing difficult. "I've never hated you," I mumbled to the ceiling.

She stared up at the same spot alongside me, silent until her fingers brushed against my knuckles, and then she was twining her slender hand in mine. She whispered, so quiet I wasn't sure I was meant to hear it, "I've never hated you either."

15

JESS

LORD, HELP ME. Logan with a sledgehammer, arms rippling as he tore through walls, abs flashing as he wiped his face with the hem of his T-shirt, was straight-up porn—and I wanted a subscription.

He'd arrived at my place just after sunrise with an older guy named Paul to help with the demolition. There was already an industrial-sized waste container in my backyard, and Logan had pored over every piece of paperwork I had for the property—blueprints, building assessments, structural reports. He'd walked me through what he needed to knock down and now the work had begun, all I could do was supervise. Unfortunately for my libido, watching Logan work was working up a sweat on *me*. It was perfectly fine to look, as long as I didn't touch, right? And there would *definitely* be no more touching.

Logan knew we'd made the right decision. I could tell from the change in him that morning. He walked wide around me and had barely looked at me in the three hours since he'd arrived, talking mostly to Paul and concentrating on throwing his energy at brick walls and bathroom tiles and kitchen cupboards. When Logan did look up, I'd quickly glance away, trying to hide the fact I'd been ogling him to the point of drool, recalling his hands on my body, between my legs, inside me. Logan had made me come with nothing but those clever fingers, and the ache between my legs wasn't letting me forget it.

What had I been thinking? As if I needed more evidence, but there in front of me, with his incredible arms and sweat-matted hair, was irrefutable proof I had zero capacity for Good Life Choices. Sleeping with Logan was the definition of a bad decision, but ... wasn't that exactly what I'd set out to do? This whole adventure started because I needed to take my mother's version of Jessica Frost and exorcise her from my life. I needed to turn my back on smart and sensible by having lots of unsuitable sex and making plans to die alone in a gorgeous house I made for myself and my horde of demonic, flesh-eating cats. From that perspective, I was making good progress.

In my orgasm-addled brain, my roundabout logic made complete sense, but more importantly, it's not like anyone ever had to know about it. The sums only had to add up to me.

"Hello? Anyone home?"

I startled at the unexpected interruption, spilling hot tea over my hands as I turned from the supervision of my work crew to find Abbie and Emily sneaking up the hallway.

"Uh, hi. What are you two doing here?"

Abbie held up her hands, a champagne bottle clenched in each fist, and opened her mouth to answer before her brows drew down and her arms dropped to her sides.

"You had sex."

A burn filled my cheeks just as Logan swung his hammer at a kitchen cupboard—and missed.

"What?" I choked out.

Emily poked Abbie in one shoulder, then rolled her eyes. "Abbie thinks she's got a sixth sense for sex, but that's not why we're here."

"No," Abbie agreed, "but we'll get back to the sex in a minute. A little birdie told me *someone* was starting her renovations today, and she didn't think it was important enough to share with her best friends. I told the little birdie he must have it wrong, but the little birdie is living with that Norse god with the hammer over there, so the little birdie was confident that he had the story straight, and eventually, I had to believe him." Abbie waved at Logan. "Hey, Reeve."

He jerked his chin at her. "Hey, Ellison. Hi, Emily. Good to see you again."

"You, too," Emily replied.

"Will has the biggest mouth of anyone I've ever met," I grumbled, wiping my tea-soaked hands on my jeans and studiously *not* looking at Logan, "and that's saying something in this town."

Emily, with a grocery bag in one hand, wrapped me in a hug with the other. "Sorry to show up unannounced, but … well, why didn't you tell us? This is a big deal, and we want to celebrate with you—and help."

I narrowed my eyes at the wine. "Bit early for bubbles, isn't it?"

Abbie started to speak again, but Emily cut her off, hefting the grocery bag. "I've got OJ in here and morning snacks, so we can drink celebratory brunch mimosas while you explain to us why you've gone from zero to sixty on the house plans and kept it all to yourself."

Sparing one last, fleeting look at Logan, who had his back to me in the rapidly deteriorating kitchen, I caved. "All right. Let's sit out front, and I'll explain about the house."

"And the sex," Abbie added. "Don't forget about the sex."

Twenty minutes later, after I'd run into Dot's house to borrow cups, plates, and a blanket, Abbie, Emily, and I had set up a picnic on the porch. Between the sounds of destruction crashing and booming every other minute, I'd told the girls everything that had happened with my parents: their insistence I sell my house, their *incentive* to have me renovate it, and my counteroffer to get it done in half the time.

"So, that's why things are moving full steam ahead." I dropped my head back onto the balustrade I was leaning against, my legs stretched out in front of me so I could sit comfortably in my mid-length khaki skirt. "I know it was a stupid thing to do, which is why I didn't say anything. I was embarrassed."

Emily reached out and squeezed my knee. "What's there to be embarrassed about? I'm proud of you for standing up to your parents the way you did. That takes a lot of guts."

I chuckled humourlessly. "I didn't do it because I've got guts. I did it because I was annoyed and because, more than anything, I wanted to do the opposite of what they wanted me to do."

"And how did you rope Logan into helping out?" Emily asked.

I thought back. "He caught me in a weak moment or two, picked a couple of fights, and bullied his way into my plans. You know how it is with us."

"I do," Abbie answered, smirking as she picked at a box of mini quiches in the pile of food we'd dumped in the middle of the blanket. "I'm surprised you haven't torn each other to pieces yet."

A premonition of my nails scoring lines down Logan's back flashed through my head, and I buried my face in my cocktail to hide my blush. "It's early days," I murmured.

Abbie refilled her glass, then added more wine to my mimosa. "Well, I love this brazen new Jessica," she announced. "It's about time your rebellious streak kicked in. You were such a goody-two-shoes all through school."

I took another sip of my drink, which was now nine parts alcohol to one part juice. "Don't remind me."

"I won't because I'm much more interested in how you've been a *bad* girl." Abbie wiggled her brows and gave me a knowing grin. "Spill, Jess. You got lucky in the last"—she squinted at me, as if she could read residues of sexual energy sparking like static in my aura—"forty-eight hours, to my best estimate, and we want to know who it was."

"Was it the guy from the dating app?" Emily asked, hiding a smile behind her drink. "And was it good?"

I wet my lips, then picked up a strawberry and took a bite. I could never admit to what happened with Logan, but part of me really wanted to talk about the sex. As I nibbled my fruit, balancing on a tightrope between the truth and a lie, I wondered if part of the thrill of being with Logan was that it felt almost illicit. He was my ex-boyfriend's best friend. The boy I'd wanted so long ago, who I never dreamed might want me back. My parents would disapprove. Even—perhaps especially—my friends would have something to say about my reckless behaviour. *His* friends would have something to say. Was sex with Logan so otherworldly because it made me feel like the woman I'd never been brave enough to be?

I recalled his hot breath on my neck, his gravelly voice at my ear. *You want to scream, baby? Then, scream.*

A shiver rolled through me, and Abbie screeched. "Oh my God, anything with a memory that makes you vibrate like that must have been off the charts. Don't make me torture you for details because you know I will."

Noting the silence coming from Emily's corner, combined with the curious sparkle in her eyes, I broke down and confessed.

"Okay, yes. I had sex."

They squealed like teenagers, jumping to their knees and clinking their glasses, then fell on me with congratulatory hugs.

"Ouch!" I said, squeezing them back. "You're going to ruin the food and break one of my ribs."

"Sorry," Emily said, drawing back and taking a seat again. "But ending a three-year dry spell is something to get giddy about."

"It's something to write a *book* about," Abbie added, going for more bubbles. "Don't be stingy with the details. I want to know everything. Who was it? Do we know him? How many times? Will you do it again?"

"Uh, it's a guy I work with." True enough to not be a lie.

"Not the online guy?"

I blanched at the memory of Zachary. "Ugh. Definitely not."

"Someone you work with, so we don't know him," Emily added, and I took another bite of my strawberry so I didn't have to correct her.

"Name?" Abbie demanded.

I said the first thing that came to mind. "Miles."

"Ooh. Cute," Emily said.

"Another teacher?" Abbie leaned in, dropping her chin and her voice. "Is that allowed?"

"This kind of thing is definitely risky," I answered evasively.

Abbie shook her head slowly. "How the hell did my play-it-safe, follow-the-rules, saving-it-for-my-soulmate best friend land in the middle of a sex scandal?"

"It's not a scandal," I replied. "It was a ..."

"One-night stand?" Emily supplied.

I turned that over in my head, uneasy with the way the description made me feel. "Yes? I mean, I think so."

"I know that look," Abbie said. "The orgasms were powerful and plentiful, and you don't want it to be a one-night stand, but you're not interested in a relationship either. You're after hot sex without the strings. Way to go, Jess. I'm proud of you."

Emily and I exchanged small smiles. My friends had polar-opposite opinions on the kind of behaviour they deemed worthy of praise.

"It doesn't matter what I want," I found myself saying. "His ... contract ... finishes at the end of the month, and then he'll be moving out of the area. I probably won't see him again after that."

The thought made the wine in my stomach churn, and I put my glass down as I swallowed a final sip. Logan would be gone soon, and I didn't want to think about him leaving or about why it should bother me. If anything, Logan going back to London was a good thing. It meant it would be easier for both of us to move on from our temporary insanity.

"Are you telling me," Abbie said, "that you've found yourself a hot guy who's not only a firecracker in the sack but comes clearly stamped with a use-by date?"

"Er, yes?"

Abbie stuck out her hand, and I shook it as she said, "Congratulations, Miss Frost. You've gone and won the jackpot."

16

JESS

ABBIE AND EMILY stayed for another two hours, but after I'd admitted what happened with my parents, plus added a bunch of vague half-truths about my encounter with "Miles", they were satisfied enough that talk soon turned to Emily's burgeoning photography business, as well as Abbie's expansion of her health and wellness studio, a place called Love, Yoga where she taught yoga and pilates. Any further conversations about sex were strictly related to Emily and Josh's escapades and Abbie's search for her next orgasm. She had a lot more luck with dating apps than I'd had.

"Let me know when I can come back and help," Emily said as she hugged me goodbye on the porch steps. "I'll clean and paint, and maybe I can take some photographs of the Bay for you to print and hang. Only if you want them. No pressure."

"That sounds amazing. Thanks, Em."

"You're welcome, and you should get together with Josh soon to talk about the yards. He'll have ideas. I guarantee it."

"That's a great idea. I'll do that."

"I'll help, too," Abbie said, taking Emily's place in my arms. "Painting and cleaning if I have to, but sex advice anytime, okay?"

I chuckled. "Okay. Thank you."

After I'd waved goodbye, I scooped up the remnants of our picnic and carried them over to Dot's house. I'd been right—my surrogate grandmother was stoked to have me as her housemate for as long as necessary, but the old woman was rarely home. She had a busy enough social life that I had to force myself to feel less envy and more hopeful that somehow I'd be having as much fun as Dot when I was in my eighties.

I packed away the leftover food and stored it neatly in the fridge, handwashed all the dishes—Dot didn't believe in dishwashers—then dried and put them away. I told myself I wasn't deliberately avoiding going home, where the only thing I had to do was try to keep my eyes and hands off Logan, but when I found myself searching Dot's cupboards for tumblers with water spots I could wash all over again, I knew I had to get back over there.

Climbing my porch steps with the kind of butterflies in my belly I hadn't felt since high school, I passed Paul on the way out. In his early forties with rich brown skin, the labourer was fit and polite, but not much of a talker. He had keys in his hand and a bag of gear on his back.

"Oh, are you done already?" I asked.

"For today. I'll be back tomorrow morning to help finish up, but I'm on loan, so back to the boss I go."

"Right. Well, thanks so much for all your work this morning. I appreciate it."

He gave me a salute and jogged down the stairs to his car while I crept inside, not sure what to expect after six hours of destruction.

Almost the entire back wall of the house was gone, and so was the kitchen. I peeked into the bathroom and laundry, both of which were nothing but shells, then tiptoed through a curtain of plastic sheeting and out onto the back porch, which was still intact. The changes were significant, and as I explored the ruins of my grandmother's old home, something tight released in my chest. What had only been a dream less than two weeks ago was now an irreversible reality, and I couldn't turn back, even if I wanted to. I'd taken a risk, and I felt a little foolish when I realised that the worrying I'd done leading up to this moment had been much worse than the worry I felt now about how things were going to work out. In fact, I hardly felt anxious at all. I was exhilarated. Could I apply this lesson to other areas of my life—other decisions I'd avoided making because of overthinking and apprehension? If I just leaped more quickly instead of peering over the ledge, would I stop obsessing so much about where I would land?

Circling back to check the bedrooms, I couldn't find Logan, so I pulled out my phone, contemplating texting to see if he'd left while I was at Dot's. As my thumb hovered over the screen, a crash sounded from the garage. He was still here … and I was going to leap.

After pausing in my bedroom to take a fortifying breath and remove my underwear, I made my way outside and found him in the workshop. He was dusty from the demolition work, his clothes worn and grimy, his hair mussed and messy, and he was washing up at the old sink in the corner. He'd never looked sexier.

"The house looks good," I said.

He turned his head, lathering up his hands under a stream of water, not at all startled by my sudden appearance.

"No, the house looks like a bomb site. Demo will be done tomorrow, then we start putting the pieces back together again."

I nodded, strolling around the edge of the room, then pulled myself up to sit on the bench next to him. I knew what I was doing. I knew I was playing with fire, but right then, I wanted to burn.

"Thanks for all the work," I said. "If you'd let me pay you something—"

"No. Absolutely not."

"Okay, but I wish you would. It would make asking you for favours less like sucking lemons."

His cheek lifted with a small smile. "What do you need from me now, Frost?"

"I've been thinking about what to get Luca and Natasha for a wedding gift, and I wondered if there's anything in the garage that can be refurbished quickly? An armchair would be nice, or a coffee table. Something worth a bit that they won't find anywhere else."

Logan contemplated me long enough that warmth started building in my cheeks. "That's a nice idea," he said finally. "I could find something they'd like, no doubt about it." Then he grimaced. "Goes to show what a great best man I am. A wedding gift hadn't even crossed my mind."

I rubbed at my nose as it twitched. "My furniture plus your skill ... We could make it a joint present."

"You mean we'd give them a gift from the both of us?"

"Yes?"

He cupped his hand under the tap, then splashed his face with water. When he ran his wet hands through his hair, inked biceps flexing, I was the one sitting in a puddle, and I bit my lip against a needy sigh.

"Okay," he murmured, turning off the tap. "Thanks, Frost."

I set my hands on the bench beside my thighs, leaned forward a little, and swung my legs one at a time, back and forth. "Is there any outdoor furniture in there? I just had to host the girls on a blanket on the porch. It would have been nice to have something to sit on."

Logan squinted at the wall of the workshop as if he could see through it to the adjoining garage and all its wares, then shook his head. "Sorry, I don't think so. You might have to buy new."

I shrugged. "That's fine."

Logan's eyes landed on me then, taking in the carefully constructed view down the neck of my shirt, travelling down over my bare calves and up again. I widened my legs a little, so my knee brushed up against him, and my skirt rode up, revealing a little more of my thighs.

"What are you doing?" he asked, low and husky, as his hands balled in and out of fists.

"Whatever it is," I whispered, "it's a very bad idea."

Surprise flared in his gaze for a second before he pushed his hips between my knees and grabbed my arse, yanking me forwards and slamming my pelvis against his bulging erection, crushing his mouth against mine. Heat and moisture sprang up at his touch. Oh, God. This was the best bad idea I'd ever had.

My hips started to circle, my core muscles throbbing and blooming to welcome him inside, but he was too busy running his hands over me to give me his cock yet. His fingers were rough and greedy, grabbing at my breasts, tearing off my shirt, gripping the back of my neck as he kissed me in a frenzied haze that had me wanting more of it all. When he pinched my nipple hard, I cried out, first at the pain, then at the shock of desire that zipped straight to my clit.

My tongue lapped at his, and our kisses grew messy and wet while his fingers dug into my hips, and I opened my legs wider as he thrust against me. Leaning back on my hands, I offered him my neck and chest, silently begging to feel his tongue on every inch of my skin.

"Jesus, Frost," he moaned against my ear, sliding his hands up my thighs. "I want this so badly. I thought about your body every minute of every hour last night."

The picture of Logan touching himself while fantasising about me sent a slick of exhilaration through my racing blood. I tried to talk between pants and moans and kisses as his attention returned to my tits, mouth on one aching nipple, hand massaging the other. "Did you— Did you—"

"Did I fuck my hand the way I want to fuck you? You bet your pretty pussy I did."

"Oh, God." I tore at his shirt, needing to run my hands over his glorious chest, then fumbled at his pants, desperate to feel that thick flesh in my hand. "Please," I begged.

Logan peeled off his shirt, then unbuttoned his pants and tore them off, taking his briefs with them, and I reached for his towering cock. He groaned, braced his hands on the bench on either side of my hips, and set his forehead against mine as he watched me wrap my fingers around him and stroke. Once, twice. Hard, harder.

I pulled, cupping his balls with my other hand, until he dived at my mouth, kissing and nipping at my lips. Then a growl reverberated through his chest as he snatched my hips, lifted me off the bench, and set me on my feet. He spun me around, hands caressing my outer thighs as he gathered my skirt around my hips. Finding me bare underneath, he groaned.

"Fuck, Frost. I always thought you'd kill me, but I didn't expect to go like this."

He held me flush against the bench, the hardness of his body pressed against my back, the tip of his dick running along the line of my arse, the warmth of his lips at the shell of my ear.

"You still think this is a bad idea?" he murmured.

"Yes," I whispered, but then I shook my head. "No. I'm not sure I care."

I whimpered as he ran a hand down the dip of my spine, neck to arse and back again, then pressed me chest-down onto the bench.

"Widen your legs, baby," he said.

I did, tilting my hips as Logan rubbed the crown of his dick along my slick folds.

"So wet for me, aren't you?" he said. "I'm going to slide right in there, and you're going to scream for me again."

"Yes," I panted. "Make me scream."

Logan stepped away, and I heard him tear open the packet of a condom, and then he was there again, teasing my entrance, running his hands over my bare back. He rested one palm between my shoulder blades as he snaked the other around my front, fingers rubbing my folds and seeking my clit, then finding it with stunning accuracy.

"Oh, shit," I gasped against the smooth timber of the bench, the sawdusty smell of it only adding to my excitement.

Logan chuckled, and I could hear the smile in his voice as he used his fingers to open me up and circle my swollen clit. "You like that?"

"Yes!"

His fingertips maintained their pressure as he pushed an inch of his hard length inside me, then retreated.

"You like that, too?" he asked.

"Mm-hm," I panted.

Another inch, and another one, slowly sinking inside me. He felt bigger at this angle, and I breathed through twinges of discomfort as I willed my walls to relax and take him.

"Can you take a little more?" he grunted, working my clit hard enough that I felt contractions in my core.

"There's more?" I moaned, already stretched by his size and on the verge of coming.

"There's more," he whispered.

"Yes," I breathed. "I can take it."

"Good girl," he replied, pushing on my hips and burying himself a little further. When I thought I'd have to tell him I couldn't take another inch, he shifted the angle of my body, pressing on the small of my back, and found space I didn't know I had. I'd never experienced such a fit before, and then his thrusts began, slow and steady.

"That's it," he said as I groaned, his dick reaching nerve endings inside me that had never been touched. "Here we go, baby."

I gasped and pushed my arse out, rocking against him.

Logan gripped my hips with both hands, and though I missed the friction of his fingers between my legs, I loved this more. He was in control, driving my body onto his, keeping me safe and steady and on the edge of ecstasy as he slammed himself against my arse, the sound of our bodies smacking into each other winding up my arousal. He grunted and mumbled incoherently, and so did I, dissolving into whimpers and single-syllable pleas. The pressure built and built, and I teetered there for long enough that he finally growled and reapplied two talented fingers to my pussy, rolling over that hypersensitive bundle of nerves and extracting an orgasm almost immediately.

"Yes, baby," he panted. "That's it. Scream for me."

And I did. I screamed because my climax was so hard and so welcome, because Logan inside me was the freest I'd ever felt, and because this man knew what I wanted, and he wanted me to take it.

I screamed because leaping felt so good that I didn't care where I landed.

The pulse of his orgasm rippled inside me, and my muscles clenched down on him, drawing out every last drop. He breathed hard and heavy, leaning over me and pressing soft, warm kisses across my shoulders and back. Logan was still inside me, I was still trembling with the aftershocks of my orgasm, and already I was thinking about how quickly we could do it again.

17

LOGAN

"ALL RIGHT," I declared, propping the broom against a wall in the living room. "That's a wrap for today."

We'd reached the end of the second week of renovations, the demolition was finished, and I'd framed up the new wall in the dining room to convert it into an extra bedroom. Paul had given me a hand, hanging the plasterboard and sanding it back in preparation for painting. Jess's order from the showroom was on schedule to arrive within the next seven days, which meant she was going to spend the weekend cleaning up while the contractors roughed in the plumbing and electrical, and I hosted Luca's bucks' night. I wasn't looking forward to being away from her because, on top of all the progress we'd made on the house, Jess had become extremely enthusiastic about exploring our sexual chemistry. I didn't know what had sparked the change in her, and perhaps I was better off not knowing. All I could do was enjoy it while it lasted.

Jess looked at her watch. "It's getting late. Do you need to get back to The Stop and help Will behind the bar?"

"I checked in with him earlier and told him we were flat out here. He's not expecting me for at least another two hours."

She blushed prettily, and I rolled my lips to stop a grin.

"Okay," she said. "Do you want to stay for dinner?"

I curled my arms around her waist, pulled her in so tight her body curved against mine, and kissed her mouth. "I could eat," I murmured, unbuttoning her denim shorts.

She giggled and nuzzled my neck as I slid a hand into her panties, teasing her with light touches as I brushed my lips over her jaw and down the side of her neck. Her fingers twisted in my hair, and I'd just started to drag her shorts over her hips when there was a knock on the front door.

Dot's reedy voice floated up the hallway. "Hello? Is anybody there?"

Jess and I exchanged frustrated smiles as she quickly buttoned up and went to the door. I stayed out of sight, thinking it would be better not to greet little old Mrs March with an unmissable bulge in my pants.

"Hi, Dot," Jess greeted her, and I heard the door swing open. "Did you want to come in?"

As much as I liked Jess's neighbour, I was not in the mood to chat. I crossed my fingers, consoled my cock, and willed the old woman away.

"Oh, no, dear," she replied. "I don't want to interrupt your work. I just wanted to let you know I have a casserole ready for you when you're done."

"Thank you. That sounds delicious. Is there enough for Logan too? I might come with you to plate up and bring it back here. We're, uh, right in the middle of cleaning up, so this way, we can eat while we work."

"Of course. Come with me, and I'll sort you out." Dot raised her voice and called to me, "Hello, Logan!"

"Oh, hi, Mrs March," I yelled back, fidgeting with my dick, which was now at half-mast. I stuck my head into the hallway. "Good to see you again."

Her mouth twitched with a knowing smile. "I'm stealing Jess for a moment to fetch your dinner. Maryanne Diaz gave me her recipe for chicken goulash. It's delicious."

There were other things I'd rather be doing than eating dinner, but Maryanne was one of Valentine Bay's most reliable cooks, and my stomach growled with anticipation. "I appreciate that. Thanks."

Jess spared me a cheeky grin as she followed Dot out the door, and as soon as they cleared the porch, I dashed to the spare bedroom, where we'd packed away all of Jess's kitchen gear. Rifling through the boxes, I finally found what I was looking for and, working quickly, I'd set up everything I needed to by the time Jess returned with two plates of something that smelled sensational.

"Come and get it! Fresh from the—" Jess froze in the doorway to the living area, her mouth ajar. "Where did you get all this?"

I took the plates from her and set them on the thick, grey woollen blankets I'd spread out on the timber floor. Old pillows were scattered around, and candles flickered in the corners of the room, so I switched off the overhead lights. Taking Jess's hand and settling her against an oversized cushion, I joined her, then handed her a glass of wine.

"I raided your linen cupboard and the boxes of kitchen stuff we packed into the bedroom, plus a few others for the candles. The wine was an unexpected surprise."

Jess picked up the bottle of shiraz and examined the label. "It was a gift, I think. I'd forgotten all about it."

I'd poured us both glasses, though little more than a mouthful for me. "Cheers," I said, lifting my glass, and she clinked hers to mine. "To a productive week."

"To a productive week," she echoed, glancing around the room again. "I can't believe you did this."

"Shh," I replied, embarrassed. "Now, are you sure you're comfortable managing the contractors tomorrow? I've already briefed Baz and Brody, and they have the house plans, so there shouldn't be any problems."

Jess took a sip of her wine, then replaced the glass with her plate, and we began to eat. "It'll be fine. You took me through the plans, too. I know what to expect."

"All right. Good. But you can call me if you need me."

She smirked, a forkful of food halfway to her mouth. "And interrupt Luca's bucks' weekend? I wouldn't dream of it. Go on, tell me what you've planned."

I rolled my eyes and swallowed my bite of food. "Fine, but you're sworn to secrecy."

She mimed buttoning her lips, and I grinned.

We talked about the boys' weekend, then a little more about the house. An hour later, she ran our dirty plates back to Dot's house and returned with bottles of water and two small cartons of ice-cream, and we stretched out on the pillows, swapping flavours back and forth. When silence finally fell, I propped my head in my hand and watched her lick vanilla ice-cream off a spoon as golden light flickered across her face and danced along the edges of her hair.

"What?" she asked, putting down her dessert and wiping at her lips. "I've made a mess of myself, haven't I?"

I shook my head. "No."

She hummed, setting the ice-cream carton to the side and mirroring my posture so we were face to face across the rugs. "Not sure if I should believe you. You're just the type to let me walk around all day with food dried on my face."

Smiling a little at the jab, I played with the fabric of a cushion, avoiding her eyes. "Can I ask you a question?"

"Oh, no. This sounds ominous."

I ignored that, nervous enough about what I was about to say. "Why has our relationship always been so hostile?"

She blinked a half-dozen times. "What?"

I rolled onto my back and stared up at the ceiling, reconsidering this can of worms, but for better or worse, I wanted to know the answer. I turned my head to find her staring down at me with a guarded expression. "Why did we spend more than ten years at each other's throats? Did I do something wrong?"

"You mean other than torment me every chance you got? You've been a mosquito buzzing around my ear for nearly half my life."

When I said nothing, Jess worried at her lip as her gaze grew distant, then she flopped onto her stomach, a cushion under her folded arms. "I overheard you once talking to Luca about me."

My hackles rose. "What do you mean?"

"It was about a year after the spin-the-bottle incident. You were obviously not interested in me—*really* obviously, always teasing me about my perfect grades, or my glasses, or the little hearts I used to draw to dot my Is—"

"I stand by that, Frost. Those little hearts looked like hard work. Who the fuck has time for that?"

She scowled. "Anyway, it was clear to everyone you thought I was a joke, and then I overheard a conversation that confirmed it. Luca was trying to reason with you, explain that I wasn't as painful a person as you seemed to think, and you called me—and I quote—*not your type*. Too smart. Too uptight. Too serious. Too much *hard work*."

I dug through my patchy memories of high school, searching for the moment Jess remembered so clearly, and came up blank, but it didn't matter. I didn't need to recall the date and time of this alleged discussion to know why I'd said those things, given who I was talking to at the time, and I grew defensive.

"You were eavesdropping on me?" I accused.

"Uh, I—" Jess swung her legs around and sat up. "That's what you're taking away from this?" When

I didn't look at her, she huffed incredulously. "Okay, fine. I wasn't *eavesdropping*. You and Luca were having a public conversation, and you didn't notice me walking behind you. Here's a piece of advice: next time you want to tear a person down simply for being who they are, maybe choose some out-of-the-way place where you won't get caught."

She didn't get it. She would never understand. Was there any point in trying to explain it to her?

"It wasn't what you think it was," I mumbled.

Silence, and when I finally looked at her, she was blinking again. "I heard you say the words. You were pretty verbal about your opinion of me, and things only went downhill from there. You took pleasure in pissing me off for years. Teasing me, making fun of the way I dressed or spoke or studied or *breathed*. Nothing made you happier than making me suffer."

I snorted and rolled my eyes to the ceiling again. "You have no idea what you're talking about."

Abruptly, Jess stood up. "Don't do that. Don't dismiss me or imply I overreact. Aren't we beyond that? I don't know what I thought was going on here between us this last week, but I assumed we'd at least moved past the sniping and the meanness." She stalked to the other side of the room and flung up her hands. "I am such an idiot! Why did I ever think you could be different? Defences, Jessica. *Defences*."

I jumped to my feet as well, hands balling at my sides, my words failing me when I needed them, as always.

"I'm not dismissing you, but just because I said those things, it doesn't mean I believed them."

She laughed under her breath, shaking her head. "Is that supposed to make me feel better? You've spent years trying to tear me down, but you didn't *mean* it?"

"No, that's not what I'm saying. Look, I was young, and I was stupid. I probably went the wrong way about keeping you at a distance, but it was the right thing to do."

Jess paused, crossed her arms, and narrowed her eyes. "Why would you need to keep me at a distance?"

"No, I mean, it was for the best. For everyone."

"What was for the best?"

I groaned and dropped my head back, knowing I should quit while I was ahead but unable to stop my mouth. "Luca is my best mate, and he liked you. I had to make it perfectly clear I wasn't interested in you, okay?"

"Holy hell, this sounds like some tribal mating ritual. I'm my own person, you know."

"No, I know, but it was just easier to give you a hard time. What else was I supposed to do? Be your friend and get my hopes up, then end up looking like a total fool?"

"What hopes?"

I dragged my hands down my face. "Can we just drop this? I'm sorry I fucking asked you anything."

"No, we're not dropping it until you tell me what you mean. Reeve, look at me."

Blood rushing in my ears and heart racing in my chest, I began bundling up the pillows and blankets. "Just let it go."

"I don't want to let it go. I want to know what you're trying to tell me."

"It doesn't matter."

"What are you talking about? Why doesn't it matter?"

"Because you loved Luca!" I yelled.

"I loved you first, you idiot!"

We stood there staring at each other, our shouts echoing off the walls. I don't know who moved first, but I couldn't get to her fast enough, and we crashed into each other in the middle of the empty room.

The kiss was desperate, but it softened quickly as I cradled her head in my hands and breathed her in, folding my lips over hers and revelling in the feel of her arms wrapped around my body. Closer. I needed to get closer, and when I pulled her down onto the pillows, she collapsed with me, our mouths never breaking away from their exploration of each other.

I undressed her, not for the first time, but this felt different. Slower. I didn't think there was an inch of her skin I hadn't already licked or sucked or kissed, but I'd been too greedy before to take my time. I was about to remedy that oversight. I was going to explore every part of her, memorise every curve and line and valley, and map the terrain of her so it would live forever in my mind.

Jess seemed to notice the shift, too. Her hands weren't frenzied, her body wasn't heaving. We weren't lost in a fog of desire. Our need had shifted, glowing bone-deep where before it blazed across skin, and it would take time to satiate—time I wanted to give her.

When we were both naked, I kissed her. I kissed her for what felt like hours. I ran my hands down her sides, the planes of her shoulders, the dip of her spine, over the roundness of her hips, along the crease of her arse. Our bodies lay close enough that my erection pressed into the soft skin of her stomach, and that was enough until finally, trailing my fingertips so lightly over her skin that I left ripples of goosebumps in my wake, I brushed her inner thighs, encouraging them to open.

As Jess widened her knees for me, I hissed in a breath as her warm hand enclosed my straining cock. That glow in my bones burned brighter. I squeezed her pussy, teased the lips between her legs apart, and moaned at the slick warmth that greeted my fingers. As I dipped a fingertip into her entrance, her grip on my dick tightened, her thumb grazed the tip, and I circled my tongue around one taut nipple, flicking it roughly and loving the way I'd grown to know her body so well I'd anticipated the familiar gasp-and-groan that followed.

"I want to ride you," she whispered, her husky voice like electric paddles on my cock, and she set her hands on my chest, pushed me back onto the pillows, and swung a leg over my body.

Stretching a hand towards my pants, where a condom lay hidden in the pocket, I grabbed onto her hip to keep her steady, balanced over my dick, ready to slide that tight pussy onto me. "We need a—"

"I'm on the pill," she said, shifting south just enough that the tip of my cock brushed against her wet heat.

I grunted and gritted my teeth, using every ounce of self-control I possessed not to slam my dick straight into her. "And I haven't been with anyone in … a while."

"I'm clean," I replied, pressing a thumb to her clit and rubbing gently, feeling like a fucking magician at the way I could conjure that glassy look of lust in her eyes. "But you don't have to do anything you don't want to— Ah, fuck!"

Jess dropped her body onto mine, sheathing my entire length in one movement that knocked the breath out of us both. The gasp that rushed from her mouth was somewhere between gratification and anguish, and I almost came at the sudden pressure of her snug, hot walls around me, nothing between us anywhere on our bodies. If you'd told me I'd died and gone to heaven, in that moment I'd have believed you.

As Jess's eyes closed, her head lolled back, and her hips started to rock. I watched in rapture as she rode me, getting off on the way she used me for her own pleasure. I palmed her soft, ample breasts, tweaking her nipples as she gasped and moaned, until she fell forwards, braced her hands on either side of my shoulders with her hair falling loose between us, and began to slide up and down my shaft. I grunted, fighting the urge to come, but I couldn't take it anymore. I needed to *see* her.

"Baby, open your eyes," I demanded. "Look at me."

She did, biting her lip, gazing down at me with masses of curls around her damp, flushed face, dark hooded eyes so soft and so beautiful something snapped inside my chest. I grabbed onto her hips and thrust hard, desperate to come deep inside her because I didn't know a way to make her mine other than this primal drive to claim her with my body. She shifted her hips, grinding into me in tight, frenzied circles, and my balls ached as her core trembled around my cock. When she dug her fingernails so deep into my shoulders, I distantly registered the sting of blood, but I didn't look away, wanting—no, *needing*—to see her reach her climax, needing her to register what I felt when I came inside her for the first time.

I was almost afraid she'd close her eyes when her orgasm hit, but her gaze bored into mine as she cried out, her pussy tightening, her fingers dragging score marks down my chest. A moment later, I poured myself into her, grunting and straining, holding her against me as if I could somehow get closer, trying to tell her with my expression all the things I couldn't say with words.

Loving me is a bad idea, but could you ever do it again?

18

JESS

———————

I WAS HUNCHED over paperwork strewn across Dot's breakfast table at six o'clock the next morning when she shuffled out of her bedroom wrapped in a lavender dressing gown, rollers in her pink hair.

"I thought I heard the shower running," she commented as she filled the kettle. "You're up early for a Saturday, aren't you?"

"The electrician and the plumber will be at the house in half an hour, and I wanted to make extra certain I'm up to speed on the plans before they arrive."

"Ah." Dot pulled out her favourite mug—the one with the pink VBFYRRRBC logo printed on the side—and held up another. "Would you like tea? Perhaps some toast to go with it?"

"That sounds great. Thanks."

As Dot made us breakfast, I returned to my study of the house plans. I was on my own today—no Logan—and although I'd assured him I had everything under control, I was nervous about supervising tradespeople without him. Against all odds, Logan had become my rock and my sounding board, and though I was fairly confident I could handle things on my own for one day, I would have liked to have him around.

It made me a little woozy when I considered how quickly things had shifted between us, and because I felt steadier with things mapped out, I'd given it some thought and was almost certain I could pinpoint the exact moment the dynamic between us changed. It was after the debacle with the curtain rod, the day I was forced to admit how badly I'd screwed up with my parents. I'd handed him what he'd always wanted: irrefutable proof that I really was the stubborn, uptight know-it-all he'd always said I was. That had been his moment to crow—and he hadn't. He'd stepped in and stepped up without ever making me ask for his help, and now, the guy who had always made me feel too self-conscious to relax in his company had the power to melt me with only a look or a touch.

As my thoughts drifted to Logan, I recalled for the thousandth time the candlelit picnic he'd set up for me, the fight we'd had about our past, and his confession that picking on me had been his backwards way of protecting himself.

I found his revelation equal parts endearing and frustrating. As kids, we'd unwittingly set a precedent for our hostile relationship, but then our lives had taken us in different directions, and we'd never had an opportunity to outgrow it. Then there was my unintentional confession that I'd loved him once and the sex that had come after it.

Oh, God, we'd climaxed together, and the way he'd met my eyes when we did, holding me there and refusing to let me turn away …

"I know that look," Dot said, setting a steaming cup of tea in front of me, then a plate of hot buttered toast. "You're thinking about a boy."

I took a sip of tea and burned my tongue while Dot took the chair next to me, watching me with a shrewd smile. "It's hot," she murmured unnecessarily.

"Mm," I replied, picking up a pen in one hand and a triangle of toast in the other, munching on it while I tried and failed to read the diagrams in front of me.

"No rush," Dot said. "I've got all day."

"No, you don't. You have book club today."

"Well, I've got a few hours, at least. Oh, come on, Jessica. Don't make an old lady beg."

I swallowed and took another tentative slurp of tea. "Yes, I was thinking about a boy."

Dot clasped her gnarled hands together on the table as her blue eyes lit up. "Anybody I know?"

I was sure she had her suspicions, but I wasn't ready to confirm them just yet. "Maybe, maybe not."

"I see. Well, tell me a little about this mystery man."

A sigh whooshed out of my chest, and I leaned back into the dining chair. "He's sweet and solid and makes me feel safe."

He makes me want to leap without worrying about where I'll land.

"All admirable qualities," Dot replied.

I pursed my lips at her tone. "Are you making fun of me?"

"Of course not, but a woman as young and spectacular as you should be looking for more than safe." She leaned in and tucked her chin. "Now's the time to be with someone sexy."

"Dot!" Heat spotted my cheeks, and she patted my hand.

"I didn't mean to embarrass you, dear, but I stand by that piece of advice. Find someone hot enough to light a fire inside you."

I cleared my throat and nibbled at my breakfast. "He does that too."

"I'm glad, and does he have the skills required to put that fire out?"

"Dot!" My entire face flooded with embarrassment, but the old woman just cackled.

"Trust me on this, dear. Having six husbands taught me a thing or two."

"Six? I thought it was five."

"No, six, so believe me when I tell you, sweet and safe are nothing to be sneezed at, but neither is what he can do between the sheets."

My heart skipped a beat or two as I relived the memory of Logan's body under mine. "Well, I appreciate the advice," I said, squeezing my thighs together, "but you've got nothing to worry about. Logan's good at everything he does."

Dot didn't say anything, and it was only when I met her smug, steady gaze I realised I'd outed myself. My eyes widened, and my mouth opened, but no words came to me.

"And is this man a keeper?" Dot asked, picking up her mug and taking a slow sip.

She was going to pretend as though I hadn't said his name? Okay, good. I could deal with that.

"Uh, no. I don't think so." I started to scoop up the plans on the table, fumbling with the handful of pens and having to pick them up one by one. "He doesn't live in the Bay, and he has other commitments elsewhere, so it's a fling. I think."

"You think?"

It was an unspoken understanding, wasn't it? This thing with Logan and me couldn't go anywhere. He didn't want it to, and neither did I ... Right?

"Well, we haven't discussed a relationship," I replied, "and we haven't told anyone about ... us."

"Was it your idea to keep it on the down low or his?"

I blinked at the question as well as the way she'd phrased it. "Uh, mine ... or his. We both agreed, I guess. There are reasons. It's complicated."

Dot nodded sagely. "It always is, but sometimes we overthink things that could be quite simple."

"You might be right," I said, finally capturing all my paperwork, "but I don't think this is one of those times."

"A man who takes care of you and can *take care of you*." Dot shook her head, her eyes growing distant. "Out of my six husbands, only one could do both, and he was my favourite."

"Which one was that? No, don't tell me now. I'm running late. I'm going to head over to the house, but we can talk about it another time. Have fun at book club."

"I will, dear, and thank you for sharing with me. You made an old girl feel young again."

I loved my grandmother's oldest and dearest friend, but our conversation confused me, not least because we both knew the man in question was Logan, and that hadn't changed her opinion. If anything, it seemed to make her more determined to encourage a theoretical relationship between the two of us. Should I be worried that the only person in my life who could possibly believe Logan and I were a good match was the old woman who'd burned through six husbands? Probably.

I stood and dropped a kiss on her temple, narrowly avoiding a curler to the eye. "Thanks for the chat, Dot. You've definitely given me something to think about."

It took the tradespeople more than five hours to finish roughing in for the plumbing and electrical. I hovered a little, tried to look busy in other rooms of the house, gnawed at my nails, and answered their questions when they asked them. Early that afternoon, when I was sending them off with the work done and no disasters to show for it, I felt almost proud of myself. Not that I'd done anything remotely heroic, but I'd handled an important day on my renovation schedule all on my own. It was empowering.

No sooner had I completed a second circuit of the house, examining the wires dangling from walls and open pipes poking out of the floors, cross-checking them against the house plans, than a knock sounded on the door. My silly stomach flipped, hoping it was Logan coming to surprise me, before my brain shut it down with a reminder that he was at Luca's bucks' party. Logan had organised a full itinerary with go-karts and paintball, followed by twilight beers and barefoot lawn bowls, then drinks back at The Stop until one or all of them passed out from too much booze. No matter how much I'd wheedled for an answer, Logan had refused to confirm or deny the presence of dancers at any of the day's events, and I tried not to let the idea of a half-naked woman gyrating over him bother me too much. We weren't together, and it wasn't up to me to police his behaviour. Still, I'd like to believe he wasn't stuffing tips into an itty-bitty G-string somewhere.

I opened the door to find Abbie and Emily on the other side. "Hey, you two. What are you doing here?"

Abbie shook a bucket of cleaning supplies at me. "Doesn't this give it away?"

"You're here to help me mop the floors and wipe down the walls?"

Emily tapped her nose. "Bingo. Let us in."

I moved aside as my friends marched past me. "How did you know that's what I was doing this afternoon? No, don't tell me. Your little birdie let it slip."

"Right again," Abbie agreed, "though Logan mentioned it as well. We bumped into the boys on their way out for Luca's party."

"Josh is so pumped for paintball," Emily added with an affectionate eye roll.

"They all are," Abbie said. "But what I want to know is, why did we have to hear about your house stuff second-hand at all? We told you to call us when you needed help."

"You don't have to do all this yourself," Emily added. "We want to lend a hand."

It was right on the tip of my tongue to say, *I've been too busy getting naked with Logan to have you poking around the place with soaped-up sponges*. Instead, I shrugged and tried to look the right kind of abashed.

"I didn't want to bother you, and this is something I've needed to do on my own. It's my way of showing my parents that I can take care of myself, you know?"

"So, do you want us to stick around and scrub walls or not?" Abbie set her bucket on the floor and dragged her hands through her long blonde hair. "Because there's a jug of bottomless margaritas calling our name somewhere in the Bay right now."

I chuckled. "As tempting as that sounds, I can't. The deadline is just too tight, and Logan is expecting me to get a lot done this weekend."

Abbie cocked an eyebrow and crossed her arms. "You'll accept Logan's help and not ours?"

"I don't think of him as a helper. He's more like an employee."

"Are you paying him?" Emily asked.

"No."

"Then consider us staff as well." She picked up the bucket Abbie had set down. "Where do you want us?"

We started with wiping down the walls in my bedroom to prep them for painting, and as much as I liked working side by side with Logan day in and day out, it was refreshing to spend time with the girls again. I'd been avoiding them, at first because of the dating app disaster, then the renovation bargain conundrum. Now I was anxious about hiding my affair with Logan. These kinds of situations were stressful for someone who wasn't a very good liar.

"So," Abbie said, running a large damp sponge over one wall using the circular motion Logan had shown me the day before and I'd demonstrated to my friends a moment ago. "What's happening with Miles?"

Miles? It took me a second to remember I'd used "Miles" as a codename for Logan.

"I'm proud of you, Abs," Emily said with a grin. "You waited a whole half-hour before hitting her up about her sex life."

Abbie stuck her nose in the air. "That's because I'm a patient person and a sensitive soul, not to mention an excellent friend."

"Right you are. So ..." Emily raised her eyebrows at me. "Any developments?"

I turned to another wall, putting my back to them, and moved my cloth in slow circles while I gathered my thoughts. Maybe talking about things would help me sort out how I felt about Logan. *Miles* was a stranger as far as they knew, and I could use the advice of someone other than my eighty-year-old neighbour.

"There's been more sex," I admitted.

Abbie screeched, and I couldn't help but laugh. I looked over my shoulder at the both of them—Abbie bounced on her toes, and Emily clasped her hands under her chin, waiting for more.

I bit back a goofy grin. "It's … off the charts."

"Atta girl!" Abbie whooped. "I feel like a mother hen or something, sending my chick out into the wild and watching her fly."

"Oh, God. Stop."

"You do seem happy," Emily said. "Not to sound like a cliché, but there's a certain glow about you."

"There is not."

"There is," Abbie replied. "Tell us what positions, techniques, and sexual accoutrements have given you this glow, and don't spare any details. You owe me at least a hundred good sex stories."

That much was true. I'd had nothing to add to these conversations in a very long time. Even when I was with Luca, I'd never volunteered much about our physical relationship. It had been nice with him—always nice—but though it pained me to admit it, even to myself, there'd never been anything between us like the primal urgency I felt being in the same room as Logan.

"There was the first time, which you already know about. And the second time, which was so hot. Then the

212

last time, he surprised me with a candlelit indoor picnic, and we did it on the floor."

Emily covered her face and squeaked out a high-pitched keen, but Abbie dropped her sponge in the bucket with a wet plop and planted her hands on her hips.

"No."

I frowned. "No, what?"

"No, I won't let you fall in love with this man."

I scoffed. "What? I'm not in *love* with him."

"Bullshit, Jessica Jane. I've known you since you were a foetus, and I know what it means when your eyes get all gooey like that. You're falling for this Miles guy."

"No, I'm not." I had no trouble denying that with a straight face. I was definitely *not* in love with a man named Miles.

"Would it be such a bad thing if she was?" Emily asked, the sponge in her hand forgotten as it dripped soapy water onto the bare floorboards.

"Yes," Abbie said. "It would be a very bad thing."

"Why?" I asked, then I bit the inside of my cheek. Dammit.

Abbie's expression grew sympathetic. "Because he's *leaving* in a month, sweetie."

Ouch. "I know," I mumbled.

"He knows there's an end date to this, and you know it too," Abbie said, trying to be gentle. "Neither of you went into this thinking it would last, right?"

Hit again. "No."

"So, the terms of your arrangement were clear from the

start. He's probably not after anything serious. I know how these things work, and I don't want you to get hurt."

Yikes. That one made me wince, so I nodded and moved up the wall a little, applying my sponge to a new section.

"Do you think, maybe, he might feel something for you?" Emily asked in a careful voice.

"I don't know," I said to the wall. "We haven't discussed it."

"And you shouldn't." Abbie walked over and squeezed my arm. "You're doing amazing things with this house, all by yourself. You're coming out of your Luca-stupor in a blaze of fucking glory, having a shitload of hot sex with a new man who makes you feel good about yourself. When all this is over, you're going to be a brand-new woman with a blank cheque of self-confidence that'll be your ticket to landing the man of your dreams. I won't let anything sabotage that, even you and your humongous heart."

I rubbed my forehead, leaving a streak of soap that I wiped away with my other hand. Abbie was more right than she realised. Letting Logan in, hoping for something real with him, was a huge risk—bigger than taking a chance on a stranger because I'd let my guard down before and walked away hurt and disappointed. I didn't know if I could trust him.

"Maybe you could look at this experience with the house and Miles as a transition period from your old life to your new one?" Emily suggested. "A story you tell your kids one day that you look back on with fond memories."

"Yeah," I whispered. "Maybe."

Looking around at the room, my eyes fell on my bed, and a replay of that first time with Logan unfurled in front of my eyes. Was that all this was between us—the makings of a wonderful memory? I'd set out to fix my house and have hot, rebellious sex so I could shed the skin of a Jessica I didn't know or like anymore, a Jessica my parents claimed to have made. Logan made me feel sexy and empowered and powerful, the way I'd hoped sex would do, so perhaps I'd feel the same way if it actually *had* been Miles instead of Logan in my bed. Maybe even Zachary—if Zachary hadn't turned out to be a total jerk.

Was I responding to Logan because he was Logan, or because sex with him ticked a box I needed to tick, the one marked sexual liberation with no strings attached?

What was real, and what wasn't? I didn't know anymore. It was one too many questions in such a short space of time, and I had answers for none of them.

19

LOGAN

THE STOP WAS closed, and it was only the five of us crowded into our usual booth at the back of the pub. It had been a long time since we'd sat down together over beers and wings, and it felt fucking fantastic.

Luca raised his glass—the twelfth time he'd done so in the last thirty minutes—and I knew he was about to toast me. Again.

"Cheers to the best best man a man could ask for," he slurred, and as we all smacked our glasses together, Luca mumbled under his breath, trying to work out if his praise made any sense.

"It was a bloody great day," Isaac agreed, tipping his glass up to his mouth and finding it empty. He stared into it, confused. "Genius thinking with the go-karts. Haven't done that in years."

"Good call on the paintball," Josh added, rolling his shoulders and wincing a little. "I love paintball." He wasn't as far gone as the other three but still drunk enough to have proclaimed his love of paintball three times in five minutes.

I reached out and grabbed Will's shirt, hauling him into an upright seated position before he fell out of the booth and onto the floor. "Glad you boys had a good day."

"We need whiskey," Will announced, trying to stand.

"I'll get it," I replied, pushing him up and out of my way, then carefully tucking him back into his seat. "But then we're done. I'm cutting you all off."

Jeers and boos sounded around the table, and I shook my head as I headed to the bar to collect a bottle and four tumblers. As I set them on the table in front of my mates, I smiled with exaggerated patience at their complaints.

"We're not *done* yet," Luca moaned. "Aren't bucks' parties supposed to have dancers or something?"

"I promised Tash there would be none, remember?" I replied, pouring everyone two fingers of expensive Japanese whiskey, then doling it out. "That said, I have it on good authority that if you ask nicely and behave yourself, she'll give you a lap dance herself when you get home."

Luca's eyes lit up. "What authority?"

"The one she gave me when she told me if I kept you out of trouble today, she'd make it up to you. I'm improvising the part about the lap dance. Feel free to use your imagination."

My best friend's face folded into a sloppy grin, and I rolled my eyes.

Beside him, Josh pulled out his phone and started tapping out a text.

"Hey!" I barked, lunging for the phone and missing as Josh swung it out of my reach. "No contact with the missus today. That's the rule."

"Yeah," Will and Isaac agreed with equal volumes of indignation, then they clinked their glasses together, united in their miserable bachelorhood.

"Fuck off," Josh grumbled, his fingers flying. "I want to ask Jones how she feels about lap dances."

Four seconds after the whoosh of his outgoing text, Josh's phone pinged with a reply. He read it with a single glance, then lurched to his feet and tried to exit the booth by climbing over the table.

"Sit your horny arse down, Ford," I ordered, and Isaac grabbed his shoulder, pressing him back into his seat. "The night's almost done, there's still whiskey in your glass, and I want to say a few words before class is dismissed."

As I stood at the edge of the table, four pairs of eyes watched me, glassy and unfocussed, squinting out of slack faces that tried to look sober. I sighed.

"I just want to tell you that there's nowhere else I'd rather be right now than here with you losers, celebrating the upcoming nuptials of our esteemed brother, Luca Rossetti."

Will's eyelids drooped closed, then opened again. "Huh?"

"I've missed you," I continued, "and—"

"Then come home, you punk." Luca climbed to his feet and slung an arm over my shoulders. His beer-and-whiskey breath puffed into my face. "Pack up that wife of yours and move back. I can't be the only one of us here with an old ball-and-chain." His face clouded, and he shout-whispered to us all, "Shh. Don't tell Tash I said that."

Isaac was shaking his head, and I watched, horrified, as his mouth opened in what felt like slow motion. "You're not married anymore, are you, Reeve?"

Ah, fuck.

"What?" Luca narrowed his eyes at me—well, sort of. He was looking in my direction, but his gaze kept sliding to someplace just over my right ear.

"Uh, no. Bek and I got divorced." I shot Isaac a dark glare. "Thanks, mate."

"What?" He frowned. "Is it a secret? I don't remember if it was a secret. Did you say it was a secret?"

I ran a hand through my hair. "It's not a secret. It's fine."

Luca pulled me in for a rough hug. His body shuddered, and I realised he was crying on my shoulder. "I'm so sorry, man. That's so sad."

I patted him on the back, then gently pushed him back into the booth. "Thanks. I appreciate that, but I'm fine."

"Sorry, Reeve," Will mumbled, echoed by Josh, and I nodded in their direction.

"Is it a secret?" Isaac asked again. "I didn't know it was a secret."

"Well, it's not now," I replied.

"I'll tell Abbie, then," Will slurred. "She'll want to know. But that's all. Nobody else. Just Abbie. I promise."

"Sure," I said with a resigned sigh. He wasn't the most obvious candidate, but Will could give Dawn a run for her money as the Bay's biggest mouth. Fifty bucks, half the town knew about my divorce by the time I walked into Tony's Place for a coffee the following morning.

"*I* know your secret," Isaac went on, stabbing the centre of his broad chest with a thick finger, then he pointed it around at everyone at the table. "And *they* know your secret. Who else knows? Is it a secret?"

"No, mate. It's fine. You know. I know. These guys know, and Frost knows."

"You told Jess?" Luca asked, his voice sounding sober for a second.

"Uh, yeah," I croaked, then cleared my throat. "It came up in conversation one time."

Isaac nodded sombrely. "She won't tell anyone. Your secret's safe with her."

"Good to know, Greene," I said with a tight smile. "Thanks."

Luca's brief grasp on reality was gone as quickly as it came. "Jess needs a man," he announced.

"All right," I declared briskly. "Bottom's up, boys. I think we're done."

All four of them threw their heads back and poured their drinks down their throats, following it with a chorus of appreciative hisses and groans, then they tumbled out of the booth, one by one. I sent Will upstairs to his bed and ushered Isaac and Josh to the door, but Luca grabbed my arm and held me back.

"Thanks for today," he said, swaying slightly. "And everything you've done for Jess while you've been here. She's not so bad, is she?"

I swallowed and tried to smile. "No, she's not so bad."

"See, I told you. Just got to give her a chance." Luca hiccupped and stumbled a little. "She should be dating by now, you know?"

"So you said."

"I want her to be as happy with her life as I am with my life with Tash."

"That's good of you to say."

He dropped his head in what I think was supposed to be a nod, but it looked more like his neck had lost all muscle tone. "She deserves to find her person. Someone good." Luca's chin jerked up, and his brows climbed towards his immaculate hairline. "Someone like you!"

I swear, my heart fucking shot up my throat so fast I thought I was about to cough it up onto the floor at our feet.

"All right. Shit like that is how I know you've had more than enough for one night." I turned him towards the door. "Go home, drink a ton of water, then tuck yourself into bed. I'll check in on you tomorrow to see how you're feeling."

Luca swung back towards me and gathered me up for another rough hug. "It's good to have you back, bro. We've missed you."

I smacked him on the back. "I've missed you, too. Now go home and sleep this off. I'll call you in the morning."

Watching my mates stumble up the road together, I considered how much we'd grown and all the things that had changed since we were kids, even while the important things stayed the same. I locked the door and began to clean up, collecting the dirty glasses from the booth first, but it was simple work that kept my hands busy while my thoughts were free to wander.

Luca's comments about Jess finding someone like me were drunken ramblings that he wouldn't remember in a few hours, but I so badly wished he'd meant what he said. What would I do if I could stay here and be with Jess, and my best friend gave us his blessing? What might my life look like if that happened?

Pulling out my phone and calculating the time in London, I scrolled through to Bek's number and hit dial. She picked up almost immediately.

"What's wrong?" she answered.

"Nothing," I replied with a chuckle. "Why do you assume the worst?"

"It's close to midnight where you are, and I wasn't expecting your call."

"It was Luca's bucks' party tonight. It just wrapped up."

"And how was it?"

"It was … good."

There was silence on the other end of the phone, then the sound of footsteps. "Hang on," she said. "I'm going somewhere quiet, so we can talk." A moment later, I heard a door close, and she said, "Okay. I'm listening. What happened?"

I pulled a chair out from under one of the tables and sank into it. "I don't know where to start."

"Tell me everything from the beginning."

So, I told her about Jess—leaving out the salacious details—then explained what had happened tonight and what Luca had said while he was intoxicated. When I was finished, I traced my fingertips over the whorls in the timber tabletop and waited.

"Can I ask you something?" she said.

"Shoot."

"Why are you still living in the UK?"

I began to reply with a smart-arse retort, then rubbed my eyes with a thumb and forefinger. I'd called Bek because I wanted to talk. This wasn't the right time for deflecting.

"It's about more than Jess if that's what you're getting at," I said, then I sighed. "It sounds stupid when I say it out loud, but I moved to London to be my own person and make my own mistakes. I needed to find out who I was outside of Luca's shadow."

"That doesn't sound stupid."

"Childish, then."

"Well, is any of it still true?"

I stared up at the ceiling, thinking, wanting to give an answer that felt honest. "I don't feel like I'm in competition with him anymore, assuming I ever really was. Nobody who knows us both would ever think he was in competition with me anyway, that's for sure."

"I wish you wouldn't put yourself down that way," she murmured.

"I don't know how to explain it. All through school, Luca had the admiration and respect of parents and teachers, while all they gave me were fleeting looks, below-average grades, and detention slips. I stopped learning and started acting up—that was what they expected from me, after all. Then, after graduation, Luca went to university and impressed everyone with his big ambition and slick suits. I picked up the tools and kept my head down, not wanting to be seen at all anymore. While Luca went from strength to strength, I stopped wanting to try. I know from experience that losing at anything feels worse when I try to win."

"Oh, Logan," she sighed, but the floodgates had opened now, and there was more I needed to say.

"When Luca and Jess first became a couple, the Bay raved about how perfect they were for each other. His parents, her parents, every dickhead with an opinion nobody asked them to share, and I got so frustrated that as the days wore on, more and more, every little thing Jess said and did pressed my buttons. I let her know it, too. I'd never be good enough for her, but I needed to be part of her life regardless, even if that made me the bad guy. It just got to be too much. Moving to London was my chance at a new life, away from both of them, but then Maggie died, and when I came back here for the funeral …"

Bek and I had talked about this before, but it felt cruel to go over it again. Knowing what was coming, she said, "Go on. I think you need to say it."

I released a heavy breath. "You know I was pretty fucked up by the fact Maggie died so young. Being back here, grieving, seeing Luca and Jess again for the first time in a long time—believing they were happy enough to spend the rest of their lives together—I bolted back to London and ..."

"You asked me to marry you," she finished.

I sighed. "I'm sorry, Bek. Life just felt too short at the time, like I was missing out on too much. Holding onto a childhood crush was the stupidest thing I could do, right?"

"Well ..." She laughed lightly, and I groaned.

"You know I loved you, right?"

"I loved you too, just not the way soulmates are supposed to love each other."

"I don't know if I've ever apologised for what happened next. All that guilt I had, feeling more lost and alone than I had before. The drinking."

"You've apologised," she murmured. "You don't need to do it again."

"I let my furniture business go under, and I let you down."

"We let each other down."

I rubbed my neck and closed my eyes. "I failed."

Bek was quiet for a minute, but the silence between us was familiar and comfortable. "You know," she said after a moment, "you sound different tonight. Like the bad stuff isn't dragging you under the way it usually does. Something's changed."

I nodded, looking for the right words. "I go over and over all my fuck-ups a lot but talking about it tonight has been easier than I thought it would be."

"Why is that, do you think?"

"Sounds like you already know the answer."

"I think I do," she replied. "It's Jess."

"I don't know," I mumbled, nowhere near ready to face what that might mean. "Maybe."

"Okay, maybe, but what if it is? You know I don't want you to leave London, but if there's a chance you can be with her and build the life you want in Valentine Bay, I think you should take it."

I forced a chuckle, trying to lighten the moment. "I don't know. Taking a chance like that sounds a bit risky to me."

"Love is always a risk worth taking."

I checked the time again and got to my feet. "I should probably let you go. Thanks for the chat and the advice."

"Anytime, and thanks for calling. I'm glad we can talk about things like this."

"Me too."

"Keep me updated on how things work out, will you?"

"You bet. Goodnight."

I hung up the phone and finished cleaning up the mess the boys had left. By the time I was done, it was just after midnight, but the boys had been drinking since noon, so the early finish made sense. I assumed Jess would be long gone to bed by now, but I wanted so badly to be near her, so I grabbed my keys and my phone, locked the door behind me, and began the walk to her house.

I often took stock of all the choices I'd made in my life and how they'd blown up in my face over and over again—it was a good way to wear away any self-esteem I'd managed to cobble together—but I was surprised that going over the inventory with Bek hadn't hit me too hard this time. Was Bek right, and was Jess the difference? Had I finally won her, and in winning her, did everything else in my life make sense?

If every bad choice so far had brought us together at this time in our lives, then all the shitty times were worth the price a thousand times over. Perhaps we were always meant to be together, just not when either of us had wanted or expected it.

Playing with the phone in my pocket, I considered texting Jess to see if she was awake, but I resisted the temptation. I didn't want her to think this was a booty call. All I needed was to stand on Dot's driveway and know Jess was close, on the other side of the closed front door. I could show her how much I wanted her tomorrow, and the next night, and the night after that ...

Every night for the next three weeks, until I was due to get on a plane and leave her behind.

As I strolled through the streets with my thoughts for company, I couldn't shy away from a possibility I'd been ignoring for more than a week now. The Bay was home, and a big part of me wanted to stay. Bek was right about one thing. If Jess said the word, I wouldn't think twice— I'd take a chance on her and us. I'd tell Luca everything. I'd risk it all to be with her.

But Jess *hadn't* said the word. She hadn't even implied it. She wanted to keep us a secret, and she hadn't said anything about me moving home permanently. I didn't know how to broach the subject or even if I should. Being with Jess now might have helped me come to terms with all the failures of my past, but they'd always be loaded bags I wore strapped to my back. I could overcome them, get past them, be a better man because of them if Jess was by my side, but what if I put myself out there and she didn't choose me after all? What if I lost this race so close to the finish?

I'd never been brave enough to put my heart on the line where Jess was concerned, and I didn't know if I could find the courage now. All my other screw-ups were hits I could live with, but asking Jess for more and her giving me a no? That was the kind of failure I'd never come back from. I needed to hear the words from her first.

It was almost pitch black along most of the streets, the neighbourhood already in bed and every other streetlight either blacked out or buzzing irritably. The closer I came to Jess's house, the more I could see brightness shining from a window on the far side. Assuming she'd left the lights on before heading over to Dot's for the night, I walked around the property intending to sneak in and switch everything off, but when I got closer, I froze in the yard.

She was still inside, in the new bedroom I'd made, dancing and singing to music I couldn't hear, using a long-handled broom to dust cobwebs from the ceiling. I watched as she laughed and spun, revealing flashes of creamy skin under her shirt while her legs flexed and her breasts bounced. Her bloody glasses did things to my dick I'd never be able to admit out loud. I did pull out my phone then. I was about to go in there and fuck her senseless, but I didn't want to spook her. I could be a gentleman before I was an animal, so I sent her a text.

Me: You're a fucking knockout, and I have to get my mouth on you right now. Get ready, baby. I'm coming.

20

JESS

THE MUSIC PLAYING through my earbuds faded in and out as my phone lit up with a notification. Snatching it up off the floor of the empty dining-now-bedroom, I smiled as Logan's name flashed up on the screen, then swiped to open his text. What I read set my heart racing and tingles rushing to all the right places. Was he outside? I peered out the uncovered window, but with full night outside and the lights on in the room, I couldn't see a thing. Then behind me, someone flicked the switch, plunging the house into darkness, and I spun around.

"Logan?"

His voice drifted to me through the blackness. "You're putting on quite a show, you know."

I snatched off my glasses and stuck them in a back pocket. "What are you doing here?"

"Party's over," he said, his voice sounding so sexy coming from the shadows, "and I felt like going for a walk."

I slipped my tongue over my lips, feeling a flicker of something at not being able to see his face—not fear, but something dangerous. Something that made me feel out of control, almost at his mercy. "Did you have a good time?" I asked with a slight wobble in my voice.

I sensed him draw closer, smelled the spicy citrus scent that was his skin, felt the heat of his breath against my jaw, and I blinked hard, trying to force my eyes to adjust to the darkness, but it wouldn't work.

He was no more than a ghost as he slid his hands over my hips and gently lifted my shirt to dance his fingertips over my bare stomach. I shivered as goosebumps erupted everywhere.

"It was a good night," he murmured, "but this is the highlight by far."

"Oh." I swallowed as the tip of his nose brushed along the edge of my jaw before he pressed his lips to the corner of my mouth, then continued along the other side of my face to my ear. He licked at the soft spot under my earlobe as his fingers tickled up my spine, and I raised my arms over my head.

Logan removed my shirt—slowly, gently, devotedly— and dropped it on the floor so he could move to the buttons on my shorts. I moaned and dropped my head back as he took one hard, aching nipple in his mouth, rolling his tongue over it and nipping it roughly with his teeth. I curled my fingers into his hair as he kissed between my

SAMANTHA LEIGH

breasts and down to my navel, then dropped to his knees and dragged off my shorts and underwear. When they were pooled around my ankles, he took hold of my hips and carefully guided me backwards until I hit the wall, where he parted my knees a little wider.

"I haven't spent enough time between your legs," he said, sliding his hands over the outside of my thighs. His hot, open-mouthed kisses started inside one knee, then moved higher, and I whimpered when he reached the top and breathed past my centre, starting again with kisses on the other side. His teasing drove me to distraction, and I squeezed my eyelids closed as my pussy grew wetter, every muscle in my core pulsing with silent pleas to *touch me*. I'd take any part of him—his mouth, his tongue, his fingers, his cock. I wanted it all, but tonight, he was taking his time. Emboldened by the dark, knowing he couldn't see any more of me than I could of him, I pulled one hand away from his hair and cupped my breast, circling the nipple with a thumb, then pinching it hard enough to make me gasp.

"Is my girl touching herself?" Logan asked, and I glanced down at him. The light in the room had shifted, and my sight had adjusted to the darkness enough that I could make out the subtle lines of his face in the shadows. We weren't blind to each other anymore, but it was dark enough that I still felt naughty—or maybe the dull light made me feel even naughtier.

I squeezed my breast harder and massaged it in my palm. "Mm-hm," I moaned, dropping my head back against the wall.

"Okay, baby, you keep doing that, but I'm not rushing things down here, okay? I intend to savour every last drop of you."

I nodded and bit my lip, another moan sounding deep inside my throat as Logan finally touched my sex.

He began with his tongue, running the tip of it along my slick seam and groaning almost immediately. "You're soaked for me, baby. Fucking soaked."

"Just for you, baby," I replied, clenching the fist I had in his hair.

"Oh, fuck," he growled before he tossed one of my legs over a shoulder, wrapped a muscled arm around my thigh to brace me against the wall, and buried his face between my folds.

He devoured me—that's the only word for it—like he would never get enough to satisfy his appetite.

I felt his thumbs on my lower lips as he spread me open, then the flat of his tongue stroked from my entrance and up again, over and over, until he finally hovered at the top, lapping and circling and sucking my clit while his hands kneaded the flesh of my thighs. Every time his lips and tongue pulled away only to return again, desire crackled anew at my core, and I couldn't help it—my hips moved, rocking and rotating desperately as I sped towards the finish line of a race I never wanted to be over.

"That's it, baby," he groaned, grazing his teeth over one lower lip, then the other. "You want to ride my face? Fucking ride it." He set a hand against my other thigh, spreading me even wider, then plunged his tongue into my centre. I cried out at the shock of it, the out-of-body euphoria of Logan Reeve fucking me with his tongue, just as he added his fingers to the performance and started rubbing electric circles over my swollen clit.

"Oh, God, Logan," I screamed, slamming one fist against the wall beside me. "Oh, fuck. I'm going to come."

"Come on my tongue, baby," he growled against me, and I flew higher at the wild ferocity in his voice. "Come on my mouth."

I looked down at him on his knees, and the vision of Logan's blond head between my legs sent me careening into darkness all over again, a darkness that exploded into stars behind my eyes and triggered wave after wave of full-body ecstasy. My orgasm kept coming, only this time when I looked for Logan, he was staring back up at me, watching me while his fingers slid in and out. I rode his hand now, chasing those last flutters of my climax, shuddering as each one sent an aftershock of pleasure through me.

As my muscles loosened and the leg I was standing on finally buckled, Logan propped me up as he pressed tender kisses across my stomach. Something that felt a little like love swam behind my eyes, so I closed them, panting and trying to call my breath—and my senses— back to my body.

"You okay?" he asked, and I heard the grin in his voice.

"You think you're a hero, don't you?" I mumbled, but I smiled into the darkness.

"Like all heroes, I live to serve," he replied, easing my other leg off his shoulder and climbing to his feet. He kept his hands firmly on my hips, holding me upright until he could lean against me, pressing me tight against the wall. "Can you walk?"

I sucked in a breath at the hard outline of his erection underneath his jeans. My body hummed with gratification, but my centre throbbed with the need to feel the snug satisfaction of his thick cock deep inside. I rolled my pelvis against him and kissed him on the mouth, delving for his tongue and tasting my arousal on his lips, before I cupped his dick and asked, "Can you?"

Our hands tore at his jeans, and he pulled them down just far enough to free his beautiful dick. I wrapped an eager hand around it, tugging with a firm enough grip that he grunted and bit at my lips as he lined himself up at my entrance.

"You ready?" he whispered, rubbing the crown along my slippery seam and groaning at the warmth.

"Don't I feel ready?"

"Oh, God, I—"

Whatever he was going to say died on his lips as he eased into me, slowly at first, the strangled sounds in his throat telling me how much restraint it took him. I went with it, waiting for my body to stretch the way it needed to before I could tell him to take me the way I wanted. He was almost there, the angle not quite right, so I wrapped one leg around his waist, tilted my hips, and grabbed his arse, pulling him into me until there was no more left to take.

Logan nuzzled my neck as he slid out, long and slow in a divine type of torture, then in again with the same melting rhythm. He mouthed my skin and made desperate little moaning noises against my shoulder that reverberated through my body. I turned my head and breathed him in, revelling in a connection between us that couldn't get any closer before I set my lips against his ear.

"Fuck me," I whispered.

And he did.

He pumped into me hard and fast, almost violently, and I loved every second of it. I loved the power of his body, claiming me and owning me and losing control inside me. He shifted his hips a little, thrusting and striking some hidden spot that detonated with every touch. I clung to him, conscious of the way my pussy clamped down tighter and tighter as the tension coiled in my middle, and I teetered on the precipice of another orgasm.

"Fuck, you're so tight," he said between gritted teeth. "And you're getting tighter, baby. Can you feel it?"

"I feel it," I gasped.

He looked down between us, and so did I, our foreheads resting together, and though the room was dark and we were clothed in shadows, there was enough light to see the way we came together over and over. Logan grunted and slammed his mouth on mine as his hips jerked frantically, coaxing me with his tongue and dick into another powerful finish. I screamed his name and cut my nails into his back, right as the pulse of his orgasm trembled inside me and his hot release spilled deep into my body. I held onto him as his body stiffened, then relaxed, and it was all I could do to keep breathing. Holding onto his shoulders, I knew that if he let me go, I'd fall into a heap on the floor. But he held me up as he carefully pulled away, his mouth never far from mine.

"Oh, God, Jessica," he said between kisses.

The thrill of hearing my name on his lips surprised me. I'd been "Frost" to him all my life, and this felt intimate in a way I wasn't expecting. I vaguely recalled calling him Logan just minutes earlier, and even with my head in a pleasant post-coital fog, I knew I'd overthink this later. Had we just crossed another line?

I rested my head on his shoulder and chuckled quietly. "I think you were right before. I'm not sure I can walk. I might collapse before I take two steps."

Working awkwardly and one-handed while the other cradled my face, Logan hiked his pants up over his hips before swinging me up into his arms. I felt silly, especially when I ordered him to detour past the linen cupboard first so I could retrieve a towel, but I let him take me to my bed and lay me down. He ducked away for a few minutes so we could both clean ourselves up a little, but when he returned, he stripped off his clothes and slid under the covers with me, wrapping a hard, inked arm around my waist and tucking me in against his body.

"Let's wait here a little while," he said, "until you regain enough strength to drag yourself back to Dot's."

"Mm," I agreed, my eyelids feeling heavy. It must have been the early hours of the morning by now, and I'd been up since five a.m. Throw in two top-quality orgasms while upright against a wall, and I was ready to sleep for days.

I registered the soothing sensation of Logan's hand grazing my forehead as he brushed my hair back from my face. It had been a long time since I fell asleep in a man's arms, and it felt so good. Safe.

I relaxed against him, unable to fight off the drowsy fantasy of falling asleep in Logan's arms every night and waking up with him beside me every morning, his cool grey eyes the first thing I'd see after opening mine. I smiled to myself and drifted away, feeling all kinds of *held*.

When I woke up an hour after sunrise, he was gone.

21

LOGAN

I LEFT BEFORE Jess woke up. With her eyes closed, dark lashes resting on her cheeks, and puffy lips parted just a little, she was too perfect to disturb, but it had been close to dawn, and I knew she wouldn't want to deal with the potential fallout of me walking out of her house in the clothes I wore the night before. What if Dot saw me? What if Abbie or Emily showed up unannounced again— or worse, Jess's parents? I was already trying to concoct a story to tell Will when he asked where I'd slept, but when I snuck into the loft just before sunlight broke over the horizon, he was snoring heavily in the loft overhead. I quietly stripped off my clothes and stretched out on the sofa, pretending I'd been there all along. He'd be none the wiser, so there was one less thing for me to worry about. Thank fuck, because, after last night, I had too much shit happening in my head to deal with more complications.

I'd almost told Jess I loved her, and damn it, part of me wished I had. Another part—a more reasonable part, a part I couldn't shake—knew that once I said those words, there'd be no getting them back. I *wanted* to say them, but not in the middle of the hottest sex I'd had in my life, and definitely not before I was sure Jess would say them back.

Did that make me a coward? Probably. But as I stared up at the ceiling, a hand underneath my head, thinking about how much I loved this woman, I couldn't imagine myself uttering those words out loud ... unless she said them first, and that was out of my control. Or was it?

A plan began to take shape in my head at the exact moment exhilaration unfurled in my gut. I didn't need *words* to show Jess how I felt about her. I could *show* her. I'd been pushing her buttons for God knew how long with burn-her-up results, so all I had to do was aim for the ones that provoked affection and adoration instead of irritation and rage and keep going until she was mine.

Knowing Jess would sleep for at least a few more hours before her day began, I closed my eyes and grabbed a little more rest myself. I had twenty-one days to win my girl— three weeks to make it clear to her that I wanted her now and forever. Three weeks to convince her to say those three little words. How hard could it be?

"Holy crap, I'm exhausted."

Jess fell onto her bed, face down, splayed like a starfish.

I stretched out over her, nudging her thighs open with my knees as I nuzzled the back of her neck, but then I groaned and rolled away, collapsing by her side, on my back with my eyes shut.

"Me, too," I mumbled.

"Things hurt," she moaned, her voice muffled by the bedcovers. "Things I never knew could hurt."

I rubbed the crick in my neck, my reward for painting ceilings and crown mouldings for two days straight. "Same here."

Over the past four days, Jess's little house had buzzed like a hive. Abbie and Emily had corralled the crew into a working bee to make sure the painting was completed and the floors were prepped for finishing before we started kitchen and bathroom installation, and while I resented sharing Jess for even a minute of that time, we never would have gotten as far as we had without everyone's generous help.

I'd done two passes with the sander on the hardwood floors. Every wall was freshly coated in smooth snowy grey paint—except where Jess had added hints of her preferred feature colour, a deep, rich turquoise that everyone *oohed* and *aahed* over. The ornate ceilings were whiter than they'd been in decades. Isaac and Josh had helped me tear down the back porch. Even Luca and Tash had come by one afternoon to clear out the yards under Josh's enthusiastic direction, and Dot popped in and out at regular intervals with bottles of water and platters of sandwiches and cakes, so we were well looked after.

SAMANTHA LEIGH

To be honest, the hard work was an exchange I was willing to make for the time I spent with my friends. It had been a lifetime since we'd had an excuse to see each other every day, possibly not since high school. There was music and jokes and laughs and embarrassing stories. The last four days had been awesome, stiff neck be damned.

On top of all that, the constant activity was the perfect cover for the secret project I had going on in the workshop. I told Jess I was working on Luca and Tash's wedding gift—which wasn't a lie; she'd picked out an awesome retro bureau and matching writing desk that were going to refinish beautifully—but there was something else I was working on in there, something I didn't want her to see.

And everyone had to go home sometime, which meant I spent nearly every night alone with Jess, just the way I liked it—just the way I needed it. If I was ever going to convince her to love me again, I figured orgasms on-tap wouldn't hurt. She had another one coming her way very soon, but it was early evening yet. I could afford a twenty-minute breather.

Jess's phone pinged with a message, and she rolled towards where it sat on the bedside table, moaning at the effort it took.

"It's Dot," she told me. "Dinner will be ready in forty-five minutes. There's enough for both of us if you're hungry."

"I'm starving," I mumbled with my eyes closed.

"She's also made Maz's glazed strawberry tart for dessert and queued up *Gentlemen Prefer Blondes* to watch

242

afterwards." Jess turned her head and quirked her mouth at me. "Looks like Dot's angling for a girls' night."

I frowned. "What? A man can't watch *Gentlemen Prefer Blondes?*"

She chuckled. "I'm sure you could join us, but I've been neglecting Dot a little, and I feel bad taking advantage of her hospitality. I should probably spend more time with her."

I feigned a put-upon sigh. "Fine." Pulling myself to a seated position, I swung a leg over Jess's hips, straddling her, and started hiking up her shirt. "Come on, help me out a little. Arms up."

She giggled and did as she was told. "What's this?"

I threw her shirt on the floor, then got to work on her shorts. "I've got forty-five minutes to deliver at least one decent orgasm. No time to waste."

Jess lifted her hips as I climbed off the bed and peeled off her pants. "I'm starting to wonder if you've set yourself some sort of sex record. I've never had this many orgasms in my life."

I quirked an eyebrow but kept my eyes down, hearing in those words what she'd never say out loud. She'd never had this many orgasms *with Luca.* I tried not to muddy my feelings for Jess with the anxiety of knowing that what she shared with Luca had been something special, but right then, I allowed myself a moment to crow and used her words to reassure myself that what we had must be special, too.

"Would you like to lodge a complaint, Miss Frost?" I asked, brushing her shoulders to loosen her bra straps, then lifting her upright to unfasten it at the back. I peeled it off her arms, and she laid back down, her breasts begging for attention.

"Mm," she moaned as I dusted kisses over her chest, grazing her tight pink nipples with my teeth. "No, I don't think that will be necessary."

"Then, if you don't mind, I'd like you to relax and let me work on that record." I swirled my tongue towards her bellybutton, grinning against her skin as she lifted her arse off the bed to meet my mouth. "Though, for your information, my record has nothing to do with sex and everything to do with satisfaction."

I pressed my lips to one hip bone, then the other, before moving down, pushing her knees apart and lightly brushing a fingertip over her wet centre. I'd never stop loving the way she literally melted at my touch.

"Oh?" she gasped, her tongue sweeping across her bottom lip and her back arching eagerly. "What does that mean?"

I lowered myself to my knees at the edge of the bed and yanked her towards me hard enough that she yelped. I swung her legs over my shoulders and tickled her inner thighs with the tip of my nose, chuckling at the way her body shivered when my warm breath hit her pussy. "It means that I'm not here to fuck you. I'm here to fulfill you." I lapped at her folds. "Every"—lick—"single"— lick—"part of you." Then I thrust my tongue into her core, triggering a high-pitched shriek of my name. My dick responded as if to a war cry—stiff, at attention, ready for duty. *Another time, buddy.*

I exceeded the expected single climax, though I worked damn hard to deliver two explosive orgasms that left her shaking and gasping for breath. When Jess realised the hour at the same time it registered that I was still fully clothed, her eyes returning over and over to where my cock strained painfully against the fly of my jeans, I insisted she head over to Dot's before the old woman came looking for her. I'd deal with my blue balls later—they were worth it to send her next door with the damp, sexy flush to her face that *I'd* put there—but now, I had work to do in the workshop. There was a hell of a lot more I could do for Jess than sand her floors and make her come, and I was determined to prove that to her before my plane left for London in seventeen days.

22

JESS

—————

I STROLLED THROUGH my favourite homewares store, starting on a third circuit to make sure I hadn't missed anything. I'd already piled a dozen scatter cushions, two rugs, three pieces of artwork, six vases and as many throw blankets near the register, and the saleswoman was guarding it while I made a final round. I enjoyed shopping as much as the next girl, but this was the third day in a row I'd left the house early and spent all day on my feet, hunting for the perfect finishing touches for the house. Marathon shopping was nothing like browsing for new shoes on payday, and I was almost as tired as I had been after all the non-stop cleaning and painting the week before. Non-stop cleaning and painting and orgasms, that is.

Logan's behaviour over the last week or more had been … confusing. I paused and ran my fingertips over a stack of fluffy towels the exact shade of turquoise as my feature walls. I stood staring at them, biting my lip, a recessed part of my mind contemplating buying them while a louder voice listed all the ways Logan had recently left me reeling, and all the times he'd lived up to his reputation for kicking me when my defences were down. Disturbingly, the first list was much longer than the second.

There was the sex, which was so unbelievably good I was beginning to wonder if I'd developed some kind of addiction, but then there were all the little things he did that made me feel looked after. He wrote lists of things to do at the house and ticked them off at the end of every day, so I could keep track of our progress. He tidied up after himself and me and all our friends when they came to help, just so things stayed neat and orderly because he knew that's how I liked it. He was kind and patient with Dot, not to mention a little flirty, which my old neighbour loved. He brought me coffee in the mornings and brushed a hand across my bare arm or lower back when he walked past, just to let me know he was there. He'd opened and checked every box that had been delivered from the renovation showroom and reassured me that the gold tile I'd chosen for the bathroom wasn't too extreme. At that very moment, he was at my house, building me a brand-new timber-decked back porch just because he wanted to.

I was in danger of believing he genuinely cared for me, and yet … I blinked my stinging eyes and ran my fingers over the soft Egyptian cotton. I couldn't forget falling asleep with his arms around me and waking up to find him gone. Logan was leaving in fourteen days, I was staying in the Bay, and I knew from experience how painful it was to be left behind. Luca hadn't chosen me after seven years of serious commitment. Why should I believe that Logan would stay after only a few weeks of great sex? He was a good guy, we had history, and we were physically compatible, but something tight and fluttery in my chest told me I'd be an idiot to read more into it than that.

Ugh. Abbie had been spot on about my stupid heart. I wasn't a casual sex and cats-are-gonna-kill-me kind of woman. I wanted a soulmate. I wanted forever. My rebellious rage had faded, I didn't care about proving anyone wrong anymore, and I was left wishing for a life well beyond my reach.

Pulling out half a dozen of the pretty blue-green towels and tucking them awkwardly under one arm, I hurried back to the counter, where the saleswoman watched me with a giant plastic bag open and ready to collect my extra goods. I paid for my order and added a little extra to have it all delivered, then left the store. It was late afternoon, not too early to return to the house, but I wasn't in the right frame of mind to face Logan. Spotting a cafe a few doors down, I walked in and waited at the front for the hostess to guide me to an empty seat.

"Jess!"

My head jerked around at the sound of my name, and my eyes landed on Miles, waving at me from a small table in the corner.

"Table for one?" the hostess asked, pulling out a menu and waiting expectantly.

"Uh." My glance bounced between her and Miles, who smiled and gestured at the empty chair across from him. "No, I'm going to join my friend over there. Thanks."

Taking the menu and carefully picking my way through the maze of people, I stopped at the edge of the table, one hand planted on my hip. "Shouldn't you be at school, Mr McKay?"

Miles chuckled, and I took a seat while he patted a stack of papers beside his half-finished cup of coffee. "Classes are finished for the day, so I thought I'd mark these assignments over a fortifying beverage. What kind of horrible taskmaster are you to set homework over the holidays?"

I grinned, meeting Miles's sparkling violet eyes, admiring the way his inky hair fell in short waves, appreciating the dark-framed glasses on his nose. I'd always thought he was cute, but never enough to give it more consideration than a passing observation. "It gives the kids something to do."

"Not to mention the substitute teacher, who has to read the bloody things."

"Sorry about that," I said with a grimace. "I didn't know I'd be taking time off when I set the assignment."

He held up a large, smooth hand. "I'm just teasing you. I don't mind."

"Thanks."

The conversation paused as I gave my order to a waiter, then Miles picked it back up again. "So, how are the renovations coming along?" he asked.

"Really well. Everything is on schedule. I mean, it'll be tight, but we'll get it done."

"We?" Miles repeated, taking a sip of his coffee.

"Er, yeah. Me and Logan, the guy helping me out."

"The man you were with at the renovation showroom," Miles added, not quite a question.

"That's the one."

"And the two of you aren't …?"

When the sentence hung in the air a little too long for me to understand where Miles was going, I prompted, "We aren't … what?"

"You aren't together?"

An odd, hiccuping chuckle burst from my throat, and I thanked the universe when the waiter returned with my coffee. I used the distraction to collect my wits, but when the waiter walked away, Miles was watching me with expectation.

"Uh, no," I said, nose twitching. "Logan and I aren't together."

Miles set down his cup, frank disbelief creasing his forehead. "I thought for sure you were going to say the opposite."

My heartbeat was too fast, and I could sense heat creeping up my chest. "Why would you think that?"

"No reason, really. I suppose I just assumed." Miles cleared his throat, picked up the red pen he was using to correct his papers, and started snapping the cap on and off. "Does that mean you're single?"

"I—" I couldn't tear my attention away from the *click-click-click* of the pen cap. "Uh, I think so, yes."

That was true, wasn't it? Logan wasn't my boyfriend, and I wasn't in a relationship. Therefore, I was single.

"You think so?" Miles frowned a little and looked at me like I was speaking a language he couldn't understand.

"No, I mean I am. Yes, I'm single."

Why did it feel wrong to say that out loud?

A relieved breath whooshed from Miles, relaxing his shoulders and bringing a smile to his mouth. "Good. I mean, you know, not *good*. Just good to know, you know?"

"Yeah, sure. Right. Of course. And what about you? Single? Not that I assume you're single. You've probably got a girlfriend. You look like you'd have a girlfriend."

I was babbling like a talking doll with a broken ring pull.

Miles smiled crookedly and finally stopped snapping his bloody pen. "What does a man with a girlfriend look like?"

"Oh, you know." I flapped my hands. "You're cute, so you're probably seeing someone, or you're gay. You know what they say—all the good ones are either taken or gay."

He laughed a little. "I'm not taken, and I'm not gay, but it's good to know I'm cute."

My cheeks were on freaking fire. "Right, well. That's great." I took a gulp of my coffee and sputtered unattractively as it burned my tongue.

"So, if you're single," he said, handing me a napkin, "and I'm single, maybe one day we could get together and be single at the same place at the same time."

I don't know what he saw on my face, but Miles dropped his eyes and started tapping the essays into a neater stack.

"You mean as friends?" I asked, a flush of panic creeping up my chest. "Or … like a date?"

He glanced at me, then looked away and back again before he shrugged, one side of his mouth lifting in a self-deprecating smile. "Either is fine, but no pressure, Jess. It was just an idea."

I'd known where Miles had been steering the conversation the moment he asked me about Logan, which I suppose explained the choking on coffee and verbal diarrhoea.

I *was* technically single. I wanted to be with someone who would spend the rest of their life with me. Logan was leaving in two weeks, and then I'd be back to where I started, only with that blank cheque of confidence Abbie told me I should use to build the life I wanted. Miles was good looking, and we were both teachers, so we had a lot in common, and in the six months I'd known him as a colleague, I'd taken note that he was cute and easy to talk to. What good reason did I have to turn this man down?

"I think … I think I'd like that," I said, ignoring the way my stomach twisted and my nose stung. "I'm too tied up with the renovations right now, but maybe we could talk about it again in a few weeks?"

"Yeah?"

Miles's eyes lit up, and I let myself feel a little rush that someone out there thought spending time with me was something to look forward to. Perhaps I shouldn't have acknowledged that little high because the next thing out of my mouth sounded much too confident.

"Yes," I told him with a decisive nod. "Let's do it."

23

LOGAN

"HAND ME THE spirit level, would you, mate?"

I reached out my hand, eyes on the cabinet I held against the kitchen wall, and waited for Conner, my temporary apprentice, to pass me the tool I needed to make sure the joinery was balanced. It landed in my palm with a dull thud, and I checked the level.

"Good to go," I said, and the kid drilled the cabinet into place.

The house was really coming together, but every day passed faster than the one before, and I raced the clock on two fronts now. There were ten days to go until Jess revealed the house to her parents, and I was eleven days out from possibly getting on a plane and leaving her behind forever. Thinking about that too often made my teeth ache and my fingertips tingle, so I kept myself busy enough that I *didn't* think about it. Things were running right on schedule and according to plan. It was true for the construction work, and it was true for my strategy to make Jess fall in love with me again.

I had to keep telling myself that.

I hadn't let up, and I hadn't dropped the ball once. I treated this house like it were my own—not hard to do, first because I loved what Jess had pulled together, and second because I was invested in the outcome. A successful renovation would give Jess the ammunition she needed to put her parents in their places once and for all. Every time I thought about her mother making Jess feel like less than the goddess she was, I wanted to put a fucking sledgehammer through another wall.

More than that, transforming this place for Jess was going to prove that I loved her. Throw in obscene levels of regular body worship—again, hardly a burden—and against all my self-preservation instincts, I'd let myself hope. I knew how dangerous that was. The fear of rejection that had been a constant companion for much of my life twisted like a corkscrew deep in my gut, but I reassured myself that nothing was on the line yet. I wouldn't say the words until Jess said them first. My heart and my pride were safe.

I stood up from where I'd been crouched on the kitchen floor and stepped back to admire the finished product, Conner a shadow at my shoulder. I'd quickly come to learn that Ryan *had* been pulling my leg about the kid needing improvement. Tall and broad with surfer hair and shrewd brown eyes, he was a prodigy—hardworking and intuitive. He took initiative, asked smart questions, put his head down and got the work done, and barely said a word otherwise. He kind of reminded me of myself at that age.

Jess was out again, this time shopping with Abbie and Emily for something to wear to Luca's wedding, and we'd made real progress in the last six hours. The sounds of tradespeople rang out from other rooms—the tiler in the bathroom, the carpet layer in one of the bedrooms. Baz, our plumber, would be back over the weekend to finish the laundry. Brody, the electrician, would follow a day after that to install appliances and neaten up the power outlets. Josh had scheduled two days off work early the following week and convinced Isaac to do the same so the two of them, plus Will, could knock the yards into shape before D-day. I'd finish the floors at the same time, then Jess would be free to stage it all for the reveal. We were due to be done with a day to spare. I was in my element, loving the energy of a busy worksite and riding a high of achievement. Now, it was all coming together.

"So, what do you think?" I asked Conner, crossing my arms over my chest.

His face twitched just a little as his eyes ran over the timber-faced kitchen cabinets, then the feature teal laminate on the surfaces. "It's different," he said, "but I like it."

I clapped him on the back. "That's because you've got a good eye and good taste. Now, there's something I could use your help with out in the garage. Come on, I'll show you."

We stepped out through the floor-to-ceiling glass stacker doors the two of us had installed earlier in the week and straight out onto Jess's new back porch. Conner had helped me finish that, too, taking it upon himself to construct a simple railing around the outside that mirrored the one out front. His technique and confidence impressed me, and knowing how well he performed when left to his own devices, I intended to set him the task of refinishing the front porch, too.

Ignoring the three porch steps and launching myself onto the lawn, landing with a thud that sounded again behind me as Conner did the same, I unlocked the garage doors and led him to the workshop at the back. I walked through the open door with my shadow close behind.

"Wow," he said, coming to a stop, eyes landing on one thing then another as he took in the tools and furniture in various states of repair. "This is awesome."

I rubbed my neck, looking around with new appreciation. "Yeah, it is. Someone must have built it years ago. It was a lucky find." I gestured to the furniture I was refinishing for Luca and Tash's wedding gift. "Here, I wanted to talk you through what I'm doing with these pieces. Do you have any interest in refurbishing antique furniture?"

Conner stared at his toes as he kicked at the floor.

"There's no right or wrong answer," I reassured him. "I'm just curious."

He looked up at me, chin still dipped, like a schoolkid who hadn't done his homework. "Not really?"

I chuckled. "Neither did I at your age, but I've done a lot of it over the years and came to enjoy it. I could use your help with these pieces. Keen to have a crack and see how you do?"

As he ran a hand over the top of the bureau, then down the side of the old writing desk, Conner nodded. "Sounds good, Boss."

It felt juvenile to get a rush from being called "Boss" by someone barely ten years younger than me—if anything, I should have been offended the punk thought I was that old—but I liked it. I'd enjoyed working with him that week, answering his questions, showing him more efficient ways to complete a task, getting satisfaction when the light of understanding flashed in his eyes after he mastered something new. I could see myself doing this type of thing day in, day out, and I could get used to being this kid's boss.

"All right," I said gruffly, turning to retrieve a few bits and pieces. "I've already stripped these pieces back and wiped them down. Here's what I need you to do next."

Once Conner had a handle on how to meticulously sand the furniture by hand, I paced to the other end of the room, where I was working on my gift for Jess. I'd been out here every spare minute I could find—and I'd had more of those minutes this week, with Conner around to pitch in—so the pieces were coming along. It had been a long time since I'd done work I loved, but it had been even longer since I'd built something original with my own two hands, so this was a labour of love in more ways than one.

I'd chosen pale Tasmanian oak and designed the outdoor setting to feature fine lines and retro shapes. The style was modern but nostalgic, and every pass I did on the timber, every cut and nail and edge and finish, was reinforced with what I felt for Jess—what I hoped she'd feel when she saw it for the first time. It had to be perfect, and I quickly lost myself in a meditative rhythm. Behind me, Conner worked in a similar, silent way.

I didn't know how much time had passed when Conner's deep voice called me back to reality. It sounded just behind my shoulder, and I jumped.

"Sorry, Boss. Didn't mean to scare you." He had an amused smirk on his mouth, but I let it go. "Just wanted to tell you it's about time to call it a day."

I checked my watch. "Sorry. I lost track of time."

"No problem." Conner reached out and ran his palm over a side of the chair I was working on. "This is nice. What's it for?"

Pushing my hand through my hair, I hefted the piece off the workbench and set it on its feet on the floor. I did the same with its twin, then pointed at a larger seat and coffee table in one corner.

"It's a surprise, all right? So if you say anything to Jess, I'll kick your arse. She doesn't have any outdoor furniture, so I made this set for the back porch. The low table, two single-seaters, then the double bench over there."

Conner frowned. "That one's a little tight, isn't it?" He pointed at the two-seater. "Is it, like, a love seat?"

"I suppose you could call it that," I mumbled, picking up a cloth and wiping over the chair I'd just finished sanding.

"They suit her," he said, surprising me. "I mean, they suit the house, so they'll suit Jess. She'll love them."

It was more words than I'd heard the kid say in the last week, and the effort wasn't lost on me. "Thanks, mate. I appreciate that."

"And you're really good. Better than the boss let on. I mean, my other boss, Ryan."

I snorted. "Oh, yeah? What did that prick say about me?"

Conner smiled a little. "Said you were an ungrateful dick who could use a kick up the arse, and could I make sure that when all this is over, you remembered where you came from?"

Shaking my head, I laughed under my breath. "He's a fucker."

"Yeah." Conner crossed his arms and tilted his head. "So, is it true you live in London?" At my nod, he added, "What's it like?"

"Are you thinking of going?"

Conner shrugged. "Maybe. The Bay's so small, you know?"

I nodded. "I know."

"So, do you like it over there?"

Finished with the furniture for now, I tucked it all away and flung an old sheet over the top to hide it from prying eyes. Not that Jess had ever come looking for me in the workshop, but it paid to be cautious.

"I like it," I replied evasively, not wanting to sound like a grumpy old man, bitter and twisted about the lemons life had given him.

"Fuck, if that's the way you sound when you like something, I'd hate to talk to you when you're unhappy."

I shook my head and faced Conner, crossing my arms. "You know, Ryan told me you didn't know one end of a hammer from the other, and you were fucking things up left, right, and centre." Conner's face fell, and I set a hand on his shoulder. "He was setting me up because you're good—really fucking good—and he knows it. He's got a dark sense of humour, and it's his backwards way of saying he thinks you've got potential. He did the same thing to me, and I appreciate it now. Stick with him, finish your apprenticeship, and see how small the world feels then. London will wait for you, I promise."

Conner grimaced, then shrugged again. "Yeah, all right."

I turned away but watched Conner from the corner of my eye, hoping I hadn't knocked his confidence too hard. His brow furrowed before he rolled his broad shoulders back and gestured to the bureau.

"So, I didn't get this all done today. Mind if I make time for it tomorrow?"

Biting back a smile, I ducked my head to put away the cloth I'd been using, then strolled over to the furniture he'd been working on. Conner had done everything I'd asked—and done it well.

"You'd be doing me a favour. Once the sanding is done, you can apply the new stain and oil, if you like?"

"Okay, I will."

"Great. Thanks for all your help today."

"No problem."

When he didn't leave, I added, "So, I'll see you early in the morning."

"As always."

I allowed the silence to sit for a second. "Was there something else?"

"Uh." Conner scratched the side of his face with short, dirty fingernails, then dropped his eyes to the floor as he pointed at my furniture hidden under the sheet. "You think, if we've got time, you could show me how you made that stuff?"

I blinked. "Yeah, I'd be happy to." His head lifted hopefully, so I had to moderate his expectations. "I mean, I'm leaving in less than two weeks, and we're flat out here, so I don't know how much time I have to spare, but whatever I've got, it's yours."

He grinned like I'd handed him a championship trophy. "Yeah, Boss. That's cool. Anything you can do. Maybe I can build a little side table to go next to the love seat. What do you think?"

"I think Jess would love that."

I watched him leave, a little envious of the hope and possibility that straightened his back, and tentatively, I let myself imagine what life in Valentine Bay might look like for me if I stayed—more than Jess, more than working in construction as a way to make a living. Maybe I'd build a business and not screw it up this time, hire an apprentice like Conner and be to him what Ryan had been to me. I could be happy.

Jess, this house, a business I loved, work I was good at—they made up a life I'd always wanted and could never quite grasp. Now, the dream was so close I could feel the whisper of it against my fingertips. I just didn't know if it was safe to hope that this time, I might catch it.

24

JESS

I POKED MY head around the doorjamb of the second bedroom, where Logan and Conner were touching up the trim now that the carpet had been laid. They were the cutest pair, silent and diligent as they moved around the house, noting little defects and fixing them up in a very workmanlike manner. I bit back a smile, rapped my knuckles against the open door, and stepped inside.

"I'm going for a run," I announced. "You boys need anything while I'm out?"

Conner glanced up at me, then returned to his examination of the skirting board, paintbrush at the ready. "Nothing for me. Thanks, Jess."

"Logan?" I asked. "How about you?"

Logan nudged Conner's shoulder, then handed him the little pot of paint and brush he was using. Conner took it and continued working, crouching over a spot that needed attention.

"Before you go," Logan said with an adorable half-smile, "can I show you something in the master bedroom? I need your approval on a change I want to make to the, uh, window frame."

"Of course," I agreed. "Whatever you need."

He followed me into the bedroom, but before I had the chance to turn towards him, he'd closed the door and fallen on my neck. As he swirled his tongue over one earlobe and kissed the spot just behind my jaw, I dropped my head back against his shoulder and sighed, welcoming the feel of his fingertips under the fabric of my sports bra, his large warm hands cupping my breasts.

"Are you aware," he murmured between kisses, "that I can see your nipples through this thing?"

I feigned a gasp. "What? I had no idea."

Giggling as he growled and spun me around, I kissed him enthusiastically, pressing my stomach against the hard length in his shorts.

"Is it just me, or do you get naughtier every day?" he asked, pulling my bra off and freeing my breasts, taking one nipple into his mouth while tweaking the other with rough, clever fingers. Desire zinged through me, hitting its bullseye between my legs.

"We should stop," I said between little moans, sliding my fingers under the short sleeves of his grey T-shirt so I could stroke the lines of his muscled arms. "Josh will be here soon to start work in the yard. He might see— oh, God."

My knees buckled as Logan pulled down my yoga tights just enough to get his fingers between my folds, where he proceeded to do beautiful things to me, things that soaked me so badly I was going to have to change my underwear before I left the house.

"Can I tell you something?" Logan whispered in my ear, fingers dancing tantalisingly close to my entrance.

"Yes," I said, breathless. "Anything."

"I like it when you're naughty."

I groaned and circled my hips, desperate to feel his fingers inside me. "You do?"

"Mm-hm. I can't tell you how many times I've laid there in the dark, my dick in my fist, imagining you wearing your long, tight good-girl skirt and your button-up good-girl blouse, your high heels, and your hair up, and those fucking glasses on your gorgeous face."

Logan's hand shifted between my thighs, his thumb pressing on my clit as he dipped one finger inside me. I nipped at his lip and tried to ride his hand, and he chuckled.

"But you know what's under the good-girl clothes?" he asked.

I shook my head, pushing him backwards and pinning him against the wall, stroking his tongue with my own, rubbing his swollen cock over his jeans, my pussy still searching for his fingers in tight, manic spirals.

"A bad girl," he growled, plunging two fingers deep inside me, wrapping his other hand around my waist and pulling me into his body. After three weeks of daily— and multiple—orgasms at this man's hands, I'd lost all inhibitions, and I rode him recklessly, bracing myself against his shoulders as I raced towards relief.

"My naughty librarian, that's how I picture you," he panted against my ear. "Uptight and hard to please until I unravel you with my fucking fingers."

"Yes!" I gasped. "I love your fingers."

"I know you do, baby."

He did that thing he did, shifting the way he touched me inside to hit the spot that drowned my pussy and sent me flying. I should have been embarrassed at the way I drenched his hand, I should have felt self-conscious when I came just minutes after he began playing with me, but I didn't. Logan made it feel too good.

I bit down on my bottom lip as my climax tore through me, silently riding the surges of pleasure and gripping Logan's shoulders so tightly it might even leave bruises. When the bliss passed, rippling through me in gentle waves that left me boneless, his arm around my waist was all that held me up.

"You have to stop doing this," I mumbled, resting my cheek on his broad shoulder. "I'm developing a dependency." Impulsively, I sucked gently on the side of his neck. I wanted to leave a little mark—and I did, though it was faint and small—and the temporary brand made me giggle.

"Did you just give me a hickey?" he asked, sounding affronted.

Circling the pink bruise with the tip of my finger, I nodded and nuzzled into him, trying to muffle my chuckles.

"Maybe."

"You branded me!"

I laughed harder. "Maybe."

His hand hit my arse so hard and unexpectedly, I jumped and then shivered as he gently palmed the sting, soothing it with small, sweet circles that sent a new flood of warmth to all the necessary extremities.

"Maybe I'll find a way to mark you, too," he said, low and gravelly.

My breath came a little faster as I imagined Logan bending me over his knee or a desk, at the mercy of his strength, his open palm striking my arse and sending shocks of arousal through my entire body.

"Again," I whispered, and he paused to look for something in my gaze. I kept my focus steady on him as his hand landed on me with a sharp crack. I yelped again, but the sting of his handprint quickly morphed into a buzz of want that had my throbbing pussy craving more than only his fingers.

"Sometimes naughty librarians need to be punished," I said with a hot whisper.

"Holy fuck, Frost. I just came in my pants. How the hell am I going to explain that to Dot when I beg to use her bathroom?"

I blushed for a moment, believing that the sexual power I had over Logan might be anything near to what he had over me. "You didn't really," I said, pressing an open palm over the hard bulge between his legs.

"No, not yet, but you keep that up, and I will."

"Well, the bathroom here is up and running again. No need to shame yourself at Dot's place."

"Lucky me." He smacked me on the butt again, playfully this time. "Are you really going for a run, or did you just put on this outfit to tease me?"

"I'm really going for a run."

"But you don't run."

"I know, but there's not enough for me to do around here, and I need to stay busy. Six days until deadline. I'm nervous."

Logan smiled, but it was small, and he blinked one too many times. Perhaps he was thinking about what I wasn't brave enough to acknowledge. I backed away, turning to my dresser and rummaging through a drawer for fresh underwear. My old high school diary peeked through the piles of fabric, taunting me with memories of the hearts I'd scribbled inside it. Six days until my renovation deadline meant seven days until Logan returned to London. It was the elephant in the room, and it loomed larger by the hour. Neither of us wanted to say what both of us were thinking, and I wondered how long we would go on living in denial.

In the end, I didn't go for a run after all. My legs weren't up for it after coming so hard just ten minutes earlier, so I set out at a pace that could more accurately be called a stroll.

I'd been looking for excuses to spend more time out of the house over the past week. I needed distance from

Logan so I could hear the common sense of my head over the pounding recklessness of my libido. I'd started to imagine a life with him in it, a life that started by me asking him to stay, and only when I was out from under the influence of his souped-up pheromones was I able to think objectively about that path.

It was too big a risk, my head told me. Too big a leap to make. It was smarter to enjoy what we had now, then let him go. Smart, sensible advice ... that only made sense when Logan didn't have his hands on me.

The weather was cool but sunny, so I headed over to Main Street to collect a cup of hot chocolate from Tony's Place, then walked up towards the lookout at the north end of the Bay. I hadn't been to the lookout in a long time—at least three years—but the ocean views from there were relaxing, and I needed time on my own to think. I lengthened my stride as the path grew steeper, finally arriving at the top of the tallest cliff in Valentine Bay, and froze.

There was a reason I hadn't come to the lookout in three years, and that reason was leaning against the guardrail, his back to me as he stared out over the water, a hot cup of something grasped between his hands. Before I could decide whether it would be best to say hello or turn and run, his head shifted, and he looked over his shoulder, almost as if he sensed someone there.

"Frost," Luca said, straightening to face me.

"Hey, Rossetti." I hesitated before joining him at the rail, standing an arm's length from him. He returned his elbows to the balustrade, squinting out at the waves.

"Cold today," he commented.

"Mm." I took a sip of my hot chocolate.

"Cocoa?" he asked, lip twitching as he nodded at my cup.

"Of course. You?"

"Tea," he said, taking a slow sip.

I noticed the paper tag then, dangling from under the closed lid. "Ah," I said.

When we were a couple, Luca and I had loved the lookout. The same could be said for a lot of people in the Bay, I supposed, but we'd made something of a tradition in wintertime, ordering takeaway cocoa from Tony's Place and drinking it at the top of the cliff, staring out across the grey water. The lookout was quieter in winter, with fewer tourists and locals brave enough to face the unpredictable winds, so we were often the only ones there. It became our place, and I'd avoided it since our break-up. What were the chances that the first time I went back, he'd be there too?

"So, what brings you up here?" I asked.

"I don't know, really," he said with a small shrug. "Just felt like going for a walk. You?"

"Same," I replied. Following an uncomfortable silence, I added, "It's hard to believe the wedding is in five days. Is everything ready?"

He tried to bite back the grin that lit up his face—and failed. "I think so. I mean, Tash runs a tight ship, and it's been smarter to stay out of her way, but she's not freaking out, so I think that means we're ready to go."

"I'm happy for you, Luca," I said, meeting his eyes.

He nodded. "Thanks."

"I don't know if Logan mentioned it, but I wanted to give you something special as a wedding gift. He's been refinishing a gorgeous old bureau that Gran left me and a cute little writing desk to go with it. They might even be ready now, so I'll have him bring them round in Will's work truck. I hope that's okay."

Luca smiled broadly. "More than okay. That's very generous of you. Thank you."

"You're welcome. Logan worked hard on them, so we decided the furniture would be from the both of us."

Luca quirked an eyebrow at me, and I bit my lip. Even I could hear the affection in my voice. There was no way Luca would miss it.

"You two getting along, then?" he asked.

"Uh, yeah. You could say that."

He smiled, then turned back to the water as he sipped his tea. "Good."

The moment of potential crisis behind me, I took a deep, relaxing breath, watched the waves heaving themselves onto the rocks below, and enjoyed my drink. We said nothing for a while, but the silence was familiar. I don't know when or how it had happened, but talking to Luca about his wedding, standing so close to him now in a place that held memories for both of us, I'd reached a place of acceptance. Peace, even. I wasn't anxious, and no part of me wished for my world to be different. Luca and I finally felt resolved. I didn't love him anymore, and I wasn't sad about it. The opposite, in fact—I was elated and strong enough to ask the one question that had haunted me since he'd first told me he wanted to leave the Bay three years ago.

"Can I ask you something?" I said. "It'll be the last question I'll ever ask you about … us … but I need an honest answer. No bullshit."

He was quiet for a minute, gazing at the water. "Shoot."

I cleared my throat, nervous about his answer but not for the reasons I might have thought. "If I'd asked you to stay in the Bay instead of moving to Sydney, would you have done that? Would you have stayed for me?"

Luca opened his mouth, but I could see the lie on his lips, so I stopped him. "The truth, Rossetti. I'm a big girl. I can take it."

He snapped his jaw shut, turned his head to look at me, and there was pain in his eyes. "No."

As soon as he said the word, I realised I'd known all along what his answer would be. My body felt numb before I remembered how to breathe.

Luca straightened from his lean on the railing and extended a hand to me, but I stopped him with palms up.

"I'm good, Rossetti," I said, and it was almost true.

He tilted his head to one side, not believing me.

I swallowed the lump in my throat, trying to work out why I wanted to cry when Luca's response didn't even hurt. "Honest. Things worked out the way they were supposed to. The two of us … We weren't meant to be."

Luca nodded slowly before he took a hesitant step closer. I let him, and he wrapped his arms around me. I allowed his hug because I needed the comfort, and there was something cathartic about resting my head against his firm, familiar chest.

I had proof that, for once, my instincts had done what they were supposed to do. I'd made the right decision letting Luca go because if he'd wanted to be with me, he would have stayed. It was as simple—and as heartbreaking—as that. My head had been right all along, and that explained the tears. I had to let Logan go. If he wanted to be with me, he'd stay, but asking him to choose me when my heart told me not to risk it? That was a bad decision I was determined not to make.

25

LOGAN

"ALL RIGHT," ABBIE declared, climbing to her feet and tapping a dessertspoon against her half-filled champagne flute so that a glassy *ping-ping-ping* rang around Jess's finished living room. "Everybody shut up so I can say a few words about our girl."

I watched as a pretty pink flush bloomed in Jess's cheeks. It reminded me of the way her face looked after she'd climaxed, and my cock nudged against my pants.

It was early Thursday evening—two days before Luca's wedding, three days before Jess's renovation reveal, and four days until I was due to go home to London. The *tick-tick-tick* of time passing was louder, more insistent, and more significant than the pounding of my heart, and the sound hadn't given me a moment's peace in the last three days. I'd come this far, and all I could do now was stick to the plan, keep my poker face in place, and wait for Jess to say the words. She was close. She had to be.

At about four o'clock, Jess had fluffed the last scatter cushion, arranged the last flower, and hung the last curtain—with my help, of course—and I'd sent alerts to Abbie and Will that it was time to gather the troops at the house for a proper celebration. We already had everyone on standby, so within the hour, Dot, Abbie, Will, Josh, Emily, Isaac, and Luca—even Tash—had piled through the door with wine and cheese platters, indoor plants, and exclamations about how incredible everything looked.

Now, in various positions on the sofas and chairs and floor of Jess's living room, we all hushed while Abbie—always in her element as the centre of attention—preened as our eyes fell on her. "Thank you. Now, a toast. Please raise your glasses to my gorgeous, clever, talented bestie, Jessica. You've done the impossible, sweetie. You've taken a rundown old beach shack with shitloads of heart, made it look like something that belongs in one of your fancy interior design magazines, and somehow added more warmth as well as a truckload of good vibes that belong to you and you alone. This is a happy place—we can all feel it—and it's fucking stunning, just like you. We're all so proud of you." Abbie lifted her glass higher. "To Jess and her hot new house. May it be the start of a hot new life!"

We all raised our drinks, and I grinned at the abashed joy on Jess's face.

"To Jess!" we chorused.

It was a good party, relaxed and casual, but two hours later, Luca and Tash were the first ones to call it a night, and everyone quickly followed. There was a wedding to worry about, a bar to run, shift work to get to. Jess gave everyone hugs as they left, at the head of a receiving line down the hallway to the front door, and each person raved about the room or feature they liked best. Luca and Tash complimented the dining furniture, Isaac called out the back porch, and Will praised the timber-faced joinery in the kitchen. Dot commented on the well-hung curtains with a sparkle in her eye as she winked at me. Josh had more ideas for the yards, and Jess promised he could get at them sometime in the spring. Emily mentioned how much she envied the home office set up in the second bedroom, just as Abbie complained that it would have worked much better as a wellness space, kitted out for yoga and meditation.

"If I did my yoga here, I'd have no reason to visit your studio," Jess replied.

"You hardly ever come anyway," Abbie grumbled, wrapping Jess in a bear hug.

Jess laughed, sounding a little strangled by Abbie's grip around her ribs. "But I still pay my membership fees like a good friend."

"Don't listen to her," Emily said, taking Abbie's place in the circle of Jess's arms. "The study is divine. I'm so jealous. That desk is lovely, and the bookcase! I can't wait until I move into my own place. I'm going to do the exact same thing."

"You guys are the best," Jess said, squeezing Josh last and letting him go. "Thanks for coming around."

"Sorry to leave you with all the dirty dishes," Emily said, glancing up the hall as though considering whether she should stay to wash up.

No way in hell that was happening. I'd kept my hands to myself for long enough.

"I'll hang back to help," I said. "You guys get going, and we'll see you at the wedding on Saturday."

"Are you sure?" Emily asked, first looking to me, then to Jess.

"He's sure," Dot answered for us, hustling everyone closer to the door and sweeping them out onto the porch. "Come along, dears. We have a big weekend coming up, and some of us need our beauty sleep."

"It's only eight-thirty, Mrs March," Josh replied politely.

"And I'm eighty-five. You do the maths."

When the door closed behind them, and it was Jess and me alone again, her lips tipped up a little at the edges, and she wrapped her arms around my neck. "That party was a sweet gesture. Thank you for organising it."

I kissed the tip of her nose. "You deserved to celebrate. You fucking did it, Frost. You renovated an entire house, and you murdered the deadline. Two days to spare! It has to be some kind of record."

She set her forehead on my chest. "I couldn't have done it without you, you know," she said quietly. "Thank you."

"Ouch," I said with a laugh. "How much did that hurt to say out loud?"

"Shut up!" She smacked my shoulder so hard it stung, and I laughed harder. "It hurt a lot. The least you can do is to be a gentleman about it."

Chuckling, I wrapped my arms tighter around her waist and folded my lips around hers in a gentle kiss. "You're welcome."

She snorted. "Just for that, you can take care of the mess in the kitchen and living room while I finish a few things in my bedroom and the home office. Then I'm going to bed. Okay?"

"Fine, as long as by 'going to bed' you mean 'have mind-blowing sex until I pass out from exhaustion'."

"Oh my God," she groaned, rolling her eyes and feigning impatience. "Again?"

I tapped her on the butt, loving the way she jumped before biting back a pleased grin. "I'm going to pretend you didn't say that."

Arching an eyebrow, she disappeared into her bedroom while I headed to the living area. I collected the dirty plates and glasses, stacked them in the dishwasher, then went back for the scrunched-up paper napkins. I did my best to straighten the cushions on the sofa, though I couldn't get them to look casually perfect the way Jess did, and then ran the vacuum over the rugs to pick up the scattered cracker crumbs. With the kitchen wiped over and the dishwasher humming happily, I checked the time.

Half an hour had passed, and Jess hadn't emerged from the bedroom, so I stuck my head in there to look for her. Finding it empty, I headed to the study, but what I found froze me at the door, my stomach dropping like I was flying downhill on a rollercoaster, my hard-on swelling so painfully fast I had to adjust the crotch of my pants.

Jess looked up at me from where she sat behind the heavy timber desk, her glossy hair pulled up into a tight, neat knot. She wore a white, long-sleeve blouse buttoned to the neck, and her plump lips were painted bright red, the kind of red she'd chosen the night she went on that hellish date with the guy she met online. Sliding her black-framed glasses down her nose, she examined me over the top, then pushed them back and returned to the book in front of her.

"Take a seat, Mr Reeve. I'll be with you in a moment."

I snapped my mouth closed, crept into the room, and lowered myself into the armchair in the corner, unable to see anything but Jess. I watched her while she behaved as though I wasn't even there. She turned a page, and I stared as her fingers moved over the paper. She picked up a pen and bit the tip, drawing my attention to her mouth. She shifted as she crossed her legs, and I got a glimpse of the tall black heels she had on her feet under the desk.

Jesus Christ. Was this what I thought it was? My dick seemed to think so. I moved a little to relieve the pressure in my pants, but Jess flicked her eyes towards me, pursed her lips, and cocked an eyebrow, so I remained still, scared that one wrong move would shatter the illusion.

A minute passed, and another one, as Jess read her book, crossed her legs, ran her tongue over her lips, and pretended I didn't exist. She tortured me deliberately—and I fucking loved it.

After an eternity, she closed the book and leaned back in her chair, then swivelled, stood, and walked around to the front of the desk, where she leaned her hips against it, crossed her arms, and watched me. She'd tucked her fitted blouse into a skirt so short I could see black suspenders peeking out from underneath, holding up a set of thigh-high sheer stockings. From the tight hair to the glasses to the heels, I took her in from head to toe and groaned.

"Is something wrong, Mr Reeve?"

"No," I tried to say, though it came out as a strangled croak. I cleared my throat and tried again. "No."

"Good. Now, tell me. What comes next in your naughty librarian fantasy?"

Fuck. Fuck. Fuck.

"You take out your hair," I whispered, heart hammering.

Jess reached up to pull the pins out of her hair, shaking it free and letting it settle in wild curls around her shoulders. "Like this?"

I nodded and reminded myself to breathe. "Just like that."

Jess started on the buttons of her shirt, unfastening the first at the neck and working her way down. "Is this okay, Mr Reeve?"

All I could manage was an incoherent nod-and-grunt combination, and I swallowed with anticipation as she shed the fabric to reveal a lacy black bra that lifted and shaped her breasts in the most obscene way. Dropping her shirt on the floor, Jess slid her hands down her smooth, taut stomach and hooked her thumbs into the top of her skirt, then paused.

"What about the skirt? Do you want to see what's underneath?"

I shifted forward on the chair, pulse racing, a line of sweat springing up on the back of my neck, my cock throwing a fucking tantrum to be let out to play. "Jesus, yes."

Jess's lips curved in a tiny smile as she shimmied her skirt over her hips, down her thighs, and over her ankles, stepping out of it as she moved away from the desk. She wore a matching G-string, lacy and sheer in all the right places, leaving everything and nothing to the imagination.

"Glasses?" she asked, putting her fingers to the frames as though about to take them off.

"They stay," I growled, getting to my feet and crossing the room in three long paces. Just as I leaned in to delve into her mouth with my tongue, she set two hands against my chest and pushed me back towards the armchair before shoving me into it. I watched in awe as Jess dropped to her knees, opened my legs, and unbuttoned my pants.

"Mr Reeve," she said breathily, in a voice that wasn't quite her own. It drove me wild. "I've been having bad thoughts about you." She looked up at me from underneath her lashes and caught her bottom lip with her teeth.

"Oh, yeah?" I asked, loving where this was headed.

"Mm-hm, and they all involve me wrapping my lips around your cock." Jess circled a gentle hand around my bare dick and stroked it from root to crown, so lightly the tease was painful.

I ran my thumb over her bottom lip, smudging her lipstick into a red smear over her cheek that looked so fucking hot. "You're a dream come true," I whispered.

Jess watched with hot, eager eyes as I lifted my hips and pushed my pants down my legs. The idea that Jess wanted to fuck my cock with her mouth was almost hotter than the actual act, and I had to grasp the arms of the chair as she brushed her fingers along the ridges of my stomach, down my V-lines and over my groin. Then she set her hands against my thighs, and I watched her descend into my lap.

The shock of her hot, wet tongue on my shaft had me jumping, and she licked it from top to bottom over and over, swirling over the tip like she savoured a melting dessert. Without warning, she wrapped her lips around me and took me quickly, deep enough that I hit the back of her throat, and I felt her battle against her gag reflex. Jesus fucking Christ, the thought of Jess choking on my cock snapped my last thread of control.

Twisting my fingers in her hair and resisting the impulse to thrust into her mouth as she bobbed up and down on my dick, I groaned and flung my head back, rocking my hips a little. When I remembered myself enough to look down at her, I found her staring up at me through long lashes, smudged red lips sliding up and down my hard length, and my fists tightened against her scalp.

"I want to fuck your mouth so hard," I growled between gritted teeth.

Jess moaned and nodded around my cock, and the vibration set off another explosion of pleasure. As she braced herself, wrapping her hands around the arms of the chair, I pumped harder into her mouth, jerking my hips against her hot tongue, hard throat, tight lips.

"I'm going to come," I moaned, loosening my grip on Jess's hair and cradling her cheeks to let her know it was time to pull away. She did, gripping my cock in her hand and working it up and down through the wetness her mouth had left behind.

"Come on me," she said, pulling me closer and pressing my cock between her breasts. That did it. My dick trembled with the threat of my climax, and then I was pulsing against her skin, shooting thick ropes of release over the slopes of her breasts, up her flushed chest, across her smooth arched neck. My orgasm tore through me, curling my toes, straining my thighs, hardening my abdominal muscles, and ripping a guttural groan from my chest as I painted Jess with my cum.

It was the most erotic moment I'd ever experienced, made all the more unbelievable because it was *her*.

As my body shuddered into release and relaxation, Jess settled back on her heels, a look of wonder around her eyes and mouth. She was a fucking goddess. Her hair was a mess, her lipstick smeared across her face, her lips puffy and swollen, and her bare skin and lingerie coated with my orgasm. It was a cliché to say I was lost for words, but there was nothing I could think to say in that moment to do it justice. It couldn't have possibly been as incredible for Jess as it was for me, could it?

I fumbled for words. "That was—"

"Really hot," she finished.

"Fuck yeah, it was," I moaned, leaning back into the chair for a second, but when Jess started to stand, I shot up and pressed her into the seat in my place. "Wait here."

Pulling up my pants, leaving them open but hitched around my hips, I retrieved a towel and ran it under warm water in the bathroom. Returning to Jess, it was my turn to kneel between her open knees as I gently wiped her chest clean. She blinked at me while I did it, and I pretended not to notice her scrutiny.

"There," I said, setting the towel aside.

"Thank you," she whispered. "I guess we should—"

"Oh, I'm not done," I interrupted, spreading her wider and applying my mouth to the sheer cotton of her panties. I groaned as the taste of her met my tongue through the fabric. "Baby, tonight's just getting started."

26

JESS

ABBIE AND EMILY picked me up the morning
of Luca's wedding. Emily pulled up in her little blue
hatchback, and she beeped the horn in my driveway two
minutes past the hour. I took an extra thirty seconds to
check myself in the full-length stand mirror I'd added to
my new and improved master bedroom.

I'd bought an expensive, deep emerald-green dress for
the occasion—green, not *cream*, and though I was braced
for what my mother would have to say about it, I took a
disproportionate amount of pleasure in this one more act
of defiance before I was due to show my parents the house
the following morning.

Knowing that Luca's wedding would be awkward
for me, if not difficult, Abbie and Emily had taken
me shopping and dragged me through a dozen stores
and just as many change rooms before giving this dress

their enthusiastic approval. It had a modest hemline just above the knee but a little more going on at the neckline, which plunged low enough to show off a little cleavage but not so low I had to worry about falling out of it. It hugged my hips and flattered my waist, and with the silver heels, earrings, and clutch I picked out to go with it, I was feeling okay about attending a wedding as the dumped woman. It wasn't a revenge dress, as such, but with the way I'd curled my hair to look wilder than usual, my sexy black lingerie on underneath, and red lips just the way Logan had seemed to love two nights earlier, I was definitely angling for a look that said, *Yes, I'm the ex, but look at me now.*

Abbie hopped out of the passenger seat as I stepped out onto the porch and locked the front door behind me, and she slipped into the back to let me ride shotgun.

"You look incredible," Emily said, a knockout herself in a tight red dress that showed off her tiny, curvy frame.

"Thanks. So do you."

"And so do I," Abbie added from behind us. "I went for electric blue. You like?"

I spun around to check her out. The hemline of her dress was much shorter than mine—Abbie had always had legs that went on for days—but the top half of the design covered her to the neck and wrists, balancing out the exposed skin on the bottom half.

"No, I *love*," I replied.

Abbie sighed theatrically. "You know what else would go well with this dress?"

I scanned her from top to toe, noting the heels, bracelet, earrings, and clutch. "No. You look perfect to me."

"I'm missing a sexually satisfied glow, which you both have too much of, if you ask me. Go easy on the orgasms, ladies. Please. I'm in the middle of a dry spell, and you're depressing the hell out of me."

Emily and I exchanged amused glances before she put the car in reverse and backed out of the driveway. "Sorry, Abs," she said. "You've got a better chance of marrying Will and having five of his babies than I have of reducing my climax quota. Josh is ..." Emily shivered, and Abbie groaned.

"You're a cruel woman, Jones," Abbie grumbled, "and quit tormenting me about Will. He knows our agreement is an insurance policy. I've made sure of that. Well, at least Jess here will be celibate again soon. We'll cry into our wines together tonight and share stories of all the times we came so hard we forgot our own names." Abbie sighed wistfully. "Ah, the good old days."

I tried to smile and said nothing, which they took for agreement, but Abbie's words lanced something that had been bubbling in my chest ever since the night in the study with Logan. Time was running out, and I had to face an uncomfortable truth. He was leaving the Bay in two days, and I didn't want him to go. More than that, I didn't want to imagine not having him around.

My heart thumped louder and louder in my ears, drowning out the voice of reason in my head, and the longer we drove, the more I thought about what my life might be like if Logan left ... and if he stayed.

SAMANTHA LEIGH

A little less than an hour later, as we drew up to the ceremony venue—a gorgeous Catholic cathedral north-west of the Bay—Emily eyed me sideways. "How are you feeling about today?" she asked.

Lost in dreams about Logan, it took me a moment to understand what she meant. "You mean watching Luca get married?" At Emily's nod, I said, "Actually, I feel fine. I feel great. Luca and me ... We're friends, and I want him to be happy. He feels the same way about me. These days, our relationship feels like another lifetime for both of us."

"You know why that is?" Abbie asked, smugness oozing from her.

"No, why?"

"The new house and the hot sex with no strings attached. It's purged Luca from your system, and today is the last hurdle on your road to a brand-new life. Get through this, and there's no stopping you, Jessica Jane. Blank cheque, remember? Oh, I love it when I'm right."

Luca and Natasha's wedding ceremony was all the things I'd expected it to be—beautiful and long, with a traditional Catholic mass. The day was cool and clear, just the right conditions for their reception at Pepperberry Hill, an exquisite wine estate in the rolling land around this part of the coast. The enormous function room featured floor-to-ceiling glass doors that led out onto a deep decked balcony with views over wine country. The long timber dining tables burst with white flowers and tapered candles, the high beamed ceilings were strung with thousands of tiny lights, and an oversized fireplace at each end of the space added warmth and atmosphere. I had to give it to Natasha. The woman had impeccable taste.

The day went off without a hitch, and I surprised myself by having a good time. The ceremony was moving, the food was delicious—the wine even better—and with a little more than two hundred guests, it was easy for me to avoid the bride and groom and focus on the company of my friends instead—my friends and a certain gentleman who looked so damn good in his black tux, my lady parts had been dancing for hours.

From the minute I laid eyes on Logan standing next to Luca at the top of the church aisle, I'd been entertaining dangerous thoughts. Some related to sneaky sex in an empty hallway somewhere—God would have been well within His rights to strike me on the spot, given the filth I was thinking while sitting in the pews—and other impulses were a little more far-reaching. The more I entertained them—the longer I watched Logan as the night wore on, laughing with people and looking illegally dashing in his suit—the more certain I felt.

As soon as I could get him alone, I'd ask Logan to stay in the Bay.

The butterflies were there. My heart hadn't stopped racing with the threat of a panic attack. I changed my mind a hundred times, a part of me screaming loudly, over and over, that this was destined to end up another decision I'd look back on with regret, but I simply wasn't ready to say goodbye.

And okay, yes. By the time I decided to take the risk, I'd had more than my usual two-drink limit. Liquid courage fired up my blood, and if Logan turned me down, I could always save face by blaming my temporary lapse in sanity on the booze. Was that common sense or drunken delirium? I couldn't tell anymore.

"Holy shit, Jess," Abbie said, leaning towards me. We'd been assigned seats at the same table, of course—me, Abbie, and Emily, with a few familiar faces from around the Bay. Josh, Will, and Isaac were at the bridal table at the front of the room, and Abbie gestured that way with her champagne flute. "Logan looks beautiful tonight."

I retained enough wits to play it cool. "Why are you telling me that?"

"Oh, I don't know," she said, quirking one perfectly shaped brow. "You two have been getting along pretty well these days, and now we know he's divorced …"

Rolling my eyes, I snuck a quick glance at Logan, who happened to look up at me at the same time. Our eyes met, and I looked away, thinking of how he'd bent me over the desk in my home study forty-eight hours earlier.

"We're friends," I said, clearing my throat and taking another sip of my wine.

Abbie set the back of her hand against my hot cheek. "*I'm* your friend, and you don't flush half as much when you look at me."

I batted her hand away, and she laughed, then nodded

at Logan again. "Turn around because your *friend* is about to make his best man's speech."

Shifting in my seat to get a better view of the bridal table, I watched as Logan pushed back his chair and got to his feet, then tapped the edge of a knife against the side of his water glass. Everyone else did the same, and as the chime of glassware sounded musically around the room, Luca and Natasha leaned towards one another to share a kiss. When they were done, I clapped as loudly as everyone, basking in the revelation that none of this hurt. I was too busy being happy for Luca—and excited about my own future—for there to be room in my system for anything other than, as Abbie would say, positive vibes.

Logan grinned at his best friend, and I marvelled that he looked so comfortable about giving a speech in front of a couple hundred people. He was charismatic and charming in crowds and always had been, but I'd made the conscious decision not to dwell on those inconvenient facts. Now, I soaked it all up.

"Good evening, everyone," Logan began, speaking into a chunky microphone handed to him by a black-clad Pepperberry Hill assistant. "Thank you for being here tonight. I know it means a lot to Luca and Tash that they were able to share this important day with people they love."

A round of applause went up around the room, and Logan waited for it to quiet before continuing.

"Now, some of you might have been looking forward to this speech tonight, expecting a Luca Rossetti roast. Isn't that what this time is for?" Logan spoke directly to Luca for a moment. "The best man gets a thirty-minute time slot to air all your dirty laundry, right? Spill your secrets, embarrass you in front of your parents, tell Tash all about the time you …"

Luca laughed as Logan left the line hanging ominously, and the guests chuckled.

"Well, I hate to disappoint you all, but I can't do it." At a few quiet boos, Logan shook his head in mock commiseration. "I know! I'm sorry, I really am, but I can't do it. Don't get me wrong. I *want* to do it, but I *can't*. The guy's as squeaky clean as a rubber ducky."

Another wave of laughs met Logan's joke, and I smiled, feeling a swell of pride at how well he worked the room.

"Straight As in high school," Logan went on. "Football team. Debate club. Voted most likely to succeed. After that came a communications degree, a wardrobe full of well-fitted navy suits, and a lifetime supply of expensive hair products. This man hasn't put a foot wrong in nearly thirty years. He's a winner, our Luca, but … not what I'd ever call a ladies' man."

Josh, Will, and Isaac chuckled, perhaps at some inside joke, and I kept my smile fixed to my face, wondering if I imagined half a dozen eyes flicking my way and praying this part of the speech would be over quickly.

"The guy's got no game," Logan added, sighing and placing a hand on Luca's shoulder, "but somehow, he managed to convince this wonderful, charitable woman to take him in. Natasha, Luca is lucky to have you." After a pause, Logan added. "You're lucky to have each other.

Luca's stupid in love with you, Mrs Rossetti, and I have no doubt you'll live a long and happy life together. Please, raise your glasses as we toast the Bay's newest husband and wife, Luca and Natasha."

"To Luca and Natasha!" the room chorused before everybody dumped filled goblets of wine down their throats.

Speeches done and dessert served, the five-piece band struck up an anticipatory note while Luca and Natasha made their way to the dance floor. Every guest watched as they twirled, him in yet another well-fitted suit, her in a full white skirt, dark hair pulled back in a smooth ballerina bun, arms covered to the wrist with exquisite lace. They looked like something out of a fairytale, and a brief pang of sadness lanced my chest before it was gone as completely as if it had never been. Other couples moved onto the dance floor, obstructing my view of the newlyweds, and I sucked in a cleansing breath. I'd done it. I'd cleared the last hurdle, and my future could begin.

I startled when someone tapped me on the shoulder, and my heart stuttered when I found Logan standing behind me, impossibly gorgeous in his tux—the bow tie and top button undone now that the formalities were over—and his blond hair a little more tousled than it had been at the start of the day.

He held his palm out towards me. "Jess, would you like to dance?"

I'd known Logan all my life, but I'd grown to *understand* him the last month and more. I knew his body—how he liked it when I ran my tongue over his bottom lip, twisted my fingers through his when I climaxed, kissed him gently behind his jaw in the minutes after he came. I also knew *him*. His self-mocking smirk when he spoke about his life and what he considered his failures. How he looked for tasks to keep him busy because sitting idle drove him mad. The tightness of uncertainty around his eyes when he thought he was about to be let down. The kind of tightness he had now.

I deliberately kept my gaze on him, not looking around to see if anyone watched us, and set my hand in his. "I'd like that. Thank you, Logan."

The smile he gave me was reward enough for my courage, and he led me to the crowded dance floor just as another slow song began. Logan hesitated for the briefest minute before he drew me in close against his body, one hand on the small of my back, the other tucked around my hand up against his chest. We swayed side to side, close enough that the tips of our noses almost brushed together.

"It's nice to see your dance skills have improved," I commented, turning his hand a little so I could rub my thumb over the sweet brown freckle on his ring finger.

"What are you on about, Frost? I've always been good."

I snorted. "Have you blocked out Year Eight dance lessons? You bruised my toes once a week for three months."

"Oh, yeah. Guess I forgot about that."

"I didn't," I murmured, caressing his skin again. "I found this freckle in those dance lessons."

Logan squinted at his hand, mild surprise creasing his forehead. "You did?"

"I liked to pretend nobody else had noticed it before. It was mine as much as it was yours."

Our eyes met, and something that felt like wonder unfurled in my chest.

"I don't think I've ever looked at it twice," he whispered, "so you might have been right."

We danced, barely more than a sway from side to side, until he dropped his mouth to my ear. "People are looking at us."

I set my head on his chest, enjoying the thrum of his heart under my cheek. "Let them."

The song passed, then another, and I refused to lift my head. I could sense the burn of my mother's gaze, the curious glances of my friends, the whispers swirling around us, and I didn't care. This was my life to live the way I wanted.

When Logan cleared his throat, I finally shifted, looking up at him with a question on my lips. He nodded, eyes on something over my shoulder.

"Looks like Luca and Tash are leaving now, and it's time to say our goodbyes. Do you ... Do you want to do that with me?"

The subtext seemed plain to me. Agreeing to this would mean something. It would *say* something, and it would change everything.

"I do," I said, and his beautiful mouth tipped up on one side, grey eyes sparkling with the glow of the lights, and a deep pit of anticipation opened up in my stomach. "I just need a moment. Meet you out front in a few minutes?"

Logan let me go and moved towards Luca and Tash while I walked in the opposite direction, head down to avoid conversations that could wait until after the wedding. If I stopped to think about things now, there was every chance I'd talk myself off the ledge. It was time to leap, and this time, I felt pretty confident about where I was going to land.

27

JESS

I FINISHED IN the bathroom stall, then stopped at the basin to wash my hands. I was touching up my make-up when the main door opened, and in walked my mother, a look of barely contained opinion on her face.

"Hi, Mum," I said, tucking my lipstick into my purse. "Are you having a good night?"

"I am, and you know why?"

"It was a beautiful ceremony, and the food was delicious?" I suggested.

"The ceremony was long, and the food was adequate," she replied. "I can only imagine how much better this event would have been if it were you getting married today and not *that woman*."

"Natasha."

"But I'm determined to move past this horrible situation once and for all, and I have just the answer you're looking for."

"I'm not looking for—"

"Your father and I are seated at a table with the most wonderful couple." Mum rummaged in her purse and pulled out a compact, then started pressing at the glow on her nose and forehead. "We're at one of the worst tables, mind you, near the back and close to the kitchen. Can't see a thing from there or hear above the clatter of pots and pans, but the company more than makes up for it."

"That's nice," I said, tucking my clutch under my arm. "I'll see you tomorrow morning for the house reveal, right? Ten o'clock still good for you?"

Mum pursed her lips, and her eyes narrowed infinitesimally. "Yes. I can't wait to see what you've done with the place, darling, but let me tell you about this couple at our table. The McKays."

I pulled up short and turned away from the door. "What about them?"

"They're old family friends of Natasha's parents. They live in Sydney, but their son lives in Scarborough Cove. He's a teacher—only a substitute at the moment—but I saw a picture of him, and he's very handsome, Jessica. Dark hair, striking violet eyes, appealing in a bookish way." She raised one eyebrow. "Single."

I was ready to dismiss her when I started putting together pieces of her matchmaker puzzle. "Did you say their last name is McKay?"

"Yes, and their son's name is Miles. In fact, he's working at your school right now! I told them it's such a shame you're on leave. Otherwise, you would have crossed paths without any interference from us, but they agree with me that we'd be crazy not to find a way for the two of you to meet."

I rubbed my forehead and put one hand on the door. "I already know Miles. He's *my* substitute teacher."

I swear Mum's ears perked up as if she were a hunting dog listening as its quarry made a break for it.

"Well, isn't that fantastic? Less work for me to do."

"Mum, leave it alone." Almost as if I'd left my body, I listened to the heat creeping into my voice with a mix of pride and horror. "No more blind dates and no more set-ups. I don't need them. Let's celebrate my renovations at the house tomorrow and start fresh after that, okay? I've done what you asked me to do. I've proved I can make good decisions and run my life on my own terms. What more do I need to do to get a little breathing space?"

Stunned silence settled over us. I'd never had the guts to speak to my mother with that kind of force before. It was exhilarating. It was terrifying.

Mum hitched her shawl over her shoulders. It was cream coloured, just like her dress.

"I saw you with Logan on the dance floor. Don't be stupid, Jessica. That path leads to ruin. Surely even you can see the warning signs. Not even thirty yet, and he's *divorced*—"

"No," I snapped. "I'm not talking about this right now. I'm going to enjoy the party, and I hope you'll do the same. I'll see you in the morning at ten, okay? Don't drink too much tonight because there'll be champagne with brunch. We're celebrating."

Heaving the heavy door open, I stalked to the reception room, searching for a familiar face and finding none. Everyone must have been farewelling Luca and Tash outside, so I slipped through a side door, shivering and wrapping my arms around my body, and made my way along a brick wall towards the front of the venue. I eventually picked up the sounds of voices and angled towards them. Two were closer than the others and getting louder, so I picked up my pace, but when I was close enough that I heard my name in the conversation, I froze and ducked into the shadows.

"You and Jess looked friendly out there tonight."

My heart jackhammered against my ribs. That was Luca.

"Uh, yeah. I guess."

And that was Logan.

I knew better than to eavesdrop, but past experience didn't stop me from hovering just out of sight, waiting to hear what Logan said about me. About us. My fingertips tingled, and I almost choked, trying to swallow my nerves.

"Listen," Luca said. "I want to thank you again for stepping up when I asked you to."

"Seriously, man. Don't mention it."

"No, I want to. You did me a favour even though you didn't want to, and I appreciate it."

I frowned, both disappointed and relieved that the discussion had moved past me so quickly. I was about to announce myself when Luca went on.

"I can't believe how long you stuck with it," he said with a wry chuckle. "I thought the two of you would have murdered each other long before now."

"Yeah," Logan replied, though he didn't laugh. "I'd have put money on that, too."

I heard the clap of a hand on a shoulder. "Thanks for helping me out and being there for Frost when I couldn't. Muscling in on the renovations was genius. We couldn't have planned a better distraction."

"We've been, uh, busy," Logan agreed. "It kept her mind off the wedding, that's for sure."

Blood pounded in my ears, and the cool air was suddenly frigid on my cheeks. It took me a moment to realise I was crying, and I couldn't stop the strangled whimper that escaped my throat. It was too loud in the thin night air.

Logan stepped around the corner, and his eyes widened when he found me standing there, within earshot of him and Luca.

"Frost, what are you—" He took a small step towards me, and I took the same step back. "Oh, God," he said, realisation dawning on his face. "It's not what you think."

"I was a … a *favour*?" I whispered. "A bet? A joke?"

"No, you weren't. You aren't. I promise."

"Oh my God." I shook my head. "We aren't real. We were never real."

"Jess, wait. If you'll let me explain—"

Desperate to get away from the man who'd almost become my next big regret, I spun and ran back to the party.

All I could think as I lurched along in heels that made my retreat more difficult was that my mother was right. I had no idea what I was doing with my life, and a renovation *I couldn't have done by myself* didn't change that. Great sex certainly hadn't changed it. Believing in Logan hadn't changed it either. I'd dropped my defences, forgotten that Logan had always thought of me as a game, and let myself believe that what we had was genuine.

What did I know from real? Logan was a bad decision, and hadn't I known that deep inside? Hadn't I convinced myself to leap anyway, believing what we'd created together made any place I landed a safe one?

He was a liar, and I was an idiot. Thank God I found out before I threw myself off the ledge because the ground beneath me had just opened up, leaving my heart nowhere to go but into an eternal, terrifying free fall.

28

LOGAN

"OH, CRAP," LUCA said from somewhere behind my right shoulder. "You think she heard us?"

"Safe to say she did," I said, fighting the snap in my voice. This was just as much my fault as it was Luca's. I should have set him straight as soon as he mentioned the *favour*, but I hadn't wanted to say too much until Jess confirmed what I hoped was true—that she wanted me to stay.

"Well, fuck," he replied. "What a bullshit way to finish the night."

"About sums it up," I replied. I wanted to go after her, and before I could decide if that was the right thing to do, my legs were carrying me forward. I couldn't stand still, knowing she was hurt by something I'd said behind her back. Again.

"Wait a second," Luca said, catching up and latching on to my arm. "This isn't how your visit was supposed to end."

"Nope," I agreed, my fists curling, releasing, and curling again as I fought the twitch in my fingers that told me I needed to put them on Jess's skin. My brain fumbled for words that could explain what she'd overheard—none of which was a lie, but also nothing like the truth.

Luca shifted, crossed his arms over his chest, and I sensed he was tossing up whether to say more. "You think she's a little *too* upset about what she heard?"

I ran a hand through my hair, noting how after a long night, my hair was a mess while Luca's remained coiffed to within an inch of its life. He still had his bow tie knotted tightly at the neck, and his white shirt looked freshly pressed. "Nope," I said again.

"Look, I get the feeling that you two have grown close this last month."

My mouth was suddenly dry, and I worked my tongue around my teeth to feel less choked. "Yeah, we've moved past some of the shit we went through as kids."

"And you're friends?"

Feeling his stare on me, I met his eyes, jaw clenched. He knew. I could tell, but I couldn't confirm it without Jess's consent, and after what just happened, I didn't think she'd give it to me. "Friends," I confirmed.

"Right."

"There you are!" Tash exclaimed, approaching from behind Luca, looking radiant in her wedding dress, a delighted glow dancing in her eyes. "The driver is here, and it's time to go. Are you ready?"

"Yes, sweetheart. I just need another minute with Logan."

She planted an enthusiastic kiss on Luca's mouth, and I looked in the direction Jess went, impatient to get to her. As Tash left to wait for Luca at the car, he took my hand in a firm, favour-asking grip and didn't let go.

"Fix it," he said.

"I'm leaving for London in two days," I answered, the words sticking in my throat. *I'm leaving for London in two days.* Only now, after weeks of refusing to believe I'd ever get on that plane, did I face the possibility that it just might happen.

Luca's hand tightened around mine. "Explain it to her. Make her understand why I asked and why you did it. Fix it. Please?"

I nodded. "Have a good honeymoon."

He pulled me in for a rough, one-armed man hug. "It was good to have you home, Reeve, even for a few weeks."

"It was good to be home."

"Promise you'll come back soon? Don't leave it so long between visits next time."

I nodded again, unable to tell him what he wanted to hear because the only promise I was willing to make was to myself. If I couldn't make things right with Jess, I swore to never step foot in the Bay again.

"And Reeve?" Luca said as I walked away, pushing my patience to the limit. I turned and watched as he smoothed his hair unnecessarily. "I'm happy for you—both of you."

"I—" Words escaped me, replaced by hope so enormous I thought my heart would implode. My breath caught in my throat. "Thanks, mate," I croaked.

Taking off at a run, my impatience now had nothing to do with my best mate and everything to do with setting things right. No bigger hurdle existed to Jess and me than Luca—not even one stupid misunderstood conversation—and we had his blessing. All I had to do was explain everything, and things would work out. Before the night was over, Jess would be mine, the way she was always meant to be.

———————

I found her on the dance floor with Abbie and Emily, but only Emily looked sober enough to still be on two feet. Jess looked incredible tonight, in a green dress that hinted at what lay beneath and hair wilder now than it was eight hours ago when she arrived for the ceremony. My heart lurched at the sight of her, knowing all that stood between us was a misunderstanding, but I had my work cut out for me. She had a glass of white wine in each hand, and she drained them both at the sight of me.

"Hey, there," I said, approaching slowly. "I've been looking for you."

"What?" Abbie asked, leaning towards me. "I can't hear you!"

"I was looking for you," I replied a little louder, my eyes never leaving Jess, who flat-out ignored me.

"And now you've found us!" Abbie cried, flinging one arm around my neck. "Dance with me, Reeve!"

"Hey!" Will exclaimed, appearing out of thin air and

snaking an arm around Abbie's waist. "Why don't you ever dance with me, babe?"

"Because, *babe*," she replied, "you only want to dance with me when you're drunk."

"No," he groaned, stretching for her as she twirled out of his orbit. "That's not true."

"I'll dance with you, Kidd," Emily said, picking up his hand and twisting herself underneath his arm.

"See?" Will said to Abbie, who was hanging off Jess now. "Jones'll dance with me."

"You make a cute couple," Abbie observed.

I manoeuvred my way around Will and Emily, approaching Jess from the other side, but she spun Abbie and used her friend as a human shield to block my advance.

"Who makes a cute couple?" Josh demanded, joining our little circle with Isaac by his side.

"Kidd and me," Emily replied with a giggle.

"Bullshit," Josh growled, wrapping a large arm around Emily's tiny waist and hauling her against him so hard and fast she squealed.

"Hey!" Will protested.

"I'll dance with you, Kidd," Jess said, throwing her arms around Will's neck in a move that looked less like dancing and more like, *hold me up, I'm going to fall.*

"And I'll dance with you, Greene," Abbie announced, swaying her way to Isaac, who grinned and took her hand.

I was the lone loser, but I wasn't going anywhere until I talked to Jess, so I crowded closer to Will and tried to get her attention over his shoulder.

"Jess, can we talk for a minute, please?"

"No."

"It's not what you think—"

She snorted. "Where have I heard that before?"

"But this isn't the same thing." I wasn't close enough, so I shuffled in against Will's back and couldn't stop the way my hands searched for Jess's hips on the other side of his body. It made Will a piece of meat in an awkward dancing sandwich.

"Leave me alone, Reeve," Jess said, her voice climbing an octave and her eyes growing wild.

"Not until you hear what I have to say."

"What's going on?" Will asked, giving me a glassy-eyed look over his shoulder. "You want to dance?"

"No." Jess tightened her hold on Will's neck. "I don't want to dance with him."

"Are you crying?" Will asked as Jess blinked back tears, then he shouted at Abbie. "Hey, babe! Get over here. Frost is crying."

Abbie darted over, leaving Isaac mid-twist. Emily wasn't far behind. I tightened my hands on Jess's waist, anticipating the moment they tore her away, and it trapped Will even tighter between us.

"Sweetie, what's wrong?" Abbie asked, trying to wiggle her way in.

"Nothing," Jess sniffled.

"It's me," I confessed. "I said something to upset her, but it's easy to fix if she'll only listen to me."

Abbie groaned. "Oh, God. Are we back to this? I thought you two had moved past this kind of crap."

"We have," I said between gritted teeth, my gaze glued on Jess as I willed her to look up and meet my eyes. She'd recognise the truth there, wouldn't she?

Jess pulled away, and I let her go. Will stumbled out of the way, and the seven of us stood in a frozen knot as the other wedding guests on the dance floor undulated around us.

Emily, the most sober except for me, bounced her focus between Jess and me. "What are we missing here?"

"You want to know?" Jess asked, finally looking at me and knocking me back a step with the unexpected pain in her brown eyes. "Okay, I'll tell you. Luca asked Logan to *look after* me while he planned the wedding, and Reeve used my renovations as a ploy to get me to sleep with him."

Someone gasped—I'm not sure who—and I blanched, nausea rolling unexpectedly in my gut. I tried not to see the look of horror on Emily's face, the shock on Abbie's, the disapproval pressing in on me. I took a slow, steadying breath through my nose.

"Jess, that's not what happened."

"Isn't it?" she snapped. "What, exactly, is inaccurate about what I just said? Were you kind to me as a favour to Luca?"

"In the beginning, yes, but—"

"Oh, God, Reeve," Abbie said, wrapping an arm around Jess's shoulders. "That's gross."

For the first time, panic shot through my system. "It's not like that—"

"And did you want to do it? Did you want to spend time with me?" Jess asked as she swayed a little on her feet. Abbie kept her upright on one side, Emily on the other.

I could tell her what she wanted to hear. I could try to solve this misunderstanding with a little white lie, but I couldn't do it. I wanted nothing but truth between us, and I needed to know she believed me. That she believed *in* me, "To start with, no, I didn't, but if you and I could talk somewhere private, I can explain everything."

"And you both think I'm such a sad, pathetic woman that I need a man to take care of me?" she went on, working herself up into higher levels of rage. "I couldn't get through this on my own—get over Luca, renovate my house, meet someone new, have casual sex? I needed *you* to do all those things, did I?"

My nostrils flared at the implication of Jess having sex with anyone but me, and I clenched my fists. "No, you didn't need me, but don't you think this is a conversation we could have without an audience?"

Her tears finally spilled over, dragging black lines of mascara down her blotchy cheeks. "I don't have anything else to say to you, and I never will. I want to go home."

"I can take you—"

"No," Emily cut me off. "Abbie and I will drive Jess home." Jess turned away, and Abbie threw me a disapproving look as Emily added, "You've done more than enough for one night."

"Jesus," Josh mumbled as he pushed open one of the party venue's heavy glass doors and led the way onto the decked balcony and into the cool July air. "I didn't see that coming."

The wedding reception was near its end, the function room was emptying out while staff tidied away dirty dishes and decorations, and Will had collected drinks for the four of us before we fled the scene of my public flaying. The girls were gone, the guys had sobered up after all the drama, and it was time for me to face the firing squad.

Will handed me a glass, and I took a sip of tonic water, eyeing the amber whiskey in the other tumblers with regret. I could have used a familiar burn in my throat right about then.

"It's not what you think," I began.

"So you keep saying," Will quipped.

"Then tell us what it is," Isaac replied, his voice rough from a long day and a big night on top of tightly held emotion. He'd be the first to break something on my body if I'd taken advantage of Jess.

I dragged an open hand down my face. "I love her."

I couldn't even smile at the sound of Will choking on his liquor. "You fucking *what?*"

Sighing, I shrugged and shook my head, a self-mocking laugh reverberating in my chest. "I've loved her for a really long time."

"So ..." Isaac squinted at something past my left shoulder. "What was all that talk about tricking your way into her pants?"

"And what's Luca got to do with it?" Josh added.

I took a gulp of water to wet my throat and buy myself a moment to think. When it came to the way I felt about Jess, I'd kept my cards close my whole life for two reasons. One, loving her had always been tangled up with a sense of betrayal, an uncomfortable pain that I was lying to my best mate while helplessly pitting myself against him in a competition he never knew existed. That wasn't true anymore—no competition, no betrayal, and for the first time, no uncomfortable pain. And two, I never believed I had a shot with Jess. I never thought she'd want me—*choose* me. And now ... Now I'd put money on the possibility that she loved me. Money or my heart.

In fact, that's exactly what I was going to do. I'd come this far, and I had to go all in.

Isaac, Will, and Josh listened in silence as I told the story from beginning to end. I left nothing out, even when it made me look like an idiot or, worse, a dickhead. I talked about our childhoods, kissing Jess at that party when we were teenagers, why I spent years tormenting her to numb my own insecurities, and running away from the Bay when her relationship with Luca caused me too much hurt. Marrying Bek for all the wrong reasons and divorcing her for the right ones. Returning to the Bay for the wedding, Luca asking me to watch out for Jess. The renovations. The revelations about our relationship. The intimacy that followed. The sex.

"Then tonight, she overheard Luca and me talking

about the favour," I finished. "He wanted to say thank you, but Jess overheard and drew her own conclusions."

Isaac grunted. "Not hard, given your history."

"Yeah," I muttered. "Thanks, bro."

"You love her?" Josh asked, one eyebrow cocked disbelievingly.

"Yes, I love her," I replied.

"Then you have to tell her."

I dropped my head back and grimaced. "Care to tell me how I do that when she won't even look at me?"

"You'll find a way," Josh offered.

I chuckled. "No offense, but you three suck tonight. I could use some real advice here, and you're failing in fucking spades."

Grinning like he knew a secret, Josh wandered over to one of the empty outdoor tables and took a seat. "You could trick her into attending your farewell party, then clear out the venue before she arrives and surprise her with a ring," he suggested.

"Not exactly original," Will muttered, dropping into another chair.

I lowered myself into a seat while Isaac took the last one on the opposite side of the table, and frowned first at Josh, then at Will. "Why do I get the feeling this is an inside joke?"

"Because it is," Isaac replied, running a hand over his dark, close-cropped beard. "It's what Josh did to convince Emily to stay in the Bay. They got off to a rough start, you might say."

My eyebrows climbed in surprise. "Seriously? You two are so happy it's kind of revolting."

"Thanks," Josh replied, slouching back and setting one ankle on the opposite knee. "Took a bit of work to get there, but it was worth it."

I leaned towards him. "So, how'd you do it? What's the secret?"

"He's not a fucking love god," Will grumbled, throwing back his whiskey.

Josh laughed as Isaac replied, "He's the only one of us four with a girlfriend, so let him have the mic."

My hope began to grow again as Josh told me about meeting Emily, how they'd faked an engagement to convince her cheating ex-fiancé to leave her alone, but when pretending to love her started to feel real, Josh freaked the fuck out because he hadn't yet let go of Maggie, his childhood sweetheart and our friend who died years ago. He'd pushed Emily so hard that he almost lost her, and he had to put everything on the line to convince her to give him another chance.

"Wow," I breathed, slumping and running a hand through my hair. "She could have told you no. You realise that, don't you? You took a big risk putting it all on the line and with the entire town waiting for her answer in the next room, too." I snorted. "Not sure if you've got balls of steel or shit for brains."

Josh grinned. "Like I said—it was worth it."

Will cleared his throat. "Uh, mind if I mention the elephant in the room? Jess is still Luca's ex, right? And he'll be back in two weeks with his new wife. Are we really suggesting that Logan declare his feelings for Jess, only for the shit to hit the fan all over again? Things only just sorted themselves out, what with all the Tash-and-Jess awkwardness we've been dealing with for months. No offense, Reeve, but it's been tense as fuck around here."

Isaac nodded quietly, and even Josh looked thoughtful as he swirled his whiskey around his glass.

"Yeah, about that," I said, a small smile tugging at the corner of my mouth. "I think Luca suspects. He said as much tonight, and he … Well, he gave us his blessing."

"You're joking?" Will spat.

"Nope."

"Then it's settled," Josh declared, raising his glass. "Tomorrow, you'll find a way to get to Jess, clean up this mess and tell her you love her, then tear up that plane ticket to London."

"It's an e-ticket. It's digital. It's on my phone."

"Shut up."

Isaac and Will lifted their drinks, and I did the same, that curl of hope in my chest unfurling a little wider.

"To Logan and Jess," Josh said as we clinked our glasses. "He might be slow, but he's catching up quick. It's time to go get the girl."

29

LOGAN

I KNOCKED ON Jess's door just before ten o'clock the next morning. Her parents would visit later in the day for the big renovation reveal, but given they'd been at Luca's wedding the night before, it was safe to assume they wouldn't arrive until at least noon. That gave me two hours to work things out with Jess—to explain exactly what happened when Luca asked me for a favour and how that one conversation had nothing to do with what we'd built over the last month.

The more I thought about Josh's advice—and I hadn't had more than an hour of sleep because I couldn't *stop* thinking about it—the more certain I was that I needed to say the words. I was all in. I'd tell Jess I love her, and she'd ask me to stay. The dice couldn't land any other way.

When Jess didn't answer the door after my second knock, I let myself around the back. Perhaps she'd gone out or slipped next door to visit Dot. Her absence wasn't terrible, I decided. I could use the time to retrieve the outdoor furniture I'd made, still hidden under an old sheet in the workshop, and arrange it on the porch. There hadn't been a good time to surprise her with it yet, and I grinned as I imagined her face when she saw it for the first time.

I rounded the side of the house, intending to go straight to the garage, but the sound of her voice pulled me up short.

"What are you doing here?"

She stood on the porch with a broom in her hands, wearing torn faded jeans and an oversized tee, her hair loosely pulled off her face, and her glasses on her nose. As lovely as she'd been in her dress and heels the night before, I'd never seen her look so beautiful than in that moment, and I cleared my throat before climbing the porch steps.

"I came to talk to you," I said.

"No." She took a few small steps back and held the broom up in front of her as if I were a stray dog that needed to be kept at a distance. "I don't want to talk to you."

"Then I'll talk," I replied, ignoring the way my heart pounded painfully enough that I distantly wondered if it was about to give up and stop altogether. But then Jess frowned and opened her mouth, so I rushed on before she could tell me to leave.

"Yes, Luca asked me to watch out for you, and yes, I agreed. No, I didn't want to do it at the time, and I know that sounds awful, but it wasn't for the reasons you think."

"I don't think anything—I *know* it. You've never liked me, Reeve, and this thing between us was all a game to you. Some bullshit boys' club handshake where all that mattered was Luca's ego and your need to be a good mate. What *I* wanted or needed or deserved was never part of the discussion."

I wanted to deny it, but Jess was kind of right, and it made me mad—at Luca, at myself, at the possibility that I'd come so close to winning Jessica. If I lost her now, it would be all my own fault—as usual. "Luca thought you needed a friend," I said. "His intentions were good."

"That's a bullshit excuse," she snapped. "Everyone in my life wants to make my decisions for me, and the two of you are no different. Everyone who knows me thinks I'm incapable of creating a happy life for myself, and the more I screw things up, the more I think they're right." Her voice cracked, and my heart splintered in a painful echo of the sound. "I thought you believed in me when nobody else did, and I was wrong. Again. What am I supposed to do with that?" She shook her head and stabbed the broom in my direction. "No. Luca wanted to sleep at night knowing he'd taken care of the *Jess problem*, and he outsourced his emotional baggage to you. Neither of you gave me enough credit, and it's not good enough."

A rush of rage and terror tipped me off balance—fury that she couldn't recognise all the things I'd done for her for and what they really meant, and fear it was too late to make her see. I had no surprise party, no ring, nothing but empty hands and a heart full to bursting. And when had that ever been enough? It was irrational, maybe, but the fact that she was ready to write me off without fighting for us snapped a wire between my brain and mouth.

"I didn't think of it like that, and it was probably a boneheaded thing for him to do—for us to do—but the reason I let him believe it was a favour was because I couldn't let him know the truth. Luca gave me a reason to live in your back pocket for a month, and even though I knew you hated me and spending all that time together would kill me, I did it. I should have said no, but I couldn't."

"Please," Jess said, squeezing her eyes closed. "Stop talking."

"No!" I took advantage of the lowered weapon to close in, backing her up until she hit the porch railing. "I didn't volunteer to help with the renovations because I agreed to a stupid favour or because I didn't think you could do it on your own. The point is, you didn't *have* to do it on your own. I *wanted* to help. I wanted to support you. I wanted to spend time with you."

"You wanted to have sex with me."

I choked on an incredulous laugh. "Is there a right answer to that question? Yes, I wanted to have sex with you. I wanted to kiss you. I wanted to touch you. I wanted to put my mouth on every inch of your body and make it mine."

I watched as her throat bobbed as she swallowed. "So, what?" she asked. "This was about being a good mate to Luca *and* satisfying some sort of twisted ego trip? Congratulations, Reeve. You have all the proof you needed that, yes, your wiles work on me, too. You're officially irresistible." She huffed out a sad, self-loathing laugh. "I'm such an idiot. I actually believed ..."

"Believed what?"

She was quiet for a second, and I thought she wasn't going to answer, and then she gave me a challenging stare. "I believed what we had was real. You obviously think I'm stupid, and maybe I am because you tricked me into believing this was honest, and it never was. Every minute we spent together was a lie."

My chest rose and fell with frustration. I was this close to winning the world, and she was slipping through my fingers.

"You're right," I snapped. The broom dropped from her hands, landing with a clatter on the decking, and I took a final step forward, close enough to wrap my hands around her arms. "Every minute was a fucking lie because I let Luca believe *he* was the reason I kept coming back here when the reason was always you. It was a lie because I spent every minute pretending that a few weeks with you was going to be enough when the thought of leaving you behind was tearing my heart out. It was a lie because every time I was inside you, I hoped it would be enough to prove how well we fit together. Every time I made you come, I was trying to show you the life I could give you. Every time I kissed you—every time I *looked* at you—was a fucking lie because all I ever wanted to do was tell you how much I love you!"

She inhaled sharply as my eyes widened, and the silence hung between us, locked and loaded.

"Hello! Is anybody home?"

I closed my eyes and held my breath, searching for patience as I dropped my hands and took a long step away from Jess. A moment later, her parents bustled out through the glass doors and onto the porch.

"Oh. Logan," Sandra said waspishly. "I wasn't expecting you to be here."

"No." I stretched out a polite hand to them both. "I didn't plan to bump into you either. Good morning, Mrs Frost. Mr Frost."

Jess cleared her throat and pushed herself off the railing. "Logan was just—"

"Oh, you'll never guess who we ran into at Tony's Place!" Sandra leaned back through the doors, half her body disappearing into the house as she reached for something—or someone. When she straightened, there was a man on the end of her arm, a man I recognised, and I ground my molars in irritation.

"Miles," Jess gasped, her eyes darting from me to the dark-haired guy and back again. "What are you doing here?"

"Uh, your mother—"

"That's what I'm trying to tell you," Sandra said. "Miles was out for breakfast with his parents at Tony's Place, and when he learned we were on our way over here to view the new house, he mentioned that he would love to see it."

"Sometime," Miles added, tucking his hands into the pockets of his pants. "I said I'd love to see the house *sometime*."

"No time like the present," Sandra replied while Jess's dad stood back a little, arms crossed over his chest, shaking his head at the ground beneath his feet. "And I know why you're so interested in this house, Mr McKay. Your mother told me all about the deal you made with Jessica."

Jess flinched. "Mum, stop. You don't know what you're talking about."

"Oh?" Sandra smiled tightly as she swanned past me, picking up Jess's hand and turning her back so I was cut out of the conversation. "From what I've been told, you and Miles had coffee two weeks ago, and you promised him another date just as soon as the renovations were completed."

I was already burning holes in Miles's pretty, preppy face, so I noticed the exact moment alarm widened his eyes. This had to be bullshit, but one look at Jess and I knew it wasn't. She looked like she'd just been backed into a corner. Uncertain. A little scared. Her nose wiggled, the telltale sign she was going to do something she considered a bad decision, and I knew that whatever she said next would destroy me.

A familiar pit of humiliation opened in my gut, and devastation sprung from my bones fast enough to make my skin prickle. I'd lost her again, without even realising there was someone out there I could lose her to.

Clearing my throat and pointedly ignoring everyone but Jess, I stepped around her mother and set my lips to Jess's warm cheek. "It's okay. Don't worry about it," I whispered in her ear. "Goodbye, Jess."

I launched myself off the porch, tucked my head, and rounded the house as fast as I could, then walked at a pace that had my muscles screaming by the time I climbed the stairs to Will's loft.

He wasn't home, so I threw my gear into my travel bag and ordered a ride. It was a lousy thing to do, sneaking out of the Bay without letting anybody know, but I sent a text and explained it all to the boys on the way to Sydney. After everything I'd told them the night before, they understood why I had to leave without any more farewells, even if it meant spending a day and a night at the airport while I waited for my flight.

There'd always be someone better than me for Jessica Frost, no matter how much I gave or how much I loved her. As the truth sunk in, deeper and deeper for every minute I spent in the car, at the airport, on the plane, in the cab on the way home to my flat in London, I wondered what had ever compelled me to hope my life could be something other than a string of fuck-ups and let-downs I brought upon myself.

30

JESS

_____

PEOPLE WERE TALKING, but their voices came to me through a tunnel—distant and muffled and echoing. I sank back against the porch railing and gripped it with two hands, unable to think of anything but Logan and what he'd said.

All I ever wanted to do was tell you how much I love you!

I couldn't make the words ... *fit*. If they were true, Logan would have said them weeks ago, wouldn't he? And wasn't it a little too convenient that now, when he had something to be sorry for, he used those magic words?

I wanted to believe he loved me but wanting something so badly you ached for it didn't make it real. That had always been my problem. I'd mistaken wishful thinking for reality, confused what should have been for what was, and then spent too much time regretting what I'd never have.

I wasn't safe behind the wheel. I couldn't be trusted on

the ledge. Forget paint by numbers—I couldn't even keep the colours between the lines.

"Uh, Jess?"

Blinking to clear the fog, a good part of it due to all the wine I'd consumed at the wedding and the sleepless night that came after, I lifted my head to find Miles watching me intently.

"Yes?" I answered.

"The house looks great, and I'd love to get the grand tour sometime," he said, "but I'm going to go."

"What?" Mum exclaimed. "No! Stay. Have brunch with us. Jess is thrilled you're here, aren't you, Jess?"

Miles barely hid a grimace. "I appreciate the invitation, Mrs Frost—"

"Call me Sandra, please."

"All right. I appreciate the invitation, Sandra, but I really do need to head off. Jess has my number, and she can call me anytime."

Mum smoothed the front of her fine woollen cardigan peevishly. "I'll make sure she does, Miles."

"Okay, then," I muttered, trying—and probably failing—to give Miles a reassuring smile. "Thanks for dropping in, and I'll see you tomorrow at school."

"That you will." Casting a quick but curious look at my parents, Miles took the porch stairs one at a time, like a regular person—so safe, so boring—and left the same way Logan had done, circling the house and letting himself out the side gate.

"Well," Dad said after the silence lingered a beat too long. "Where does the renovation reveal begin?"

I took my parents through the house—the kitchen, the dining nook, the new bedroom and the old ones, the living room, the bathroom—and heard myself describe every paint colour, every piece of furniture, every rug and cushion and artwork and curtain as if listening to my voice from somewhere outside my body. I didn't want to be there. I wanted to run after Logan, and it took every shred of self-discipline I had to keep myself inside those walls.

Lead with your head, not your heart.

When I'd explained to my mother at length about the back porch, choking on the description of Logan ripping the old structure down and building me a new one, Dad disappeared for a moment and returned with three glasses of the sparkling wine I'd set out in an ice bucket on the table for this very moment. He handed a flute to me, then to my mother, and raised his own glass in preparation for a toast.

"You've brought this house back to life," he said, smiling and blinking glassy eyes. "It's beautiful, sweetheart, and we're proud of you."

"Yes," Mum agreed, pursing her lips and tucking a loose strand of blonde hair behind her ear. "It's lovely, and I'm … very impressed."

My victory felt hollow. "Thanks," I murmured, tapping my glass against theirs.

Dad took a slug of his drink, then paced to the end of the porch, running his hand along the smooth rail.

"Logan did an excellent job on the woodwork out here," he commented. "It's a shame he didn't stay for a tipple."

"Oh, Michael," Mum muttered, sniffing at her wine before crossing her arms over her chest and scrutinising the porch all over again. "Will you give it a rest, please?"

"All I'm saying is, I think he did a wonderful job on the house"—he glanced at me—"not to overshadow all your hard work, darling."

"No, you're right," I replied, barely loud enough to hear. "Logan was a huge help."

"Now, Jessica," Mum said. "Logan might have been useful to have around these last few weeks, but don't confuse a new bedroom wall and a back porch with reliability. That boy cannot be trusted."

What was I supposed to say to that? She was right, so I hummed in reply, which she took for agreement, of course.

"He's always been inconstant, hasn't he? Never where he was supposed to be, never doing the things he was supposed to do, never finishing the things he started. He was the same as a child. I blame his mother. She never kept a job for longer than a year, and was always taking her family on extra holidays, even when they should have been at school."

I tossed my drink down my throat, ignoring the way the taste made my queasy stomach turn. Hair of the dog and all that. I'd either thank myself or hate myself later, and right then, I didn't care which.

"I don't want to talk about Logan," I snapped.

"What?" Mum narrowed her eyes at me. "Why not? What has he done?"

"Nothing," I said, walking away from her and back into the house.

Mum followed me. "Don't lie to me, Jessica. I can tell when you're hiding something. Did something happen?"

My nose began to sting, and my eyes welled up. I dashed them dry as I headed to the kitchen, yanked open the dishwasher, and stowed away my dirty glass.

"No, nothing happened. Just forget it."

Mum set a hand on my shoulder and turned me to face her.

"What's he done to you?"

"Nothing! Can we talk about something else, please?"

Mum frowned, then smoothed my hair back from my forehead. "We did you a favour pushing you to complete these renovations. You can see that now, can't you? We were right about the house, we were right about Luca, and I was right about Logan, wasn't I?"

I took a wide step around her, stalked out of the kitchen and then through to the hallway. Mum and Dad followed.

"You know we only want what's best for you," Mum said as I collected her handbag from the hallway table and opened the front door. "Listen to me, darling. Forget Logan. Get in touch with Miles about that date—he seems like a nice young man." She fished a business card out of her purse and handed it to me. "Call the real estate agent about the house. Now that it's not so dilapidated, you could get an excellent price for it—better than we first thought. It's time to start over." When I said nothing, she grabbed my hand. "Listen to me. I know what's best."

Pulling my hand free, I glared at her, feeling a surge of the rebellion that had swept me up and away just five weeks earlier. "Did you read my diary?" I demanded.

Her eyes widened a little. "No. What diary?"

"My high school diary."

"I— No, I would never read your diary."

"Then what has you so convinced I'm in love with Logan?"

Her face paled. "Who ever said anything about love?"

"It doesn't matter." And just like that, the puff of rebellion fizzled out as fast as it had ignited. In the end, what was I fighting against? My mother had been right all along. I was the fool, not her. "Logan's leaving tomorrow, and I'll probably never see him again. I'll think about calling the agent." My gaze roamed back to the inside of the house, almost like if I looked hard enough, I'd find Logan standing there. "Maybe you're right. Maybe it's time for a fresh start."

Mum's panic passed quickly, too, and she brightened considerably at the possibility of my selling the house. "And you'll make a date with Miles?" she prompted.

"I don't know," I hedged, deliberating if I had the energy to argue or if it was even worth it. "I'll think about that, too."

Dad gave me a kiss on the cheek as he left, and Mum waved enthusiastically from the car window. It felt like forever as I waited for them to reverse out the drive and roll away down the street, and then I shut the door, rested my back against it, and sank onto the floor.

I cried for a long time as my heart begged me to chase after Logan and make things right. But no matter how strong the pull grew inside my chest, my head wouldn't let my legs cooperate.

───────────

Knocking on the front door woke me. I crawled out from under the bedcovers, noted that the house beyond my bedroom door was dark, and then checked the time on my phone. It read eight o'clock. I'd slept six hours or more and could have happily remained unconscious for another twelve hours, at least.

The banging sounded again, and possibility spun my gut into knots. Logan. Tripping over my bed sheets in my rush to get to the door, I stumbled and fell, then dragged myself to my feet, practically hanging off the doorknob for support.

I flung open the door, switched on the porch light, and came face to face with Abbie and Emily.

"Oh," I said, despair unravelling the tangles of anticipation. "What are you doing here?"

"Nice to see you, too," Abbie replied, sweeping past me. She went straight to the living room, drew the curtains, and flicked on a lamp, then went to the kitchen and started rattling around in the cupboards.

"I have to work tomorrow," I mumbled. "And I think

I'm still a little drunk from last night. No wine for me."

Emily hoisted the grocery bag she held. "We thought sugar would work better tonight. I didn't know what you liked, so I bought vanilla, salted caramel, and strawberry ice-cream, a can of whipped cream, a jar of sprinkles, and a packet of chocolate buttons. All major food groups accounted for." She took my hand and led me into the living room, where Abbie had set bowls and spoons on the coffee table. "Take a seat, and we'll serve you a triple shot."

"How are you doing?" Abbie asked, pulling cartons out of the grocery bag and arranging them on the table. She took a seat on the rug, folding her long legs underneath her, and I did the same.

"I'm fine," I replied, watching as Emily scooped a little of each flavour of ice-cream into the bowls, then decorated them with modest amounts of toppings. I flapped a hand to indicate I'd need more sprinkles, then she pushed one towards me.

"Josh filled us in a little about what's been going on between you and Logan this last month," Emily said, helping herself to a mouthful of dessert. "It sounds ... intense."

I nodded slowly, staring into my bowl as I pushed the creamy colours around with a spoon. "It was."

"I can't believe you never said anything." Abbie said. "No, scratch that. I can't believe you lied so well. Your poker face is woeful, but you pulled it off this time. Hate to say it, but I'm proud of you."

"Uh, thanks?" I replied, then sighed. "It's complicated,

you know that. We had to keep it under wraps. There was Luca to think about, and Logan and I have always had an unconventional relationship. Plus, he was never going to stay in the Bay. Nothing about us was simple."

"But something between you must have worked," Emily said.

My lips quirked despite my low mood. "Yeah, a few things worked."

Emily grinned a little. "So, am I right to assume that 'Miles' was a codeword for Logan this whole time?"

"Yes." My cheeks flushed.

"Evil fucking genius," Abbie muttered into her ice-cream.

I ignored her. "It seemed sensible to keep it a secret. Just a fling that was supposed to end when he returned to London."

"Oh, you don't owe anyone an explanation," Emily reassured me. "I went through a similar thing with Josh, and it took me a long time to open up to you and Abbie about my feelings. It was safer to prepare for the end rather than hope for a beginning."

"That's exactly it," I replied.

"But I can tell there was more to it than the sex," Abbie guessed, her eyes narrowing at me. "And you don't have to hide it anymore. So, spill. What's really going on?"

With their rapt attention, I told Abbie and Emily about my affair with Logan—how we'd grown close, how I'd come to depend on him, and how I'd fought every instinct I had before finally deciding to ask him to stay.

332

"And that's when I overheard him and Luca talking about me like I was some kind of prize hog." I put on a rough, manly voice. "'I can't take care of her anymore. She's hard work. Can you take her off my hands?' And Logan says, 'Well, I really don't want to. She's an uptight shrew. But if it'll help you out, bro, I'll suffer through it.'" I shovelled a spoonful of ice-cream into my mouth and spoke around it. "It's like it's always been. I'm a joke to that man. My whole life is a freaking joke."

I pretended not to see the bewildered looks that Abbie and Emily exchanged over my head as I went in for more ice-cream.

"I think we all agree that Luca and Logan might have handled the situation differently," Emily said warily, "but I don't quite understand why you're this upset over it."

I scowled and snatched up the packet of chocolate drops, dumping half of it in my bowl. "The part about my lack of good judgement is the problem. There's no coming back from thinking I knew what I was doing only to find out he'd made a fool of me. It's the same story over and over. My heart wants the wrong things. I believe in the wrong people. I go left when I should go right. I jump, and there's nowhere safe to land."

"Oh. My. God," Abbie said, a hint of exasperation in her voice. "What are you talking about? You're the smartest woman I know. No offence, Em."

"A little taken," Emily said, "but we'll talk about it later."

"I'm talking about my track record," I said, throwing up my hands. "I'm talking about my mother telling me to do one thing and things going badly when I do the opposite. I'm talking about loving Logan even though I know it's emotional suicide."

Emily gasped. "You love him?"

"I—"

"Why is it emotional suicide?" Abbie interrupted.

I groaned. "Because just when I think he won't let me down again, he does something to completely devastate me. How many times do I say, 'Here you go, Logan. Have my heart. Just don't stomp all over it this time'?"

Abbie set her bowl aside and crossed her arms. "You know why he keeps fumbling things?"

I snorted, wanting the answer and dreading it at the same time. "Sounds like you're going to tell me."

"Because the poor guy is fucking head over heels in love with you."

My heart must have stopped beating for a full six seconds, because it hurt like hell when it started up again. "Why do you say that?"

"I've known it for years. Oh, don't look at me like that. It's not like he ever said, 'I love Jessica', but it was obvious. He looked at you like you were a glass of water, and he was a man dying of thirst. He was always around, always extra obnoxious, always down on himself, always putting himself in your way then darting out again when you got too close."

"He— I— No, it wasn't like that." But I heard the lie. It was exactly like that.

"And he always believed Luca was a better fit," Abbie

added. "He wasn't ever going to get in the middle and ruin things for either of you."

She made sense, and I didn't want her to make sense, so I shook my head.

"It doesn't matter," I said. "Don't you understand? Love isn't enough. Logan is wrong for me, and you know how I know that? I want him, and I always want the wrong things. When I follow my heart, it leads me down the wrong path. I have to let him go and start again."

"Logan's plane doesn't leave until tomorrow," Emily suggested, and I glanced away from the concern that crinkled her brow. "Maybe if you sleep on it, you'll feel different—"

"I won't," I cut in.

Emily reached over and squeezed my hand. "You might—"

"I'm not going to change my mind."

Abbie sat up on her heels and tipped the rest of the chocolate into my bowl. "You can wallow for another twelve hours, and then we're sorting this out."

"Stop it!" I snapped. The more they talked, the more they confused me, and the more I felt like that child I didn't want to be anymore, the one who needed to be told where to put her feet and when. A familiar sense of helplessness rose up from the outside. Blinking away tears, I took a slow, soothing breath. "I appreciate what you're trying to do, but I can make this decision by myself. I don't need you, or my mother, or anyone else telling me I'm wrong about this—or that I'm right, for that matter.

I can do this on my own without the unsolicited advice. I've fixed the house, I've had lots of sex, and I've purged Luca from my system. I've ticked all the boxes I set out to tick, and now I've got a blank cheque of confidence to cash in, remember? A new life to begin."

Abbie and Emily swapped one of those looks again before Abbie kissed the crown of my head and settled back on the floor, and we finished our desserts in a cocoon of awkward silence.

We all knew the truth. I had no confidence. I had nothing to cash in and no shiny new life waiting for me. I was back where I started, living in an empty house, and loving a man who had let me down. I needed to let go.

Could a herd of flesh-eating cats be very far behind?

31

JESS

THE REST OF the week passed in a blurry haze of depression and denial. On my first day back at work, I met Miles early so he could hand over his class notes for the previous two weeks. After a few failed attempts to raise my spirits, he kept things professional, and we were able to wrap things up in less than an hour.

I had his number, he told me, and I could use it whenever I wanted. I thought I smiled at that, but I couldn't remember, and I couldn't bring myself to care.

Later that first day, I was in class at the time Logan's plane was due to take off. When I looked up at the clock on the wall and saw that the hour of take-off had come and gone, I realised with a sinking feeling that he was gone as well. Something dropped in my chest, landing with a thud in my gut like a vault door dropping closed.

Logan was gone. I'd done nothing to stop him, and whatever we'd had together really was over.

The next day, and the days after that, passed me by as I went through the motions of my life. I woke up. I went to work. I remembered to eat, sleep, and repeat. Abbie and Emily joined me for dinner twice and dragged me out for drinks once, but I wasn't good company. Still, the distractions weren't wasted because I was itching to get out of my beautiful house, and any excuse would do.

When I woke up in the mornings, the first thing my eyes landed on was the curtain rod above the window. Logan had insisted I install it myself under his supervision, and he'd patiently explained how to measure the height of the brackets, check the balance, and use the power drill. He hadn't made fun of me once, even when he'd had to repair a hole I made in the wall, but the grin he'd given me when I finally got it right had been like sunshine. So, now whenever I looked at the curtain, I groaned and turned my head into my pillow and threw the covers over my head, only to wonder if I could smell Logan on my sheets or if it was wishful thinking.

Every time my feet hit the smooth timber floorboards that Logan had so meticulously refinished, I thought of him sweaty and dusty, a sexy frown of concentration on his face. Every time I opened or closed a kitchen cupboard, I remembered how he approved so enthusiastically of the timber cabinetry and unusual teal laminate. Every time I stepped into the shower, I remembered the afternoon I tried peeking around the door to watch him soap himself up after a day installing the rear glass windows and how he'd spotted me there and invited me to join him.

I couldn't step foot on the back porch because he was present in every line of the wood. I'd avoided the garage as though there were demons trapped inside—and it wasn't too far from the truth. The idea of entering the workshop made me physically ill. If there was any part of this home that belonged to Logan, that was it.

And that's what I couldn't bring myself to look at too closely. My home didn't feel complete without Logan in it. Every colour, every tile, every fabric, and every surface reminded me of him. It reminded me of *being with him*.

The door to my home office had been closed since he left, and ten days later, I was certain I'd never have a good enough reason to open it again.

Two weeks after the wedding, I was sitting on the front porch steps nursing a cup of tea between two hands when Dot slipped out her front door and strolled along the front path towards me. She wore an aqua-blue waterproof tracksuit and had a foil-covered dish in her hands. I smiled as genuinely as I could as she made her way over.

"What have you got there?" I asked.

"I made enough spaghetti and meatballs to feed a football team," she said. "And you're looking too thin these days, so I brought half of it over for your dinner."

She set the dish on the decking, then slowly lowered herself onto the step beside me.

"Thank you," I said, inhaling the fragrance of tomato and oregano. It should have made my mouth water, but

Dot was right about one thing: I'd lost my appetite. "It smells delicious," I remarked to be polite.

Dot patted my knee, and when I set my hand on hers, she took it and held on tight. "I don't like seeing you so sad, Jessica."

I sucked in a heavy breath, then blew it out again. "I'll be fine. It's not my first rodeo."

"Do you mean Luca?"

I shrugged. "I'm good at picking the wrong guys, I guess."

Dot said nothing straightaway, and I sipped on my tea as we watched the breeze ruffle the leaves on the gum trees that lined our street.

"I've seen you out here a lot the last couple of weeks," Dot observed. "And I know my bones are old, but I still say it's too cold for sitting outdoors as much as you have been."

"It's not that bad." The wind chose that very moment to pick up, and I shivered as the cool air got under the layers of clothes I needed to wear to stay warm outdoors for so long.

"If you say so," Dot replied, arching a knowing brow in my direction. "I ran into your mother and father at the supermarket two days ago."

Taking a sip of tea to muffle my groan, I said, "Oh, yeah?"

"Mm. Sandra is under the impression you're going to sell this place now that the improvements are finished. I told her I didn't believe it."

I stuck my hand in my pocket and pulled out the business card Mum had given me for the real estate agent, then handed it to Dot. "Honestly? I've been thinking about it."

Dot took the card but didn't look at it before she tucked it up into the sleeve of her jacket. "Why on earth would you sell this house after all the hard work you've put into making it so lovely? And it *is* lovely. You've done a marvellous job with it. Everyone thinks so—even your mother."

I smirked at the begrudging grumble in her voice, but my smile faded quickly. "Can I tell you the truth, Dot?"

The old woman squeezed my fingers and waited for me to meet her eyes before she replied. "Yes, you can always tell me the truth."

I bit my lip and blinked back the sting of incoming tears. "I hate being here. Every corner of this house reminds me of Logan. I know he was only supposed to help me with the renovations, and it was all my vision, but that's not how it feels. If I'm inside and forget myself, even for a second, I look up and expect to see him there. I *want* to see him there. The house doesn't fit me without him. *I* don't fit the house without him." I set my tea down, pulled my fingers free from Dot's grasp, and dropped my face into my hands.

"You have to help me understand, dear. Why is Logan in London if he loves you and you feel this way about him?"

"You know the story," I mumbled into my palms.

"I know he made a dubious agreement with Luca, and that was a mistake, but I also know that he apologised, and I know what I saw when he was here. That boy is smitten with you, and if you'll forgive me for saying so, I think you feel the same way about him."

I raised my head, wiping away my tears as I did. "You've had six husbands. Did you love all of them?"

"Absolutely," she answered without hesitation. "I wouldn't have married them if I didn't love them."

"But they didn't last. Don't you look back and think some of them were wrong choices? Mistakes?"

Dot frowned and brushed a tear from my cheek. "What is this all about, Jessica?"

I dropped my head back. "Every time I've tried to do what I want or follow my instincts, things haven't panned out the way I'd hoped they would, and Mum says I don't know how to make the right decisions, the kind that add up to a good life. God! Why do I always feel like a child around her? She treats me like a teenager, and in some ways, I've never stopped feeling like one."

"Your mother is *wrong*," Dot replied, shifting irritably.

I stuck my hand out, one finger extended, as I began to list proof to the contrary. "I let my parents run my life longer than I should have but look what I had to show for it when I did. A good boyfriend. Good grades, which turned into a good career. Mum even set up the job I have now, and the joke's on me because I love it. I inherited this house with all the potential to renovate it and make it a home for Luca and me. I was set, Dot, and then everything went wrong. I refused to move to Sydney with my boyfriend, and he dumped me. It knocked my confidence so badly I didn't date again for three years, and all the while I let this house tumble into ruins around my ears. The only reason I did all this"—I waved my hand at the house I'd put so much hard work into—"was because my mother forced me. I knew Logan was a risk, yet I let him get close and what did he do? He let me down, just like Mum said he would. Oh, and let's not forget Zachary." I shuddered.

"Who is Zachary?" Dot asked before she shook her head. "Never mind. It doesn't matter. Listen to me, dear. What you've given me there isn't a list of failures or mistakes or things you could have done better. That's a list of *life*."

"A crappy life," I sulked.

"How can you say that?" Dot wrapped her fingers around my chin—hard—and lifted my face. "You have a gorgeous home, friends who would commit murder for you—even Isaac, though he'd never admit it—and a neighbour who loves you like her own granddaughter. You had a beautiful relationship with Luca, and *you outgrew it*. You outgrew *him*. Where's the error in that? If anything, I think you made the exact right decision letting him go the way you did. Could you imagine a life with him in this home? Right now, Luca sharing this life with you?"

I glanced up at the front door of my house, trying to picture Luca inside, but he didn't fit. "No. I can't imagine it."

"And would you *want* it?"

I blinked at her, the bone-deep truth of my answer momentarily stunning me. "No, I don't want it."

"So why are you second-guessing yourself? Why are you regretting choices you made that were right at the time and led you to this place where you've got the world at your feet? Why write off as a failure something that was clearly one of your greatest successes?"

"I don't know," I said.

"I do. Nobody ever gave you permission to think for yourself, so you have trouble trusting your own judgement. You think detours and obstacles indicate wrong choices?" Dot snorted loudly. "Detours and obstacles are evidence of a life well lived. Who wants to take a path where the finish line is in sight from the start? I'll take the curved road, thank you, the one where your next great adventure is always just around the next bend."

My mouth twitched in a small smile. "Does that explain the six husbands?"

Dot cackled, but then she sighed, and her smile was wistful. "Every one of those men was an adventure, and I regret none of them—even the three I divorced. Even the one I could have gladly skinned alive. He showed me the meaning of passion, that one." Her eyes grew distant. "He was fire."

"And you wouldn't go back and do any of it differently if you could?"

She thought about it before answering, then looked at me so steadily I knew she'd only give me the truth. "No, not a single thing."

I nibbled at my lip. "So, how do you know which way you're supposed to go? Where are the signposts? And when they're telling you two different things, are you supposed to follow your head or your heart?"

"Depends on the situation," Dot replied. "Sometimes

the signs are right there in front of you, but more often than not, it's about trusting yourself." She tapped my temple. "If you need to apply for a loan, take the shortest route, hire an accountant, you use your head." Dot picked up my hand and pressed my palm against the centre of my chest. "When you need to renovate your home or let go of an old love and take a chance on a new one …" She set her hand over mine and whispered, "That's when you listen to your heart."

32

JESS

THE SOUND OF someone clearing his throat startled me, and both Dot and I dropped our hands. Conner stood on my garden path with a piece of light timber furniture held in his tanned, callused hands. It looked like a small table.

I wiped a tear from the corner of one eye and stood up. "Hi, Conner. What brings you here?"

He hefted the table as if that answered my question, but I shook my head in puzzlement.

"It took me longer than I expected to finish it, but I wanted to get it perfect," he said, looking down at the little table and grimacing slightly. "Still not convinced it's good enough, but maybe you can tuck it away in a corner or something. It doesn't have to sit out with the pieces Logan made."

Swallowing the lump that caught in my throat at the mention of Logan's name, I stepped closer and ran a hand over the smooth wood. It was a simple piece, with slender spokes holding up a plain tabletop, but each line had a gentle, retro curve to it that I loved.

"It's beautiful, Conner, but I think there's been a misunderstanding. I'm not expecting anything, and Logan didn't make me any furniture. He did refurbish a couple of pieces for Luca and Natasha's wedding. Is that what you mean?"

Conner frowned, then his eyes landed on Dot over my shoulder. She was struggling to get to her feet, and Conner set the table down so he could rush over and help her up.

"Thank you, dear," she said, winking at me as she clung to his arm a moment longer than necessary.

"No problem, Mrs March." Conner ran a hand over his lightly stubbled chin, then squinted at the house. "I helped Logan refinish the pieces for Luca, but that's not what I'm talking about. That table there matches the outdoor setting Logan made for you."

I exchanged a glance with Dot, but she appeared as confused as I was. "There is no outdoor furniture, Conner. I'm sorry. But I love this table, and I'd like to buy it from you. I can find somewhere for it inside."

Conner took a step towards the side gate. "I can ... I mean, would you mind if I took a look in the workshop?"

I wanted to say no. That was Logan's workshop, and as much as I didn't want to trespass on it, I didn't want anyone else in there either. It felt like desecrating a sacred space, but I couldn't very well say that, could I?

"Sure," I replied. "Let me find the key."

Three minutes later, I stepped off the back porch and made my way, key in hand, to where Dot and Conner waited at the door to the workshop. I slipped the key into the lock and pushed open the door, then stepped inside and turned on the light. The first thing I looked at, of course, was the stretch of workbench where I'd seduced Logan the day I'd decided he was a safe place—safe enough I could leap without worrying about where I landed.

Dot's words came to me at the same time. Detours were not mistakes. Unexpected results didn't need to be regrets. Proof of a life well lived. Adventure around the bend.

Life wasn't about the landing. *Life was about the fall.*

And hadn't I fallen for Logan a long time ago? Yes, I'd fallen, and I was still falling.

Tearing my focus from the workbench, I scanned the rest of the room. It was neat and tidy, tools packed away, dusty old sheets covering piles of scrap materials.

"See?" I said. "I'm sorry, Conner. There's nothing here. You must have your wires crossed."

Conner stalked straight to the back corner of the workshop and yanked at one of the sheets, then another. He balled them up and stepped to the side, and I gasped at what he revealed underneath.

Furniture. Stunning, clearly artisan-made pieces made with smooth pale timber. Two single seats, a low table, and a larger seat just wide enough to accommodate two people.

The little table Conner had made was lovely, but beside these pieces, it was an obvious imitation. I couldn't mistake this work for anyone's but Logan's, and I could see the thought he'd put into it. The colours and lines and shapes complemented everything I'd chosen for the house, a magical mix of mid-century and modern styles in a light contemporary finish.

I crept forward and hesitantly reached out a hand to touch it. It was like running my hands over Logan's skin. If there could have been a physical manifestation of his heart and soul outside of his body, this would have been it.

"I don't know why he didn't give it to you," Conner said, breaking the spell. "It's too nice to sit in here under a sheet."

"You're right," I agreed. "Will you help me get it out and onto the porch?"

I heaved one of the single seats into my arms while Conner picked up the coffee table with a lot less effort. Dot ambled out of the way and watched as we settled those pieces on the porch around the outdoor rug I'd already laid out, then went back for the others. Conner had no problem handling the two-seater on his own while I carried the remaining single chair. He helped me rearrange the configuration three times before I was happy with the set-up, and then we stood back to admire the end result.

"Logan is a talented man," Dot murmured. "Shame he's not here. I'd have asked him to make something for my porch, too."

"He's awesome," Conner agreed. "I'd have jumped ship to work with him if he'd stayed."

My head whipped around. "Did Logan say anything to you about moving back to the Bay?" At my side, Dot latched onto my hand.

"Not exactly," Conner said, rubbing his neck, "but the way he talked about his life sometimes, what he *would* do if he didn't go back to London, sounded a lot like wishing he had a reason to stay."

I blinked at the furniture, wondering if that should mean as much to me as it did.

"Logan would kick my arse if I left here without checking a few things out," Conner said, interrupting my thoughts. "Mind if I take a look around and make a list of any defects that need fixing?"

It sounded so much like something Logan would have said that I had to smile. "Uh, sure. I appreciate that. And don't forget to add your table to the porch when you're done. It's the perfect thing to finish it off."

The grin that split his face warmed me from the inside. "Yeah, I will. Thanks, Jess."

Dot waited for Conner to clear earshot before she said, "Well, this is a nice surprise."

I circled the furniture, running a hand over the surfaces, loving every detail, loving Logan for making it for me. "It really is."

"And?" Dot prompted, her eyes sparkling. "What are you thinking? Or, more importantly, how do you feel?"

"I feel …" My fingertips, gliding easily over the smooth

350

surface, caught on a rough patch on the back of the love seat, and when I stopped to look at what it was, my heart skipped a beat. "Oh my God."

Crouching down to get a better look, I traced a finger over a patch of carved lines. Dot walked around to join me, then she set a hand on my shoulder and clucked her tongue.

"I don't have my glasses on," she said. "What is it?"

I laughed, not quite believing what I was seeing. "Logan carved a heart into the back of the love seat, and inside it, he added 'LR + JF'. Here, come a little closer. Can you see it now?"

Dot hunched over and squinted at the chair. "Oh, yes. I think so." The smile on her face grew wider. "Looks a lot like that boy loves you, dear."

I stared at the carved heart, recalling the identical drawings I'd scrawled in my diary fifteen years ago. I remembered the way my body responded to his touch, the way my stomach flipped whenever he was in the same room, and I asked myself if I believed he loved me. I did, but the more important question was, did I have enough faith in him—and myself—to leap one more time?

"I love him, too," I murmured to myself.

Dot's hearing was apparently better than her eyesight. Behind me, she clapped her hands and laughed. "Finally! So, what are you going to do about it?"

I jumped to my feet and stared around wild-eyed. What was I going to do about it? For the first time ever, my head and my heart agreed there was only one answer.

"Help me pack my bags, Dot. I'm going to London."

By the time I'd filled a suitcase, found my passport, and booked the next available flight, Conner had left, and Dot was fluttering around like a hyperactive butterfly. I was about to fly halfway around the world and tell the man I loved that I wanted to spend the rest of my life with him because that's what this was. I wanted Logan forever, and I wanted him to know it.

"Do you have everything you need?" Dot asked as I locked the door behind us.

"Everything but a ride to the airport," I said, panicking as the local rideshare app let me know there was nobody available to pick me up. Neither Abbie nor Emily had answered my half-dozen calls and texts. "Dammit! What am I going to do?"

"Oh, it's times like this I wish I could drive," Dot muttered, then she turned me around and pushed me towards my car. "You'll have to do it yourself, dear."

I threw my phone in my handbag and collected Dot's little body in a quick, tight hug. "Thank you for everything. I'll call you when I get there, okay? I love you, Dot."

"I love you, too, dear. Now don't give me another thought. Go get your man!"

Settling my suitcase on the back seat and slipping behind the wheel, letting adrenaline course through my blood and enjoying the rush, I checked the time again and made a last-minute decision to pull in at The Stop. Will wouldn't be anywhere else on a Saturday, and if I let him know I was heading out of town, the whole crew would know soon after that. I'd ask Will to keep it just between the few of us, but I didn't feel right flying all the way to London without letting my friends know I'd be gone—and why.

As soon as I stepped into the bar, I wished I'd just kept on driving.

Luca and Natasha were snuggled up in a booth, and the option to ignore them was dashed when Natasha glanced up and spotted me hovering in the doorway. I waved awkwardly, looked for Will at the bar and couldn't find him, then froze, nausea curling in my gut.

Was I really going to go to London and tell Logan I loved him and still be afraid of Luca learning the truth?

No, I wasn't. I wanted to be with Logan, and Luca would have to deal with it. I wanted forever, and forever started now.

I strode over there and smiled. "Hi, you two. I didn't realise you were back. How was the honeymoon?"

"Really great," Natasha replied, swapping a guarded look with Luca. "And how are you?"

"I'm good," I said as nerves assaulted me. "I'm okay. I'm fine."

Luca took a sip of his beer, and his eyes narrowed at me over the rim of his glass. "What's up, Frost?"

I sucked in a breath. "I'm in love with Logan, and I'm flying to London today to tell him and ask him to come home. So that we can be together. Because I love him. And I want him here. With me. Forever."

My fortifying breath was still trapped in my lungs, and I held it while I waited for their reactions.

Natasha's eyes widened at Luca, while Luca's face gave nothing away until he said, "It's about time. How are you getting to the airport?"

My focus darted between them both as I tried, in my heightened state, to understand what was going on. Natasha just grinned, and Luca waited patiently for my answer.

"Uh, my car's out front. I'm driving myself."

"You'll waste too much time looking for a place to park," Natasha said.

Luca nodded, then he pushed his drink away, scooped up his keys and wallet from where he'd stacked them on the table, and stood. "Go get your stuff, Frost. We'll take you."

I was flying halfway across the planet to tell my ex-boyfriend's best friend I was in love with him, and if there was one thing that could make that statement sound even wilder than it already did, it would be to add that my ex-boyfriend and his new wife were driving me to the airport.

It took less than two hours to make the trip down the freeway to Sydney, but soon enough, I was flinging myself from the car at the drop-off curb, stopping only when Luca and Natasha both got out as well and wrapped me in a warm group hug.

"We'll let everyone know where you are," Luca said.

"Care to tell my parents as well?" I asked, only half joking. I couldn't think of a better—or worse—person to break this news to my mother, and I certainly wasn't looking forward to that conversation.

Luca grinned. "Actually, that would be my pleasure."

I forced a chuckle as the brief good humour swam like oil over the stress in my system. "Be my guest, Rossetti. You'd be doing me a huge favour."

"Good luck," Natasha said, looping an arm around Luca's waist. "At the risk of sounding completely out of line, I'm kind of proud of you."

"Thanks, Tash. I appreciate that." I glanced at her arm around Luca and his around her shoulders, and horror engulfed me. "Holy shit," I whispered. "What if he says no?"

Luca took the handle of my suitcase and put it in my grasp. "He won't, and if he does, I will get on a plane so I can personally kick his arse."

"We all will," Tash agreed.

Taking a deep breath, I gave them one firm nod. "Right. Okay. I guess I really am doing this."

Luca gave me a satisfied smile. "Go get him, Frost. Bring back our boy."

The wait at the airport went on forever. The flight—all twenty-two hours of it—was never-ending claustrophobic torture. No music or movie or book could distract me from the task I'd set for myself and all the ways it could go wrong. The more exhausted I grew, the more my thoughts spiralled out of control—rage, rejection, humiliation all waited for me—until I finally wrote a mantra on a napkin to remind myself of what I was doing and, more importantly, why.

Life isn't about the landing. Life is about the fall.

The same could be said about love.

At Heathrow, I impatiently stood in line at customs, collected my baggage, and then did the best I could to fix myself up in the public bathroom. I brushed my teeth, retied my hair, changed my clothes into something cleaner and prettier and, at the last minute, chose my glasses over my contact lenses. It might have been playing dirty, but I was leaving nothing about this to chance.

It was early morning London time, and I had Logan's address. I could only assume he had returned to working nights in the local pubs, so I was quietly hopeful he'd be home when I knocked on his door. I had nowhere else to go, so if he wasn't there, I'd sit on his front steps until he got home.

That was it. That was my grand plan. Knock on the door, tell him how I felt, and beg him to come home. In the taxi on the way to his flat, it felt embarrassingly underwhelming.

"All right, love," the driver finally announced, pulling to the curb on a tidy inner-city street packed with art-deco apartment buildings. "We're here."

For a journey that had taken an eternity to complete, I was unprepared for the moment I exited that cab, walked to the door, and rang the bell. My breath came in such short, fast bursts I was at risk of hyperventilating.

And yet, amid all the panic, I was desperate to set eyes on him again. Only now did I realise how big a part of me was missing.

I had to leap. I *wanted* to leap. And after my conversation with Dot, I realised something important. As scared as I was, and as much as I wanted to have faith that Logan would never let me down again, more than that, I had to have faith in myself.

If things went sideways, if our road held more curves ahead than we'd already left behind, I would be okay. I would make it around the bend, and I would run towards the next adventure. I wasn't making mistakes. I was making a life.

The short, shrill ring of a doorbell sounded inside the building, and then a static *buzz* replied to indicate that someone had pressed the button on the security intercom. I opened my mouth to announce myself, but the door clicked open, and the intercom cut out. Pushing on the door and dragging my suitcase up a flight of stairs, feeling equal measures of anticipation and terror, I found his apartment, took a shaky breath, and knocked.

It swung open, and a woman stood on the other side—a gorgeous woman with tousled blonde hair and wide blue eyes and a light sheen of sweat on her flushed cheeks. Her chest rose in quick pants.

"Can I help you?" she asked in a British accent.

I glanced at the brass apartment number attached to the wall beside the door. Number 14. I looked at my watch.

It was seven in the morning. I was in the right place, and my heart took off so fast I was never going to catch it.

"Who are you?" I blurted.

"Bek," she said, a confused smile curving her lips as she wiped her forehead with the back of her forearm. "And who are you?"

Bek. The ex-wife. Of all the things that could have gone wrong, I had not planned on this. She was not the adventure I was running towards.

"Oh, crap," I muttered as my nose tingled with incoming tears. "I forgot about you."

33

LOGAN

AS I WALKED from my bedroom down the hall, curious about who had rung my doorbell, I peeled off my damp T-shirt and used it to mop the sweat from my face. Damon and Bek had ambushed me every morning for at least a week, insisting I join them for an early morning workout no matter how much I objected. Perhaps they thought it would distract me from my heartache or move pent-up pain through my system, but it did neither of those things. I wouldn't let it. Depression and resentment were all I had left, and the only reason I went along with them was that I was pathetic and had nothing better to do.

"Oh, crap," said a voice at the front door, and I froze, my heart stopping dead in my chest. "I forgot about you."

"Excuse me?" Bek replied as I stepped around a corner and into the living room.

It was her.

My legs propelled me forwards, though I had no concept of walking anywhere until I stood just behind Bek's shoulder.

"Jess?" I asked. "How did you … What are you doing here?"

"This is Jess?" Bek asked, cocking an eyebrow. At my distracted nod, Bek collected her bag from the coat rack by the door and slipped around Jess into the hall outside. "I'll catch Damon at the coffee shop and tell him plans have changed." Bek glanced at Jess again, then back at me, rolling her lips to hide a grin. "Bye, Logan."

I waved her away without looking. "Yeah. Bye."

And then we were alone. Jess clasped her hands in front of her, and I noticed the suitcase at her side. Her gaze ran over my face, then dropped to my chest before she closed her eyes and took a deep breath. "Can I come in?"

"What? Yeah, sure. Of course."

I stepped aside, and she passed me, wheeling her luggage behind her, then stopping in the middle of my sparse living room. Under different circumstances, I'd have been embarrassed to have her here. I hadn't made much effort in the decorating department, never tried to create a home. It was a place to crash. A stereotypically sad bachelor pad. If Jess noticed how bare and boring the place was, it didn't show on her face.

Holy shit. Jessica was in London, standing in the middle of my little flat, wearing those fucking glasses, and she was more beautiful now than she had been when I last saw her two weeks earlier, for what I thought would be the last time. She was sunshine, and a weed of hope sprouted from the gloom inside my chest. It reached for her without any instruction from me. Heart and soul, I couldn't help but want her, and I couldn't stop myself from hoping she wanted me too.

I shook my head, trying to find the right words. "I don't understand what's happening here. What—"

"Could you put your shirt on, please?" she asked.

Clutching the fabric in my hand, I glanced down at my bare chest and low-slung grey gym shorts, and let a smile tip up one corner of my mouth. "You want me to put my shirt back on?" She nodded, blushing, and I took a step closer, tossing my shirt on the sofa. "Why?"

Jess flapped a hand in my direction. "Because I can't think straight with all that going on."

"All what going on?"

She groaned and dropped her head back. "You're not going to make this easy for me, are you?"

Hope bloomed brighter, and I moved closer.

Jess took a step back and flung up a hand. "Wait. There are things I need to say."

Crossing my arms over my chest, I paused. My strongest impulse was to touch her, but there were reasons I'd returned to London a fortnight ago, and if Jess and I stood a chance of having something real, we were going to have to resolve them. The sadness I'd been swimming in surged up again, dousing my brief euphoria and bringing me back down to Earth.

"Okay," I said. "I'm listening."

Jess licked her lips, and I resolutely ignored the way her tongue stirred things in my pants while she cleared her throat. "First of all," she began, "I never went on a date with Miles."

Rage fired in my blood at the mention of his name, and Jess seemed to notice.

"I bumped into him one day at a cafe," she hurried on, "and I sat at his table while I drank my coffee. He asked me out"—she blinked rapidly as her nose twitched—"and I did agree to see him again when the renovations were finished. Not as a date, but not as a non-date either. It was vague, and I don't feel good about what I did, but you deserve the truth. I never should have done it, but I thought I was future-proofing my heart against the day you left. By the time Luca's wedding came around, I knew I'd never go out with Miles—or anyone else, for that matter. Only you."

Only me. I was ready to forgive everything, but when I took a step towards her, she took another one back.

"The house feels wrong without you. I keep expecting to find you in the next room or beside me in bed, and every time I remember you're gone, it's like losing you all over again."

I had to hold her. One step closer, and she took a step away.

"Conner came over and told me about the furniture you made," she said, opening her handbag and riffling through it as she searched for something. "He helped me pull it out and arrange it on the back porch." She paused digging around in her bag long enough to meet my eyes. "It's beautiful, Logan. I love it."

Red-hot heat crawled up the back of my neck. I hadn't forgotten about the furniture. Just the opposite. When I hadn't been hoping it would stay hidden until it rotted away, I'd been dreaming of Jess discovering it and realising she did, in fact, love me after all. In a third scenario, I'd been terrified she'd find it one day in the not-so-distant future while clearing out the workshop to make space for a new boyfriend. I replayed *that* particular possibility on repeat when I was due a good round of mental anguish. Happened daily. Worked like a charm.

Jess pulled a small spiral-bound notebook out of her bag and threw it to me. I looked at the cover—a pale pink hardback with tiny white-and-yellow daisies printed over it—then back at her. "What's this?"

"Open it to one of the pages I've marked with a little tag."

There was a fan of yellow and purple paper flags sticking out the side of the notebook, so I flipped to one at random and opened it. There on the lined page was a hand-drawn red heart with "JF + LR" scribbled inside it. My pulse pounded in my ears, and I turned to another flagged page. Another heart, larger this time, with "Jessica Frost loves Logan Reeve" printed over the top of it. Again, I opened a page, and this one read "Logan Reeve 4EVA".

"That's my high school diary," Jess said as I flipped over page after page after page, finding more and more of the same. "I was carving hearts with your name in them long before you did it."

I was going to kiss this woman now. No force on the planet could stop me.

Jess stumbled backwards as I closed in on her, then she rushed around to the other side of the sofa and put the bulky piece of furniture between us.

"I told Luca about us," she said in a rush as she backed away from me, and I shadowed her around the living room. "I told him I'm in love with you, and I want to be with you forever. He's happy for us. He drove me to the airport."

Every word she said was fuel for the fire under my skin. I launched myself over the sofa, and Jess let out a tiny squeak as she backed herself up against the wall. I followed, standing so close there was less than a hairsbreadth between her chest and mine. Looking down at her, I grinned at the way her chocolate eyes rounded, and her breath came faster as she stared up into my eyes.

"He's doing us both a favour and telling my parents about us while I'm out of the country," she murmured.

I brushed the back of my fingers over her cheek, and her eyes floated closed before they opened again.

"Is there anything else you need to say before I kiss you?" I whispered.

She nodded and bit her lip. Her nose didn't twitch. Not once. "No matter where life takes me next, I want to go there with you. You're it for me, and if there are any detours in the road ahead, I can't wait to walk them with you by my side. I love you, Logan."

A rush of air left my lungs, and my shoulders dropped as she rested her forehead against my chest. "I love you, too," I said.

Saying—and hearing—those words was the best fucking feeling in the world, and I cupped my hand around her head so I could tip her mouth up to meet mine. It opened the way I remembered, her taste setting off alarm bells in my blood as her tongue met mine with a touch that was exhilarating and familiar. Her body curved against me like she was meant for me. Like she was meant to be there always.

"Jess?" I asked, pulling back just enough that I could drink in her face.

She looped her arms around my waist and brushed her lips against mine again. "Mm?"

I tickled the tip of her nose with my own. "Let's go home."

34

LOGAN

WE DIDN'T LEAVE immediately, of course. There were urgent things I had to take care of before we boarded a plane. First order of business was dedicating enough time to exploring Jess's body. It felt like discovering her for the first time all over again.

We spent three full days in bed—jet lag, you understand—before we checked in for a flight bound for Sydney, and I left London without any intention of going back.

Bek gave me her blessing. Well, no, that's not exactly accurate. Bek packed my bags and drove Jess and me to the airport, and though both Bek and I shed a couple of tears saying goodbye at the gate, neither of us doubted for a minute that it was the right thing to do. Jess made Bek promise she'd visit us in the Bay as soon as she could get the time off work.

And then we were home. Almost two months to the day I stood outside The Salty Stop for the first time in four years, desperate and terrified to see Jess again, I was back on Main Street, staring up at Will's pub, preparing myself to step inside. Only this time, Jess was right there by my side.

"Can't we just go home?" I grumbled as Jess slipped her hand through mine, and I twined my fingers around hers. We'd come straight from the airport, and we still had our luggage with us. "Aren't you tired?"

"Not really," she said. "I'm oddly wound up."

Cocking a suggestive eyebrow, I dipped my head against her neck. "I can think of better ways than a night out to work off any excess energy."

She turned her head and planted a lingering kiss on my mouth. "Let's have a quiet drink and something to eat, then we'll go home, and you can show me what you mean."

I nipped her earlobe with my teeth, and she grinned, so all I could do was roll my eyes and pretend to pout. "Fine, but we're hiding in the back somewhere and then slipping out the side door when we're done. I want you all to myself for at least another day. I like not having to share you."

"I like that, too," she said, pressing herself against me and tapping my bottom lip with a fingertip before she stepped back much too quickly and yanked on my arm. "Come on," she said. "I'm hungry."

Helping her push open the heavy timber door of The Stop, Jess walked in first, and I followed, freezing immediately at the person waiting for us just inside.

"Welcome home, Reeve," Abbie screeched, throwing herself at me hard enough I stumbled back a step. "Back where you belong. Finally!"

"What's this?" I asked, noting a crowd of familiar, goofy-looking faces deeper inside the room. I narrowed my eyes at Jess, who had the audacity to shrug innocently even as her eyes sparkled.

"It's your welcome home party," Abbie replied, picking up my hand and dragging me towards our regular booth.

I searched back over my shoulder for Jess and reached for her so that we moved like a three-linked snake towards the crew, and they piled out of the leather seats at the sight of us. Overhead, a couple dozen helium balloons in a rainbow of colours crowded the ceiling, each one dropping a tail of silver ribbon long enough to tickle our heads. The table was piled with jugs of beer and bottomless margaritas and plates of hot tapas. It was a tight fit for the people and catering alike, and as far as welcome home parties went, it was small and understated—and just about perfect. As much as I wanted to go straight to Jess's place—*our* place, our *home*, because she'd asked me to move in with her and of course I'd said yes—my chest felt lighter seeing my friends again. Luca especially, who pulled me in for a hug.

"Good to have you back, bro," he said, slapping me on the back before releasing me.

"Thanks. It's good to be back." I ran a hand over my jaw. My scruff was a little longer than usual, but Jess seemed to like it. "Listen, I'm sorry I didn't—"

"We're good, Reeve," he said, sticking out his hand. I gripped it and nodded, but then he didn't let it go.

Jess tucked herself under my free arm and cuddled against my side, grinning up at Luca. "What's going on here?"

"Rossetti's about to ask me for a favour," I replied, watching my best mate's face and daring him to deny it.

He only chuckled. "All I was going to say is keep doing what you're doing. It's good to see you both happy."

I gave his hand one last shake, then dropped it and pulled Jess in tighter, needing both arms to envelop her the way I wanted to. "Thanks. We appreciate it."

Who'd have thought I'd get a thrill saying "we" about Jess and me? Fuck, it was among the best highs I'd ever experienced.

Tash was next with the hugs, giving me a quick, tight squeeze before doing the same with Jess. Isaac wasn't far behind, with enough strength to make my ribs creak and lift Jess clear off the floor. Josh and Emily were all smiles just as Will arrived with another tray of drinks. Abbie shoved a tumbler of water into my hand, then pulled Jess and me into the booth alongside her before everyone crowded in, though there was barely enough room for the nine of us.

As Jess and I shared the story of her dash to London, and we shared some of what transpired between us, I slowly drew back and let her take the lead. I wanted to watch her laugh. I wanted to appreciate the feeling of her hand on my thigh and her body pressed up against mine like she was meant to be there. We didn't have to hide anything. *I* didn't have to hide anything. For the first time in my life, I could show the world the way I felt about this woman, and the next time she settled against me, a lull in the conversation gave us both the chance to breathe a little, so I ran my nose over her jawline and pressed my mouth to the soft spot under her earlobe.

"You smell delicious," I murmured against her skin.

She smiled and turned her head into my shoulder. "No, I don't. I smell like planes and airports."

"You smell like you," I disagreed. "And you always smell delicious."

She stared up at me through dark lashes, and I dropped a kiss on her mouth before wrapping an arm around her shoulders and pulling her in tighter against my side. Around us, our friends talked and joked and laughed like things had always been this way.

In some ways, that was true. There was a sense of *déjà vu* about that moment, the feeling of reliving a night I'd experienced a hundred times before, with friends who were my family, in a place that owned my heart. Only this time, the girl I'd always wished could be mine was snuggled under my arm. I didn't have to look for her or brace myself against the hurt of watching her hold a man who would never be me. I didn't have to wonder if I could be good enough for her or if there'd ever be a time she'd choose me because she'd already given me the answers.

I didn't have to worry about losing a race nobody knew I was in, because Jess had taken everyone else out of the running.

She had flown halfway around the world to tell me she loved me, then she'd taken my hand and brought me home.

ONE YEAR LATER

JESS

I'D LAST VISITED this church the day Luca and Tash were married, and again I sat in the pew, staring up at Logan, who stood at the altar dressed in a suit that fit him so well it should have been illegal. Unlike his groomsman's tux, this one was light grey, and he wore it with a crisp white shirt and navy tie. If the rare sight of Logan in a suit wasn't enough to set off flutters in my chest, the tiny baby in his arms was nearly more than my heart could handle.

He looked awkward and nervous as he balanced the tiny boy over a basin of holy water. The baby—little Leonardo Luca Rossetti—was wrapped in a traditional, long white gown, which made holding him a little bit harder. Logan handled Leo as if he were a football made of glass, and he hadn't taken his eyes off him for a moment.

My ovaries were rioting.

Or they would have been, had they not already sent a scout out on a stealth mission a month earlier—a scout clever enough to neatly evade all defences and get herself captured by the enemy.

Yes, I was pregnant.

It was early days, but I was already feeling nauseous in the mornings, and Logan had busted me crying at a toilet paper commercial two days earlier. I wanted to tell him, but I'd been working through the way I felt about becoming a parent. It was hard to be sensible about it because no matter what way I looked at it, I could only be certain of one thing. I was thrilled. Ecstatic. More than ready to have a baby, and there was nobody I wanted to do it with more than Logan. He was going to be an amazing father, and if I'd ever had any doubts about that—and I hadn't—they'd have been pulverised over the last three months as I watched him with Luca and Tash's firstborn. Logan doted on that baby, and when Luca had asked him to be Leo's godfather, Logan walked around with a grin on his face for days.

That night would be the perfect time to tell him after he'd spent the day soaking in father-figure hormones with his godson in his arms. I was almost positive he'd be as happy about the news as I was, but an inkling of worry still tickled my nose. Telling a man he was going to be a father was not the kind of thing that usually went well with *surprise!* attached.

After the ceremony, Luca and Tash hosted a reception at Honeysuckle Pavilion, a stunning venue in the heart of the Bay favoured by out-of-town brides who wanted small destination weddings as well as locals who needed something a little fancier than a bonfire on the beach. I hadn't been invited to an occasion at the Pavilion since Dot and her sixth husband had their ten-year anniversary party there five years earlier, and I'd forgotten how pretty it was. The wall facing the ocean was made entirely of glass, framing sweeping views out across the water. Every other surface inside was white—the walls, the chairs, the table linen, the flatware, the flowers, the waitstaff uniforms. The lighting was subtle enough to let the natural glow of the Bay bounce from every corner. It was understated and elegant, and it had always been one of my favourite spaces.

Once Logan and I found our seats, we had a moment to ourselves among all the commotion, and I leaned into him and whispered, "Have I told you how dashing you look in that suit?"

"Yes," he replied, his mouth twitching in that cocky smirk that had always sent me wild, only now, I didn't need to pretend to hate him for it. I could acknowledge that the wild I felt was the kind that ended with my hands in his pants and my knickers around my ankles.

The kind of wild that put a baby in my belly.

"Fine," I replied, arching a brow and sitting back in my chair. "No need to say it again, then."

Logan grinned and followed me, taking his turn to set his lips against my ear and murmur, "Have I told you yet how beautiful you look today?"

The heat of his breath on my neck sent a wave of goosebumps rippling across my body. "Yes," I whispered.

Under the table, his hand settled on my knee before it slid up my thigh and swept under the hem of my dress. "No need to say it again, then," he teased.

"Hello, Logan," my mother said, pulling out a chair on the other side of the round table.

Logan smiled regretfully as he pulled away and turned to my parents. "Sandra, hello. And Michael. Nice to see you. Did you enjoy the ceremony?"

"It was a little long," my dad replied, hanging his suit jacket over the back of his chair.

Tugging the hem of my dress lower down my thighs, I poured water into glasses for myself and Logan and waited out the awkward small talk between my boyfriend and my parents.

"How's business this week, Logan?" Mum asked, flinging her napkin onto her lap and breaking into one of the bread rolls on the table. "Did you call Mrs Boxwell? I said you would. I don't want to let her down."

"I called her the day you gave me her number," Logan said. "She put in an order for six new dining chairs, and I'll be working on her front porch later in the year."

"She'll need it done before the summer," Sandra replied.

"I'm on it," Logan assured her, and when she opened her mouth again, he added, "And I've got Conner on it too. It's under control."

My mother had come to accept Logan in my life, somewhat begrudgingly and in the oddest way. Her mouth still pursed at the sight of him, as though she'd been sucking lemons, but she'd single-handedly set up his new business in the Bay by recommending Logan's contracting services and artisan furniture hustle to anyone within shouting distance. Actually, *recommending* was too generous a description. *Bullying* might have been more accurate.

At first, her attitude had bothered me, but whenever I'd spoken to Logan about it—apologised for her behaviour, offered to intervene—he told me he didn't mind. In fact, he enjoyed delivering way beyond her expectations and proving he could fulfill all the business she drummed up. It had become one of his favourite pastimes.

"Logan, you're a natural with that baby," Dad commented, signalling to a waiter and ordering himself a beer.

Logan chuckled. "Hardly. I was terrified I was going to drop him in that enormous bath."

"You did good," Dad said, glancing slyly at me. "Made me wonder if you two might make me a grandfather one day soon."

"Dad!" I exclaimed at the same time my mother gasped. If she'd been wearing pearls, she'd have been clutching them.

My dad laughed, and Logan reached out to hold my hand on top of the table. "Seems the sensible way to do things would be to get married first."

All colour drained from my mother's face, and I wondered if mine looked similarly peaked. Logan winked at me, his thumb rubbing soothing circles over the back of my hand, and I tried to smile, but my intermittent nausea had flared with a vengeance.

Oh, boy. Marriage, babies, Sandra Frost becoming a grandmother ... Would Logan be grinning so easily when he realised none of this was a joke?

LOGAN

AS I PULLED The car into the driveway of our home—
the home we'd created while we built the bones for a
relationship that would last a lifetime—I turned off the
engine and used the cover of relative darkness to suck in a
calming breath.

I'd never felt so sick in my life or spent a day working
so hard at keeping my cool. Leo's baptismal ceremony was
one thing—for most of the morning, I barely thought
of anything other than *do not drop this child*—but the
reception had dragged on forever. My head kept rehearsing
what I had planned for afterwards, and Jess's father read
my nervous energy like a book. Any other time, I'd have
appreciated his attempt to make light of a serious situation,
but I'd almost sunk to the floor when he made that quip
about having babies with his daughter.

Had I done the wrong thing by asking for Michael's blessing before I proposed to Jess?

It wasn't the type of thing I'd ever imagined doing—Jess was a grown woman, and she didn't need her parents' permission to get married—but I'd known since the moment she showed up in my London apartment that I wanted to be with her forever. Hell, I probably knew way before that, maybe even years before, and now the time had come to ask the question. I didn't want to put a foot wrong—not with Jess and not with her parents. I was working bloody hard to prove to them I was good enough for their daughter, and talking to Michael before I popped the question had been less about asking for his blessing and more about getting advice on how to manage Sandra. I wanted her to be happy about it—not for my benefit, but because Jess deserved it. Unexpectedly, Mr Frost had shaken my hand, told me I was the best thing that could have happened to Jess and that I wasn't to worry about his wife. It was a weight off my shoulders, leaving me the brain space to concentrate on sweeping the woman I loved off her feet.

And that's what I was hoping to do tonight.

"I thought I left the porch light on," Jess mumbled as we exited the car.

"Must have forgotten," I replied, squinting over at Dot's place. The curtains in the front bedroom twitched, then opened just enough to reveal two silhouettes—one small and slight, the other broad and tall enough to tower over the other. A light flickered inside—on, then off—and the old lady closed the curtains again.

Okay. The first part of my plan was ready to go. If only the rest of the night went so smoothly.

"The front door is open," Jess commented, pulling her hand back from the knob as if burned. "Oh my God, do you think we've been burgled?"

"Unlikely," I said, pushing the door open and stepping into the hall, my anxiety settling a little more as I took in the fluttering shadows against the walls. After pulling Jess into the house and guiding her to the living room, she gasped and covered her mouth with her free hand.

"What's all this?"

The room had been cleared of all its furniture, and in its place were layers of rugs, piles of pillows and cushions, and dozens of candles. There was a bottle of red wine in the middle, along with warm plates of chicken casserole and a carton of vanilla ice-cream with two spoons.

"A picnic," I answered, drawing her in and settling her onto a mound of cushions.

Her eyes darted around the room, and though I couldn't be sure in the flickering light, I thought she might have been about to cry. "But ...how?"

"I had help. Dot and Conner did all the hard work while we were out."

"It's just like that night when we were renovating," she croaked.

"Is that okay?" I asked, only almost sure she was crying happy tears.

Nodding, she smiled as her eyes spilled over. "It's perfect. But why?"

I'd planned to wait until after dinner, after wine, after dessert, but I couldn't fathom spending another minute without my ring on this woman's finger, so I sank to one knee and pulled out the little box. A little sob escaped her throat, and I bit my lip to stop a grin.

She smacked my arm. Hard.

"Ow! What was that for?"

"Stop laughing at me," she said—or tried to say. It was hard to understand her with all the crying going on. "This is supposed to be serious."

"Press pause on all the waterworks, and I won't laugh," I replied, opening the box to reveal the ring I'd so painstakingly designed for her—a round, brilliant-cut diamond set with pear-shaped stones to either side. It was new, but it had an art-deco feel that was all Jessica.

Jess sobbed louder. "It's beautiful!"

"So, is that a yes?" I asked, amused by the theatrics but desperate to make this official.

"You didn't ask a question!" she wailed, holding up her left hand.

I plucked the ring from its cushion, set the box aside, and took hold of Jess's hand. "Jessica Frost. I want to spend every minute of every day of the rest of my life with you. Will you do me the honour of becoming my wife?"

"Yes!" she sputtered, and I slid the ring on her finger. It had dazzled in the box, but on her hand, it looked finished. Complete. Like it was meant to be there.

Jess flung her arms around my neck, and I rubbed her

back as she nuzzled her wet cheeks and snotty nose into my shoulder.

"I'm going to assume those are tears of uncontrollable joy," I said, pressing my lips against her hair.

"They are," she said, nodding against me.

"Glad to hear it, though I'll be honest. This is not how I thought tonight would pan out."

"It's not?" Jess drew back to look at me, though her arms stayed wrapped around my neck.

"I thought there'd be more smiling and smooching and less ... snot."

She whacked me on the arm again, and I feigned a wince, but then her expression turned serious. "I'm pregnant," she whispered.

The smile on my mouth froze in place, forgotten as I blinked. "You're ... what?"

"I'm pregnant," she repeated, her brows drawing inwards as she searched my eyes for a reaction.

"You're pregnant?"

Jess's chin wobbled as she nodded.

And then my hands were cradling her face, and my mouth was on hers, and I was kissing the woman I loved, who in the space of ninety seconds had given me everything I'd ever wanted. Herself. A *child*. Our very own forever.

"I love you," I said as I kissed away the tears tumbling over her cheeks. "I love you. I love you." Dropping my head to her middle, I rained kisses over the fabric of her dress right where I thought our baby might be snuggled up inside. "I love you," I told him. Or her. I didn't care.

"I love you, too," Jess said, dropping her head back as I straightened and applied my lips to her collarbone while peeling her dress from her shoulders. She moaned as I freed one stiff, straining nipple from her bra and covered it with my hot mouth, then set about making love to the woman who was giving me the world. "I love you, Logan. Oh, so much."

BONUS SCENE

Logan and Jess's story doesn't end here!
Visit my website at samanthaleighbooks.com/books/
bonus-content or use the QR code to download
a bonus scene set ten years in the future...

UP NEXT: PERFECT FOR YOU

Do you want to find out why Isaac Greene is so unlucky in love—and have a front-row seat when a book club of senior citizens and the girl next door show him how to turn it all around? Here's what you're in for...

He's a small-town cop with absolutely no game... until the girl next door teaches him how to play.

After another crash landing in the friend zone, Isaac Greene realises he's clueless about women. Desperate for help, he's got two options: join Valentine Bay's secret senior citizens' romance book club and hope a bunch of randy octogenarians can give him some advice, or risk humiliation and ask the girl next door to improve his moves.

Naturally, he does both.

Birdie Maxwell is a genius with numbers but terrible at relationships. Smart, sassy and self-sufficient, she's great at keeping people at a distance—until she strikes a deal with the sexy cop who's determined to get close in more ways one.

As their spice lessons heat up and Birdie's walls fall down, Isaac's ready to risk it all...

But is Birdie willing to bet on him too?

Perfect For You *is a first-person, dual POV contemporary romance with lots of steam and a satisfying happily ever after.*

ACKNOWLEDGEMENTS

Thank you for reading *Meant For You*. This was one of those books that jumped from my fingers to the screen, and writing it brought me so much joy. I'm thrilled to finally be able to share Jess and Logan's love story with you, and I can only hope you fall in love with them the same way I did—one word at a time, and a little more with every page.

And here's where I get to tell everyone how much I appreciate all the wonderful people who helped me get this book ready for the world.

My brilliant book coach—Dawn Alexander.

The best beta reader and cheerleader an author could ask for—Shay Laurent.

My wonderful and eternally patient editor—Gina Salamon.

My smart and supportive proofreader and PA—Brandi Zelenka.

My sister—the one who read the book, even though you're all beautiful and I love each of you just the same.

Thank you Carole and Krista for your input on my early drafts.

A truckload of gratitude to all the ARC readers, bloggers, and influencers on Facebook, Instagram, and TikTok who championed this series from day one, and especially Mindy, Siena, Abbey, Carolyn, Sammy, Sarah, Kylie... Thank you!

And finally, to my husband for your limitless love and support.

ABOUT THE AUTHOR

Samantha Leigh is an Australian author of steamy contemporary romance. When she's not playing matchmaker in imaginary worlds, Sam is reading books with all the feels and all the spice. In the tiny slices of time she has between word wrangling, Sam likes to hit her yoga mat, go for walks in the bush or on the beach, continue her search for the perfect poke bowl, drown herself in coffee and hot cacao, and binge-watch nineties television.

samanthaleighbooks.com